USA _____ orth Texas w____ _____ _____ _____ _____ sband, three beautiful children, a spunky golden retriever/standard poodle mix and too many books in her to-read pile. In her downtime, she plays video games and spends much of her time on or around a basketball court. She loves interacting with readers and is grateful for their support. You can reach her at barbhan.com.

Julie Miller is an award-winning *USA TODAY* bestselling author of breathtaking romantic suspense—with a National Readers' Choice Award and a Daphne du Maurier Award, among other prizes. She has also earned an *RT Book Reviews* Career Achievement Award. For a complete list of her books, monthly newsletter and more, go to juliemiller.org.

Also by Barb Han

Sudden Setup
Endangered Heiress
Texas Grit
Stockyard Snatching
Delivering Justice
One Tough Texan
Texas-Sized Trouble
Texas Witness
Texas Showdown

Also by Julie Miller

Beauty and the Badge
Takedown
KCPD Protector
Crossfire Christmas
Military Grade Mistletoe
Kansas City Cop
APB: Baby
Kansas City Countdown
Necessary Action
Protection Detail

Discover more at millsandboon.co.uk

KIDNAPPED AT CHRISTMAS

BARB HAN

RESCUED BY THE MARINE

JULIE MILLER

MILLS & BOON

First Published in Great Britain 2018
by Mills & Boon, an imprint of HarperCollins*Publishers*
1 London Bridge Street, London, SE1 9GF

Kidnapped at Christmas © 2018 Barb Han
Rescued By The Marine © 2018 Julie Miller

ISBN: 978-0-263-26597-2

1018

MIX
Paper from
responsible sources
FSC® C007454

This book is produced from independently certified FSC™ paper to ensure responsible forest management.

For more information visit: www.harpercollins.co.uk/green

Printed and bound in Spain
by CPI, Barcelona

KIDNAPPED
AT CHRISTMAS

BARB HAN

Brandon, I'm amazed by your brilliance and kindness. I'm so very proud of you. Jacob, I can't wait to play the games you're working so hard to create. Tori, I love to watch you dance. From Twinkle to Transformation to It Is Done you have so many stories to tell.

Babe, my guy, for being my best friend and partner in crime. I love you.

To Michelle Spall for helping me see a new way to define home. I'm so grateful for your friendship and am looking forward to many more dance mom antics together.

Chapter One

"Why can't I think of one word to say to him?" Meg Anderson looked down at her sleeping angel, trying to psych herself up for the conversation that needed to take place with the baby's father.

"You're the best child advocate in Texas, Meg. The words will come." Meg's best friend and business partner, Stephanie Gable, walked over and ran her finger along two-month-old Aubrey's cheek.

"He deserves to know about her, right?" Meg already knew the answer, but she asked anyway. She'd do just about anything to gain a few more minutes of courage before walking out the door.

"He does." Stephanie's sympathetic tone struck a chord.

"I'm being totally unfair to her by keeping her from her father." Tears burned the backs of Meg's eyes.

"That's right. If you can't do it for yourself, think of Aubrey." Stephanie seemed to be catching on. "It'll work out."

"What if he rejects her?" Meg tamped down the panic causing her heart to gallop.

"Then it's his loss." Stephanie didn't hesitate.

Meg made eyes at her friend. "You're absolutely right."

"What's the worst he can say?" Stephanie shot her what was supposed to be a nerve-fortifying look.

"I don't think I want to go there, not even in theory," Meg answered honestly. The rejection from her mother still stung even ten years after she'd walked out.

"You face bigger challenges every day and win." Stephanie was making good points, and yet Meg's courage still escaped her.

"Work challenges. This is personal." She twisted her fingers around the corner of the baby blanket swaddling her infant daughter, Aubrey. "And I'm pretty sure the statute of limitations and good taste has run out considering our daughter is two months old and I still haven't told him about her. How am I supposed to explain that?"

"If he's too stupid to figure out how you guys made a baby, he's definitely not worth all this stress." Stephanie laughed.

The joke was meant to ease the tension, so Meg smiled as she rolled the edge of the blanket in between her thumb and forefinger.

Normally the ploy would work. Not today. Not when Meg's thoughts were careening out of control.

"Okay, I can see my bad attempt at humor isn't helping. How about this? I'll take Aubrey to the park while you feel him out. See if he's ready." Stephanie's calm demeanor had little impact on Meg's frayed nerves. "You had good reasons for waiting. And he'd be crazy to turn his back on that little girl."

"A total nutcase," Meg agreed, gazing down at the sleeping bundle.

"She's perfect." Stephanie could hold her own with anyone in an argument. She was a huge asset to One Child—One Advocate. "She might just be the best baby in the world, bar none, and it would be his loss if he walked away from her." Stephanie smiled at Aubrey with the kind of sheer adoration reserved for aunts. She might not be a blood relative, but Stephanie was the closest thing to family Meg had aside from her daughter.

"The man should be given the option to be part of her life." Meg was steeling her resolve by picking up Aubrey. Holding her daughter, so much innocence, inspired her to do the right thing even when her nerves were frayed and her stomach threatened to revolt.

"I'll be right down the street with her at the park. You give me the green light and I'm there at the restaurant. If you don't pick up on the vibe that he wants to know or if he makes one wrong move before you tell him you can always do this another time."

"Will you text me first so I don't seem rude or obvious if I have to whip out my phone in front of him?" Meg hedged. Thinking through an exit strategy made her feel less trapped.

"Great idea. I'll take the baby for a lap or two before checking in." Stephanie picked up her purse. "The fresh air will be good for us both, and the park is so pretty this time of year. Plus, the mayor's lighting the Christmas tree at noon."

"She'd love that. It's probably just all these hormones and this time of year giving me jitters." The first part was true enough. Meg didn't want to acknowledge how much the thought of seeing Wyatt Jackson again affected her. This was the first time the Christmas season had brought a feeling of renewal and hope instead of sadness and dread. The magic of the holidays had always escaped Meg until having Aubrey. Facing Wyatt with the news he was a father stamped out all the newly gained warm-and-fuzzy sentiment.

Stephanie shot a sympathetic look. "I know. Everything in town's been strange ever since Maverick Mike Butler's death this summer. The whole town's been on edge. But everything's calming down and slowly returning to normal. It's only a matter of time before the sheriff finds the person responsible and we can put all this behind us. You have a new baby and lots of memories to look forward to. And it's nice to focus on something besides murder for a change."

Meg nodded. The town had been through a lot since its wealthiest and most infamous resident was killed on his ranch this past summer. But it was more than that. The holidays brought back a memory of being interviewed for hours. The unspoken accusations had been so obvious that even a ten-year-old girl had understood them. Meg shivered involuntarily, thinking about the past. She couldn't bring herself to talk about it with anyone. She needed to focus on something else. Bad thoughts had a way of multiplying, causing her to tumble down a slippery slope of pain and regret.

Meg turned her attention to her sleeping baby. The change in Meg this year was because of Aubrey. That little girl brightened everything she touched. Her baby held a special kind of magic that made Meg want to believe in miracles again, precisely the innocent sentiment that would end up crushing her in—she checked her watch—less than five minutes.

She shouldered the diaper bag. "Ready?"

When Meg had become too sick to drive herself to a doctor visit, Stephanie had stepped up to help. Not long after, her work partner had found herself in a bind when her two-year relationship ended and she had no place to live. Meg had volunteered to room together and the friendship had blossomed from there. It was nice to have that in her life after keeping herself isolated for so long.

Stephanie examined Meg with a questioning look. "I am."

"It's just a conversation," Meg said to herself as she walked outside, bracing herself against the blast of frigid air. Her small SUV was parked in the lot behind the office. "I speak to people every day."

"And you're pretty darn good at it, too." Stephanie closed and locked the door behind them. It was Friday and they'd let the receptionist go early so she could watch the tree-lighting ceremony. "But anything about this guy gives you pause and I'm only two blocks away. I can be at the restaurant in less than five minutes." Stephanie snapped her fingers.

Meg froze as an awkward thought struck. "What if he doesn't remember me?"

"It's only been a year, Meg. You said that he'd been clear about not being the type to settle down, but I seriously doubt you'd spend time with anyone who was that much of a jerk." Stephanie jangled her keys. "Besides,

I'm following you in my car in case you both remember all too well and decide to get to know each other again while I babysit." Stephanie wiggled her eyebrows.

Meg held back the laugh trying to force its way out of her throat. Wyatt Jackson didn't want anything to do with her.

"I had to email him half a dozen times in order to get a response. If he remembers me at all from a year ago, he obviously wasn't too impressed." Meg secured Aubrey in her car seat in Stephanie's car. The baby stretched but didn't wake. She'd had a bottle twenty minutes ago so, fingers crossed, that should buy Meg a couple of hours to do what she should've done months ago before the baby arrived. Shoving the guilt aside, she climbed into the driver's seat.

Meg glanced around with that awful feeling of someone watching her. Her stress levels were already on an upward trajectory and this made it worse. It was probably nothing more than the thought of facing her baby's father that had her insides braided and the tiny hairs on her arms standing at attention. Or maybe it was the time of year. The holidays. The cold. The memories...

Meg glanced at the rearview. No one was there. She started the vehicle.

Wyatt Jackson was just a man like any other. This wasn't the time for her brain to point out that he was intelligent, successful and unnervingly gorgeous. In retrospect, the man seemed almost superhuman to her. But then, he'd given her the absolute best gift in her life, her daughter, and that was likely the reason she'd built him up so much in her mind.

Meg checked the rearview one more time, making sure that Stephanie had cleared the parking spot behind her. She glanced at the backup camera as she pressed the gas pedal. Something crossed the corner of the screen.

Heart jackhammering, she touched the brake.

What was back there? An animal?

A tiny little thing darted toward the trees, yellow stripes streaking past the driver's side. It was just a cat, barely more than a kitten.

Hands shaking, Meg white-knuckled the steering wheel, trying to calm her rattled nerves by sheer force of will.

There was nothing to be afraid of.

Right?

CHRISTMAS MIGHT ONLY be weeks away, but the holidays were something Wyatt Jackson would have no trouble skipping over altogether. New Year's was more his style with its all-night partying and the attitude of ringing in the New Year with free-flowing booze and a carefree attitude.

Speaking of which, receiving an email from the blond-haired beauty Wyatt had spent time with last year had caught him off guard. She'd made it look easy to ignore his repeated phone calls this time last year, so he'd returned the favor by deleting her messages when she'd first contacted him.

In fact, in the past twelve months he'd done his level best to forget she existed. Although part of him had known that would be impossible given that he couldn't

seem to shake the feel of her soft skin on his fingertips, her intellect or the easy way she made him laugh.

The last email from Meg had seemed urgent, and
to make matters even more interesting Maverick Mike
Butler's lawyer had been hot on Wyatt's tail to get him
to come to Cattle Barge. Mike Butler had been one
of Texas's most colorful citizens. A billionaire cattle
rancher who'd been murdered on his own property this
summer had sent the media into a feeding frenzy.

Ed Staples, the family's lawyer, had seemed down-
right shocked that Wyatt already knew he was Mike
Butler's illegitimate son. Probably because Wyatt
hadn't made a single attempt to contact the estate—
and thereby claim his right to the Butler fortune. Wyatt
had made a success of himself on his own terms and
had no need for a handout from the family who'd left
his mother pregnant and destitute.

The first thing Wyatt had noticed when he hit Cattle
Barge city limits was the swarm of media people. The
town was still overrun months after Butler's murder,
although reporters were starting to write fluff. News
about the famous will being read on Christmas Eve
splashed across headlines on every outlet. Maverick
Mike could take his money and shove it up his...

Wyatt realized he'd white-knuckled the steering
wheel and laughed at himself. The holidays had soured
his mood, and he had no plans to let emotions get in the
way of what he hoped would be a hot reunion between
him and the blonde. Besides, he couldn't imagine that
Maverick Mike's legitimate kids would welcome him
with open arms. Making the Butler heirs uncomfortable

wasn't the main reason Wyatt had hit the highway leading to Cattle Barge. He saw it more as a fringe benefit.

Wyatt knew the reason he'd been summoned, and to say he had mixed feelings about Maverick Mike Butler being his father was a lot like saying ghost peppers burned the tongue. Was he a Butler? His mother had said so, but in his heart he could never be connected to the man who'd walked away from her, from *him*.

Wyatt didn't want the man's money. His twenty-fifth Tiko Taco restaurant was about to open and he didn't need a handout from anyone. Wyatt had learned how to work hard for his successes and he enjoyed the fruits of his labor to the fullest.

The Butlers weren't the real reason he'd accepted the invitation to meet the family. There was another benefit to coming to Cattle Barge—seeing Meg Anderson again. He'd needed a good reason to show, convincing himself that a reunion wasn't pull enough and especially with the way she'd left things. To prove a point to himself—the point being that he didn't need her—he'd taken his time to return her emails.

That her tone had intensified, saying that they needed to meet got his curiosity going. They'd spent time together and—according to his memory—had one helluva good time before she'd ditched him. She'd cut off communication a few months after their smoking-hot affair started, leaving him scratching his head at what he'd done wrong.

Granted, he wasn't the relationship type by a long shot and he'd been up-front about it with her. He was always honest. And he knew deep down that one of them was bound to walk away first sooner or later. Normally he hit the door, not the other way around, and that was most likely the reason she was still on his mind a year later. He could make that concession.

He'd been clear about his intentions, and although he'd enjoyed her company—he could further admit that *enjoyed* put it lightly—they hadn't been together long enough for real heartbreak. And yet there'd been an uncomfortable feeling in his chest that felt a lot like a hole ever since she'd walked away.

Wyatt flipped the radio channel to his favorite country-and-western station. The breakup song playing reminded him of how he'd felt when Meg cut off communication. Now he was a bad cliché, and that just worsened his mood.

And even though Christmas was coming, he was most definitely not a ho-ho-ho type. Kris Kringle had never been more than a fat man in a silly suit. Wyatt tried to convince himself one more time that he didn't care what Meg had to tell him. He was doing her a favor by showing up to hear her out and he needed to be in town anyway, so he might as well see what she wanted.

He parked at the Home Grown Foods Restaurant and ignored the fact that his pulse kick-started with each forward step toward the door. What was he—a teenager again? That ship had sailed long ago, and Wyatt didn't appreciate the blast from the past making his collar feel stifling and his palms warm and sweaty.

The restaurant, located in the center of Main Street, had all of seven patrons. Traffic alone should've dictated a full house, although he remembered spotting a sign on his way in with details about a tree lighting at the park. He'd only been half paying attention.

Meg was hard to miss in her spot at the four-top table dead center in the room, and it was more than just her beauty that drew him toward her, although she looked even better than he remembered. She gave him one of those awkward morning-after smiles, the nervous kind with thin lips and scarcely any teeth showing. Even so, she was stunning and his heart reacted to seeing her by ratcheting up a few notches.

Acknowledging her with a nod, he removed his Stetson and closed the distance between them.

"Thanks for coming." She motioned toward the chair and quickly pulled her hand back like an alligator might bite it. "Please, take a seat."

The muscles on her forehead were pinched, which did nothing to dull her beauty as she sat on the edge of her seat. All hope this was going to be fun-filled day of reunion sex after a quick greeting and a decent meal died.

"You said this was important." He took the chair opposite her, reminding himself not to get too comfortable. He leaned back, crossed his legs and touched his fingertips together, forming a steeple. The most beautiful pair of sky-blue eyes framed by thick dark eyelashes stared back at him. Her eyes were the color of summer.

"It is." Blond locks spilled down her back. Was she this stunning before? Damn. She was and more.

Seeing her again awakened cells he thought were beyond resuscitation. Too bad she wanted something from him. And then he thought about it. News must be out that he was a Butler. A small town like Cattle Barge would have trouble keeping anything secret for long. Was she making a play for his inheritance? His heart argued against the idea even as the thought made him frown. Besides, he had no plans to claim anything about being a Butler, so she'd be out of luck.

A waitress brought over a menu. She was short, maybe five-feet-three inches, and had mousy brown hair. Her name tag read Hailey. The woman was the complete opposite of Meg, who had those long legs and shiny blond locks.

"Can I get you anything to drink?" Hailey asked.

"No. Thank you, Hailey." He didn't figure this conversation was going to take long enough to stick around. Meg would make her demand. He'd say no. Problem solved.

Ignoring the tug at his heart, he said, "I'm not staying."

Meg let out a little grunt.

"You sure about that?" Hailey asked with a smile and a wink.

"Never been more certain of anything in my life." Out of respect for his companion, he didn't flirt back.

"Let me know if you change your mind," Hailey said with a pout.

There was another emotion radiating off Meg—impatience. Or it could be jealousy, but that was most likely wishful thinking on his part. Sue him. She was even more beautiful than he remembered, and another pang of something—remorse?—hit as he acknowledged to himself she didn't seem to want to be there any more than he did. At least he was trying to make the best out of a bad situation. What was her excuse?

Her arms were crossed and her gaze laser focused.

"Might as well go ahead and spit it out." He didn't bother hiding his impatience. "What do you want from me?"

A sound ripped from her throat and she made a move toward her purse.

"Do us both a favor." She looked him square in the eyes. "Forget I called."

"Suit yourself," he said without conviction as he stood.

Wyatt turned around and walked right out the door.

Chapter Two

With every step the handsome cowboy took toward the parking lot, Meg's pulse climbed another notch. Let him leave and it was all over. She couldn't imagine finding the courage to contact him again, and even if she did he wouldn't take her calls.

Seeing him again, all bronzed hair and steel-gray eyes with thick lashes, had thrown her off. The restaurant should've been full over the lunch hour but she'd forgotten about the midday tree-lighting ceremony in the park. The place must be bustling about now, and she figured that was half the reason she hadn't heard from Stephanie yet.

Meg pushed off the chair and followed Wyatt. A young guy held the door open for her, but their feet collided and she had to take a couple of steps to recover her balance.

She acknowledged his mumbled apology with a nod. Her gaze was locked onto Wyatt's back side as she ignored the sensual shivers running through her.

The fact that he'd been clear about flying solo had

been the exact reason she'd ended their fling last year and walked away before her emotions got involved.

"Wait," she said to his back, a strong one at that. Birds fluttered in her chest. When he didn't stop, she added, "Please."

Wyatt slowed his pace, which allowed her to catch up to his long strides without breaking into a run.

"I'm sorry about before…" Now at his side, she could see him smirking. Meg stopped. "I have something serious to say, but if this is just a game to you then forget it."

Wyatt turned to face her and put all signs of his playboy swagger in check.

Wow. Meg had been nervous before, but she had totally underestimated how much harder this was going to be in person while staring into his eyes. Her legs threatened to give.

"Last year, I stopped returning your calls—"

He brought his hand up to stop her.

"If that's why you called me here, save it. It was a long time ago and I don't need an explanation. We had fun. You moved on. End of story." Was there a momentary flicker of…*hurt?*…in his eyes? Meg must be crazy and seeing imaginary things. What was next? Unicorns? She'd been reading too many fairy tales to her daughter because her mind was flirting with believing them.

He made a move to walk away again, and the pressure mounted…

"We had more than fun. We had a baby," she blurted out, her pulse pounding wildly in part because of what she'd just shared and in part because of the strong virile male standing two feet in front of her.

He looked her up and down like he was evaluating her for a trip to the psych ward. His eyes grazed a hot trail as they lingered on the curve of her hips and then the fullness of her breasts. An unwelcome sensation of warmth slid along her belly and heated her inner thighs despite the frigid December temperatures.

"How do you know it's mine?" That question was the equivalent of a bucket of ice water dumped over her head.

"You were the only possibility." She brought her fisted hand to rest on her hip and her body shivered to stave off the cold.

Wyatt glanced around. "I don't exactly see a baby, so…"

"She's at the park." Meg fumbled inside her purse for her cell, willing her shaky hands to calm down. After his accusation, they were trembling with anger. She needed to check her texts to see if Stephanie had tried to reach her. "She's eight weeks old and I haven't slept since she was born, so excuse me if I'm a little rattled." She threw one of her hands up in the air.

"If you're after the Butler fortune you're going about it the wrong way." The words knifed her chest. She'd expected him to be surprised but not condemn her as money-grubbing crackpot, but hold on a minute. Had she heard him right?

"What does my daughter have to do with the Butlers? Your last name is Jackson." Now it was Meg's turn to look at him like he'd lost his mind. Although, she shouldn't be surprised at the news. Maverick Mike

Butler had fathered at least one other child that no one knew about.

Wyatt stared at her, same as before, with a raised brow and unbelievable expression.

"No, I'm not in need of psychiatric care." She located her cell and white-knuckled it. "And I do have a baby."

Meg entered her screensaver password and noticed there was still no text from Stephanie. An uneasy feeling gripped her as she stuck her phone out at Wyatt. A picture of Aubrey was her wallpaper and, therefore, proof. "See."

He nodded as he scrutinized the image.

"You still haven't answered my question. What does Aubrey have to do with the Butlers?" Her patience was running thin and she really was starting to get worried about Stephanie.

Wyatt looked at a loss for words.

"Never mind. Excuse me for a second while I make a call. My friend took my—" she flashed eyes at him "—*our* daughter for a walk around the park. She was supposed to text me in case things went sour…" Meg ran her finger along Stephanie's name. She didn't dare turn her back on Wyatt for fear he'd disappear even though she wanted to make this call in private. The cell ran straight into voice mail and her pulse shot up a couple more notches. "Stephanie, give me a call as soon as you get this. Hope everything is okay."

Wyatt, who had been quiet until now, said, "I'm sure everything's all right."

"It's not like her not to do something if she says she's going to." Meg started to pace, torn between walking away from him—and possibly never seeing him again—and checking on her daughter.

"Do you trust your friend?" he asked.

"Absolutely."

"Then you have to believe that she wouldn't do anything to put your daughter in harm's way. That's really what you're worried about, right? Something bad happening to…" He seemed to be searching for the name so she supplied it.

"Aubrey."

His jaw muscle ticked. "Right. You said something about a tree-lighting ceremony and that's probably what the traffic I drove in to get here was for. Thus, the reason I was late. They could be playing holiday music. She most likely can't hear her cell."

"Wouldn't we hear if it was *that* loud?" she asked.

"It's two blocks away from the restaurant. I doubt it." He was making sense, being rational, while her over-the-top protective instinct was waging war on her insides. The two had driven separate vehicles because Stephanie had errands to run later.

"I have a bad feeling." She couldn't shake it no matter how hard she tried.

"You and every mother I've ever known." Wyatt's steel gaze intensified.

She looked at him, shocked.

"What?" He lifted a shoulder.

"How many like me have there been?" Astonishment flushed her cheeks.

"Like you?" He shot a look. "None."

"Then how do you… Oh, right, you had a mother."

She didn't figure him the type to notice the little things. "Everyone does. Even someone like—"

"You really don't like me very much, do you?" he said with half a smirk and that infuriating twinkle in his eye that had been so good at seducing her.

"I'm sorry. It's just ever since my—" she glanced up at him "—*our* daughter was born I've been on high alert, afraid something could happen to her. She's so tiny and fragile except when she cries. Then I know there's a tiger in there waiting to come out. But the rest of the time she's just this little thing who's totally dependent on me and I'm trying my best not to mess everything up." Had all that really just come out? Wow. Meg was on the verge of a meltdown. She was normally more of the quiet type.

Wyatt seemed too stunned to speak.

"None of which is your problem." She glanced at the time. More than half an hour had passed and still no word from Stephanie.

"We can head down there to the park, to see for ourselves." He was extending an olive branch and she would take it.

"Thank you. I'd like that a lot actually." Meg started toward the park, remembering that although he might have the swagger of a playboy and was all alpha male, she'd been drawn to his kindness in the first place. There wasn't anything sexier than a strong man who wasn't afraid to show he had a beating heart in his chest.

"I'm not claiming responsibility for her," he clarified, and it was so cold outside she could see his breath. So much for the warmth.

WYATT STARED AT the woman who was walking so fast he had to hustle to keep pace. His judgment with people and especially women was normally spot-on, and he hadn't pegged Meg Anderson as unstable or a gold digger.

In fact, she'd seemed like the most grounded, intelligent woman he'd been with in a long time, possibly ever. Her sharp mind was what he'd missed most about her. Since their tryst he'd compared every date to her and no one seemed to measure up. Even sex had been lacking, but that was a whole other story that made him think he might be losing his edge. So, he was even more shocked by her whipping out the baby card. Was there even a child? *His child?* This whole conversation left him scratching his head and an unsettled feeling gnawed at his gut.

He took off his coat and placed it around her arms, realizing she didn't have any covering on her shoulders. She must've left her jacket on the chair back where he'd last seen it.

He didn't have the heart to walk away while she was so distraught. Even though she'd shown him the pic of the cute infant on her phone, he couldn't ignore the possibility that she'd jumped off the deep end. Maybe she'd been on mood-regulating drugs when they'd spent time together. Maybe she'd stopped taking them and this was the real her.

His logical mind wrestled against the possibility, but that could just be his pride unable to accept that he'd made such a wide turn with his judgment before. Wyatt had always considered himself more intelligent than that. As they said, the proof was in the pudding and this "pudding" was starting to unravel in front of his eyes.

When he really looked at her, he couldn't ignore the changes in her body. Her hips had more pronounced curves, which were even sexier now. There were definite changes in her breasts. They'd been full before but not quite this generous.

Even tired, she was still one of the most beautiful women he'd ever seen. He told himself the only reason he was noticing any of the changes in her was because he was trying to determine if she needed to be driven to Kruger Belton Mental facility for evaluation and not because he cared or was still attracted to her. His heart had fisted a little bit when he'd first seen her. He did care, generally speaking.

The park was crowded. Holiday music filled the air. Families walked in clumps, smiling and singing along with Christmas carols. It was something out of a Norman Rockwell painting and definitely not Wyatt's scene.

"They aren't here." Meg stopped and looked at him, clearly flustered. She had that panicked-mother look even though he wouldn't know from personal experience. His had been too exhausted working to keep food on the table to get too emotional. He'd known his mother loved him and the fact he'd grown up in poverty was all the more reason to be proud of the successful taco franchise he'd built from a food truck.

Meg dug in her purse and pulled out a baby's cloth with little owls on it.

"Was she supposed to bring the baby to the restaurant?" He had no idea of the protocol in dealing with a nearly hysterical woman, but he could see from the way she twisted the baby's cloth in her hands that she was working herself up. Experience with women had taught him that this was not the time to tell her to *calm down*.

"Stephanie was supposed to text first." Meg worked the cloth in her hands.

"Her battery could've died." She winced at that last word.

"I guess." That cloth in her hands was about to become pulp.

Wyatt reached out to touch her shoulder in an attempt to reassure her but was left with a sizzle on his fingertips. He almost pulled his hand back but decided to ignore the frissons of heat.

Hot or not, this one was off-limits, and especially with the bomb she'd dropped on him earlier.

Still, he couldn't help but feel sorry for her. The child, real or imagined, was obviously very important to her. So much so that she was trembling.

And then she looked up at him with those blue eyes that he'd liked looking into right before he fell off the cliff during sex. *Okay, not the time for that thought, Jackson.*

"I can't imagine how all this must look from your point of view. Thank you for the coat. I must've left mine in the restaurant. I was in such a hurry to catch you because I knew if you left it was over. I'd never have the courage to email again. You should know that I don't want anything from you. I just thought you had a right to know about your daughter."

Whether he believed her or not didn't matter. She seemed vulnerable, and that pierced his armor. "We'll figure this out."

Her phone buzzed and her ringtone sounded, same ones as before. He should know. He'd been the one to program the song into her new phone when she couldn't figure out how to change the basic sound.

A look of sheer relief flooded her tense expression as she checked the screen. "It's Stephanie."

Wyatt needed to clear his head so he could face the Butler family this afternoon. To say this day was throwing curveball after curveball was a lot like saying Texas highways were crowded. At least Meg had received the call she'd been waiting for and that was a relief.

His respite was short-lived as Meg dropped to her knees.

"Tell me where you are and I'll be there in two seconds." Her voice shook and panic radiated from her.

He offered a hand up, which she took. The color had drained from her face as she glanced around. "The Butler Fountain?" She paused. "I know exactly where that is."

Whatever her friend was saying wasn't good, and he figured this day was about to get even longer.

"Did you give the sheriff your statement?" She paused again. "Do it right now. Tell them everything you just told me. I'm almost there."

Now his curiosity was getting the best of him as Meg broke into a run.

He followed, easily keeping pace even though Meg was still obviously in shape. She gripped her cell as she raced toward the planned site of the Mike Butler Memorial Fountain.

A small crowd had gathered, facing away from the tree. There was a woman on the ground, her legs curled up and her face scrunched in pain and panic.

"What's going on?" he asked Meg as they neared the woman.

"I'm so sorry. I don't know what happened," the woman he presumed to be Stephanie said through sobs. "I was walking along fine and then I blacked out." Her hand came up to the back of her head to rub. "Ouch…" She blinked in panic, tears welling. "I came to and she was gone. Someone took her. Someone kidnapped Aubrey. They must've taken everything, the stroller and the diaper bag. All I remember is blacking out."

The most heartbreaking sound tore from Meg's throat.

Wyatt's head nearly exploded and an ache ripped through his chest. He couldn't figure out why he'd have such a strong reaction to a child's kidnapping when, first, he'd never even met the little tyke and, second, he still wasn't convinced she belonged to him.

His heart didn't seem to need confirmation one way or the other.

Chapter Three

"Did you call the sheriff?" Meg asked, looking like her world had just tipped on its axis in the same way Wyatt's just had. But there was no way he could care this much about a child he'd never met. He chalked his feelings up to sympathy for the mother and the heart-breaking situation.

"I did." A woman stepped forward. She was young, mid-twenties, and clutching a small child's hand. The little boy couldn't be more than three or four years old. "I wish I'd seen more. I heard someone scream and ran over to see what happened. I was too late."

Meg thanked her.

"He's on his way." Stephanie glanced around at the gathering crowd, looking bewildered. "There was a guy—he was wearing one of those forest green park-maintenance uniforms—and he said he saw everything before taking off in that direction." She pointed east. "Said he'd be right back."

Meg looked on the verge of crumpling. The more people who gathered around the less likely it would

be for him or Meg to see someone escaping with the
stroller. Wyatt glanced at Meg.

"What color stroller am I looking for?" he asked.

"Red with big wheels to take it jogging." She glanced
from him to Stephanie with the most sorrowful look
on her face.

Wyatt glanced around at the small crowd. "Did any
of you see anything unusual or anyone hurrying out
of this area with a red stroller?" The odds were slim
anyone would notice details like that, but it was worth
asking.

Heads shook.

"There was a lot going on and the music was too
loud. I was afraid to wake her, so I stayed back here by
the benches. I was worried that Meg would text and I
would miss it." Stephanie sobbed.

"You did the right thing." Wyatt had no idea what
to say, but he wished he could make the situation okay
for both of them. Stephanie seemed like a nice person and he already knew Meg was. At least she hadn't
been lying about there being a child. Obviously, there
was. No one would go through this much trouble to
set up a lie.

"Go. Look for her. I'm fine," Stephanie said, trying
to push to her feet. She wobbled and a Good Samari-
tan steadied her by grabbing her arm in time before she
landed on her bottom. She thanked him.

"We'll stay with her," the woman with the child said.

"Did you see anything?" Wyatt asked Stephanie.

"No. I was walking with the stroller before I felt
something hard hit the back of my head and then I

blacked out. Next thing I knew the park worker was beside me asking if I was okay and I had a blinding headache." She touched a spot behind her left ear.

Meg hopped onto a nearby bench and scanned the area.

"See anything up there?" Wyatt asked. He tried to convince himself that he'd feel this panicked whether the child might be his or not. An infant had been kidnapped, and he could admit that he still had residual feelings for the baby's mother. The little girl didn't have to belong to him for his heart to go out to Meg. If he could help her find her baby he would. And if she kept on insisting the baby was his, he'd ask for a DNA test before he got too worked up. Keeping a level head in challenging times had earned Wyatt his solid reputation in the business world and helped him expand to twenty-five locations. This was no different.

He joined Meg on the park bench. There were too many people spreading in all different directions. The ceremony had ended, which was the perfect time to execute this kind of crime because there was chaos while families exited the park area and spilled into the parking lot.

There was no way he was going to find the person responsible at this rate. He couldn't justify standing around and watching all this heartbreak, either.

"Text me and let me know what the sheriff says. I have to do something," Meg shouted to her friend, and he completely understood the sentiment. He was having the same conversation in his head.

Meg was on the verge of tears as she turned to look at him. "I don't see any sign of her."

"If I was going to commit the crime, I'd park in the closest spot." He pointed to the nearest parking lot, which was slowly emptying. There was a line to exit, and the park's location in the center of town off the main square caused traffic to move slowly. "Maybe we can spot your daughter in a car on the way out of the lot."

"It's worth a try." Meg sounded hopeless as he held out his hand. She took it. A simple gesture really, but when their hands made contact a fire bolt shot straight up his arm. He ignored it as best he could and took off running. With their hands linked, Meg kept pace and he was pretty sure it was from pure adrenaline.

"Maybe there," she said through gulps of air as they darted toward the light that regulated the exit. "I see the handle of a stroller in the back window and it's red."

Wyatt let her hand loose so he could push forward and catch the white minivan before the light turned and the vehicle disappeared. From this angle, he couldn't get a good look at the plate. He pushed his legs harder, leaving Meg several strides behind. If he could get to the minivan in time maybe he could put this whole ordeal to rest.

The minivan was close, but the light could turn at any second. Wyatt pushed harder until his thighs burned and his lungs threatened to burst. He could see there was only a driver and the figure was large enough to be male.

"Hold on," he shouted to the van's driver. The window was up and the man didn't so much as flinch.

As the light changed, Wyatt closed in on the van. He was so close. Dammit. There were three cars ahead of the minivan, not close enough for Wyatt to catch. The cars moved and the minivan turned left, which was the opposite side of Wyatt. What an unlucky break.

Wyatt shot in between two cars. One of the drivers laid on his horn and shouted a few terse words. Wyatt had no idea where Meg was and he didn't risk turning back to look. The minivan was going at least thirty-five miles an hour. If he could catch a break and the light at the corner turned to red… Scratch that. Wyatt had never been lucky and that's how he'd learned to work hard for everything he'd built.

Brake lights renewed his hope as he turned on the speed he'd known as a runner in high school. Although that had been a long time ago, he worked out and kept in shape.

The van disappeared around the corner before the light changed.

"Wyatt." Meg's voice rippled through him. There was a mix of hope and relief in the sound of her tone. "I got her."

He immediately turned tail and saw a man in a forest green uniform standing next to Meg, who was holding a baby. He made a beeline toward the trio, driven by something deep inside. Was it a primal need to see if her child belonged to him? Would he even be able to tell by looking at her one time?

Meg stood there, baby pressed to her chest and her face awash with relief. She was gently rocking the crying infant. An odd thought hit: No one had better get close to her or the baby. He was struck with something else that felt a lot like longing, but Wyatt didn't go there. He'd missed Meg. He could own up to it. That's as far as his feelings went, he reminded himself.

"I'm Wyatt Jackson." He stuck out his hand to the park worker. "And I can't thank you enough for what you did."

The man bent forward, panting as he took the outstretched hand. "Name's Cecil. And I'm just—" he paused to take a breath "—glad I was there to help." Cecil grabbed at his right side. "He got away, ditched the stroller by pushing it toward traffic. I had to make a choice to save her or catch him." He paused long enough to take in another breath. "His back was to me the whole time. I couldn't get a good look at his face."

"You did the right thing, Cecil." Relief washed over Wyatt. This morning had been right up there with… He didn't want to think about the other depressing event that came with the holidays.

The baby was in her mother's arms, safe. Crisis averted. That was all he would allow himself to focus on.

"Are you okay to walk?" he asked Cecil.

The man nodded.

The crime scene had been cordoned off, and a deputy was asking people to go back to work or home. Stephanie flew toward Meg and the baby; tears streamed down both women's faces.

A man by the name of Clarence Sawmill introduced himself as the sheriff. Cecil recounted his story to Sawmill, who shook his head as he recorded details. His lips formed a grim line. Middle-aged, his eyes had the white outline of sunglasses on otherwise tanned skin. Deep grooves in his forehead and hard brackets around his mouth outlined the man's stress levels. He was on high alert and, from the looks of him, had been since news broke of Maverick Mike's death five months ago.

"Our family-oriented town doesn't usually see much of a spike in crime." Sawmill shook his head. For a split second his gaze stopped on Wyatt and he seemed to be sizing him up. The sheriff looked like he hadn't slept in as many months and he probably hadn't, considering Mike Butler's murder still hadn't been solved. Sawmill seemed like the kind of guy who would take his citizens' welfare to heart.

The sheriff was holding an evidence bag.

"What did you find?" Wyatt asked.

"A child's hair ribbon. It's probably not connected. More than likely came out of a little girl's hair while she was attending the tree lighting." Sawmill pinched the bridge of his nose like he was trying to stem a raging headache. "My deputies will process the scene and we'll keep you posted if anything relevant turns up."

Meg thanked the sheriff as she gently bounced the baby, who had settled down in her mother's comforting arms. He had to admit Meg seemed content with the job of mother.

The sheriff asked Meg a few routine-sounding questions. Her body language tensed when she spoke to Sawmill, but Wyatt figured it was justifiable under the circumstances. She was being asked if there was a reason anyone she knew would try to kidnap her infant child.

"We have a potential witness already on his way to the station to work with a sketch artist while the details are still fresh," Sawmill said. "We'll want you to come in and take a look as soon as we have an image in case you can identify him."

Given the person had tried to take the baby while she was with Stephanie, Wyatt doubted that was likely.

Even so, he planned to reschedule his meeting with the Butler family lawyer. This day had taken unexpected turn after unexpected turn and, after getting a good look at Meg's daughter, he had a feeling the day wasn't done with him yet.

DINNER WAS HOURS away and yet all Meg wished for was a hot bath, a warm bed and sleep. Wyatt had said he'd been called away to a meeting, but Meg figured he needed air after the day's events. Meg and Stephanie returned to the office since it was closer to the sheriff's office and Aubrey had a pack-and-play crib there.

Stephanie had insisted on sticking around even though Meg had begged her friend to go to the ER instead. The most she would agree to was allowing an EMT to check her out at the scene.

"How's your head?" Meg asked her friend.

"It's been worse," Stephanie said with a crooked smile.

"I still think we should swing by the hospital," Meg said.

"My name is Stephanie Gable. It's three weeks until

Christmas. I live at 1212 Farm Road 236. With you, who should learn to relax a little more and stop washing every dish before it hits the sink, by the way." She made eyes at Meg. "How's that?"

"I think you took a bigger hit than we first thought," she quipped, and they both smiled. Meg's died on her lips the minute her cell rang.

A glance at the screen said it was the sheriff's office. She took the call.

"We have an image to work with but, to be honest, it isn't much to go on," he said. Any hope this case could be sewn up and a criminal taken off the streets soon died.

"I'll let Wyatt know and we'll be there as soon as we can," she informed him before ending the call and texting Wyatt.

An immediate response came: Stay where you are and I'll pick you up.

"What did the sheriff say?" Stephanie was studying Meg's reaction.

"He didn't sound encouraged," Meg admitted.

"We'll figure this out." Her friend's words were meant to reassure, but did nothing to ease the knot braiding her stomach.

Meg glanced down at her sleeping baby. She'd been unable to move from the little girl's side since... Meg couldn't even think about what had happened, what *could* have happened, without tears springing to her eyes. She was so grateful to have her daughter back where she belonged.

What kind of person tried to take a baby from her

mother three weeks before Christmas? Granted, the person had tried to take the little girl from Stephanie, but the attacker didn't know the difference.

Skipping lunch had been a bad idea even though Meg doubted she could get or keep anything down. A headache was trying to form in the spot right between her eyes.

Within fifteen minutes, Aubrey had been fed and the diaper bag packed.

"He's on his way?" Stephanie paced in the kitchenette of their office.

"He should be here any minute." Meg cradled the warm, sleeping baby in her arms. Her miracle, considering she'd never expected to have a traditional life of marriage and a family. "You should sit down."

Stephanie shot her an apprehensive look.

"Well, then maybe you should rethink going to the hospital to get checked out." Meg eyed the cup of coffee in Stephanie's shaking hand, wishing her friend had gone for the calming tea, instead.

"The ibuprofen is already kicking in. I'll be fine. I'm just so glad…" Another stream of tears slid down Stephanie's cheeks. She turned her back and sniffed.

"Let's not even go there. None of this is your fault." Meg held her baby a little closer. "And she's right here. Fine. Look at her."

A knock on the glass out front startled them both.

"That's probably him," Meg said.

"Stay right here. I'll check." Stephanie was out of the room in a flash and Meg figured her friend needed to work off some of her stress energy. The adrenaline would wear off soon, and she was afraid Stephanie was in for one monster headache when it did.

Her own nerves were on edge after the day's events and thinking about seeing Wyatt again didn't help. Based on his actions earlier, he planned to be in Aubrey's life, and Meg would have to get used to her body's reaction to him. Her heart seized a little bit at the thought he didn't want to be in hers, too. What did she expect?

Sure, they'd connected last year with chemistry she'd never experienced before, and that spark between them, mentally and physically, had produced amazingly hot sex. *And a baby*, a little voice reminded, grounding her.

"Ready?" Wyatt examined her and the baby in her arms. He was the kind of man who would do the right thing by his child no matter how he felt personally about the child's mother. On the one hand, there was something encouraging about the sentiment. At least Aubrey would have a father.

Meg stood and reached for the diaper bag. Wyatt moved beside her in a beat, taking it from her. He hadn't asked to hold the baby yet, and this was the closest he'd been to her since they'd found her. Not exactly encouraging, but it could've been so much worse.

Based on the crease in his forehead, the one he got when he was deeply contemplating something, he needed a little time to process. His daughter had almost been kidnapped.

"Wyatt, meet your daughter, Aubrey," Meg said.

A flash of emotion passed behind his eyes as he

looked at her but he seemed to get hold of it. "She's a pretty little girl."

"Do you want to hold her?" she asked.

"Not yet," he said.

Fifteen minutes later, the four of them arrived at the sheriff's office.

Janis, the sheriff's receptionist, rose to her feet. "We've spoken on the phone a few times. Come on in. The sheriff is waiting for you." She wrapped Meg and the baby in a big hug before leading them down the hall.

Sawmill got to his feet and extended his hand. "Please, sit down."

The sheriff's office was large, simple. There was a huge mahogany desk with an executive chair and two flags on poles standing sentinel to either side. A picture of the governor was centered in between the poles. Two smaller-scale leather chairs nestled up to the desk. A sofa and table with a bronze statue of a bull rider on a bull were on the other side of the room. Meg and Stephanie took the leather chairs across the sheriff's desk. Wyatt stood a few feet behind Meg's chair, arms crossed, leaning against the wall.

"I wish I could remember more about the man who attacked me. I'm just so glad everything turned out okay." Stephanie's shoulders seemed set in a forward slump. She shot another apologetic look at Meg as more tears welled.

"You were brave today. Without you, this could've turned out very differently," Wyatt said, and there was admiration in his otherwise tight voice. It was probably easier for him to sympathize with Stephanie, or anyone who wasn't Meg considering the bomb she'd dropped on him.

He put his hand on Meg's shoulder and she ignored the sensual zing of electricity that always came with his touch. After a year, it hadn't dimmed and that caught her off guard. She'd had the same reaction in the parking lot of the restaurant but was too stressed to acknowledge it.

"Mr. Daron, the park worker, gave the sketch artist very little to work with, so we're hopeful his build will seem familiar to one of you." Sawmill picked up a folder on top of a stack of papers on his desk. He showed them the sketch.

Stephanie balked. "He could be half the town. I wouldn't be able to pick him out of a lineup if he was standing right in front of me and I actually knew what he looked like."

Meg stared at the image. It was like a bomb exploded in her brain and yet she had no idea why. She could feel Sawmill's eyes on her, examining her. The blast from the past nearly crippled her. She remembered being in this very office, although the furniture was different then. There had been a different person in the chair opposite her and an overenthusiastic rookie investigator grilling her for answers.

A scared ten-year-old had sat in the chair in Meg's place. Being here, sitting in this very spot caused a lot of bad memories to crash down around her.

Meg took in a fortifying breath. She was no longer an innocent kid being railroaded by a system that too often protected criminals' rights more than victims'.

Besides, she'd grown into a woman. Everything in her life had changed since then.

The baby stirred in her arms and looked like she was winding up to cry. Like a balloon deflating, she blew out a breath and made a sucking noise before settling into her mother's arms again.

Meg forced the old thoughts out of her mind—thoughts that had her feeling vulnerable and alone.

"I don't know. Nothing about him looks familiar at all and yet I feel like I should know who he is." She scooted closer to the image, but Sawmill was already up and coming around his desk with the paper in hand.

She took the drawing from him and studied it. Her brain hurt from thinking so hard and she was coming up empty. "All I'm getting is a headache."

But then Stephanie had been the one with Aubrey when she'd been taken. She turned to her friend. "Does he look familiar to you?"

"You've never seen him before?" Sawmill said to Meg, a hauntingly similar note of disappointment in his voice. He had been hoping for better news, based on his tone.

Meg pushed but nothing came except more pain that felt a lot like a brain cramp. "I'm sorry."

Sawmill turned to Stephanie. "What about you, Ms. Gable? Do you know anyone with a similar shape or build?"

She was already shaking her head before he finished his question. "No, sir. Not one person in particular."

"Do you have any idea what age he might be?" Wyatt asked.

"Twenty-five to forty-five," the sheriff supplied.

Not exactly reassuring.

"There must be more to go on than that," Wyatt said. All signs of his casual swagger were gone, replaced by chiseled facade.

"White, male," the sheriff added.

"What about the hair ribbon?" Meg asked, hoping for some good news. "Is it connected to the case?"

"There's no information from forensics yet, ma'am. It might take a few weeks. I called in a favor to see if the results can be fast-tracked. The town's been through enough already without citizens feeling like their families are no longer safe here." The flash of frustration was quickly replaced by determination.

Meg studied the image on the paper in front of her. Fear rippled through her. But why? What was it about him? Was it the fact that this man had tried to kidnap her daughter? Those words were like gut punches.

There was something hauntingly familiar about the outline of his face. But Meg was certain she'd never seen this man before...

Right?

Chapter Four

One look from the sheriff and Meg had to fight her instincts to draw away from him. That look, that same damn look of disappointment bore down on her.

Did he think she wanted the maniac who'd tried to kidnap her daughter to go free?

It made her sick to think this person could try again with another unwitting mother.

Based on his expression, he felt the same way. Another crime in his town, under his nose. They were racking up and she could see every stress crack in the dark circles cradling his eyes. But she also knew in her heart that he couldn't help her or her baby.

Wyatt's eyes were different. His were harder to read than the sheriff's. Hesitation? Yes…well, maybe. Skepticism? Certainly. And something else she couldn't make out. Or, more accurately, didn't have the heart to try. Because it was disappointment in *her*.

Seeing that look in Wyatt's eyes would crush her. And how stupid was that? They'd had a fling and Aubrey was the product. Meg couldn't imagine life without her baby now that she was here, but she hadn't exactly planned for any of this and was still winging the whole parenting thing.

"Mind taking one last look at the sketch?" the sheriff asked Stephanie, and Meg was grateful he'd redirected his attention.

Instinctively, she held her daughter a little closer to her chest, grateful this day hadn't been much worse. Just the thought of anything happening to Aubrey...

No, Meg couldn't go there. Not even hypothetically. Another pang of guilt struck like a physical blow because this whole scenario was too close to home. She had been ten years old when her best friend was abducted right before her eyes and Meg wasn't able to remember a single detail. It had changed her life.

In this case, Meg was the mother who'd almost... *almost*...lost her child. A fresh sense of shame for not being able to bring peace to Mary Jane's family washed over her, threatening to drag her to the ocean floor.

If only she'd been able to remember what had happened. Mary Jane's family would have the closure that Meg could never give them. She'd seen the Fjords a handful of times after Mary Jane's body had turned up. They'd seemed...*hollow*.

Mary Jane's older brother, Jonathon, had been so affected that he'd had to be pulled out of school and, if memory served, he'd been too traumatized to return. She'd heard rumors that he was homeschooled after because he couldn't bring himself to leave the house.

After this experience of almost losing her own daughter, Meg could certainly understand the Fjords taking extreme measures to keep their son safe. Icy fingers gripped her spine thinking about the past.

All Meg wanted to do was take her baby home and shut out the rest of the world until she could stop trembling.

"I understand the work you do puts you in a precarious situation with folks." Sawmill seemed to realize that continuing to ask her or Stephanie to recognize the kidnapper from barely a sketch was as productive as squeezing water from a cell phone. Meg appreciated the redirection. "Have either of you had any disagreements with clients or been threatened in any way recently?"

Stephanie issued a grunt as Meg shot him a look.

"We help women and children leave abusive households, Sheriff. Being cursed at and threatened comes with the territory," she said.

He nodded and pressed his lips together in a look of solidarity.

"Does a particular incident stand out in your mind?" he asked, and there was a hint of respect in his voice.

"Are you saying this might be personal?" Meg asked. The case she would be testifying for in two weeks had been her main focus since having the baby.

"I wouldn't be doing justice to this investigation if I didn't come at this from every angle," he defended.

He had a point.

"I'm working a case involving a ten-year-old. Kaylee Garza has been physically abused by her soccer-coach father, Randol Garza. It's a typical abuse story in that the little girl has become a master at covering her bruises for school." She looked up at the sheriff in time to see his jaw clench. Hearing about abuse was never easy, especially when it involved children.

Out of the corner of her eye, she also saw that Wyatt's body language was intense. Lines creased his forehead, and tension brackets formed around his mouth. Any decent man wouldn't take hearing what she was about to say lightly and he seemed to know what was coming. She wondered if he'd been subject to abuse as a child and that's what made him seem so sympathetic now. "That is until he whipped her with a cord and she couldn't sit down in class. The domineering father had been abusive to the mother and child for a few years. But this time, he went too far and Kaylee's mother, Virginia, reached out to us for protection and legal help."

"I'm familiar with that story. One of my deputies arrested Mr. Garza. I don't mind saying we were shocked. He seemed like a decent man. Reverend Dawson spoke up on his behalf," the sheriff admitted. "I didn't realize that case was one of yours."

"Garza is fighting the charges against him, and—" she glanced at the sheriff "—he has a lot to lose if Kaylee and her mother's claims turn out to be justified, which they will."

The sheriff stared at her for a long moment. "He coaches the reverend's daughter on that team."

"That's right. There are a few prominent members of the community who have daughters who play for him, as well. Doesn't mean he didn't beat his daughter so hard there were blood blisters on her bottom and legs. Her mother has fallen down the stairs or into a cabinet five times in the past eighteen months, which makes her one the clumsiest people alive or a victim. Given that she was once captain of her college long-distance track team, I seriously doubt she has issues with coordination."

The sheriff leaned back in his chair, examining her as though he was checking her sanity or truthfulness. "My office is aware of the claims."

Hearing about and being witness to such abuses, especially with children, was by far the most difficult part of Meg's job. She couldn't allow herself to focus on that side of the equation for too long or it would be crippling. The bright spot—the good that she would cling to in situations like these—was how much Kaylee and Virginia's lives were going to change. Meg had a chance to guide them to a better future and a more fulfilled life. She couldn't erase their pain, but she could give them the blueprint for their future. In her five years of working for One Child—One Advocate that was the part that kept her going, kept her fighting even when a case seemed hopeless.

"One of your deputies is married to Alysa Estacado," Meg fired back. "She's Garza's cousin. My client asked for this case to be handled by another law enforcement agency and we petitioned the judge on her behalf."

"Mrs. Garza had a tough upbringing. Seems I remember there were drinking problems in her family," Sawmill said.

"If you're saying what I think you are, yes. My client has had her difficulties with alcohol. She's sober now and ready to work," Meg defended.

The sheriff seemed to be contemplating what she

said. She could see the road ahead with this case was going to be difficult based on his reaction to the allegations and her client's history. She could only pray the case would be moved, as requested. It was a challenge she accepted with open arms because she could make a difference in Kaylee's life. She could give Virginia a fresh start so she could be the mother she said she wanted to be. Fighting for that was worth every sideways stare she got from people—from the reverend to the sheriff himself.

"I'm not trying to convince you of the merits of this case," she finally said.

Sawmill hesitated like he was about to say something, but his lips thinned and he nodded. "Any other cases I should be aware of?"

She didn't have the heart to defend any more of her clients, considering only the most difficult-to-prove cases ended up on her doorstep. "I'll send a list of names who might be worth investigating."

"I'll need more than that. I want histories, too. I'm especially interested in the past few months. Anyone you think might have a vendetta against you or Ms. Gable," he said. "There's a possibility someone targeted your child in order to show you what it would feel like to have your baby ripped from your arms."

More icy fingers gripped her spine at the suggestion somehow her work was putting her daughter in danger. A scary thought struck. Could Wyatt use that in court to take Aubrey away from her?

Would he?

"I'll email the list with as much detail as I can provide as soon as I get home. I don't have to remind you everything I share is confidential." This was over. Aside from the fact that she had nothing else to contribute, he had already given up on her ability to help. Besides, what happened earlier most likely didn't have anything to do with her current caseload. She'd barely been back to work since having the baby.

There'd been threats before and they were idle. She was always quick to point out to the abusers that if anything happened to her they would be the first stop for the sheriff.

A little voice in the back of her head said that this time no one was threatening. Someone had taken action and they'd done it while the baby was with Stephanie, which would make it harder to tie the crime back to revenge against Meg.

If Meg didn't know any better, she'd get excited about the possibility of forensic evidence nailing the kidnapper. She knew enough to realize that, unlike crime shows on TV, forensics wasn't the be-all and end-all answer for most crimes. Furthermore, it took time to process a crime scene. She could only pray that this whole episode was random and that the attacker would be caught before he could make an attempt on another innocent child.

Meg wanted, no, needed to take her baby home. She stood. She knew the drill, so she preempted the sheriff. "If I can think of anything else, I'll call."

Wyatt caught her arm as she walked toward the door. "Where are you going?"

"Home. Let's go," she said with a finality that he should know better than to argue against.

One glance at him said he fully understood. He released his grip, and she didn't stop walking until they made it into the lobby. Facing the sea of journalists out there looking for a story wasn't exactly her idea of reducing stress.

"Maybe we could huddle together and shield the baby," she said to Stephanie.

"Hold on a minute," Wyatt argued. "What do you think you're doing?"

"Walking out the front door," she said slowly, like she was talking to a two-year-old.

"I can see that. The question is why?" Something about Wyatt made her want to stick around and tell him what was going on. Was it a look? His body language? The sympathy she believed she saw in his eyes?

"Because I can tell when I've lost a battle," she said with a little more heat than she'd intended. "There's nothing else we can do or say in there."

He stood for a long moment in what seemed like a dare. The first one to move lost.

Wyatt took in a sharp breath, a concession breath. "Fine. Let me take you and the baby out the back way to avoid media attention."

Meg held her ground. Her heart thundered against her rib cage as Wyatt disappeared into the sheriff's office. He returned a few seconds later as a deputy motioned for her to follow him toward the opposite hall.

"I'll grab the truck, circle the block and pick you up." Wyatt was a study in determination. His outer appearance was calm, too calm. There was a raging storm swirling beneath the surface and Meg didn't have the energy to withstand the gale-force winds. Not tonight.

Emotions torpedoed through her so fast that she didn't have time to process them. Aubrey was stirring and she didn't want her little girl to pick up the tension in her mother when Wyatt spoke.

Before she could agree or argue, he disappeared. He was probably trying to help, but she didn't need someone walking into her life and taking over. She could think for herself and he needed to see that she'd been fine on her own and especially if the two of them could end up in a courtroom someday.

They could talk in the morning when she had a better perspective and time to gather her thoughts. Meg never fared well when she was caught off guard. She needed to mull things over because all her best decisions came out of respecting her need for time to process information.

As Wyatt walked away she turned to the deputy. "Can you take us home?"

He hesitated and then nodded before leading them out the back and to his SUV. Meg buckled up and held on to Aubrey.

Stephanie flashed eyes at Meg and asked under her breath, "What are you doing?"

"Taking my daughter home," she said plainly.

"What about him?" Stephanie motioned toward the truck that was now behind them.

"Aubrey comes first. She needs to eat, and both he and I need a minute to cool down. There's been a lot thrown at both of us today and we need time to process everything before we make an attempt to figure this out," she said.

"Does that mean he's planning to stick around?" Stephanie's brow went up.

"I have no idea what his plans are. He accused me of trying to use Aubrey to get at the Butler fortune." The accusation still stung and she hadn't had time to process the fact that he was a Butler.

"What does he have to do with the Butlers?" Stephanie didn't hesitate.

"Turns out he's one of them but he didn't seem happy about it," Meg said. A self-made man like Wyatt wouldn't care about the money. The family had been through a lot of trauma since Mr. Butler's murder. The eldest Butler, a female, had been attacked. Another person, Madelyn Kensington, had been summoned to town by the family lawyer in order to be told Mike Butler was her father. A jealous ex had followed Madelyn and nearly killed her. And one of the Butler twins, Dade, had gotten involved with a local woman who barely survived a stalker.

"That family has certainly had their troubles. But he couldn't have meant what he said to you," Stephanie said.

"What makes you so sure?"

"Did you see the way he looks at you?"

Her friend was hallucinating if she thought Wyatt had any feelings left for Meg. He'd been clear about enjoying his single life before. Heck, the times she'd slept over at his place she realized he didn't even have two coffee mugs. What person didn't have two coffee mugs? One could be dirty. Meg didn't have the energy to analyze it again. The message had been clear. Wyatt preferred the number one.

The realization had been a good wake-up call for Meg because she'd been starting down a slippery slope of developing actual feelings for the cowboy-turned-restaurant-mogul. What a disaster that would've been.

"I wish someone looked at me like that," Stephanie said under her breath.

Yeah? Wyatt's steel eyes had been serious, intense. Stephanie was probably misreading the situation.

Aubrey yawned before starting to fuss. Meg repositioned her daughter and spoke in a soothing tone.

The deputy pulled onto the parking pad and Meg thanked him for the ride.

Aubrey fussed and fidgeted as Meg climbed out of the back seat. "Will you deal with him? I need to take care of her. She's hungry and I'm exhausted."

"I'll take care of the cowboy," Stephanie said, and Meg's heart squeezed. Would Wyatt be attracted to Stephanie? She was beautiful. Was Meg seriously jealous of her best—Meg couldn't bring herself to say *only*, but it was true—friend? "Besides, we need to get the cars home. We left them at work, remember?"

"Yes. Right. Thanks." Seeing Wyatt again was throwing Meg for a loop. She buried those unproductive thoughts and darted inside the house before Wyatt could catch up to her.

Inside, she made a beeline for the kitchen to prepare a bottle, which was difficult while trying to soothe a crying baby. Meg had more experience than she cared to think about, and a rogue thought had her wishing for a partner to help. Not just a partner, her mind protested—the child's father. Wow, her thoughts were careening out of control.

Aubrey belted out a cry that made Meg's heart fist.

"You're okay," she soothed, gently bouncing up and down while finagling the formula and the bottle. She couldn't breastfeed and feared that was one hit in what would be a long line of disappointments for her daughter.

Meg also noted that in seeing the cowboy, as Stephanie had called him, again that she longed for ridiculous things like a family and a home. What would she want next? A minivan? A dog?

Where would that leave all the families who depended on her? And where would that leave her heart when the fairy tale didn't come true?

If her own mother could walk out on her and not look back, why would anyone else stick around?

"I HAVE A right to see Meg and her baby," Wyatt insisted. He already realized convincing Meg's friend to let him inside the house was a losing battle and he should walk away, give the situation some breathing room. He could admit to being part bull when he decided to dig his heels in. His were firmly ground this time.

"I'm really sorry. She needs time," Stephanie said.

Arguing wasn't going to do any good, but Wyatt almost laughed out loud at the thought Meg needed time.

"How much? Another year?" There was more anger and frustration in his tone than he'd intended.

Stephanie shrugged.

"She's already had…what?…nine months, plus the baby is how old? How much more time does she need," he countered, clinging to his sinking ship. Wyatt didn't normally lose his cool. He'd built a million-dollar chain of taco stands because of his ability to make good decisions under pressure. As much as he tried to convince himself this was no different, he failed.

Another helpless shrug came from Stephanie.

The timer he'd set on his phone beeped. If he didn't get going he'd miss his meeting with the Butler family. He was tempted to walk away from all of this, from all of Cattle Barge, and never look back. Hell, he had enough on his plate as it was with the expansion of his taco chain. His intention in Cattle Barge had been simple. Put to rest once and for all the fact that he wanted nothing to do with being a Butler, and maybe have a little hot sex with an old flame. Okay, since he was baring his soul, he wanted to have a lot of hot sex with the woman he couldn't seem to keep out of his thoughts in the past year. But that was about as realistic as getting water from a rock. Or, in this case, walking inside that house.

Seeing Meg hold a baby—potentially his baby—should've been a bucket of ice water on the fire between them. Should've been. He was scratching his head as to why that didn't seem to be the case.

"She has my cell. If I don't hear from her in the next

few hours I'm coming back and I'm walking inside that door," he warned.

"Understood." Stephanie's hands came up, palms out, in the surrender position. "Like I said before I'm sorry for my friend. I think we've all had a rough morning and need a little time to calm down and sort this mess out."

Since pressuring Stephanie for answers was as smart and productive as firing the guy who runs the cash register because the girl on the line messed up, he decided to cut his losses.

"Fine. I'll be back," he said, realizing it came off more as a threat than a promise.

Wyatt stalked to his truck and took his seat, white-knuckling the steering wheel.

Next up?

Deal with the Butlers.

Wyatt would thank Stephanie for her help when he returned. After all, it wasn't her fault he was in this predicament, and he didn't need to take his frustration out on her. He could've done a better job handling his emotions when talking to Meg. There were a few words he'd take back if he could in hindsight.

In his defense, this situation was emotionally charged without the attempted kidnapping. This also made him wonder if Meg and her baby were safe. He scanned the area. There weren't many houses on this stretch of farm road. He'd been grateful for his truck, given the drive in. Stretches of road needed maintenance. Maybe he could convince Meg to move closer to town when she was thinking straight again. Being closer to supplies and conveniences would be better for her and the baby.

Whoa. Where'd all that come from?

Where Meg chose to live with her daughter was her business. The little girl in the house had gotten to him. He could admit it. Even though he still wasn't ready to believe she was his child, she seemed like a good baby. A sweet helpless little thing. She'd done nothing to provoke a criminal to rip her out of Stephanie's arms. Something had been bugging him since leaving the sheriff's office. The sheriff seemed intent on Meg, but the baby had been taken from Stephanie. What was going on with Sawmill?

If the attempt was related to the kind of work she did—and that was a logical possibility—why not take the baby from Meg, instead? Or had the person been targeting Stephanie? Considering Meg and Stephanie lived under the same roof, it was at least possible that a person could mistake the baby as Stephanie's. *Right?*

Heck, the two lived and worked together so the person could be targeting either of them, based on the work they did.

A rogue thought struck him harder than a sucker punch. Did someone know the baby might be a Butler? Who inside Meg's circle knew about their circumstances? There were a lot of unanswered questions and he was frustrated that his access to Meg was being blocked.

She was trying to protect her daughter, a voice in the back of his mind reminded. He'd seen that fierce look of determination in her eyes, the fire. Justly so.

Her daughter was innocent in all this and couldn't exactly fight for herself.

Anger brewed under the surface as he thought about the kind of jerk who abducted little babies. Thinking about how helpless an infant was got all his protective instincts flaring. That's probably what was bugging him the most about this situation and not that he gave any credence to the fact that the little bean shared his DNA.

Until he had definitive proof he wouldn't put too much stock in the idea. Keeping a cool head when everyone else overreacted was another one of his core strengths. He'd call on every skill that had made him the successful man he was today in order to help Meg and her baby while keeping the situation in perspective.

Since patience wasn't one of those skills, he used Bluetooth to call the number on the for-rent sign he'd memorized next door to Meg's place.

Chapter Five

Wyatt leaned forward in his chair, resting his elbows on his knees while waiting for the rest of the Butlers to arrive. He balled one of his hands and gripped it with the other. His thoughts kept drifting toward Meg, her child and the attempted abduction.

An unsettled feeling had gripped him since visiting the sheriff's office and he felt oddly off balance.

Every attempt to bring his thoughts to the present pushed him onto an endless loop. Meg. Baby. Butlers.

He hoped like hell the three weren't connected but couldn't ignore the possibility. Would someone abduct the little girl and then demand ransom?

As much as he'd tried not to care about the Butler family's personal business, they'd been all over the news lately. Living in Texas, he couldn't escape hearing about them or Maverick Mike since his death.

Driving up to the ranch, he was conflicted. He didn't want to like the place. The main building looked like an oversize log cabin. It had a high-end Western-resort feel. And, dammit, he did like it.

A housekeeper led him a short walk down a hall to

the dining room. He took a seat, waiting for the rest of the bunch to arrive.

The Solo cup filled with the dark brew he'd picked up on his way over sat on the table. The room itself was decorated to the nines. A long table sat dead center in the room. It looked like one of those hand-carved jobs. A family photo covered the back wall. In the picture, everyone wore jeans and white shirts. They looked to be out on the front lawn. Maverick Mike was in the center and his children flanked his sides. They were younger, maybe early teens, and their father wore a collared shirt along with a white Stetson.

If Wyatt had his druthers, he would be in non-Butler territory for this meeting, a neutral location like the restaurant from lunch. Was that really only seven hours ago? A world of change had happened since then.

"There was something on the news about an attempted kidnapping at the tree-lighting ceremony," the Butler female he recognized as Ella said as she entered the room.

Wyatt stood as twins Dade and Dalton strolled in behind her. Neither commented about this being the first crime in months that didn't have to do with a Butler, so he didn't mention the possibility even though it hovered in a dark corner of his mind.

"I'm Ella," she said to Wyatt as she offered a handshake. Her voice was unreadable, although he'd fully expected a chilly greeting.

He took the offering.

The twins introduced themselves next. They were tall, around Wyatt's height, and he couldn't ignore the fact they shared the same steel eyes and nose as him. Another female entered. She introduced herself as Madelyn Kensington—but he figured she should say Butler—as she took the seat next to his. Solidarity?

Spare him.

Had the seating been arranged on purpose, putting the other bastard Butler next to him in order to make him feel a sense of kinship? Put the two outsiders together so they could form a bond. No, thanks.

Wyatt positioned his body toward Ella, who was chatting easily with her newfound sister. Wasn't that cozy?

One of the twins acknowledged Wyatt with a sharp nod. Anger. That was more Wyatt's speed.

The family lawyer walked in, taking a seat on the other side of Wyatt. Cozy.

"Thank you for coming today," Ed Staples said after a formal introduction.

"You already know I'm only here because you summoned me," Wyatt informed the group as he looked toward the lawyer.

A few exchanged glances.

"Mr. Jackson has made his position clear," Ed reiterated to the group. "It took some convincing to get him to show today."

"I'd appreciate getting down to the reason for this meeting," Wyatt said to Ed.

"We're waiting for one more person," Ed responded.

Wyatt glanced around. How many more Butlers did they need to have a meeting? As it was, he felt surrounded by them, and an unfamiliar feeling of claustrophobia edged its way in. His chest started feeling tight and oxygen was in short supply.

He checked the time on the screen of his cell phone, chalking up part of his reaction to being away from Meg and not knowing if everything was okay on her end. "With all due respect, I have other business."

"I'll get my sister." Ella flashed her eyes at him. "*Our* sister, Cadence, on the phone."

"I'm an only child," Wyatt said through clenched teeth. He was ready for an argument, but none came. In fact, he was pretty damn sure one of the twins had just winked at the newest member of the Butler clan, Madelyn. Ignoring the protests rising up in his chest, he palmed his phone and checked his in-box. There were 1,256 emails. His email had blown up overnight. He used his thumb to scroll through the names, swirling around in his chair until his back was to the dinner table.

Wyatt had arguably one of the best poker faces in Texas, but his emotions were in high gear with the whole him-maybe-being-someone's-father bomb that had been dropped in the last twelve hours. He was distracted. His mind wasn't on business or the Butlers, and especially not this meeting.

Being here was a bad idea.

He skimmed a few key emails. Construction on the new location where they'd just broken ground had been stopped by the city. Crews had been sent home, and without the proper permits a nice chunk of money that Wyatt had already spent would be for nothing. Granted, he didn't need the cash. But if he couldn't get this project off the ground a lot of jobs would be compromised and people would be out of work. He'd already hired most of the staff for the new taco restaurant and they were training in Houston so they could get up and running on day one, which was supposed to happen in seven weeks. What was he supposed to tell them? They no longer had jobs because the city changed its mind?

This location had been strategically chosen because the rubber plant that had given half the town jobs was closing down. Wyatt believed in creating jobs in small communities so families could stay intact and small dots on the map where people had lived for generations wouldn't end up ghost towns in a few years when all the young people had to move to a bigger city for work. He and his mother had moved around a lot before settling in Austin where she waited tables. During his childhood, they'd always returned to a lake house near Bay. He was never sure how his mother had pulled it off, but every year no matter how difficult their circumstances were they'd spent a week there during the summer.

There was something extra special about Bay, Texas. Bringing his successful business there to give reasonable-paying jobs to people—unlike when his mother worked for the rubber plant—meant more than it should. He knew better than to mix business with emotion, and now it was coming back to bite him. And especially since he'd decided to look into buying the place where he and his mother had built so many happy memories.

A better business location would be to stay southwest, where he already had friendly politicians who appreciated him bringing work to their constituents.

Thinking with the beating heart in his chest instead of his hard-won intelligence was proof that he was losing his edge. He deserved the backlash.

Another troubling email caught his attention. His lawyer said no one owned the house in Bay by the lake. It was owned by a conglomerate in the Cayman Islands. All that said to Wyatt was that some CEO, probably a wealthy guy in Houston, was using his company to shield ownership of the house on the water. Fine. Dealing with a businessman was much easier than a new mother. In that arena, he knew exactly what he was doing.

He excused himself into the hallway and made a quick call to his lawyer, Alexander Kegel.

"I got your email about the Bay property," Wyatt said after perfunctory greetings.

"How do you want to proceed?" his lawyer asked.

"Find out who the company belongs to and which CEO is hiding behind it. Once you do, I need to find out what's important to him or her." Business was all about finding the right leverage.

"Done. I'll have a report to you in the morning," Alexander said.

Wyatt thanked his lawyer as he heard a voice coming through what sounded like a speaker in the room behind him. He turned to find five sets of eyes on him.

"Ready?" Ed Staples asked.

"Let's get on with it," one of the twins said, and his words were like fingernails on a chalkboard to Wyatt. Did he have any idea how little Wyatt wanted to be in this room with all of them? Clearly, the answer was no.

His skin itched being inside Maverick Mike Butler's home staring at four people who looked so similar. They had the same nose as their father, and Wyatt
had instantly realized it was like staring at his own. It
was all a little too close to home for his comfort. He
wanted to know what Meg was doing.

"I'm not sure why I let you talk me into coming
here." Wyatt looked squarely at Ed Staples. "I don't
want any of this."

With that, he walked down the hall and through the
front door. He heard the click of boots on tile behind
him, but he didn't stop to find out who they belonged to.

"Hold up a minute." It was one of the twins.

Wyatt stopped but didn't turn to find out which one
had followed him. He didn't care.

"Look, I know my, *our*, father didn't do the right
thing when he was alive, but—"

"Save it." Wyatt whirled around, staring into eyes
that looked a little too much like his own. Déjà vu from
earlier, from being with Aubrey, assaulted him. His sour
mood intensified.

The guy's hand came up. "I won't pretend that I know
what this must be like for you because I don't. I grew
up with the man and, until recently, had the same look
you do when anyone brought him up."

At least the guy was smart enough not to go down
the road of wondering why Wyatt didn't want to be
there. That eased a little of the tension stringing Wyatt's shoulders so taut they might snap. Business was
responsible for at least part of his high strung emotions.

But his thoughts also kept rounding back to Meg and that little girl.

"I'm sorry for how this has all played out," Dade said.

Wyatt listened mostly because he didn't want to come off as a jerk with someone who'd done nothing wrong. The man's father was a whole other story.

"Why not listen to what Ed has to say? Whatever feelings you have toward our—" he glanced at Wyatt and seemed to decide to change his tack "—toward Maverick Mike have nothing to do with him."

Wyatt's brow shot up as anger burned his chest.

"Really? Isn't he here to speak to me on behalf of the man who walked out on my mother, leaving her to fend for herself?" Saying those words out loud hit him like a sucker punch to the gut. Was that what he'd done to Meg? Was doing?

This was different. She'd pushed him away. He'd been more than willing to stick around and do whatever was necessary to pitch in until this whole ordeal was sorted out.

"We're not trying to mess with you. We have no idea what the old man wanted to say, but it might not be his fault that your mother lived the way she did."

Those words were gasoline on a fire. There was no way his mother wanted to live in poverty, paycheck to paycheck, with no medical insurance and no security. No one could convince him that she didn't want to be able to load the Christmas tree with presents every year instead of relying on the kindness of strangers through a church program. He was grateful—don't get him wrong—but his mother would never have chosen the life they'd lived if she'd had another option. Sure, she was a proud woman. But there was nothing empowering about standing in line in twenty-degree weather during a cold snap on Thanksgiving morning in order to get a plate of turkey.

"I don't need any of this in my life. I'm done." Wyatt swept his hand across the air.

"That's understandable under the circumstances," Dade admitted. "But my father has surprised us more than once recently. He might have something to offer you, too."

"No. I don't care about him. I don't need anything from him or any of you," Wyatt managed to get out through clenched teeth.

"Then by all means walk away." Dade started to turn.

For reasons Wyatt couldn't explain, he shouted, "I don't want his money, either."

"Neither do I," Dade countered. "But you know, life sometimes deals one helluva punch and you might just need a family to lean on."

"I've done all right by myself so far," Wyatt ground out, thinking Dade was sorely misguided if he thought Wyatt needed a Butler to make his life complete. Meg came to his mind, but he quickly shot down that idea as mental treason. He had a successful business to occupy his time, more money than he could spend and a beautiful home in the hills outside of Austin along with several other homes in Texas. What more could any man ask for?

Did he have regrets? Sure.

"Then you don't need to stick around." Dade was walking a thin line. Wyatt thought about hooking a right fist over that left eye of his.

But what did he care?

Wyatt wasn't now, nor would he ever be, a Butler. It was time to walk away.

Meg was up before the sun. She thought about the list of names she'd sent the sheriff yesterday, hoping she'd covered every threat. Wyatt had stopped by again last night, but Meg had been sleeping so Stephanie left a note on her bathroom door—a note that Meg had read at two o'clock in the morning. Even then, her heart pounded thinking about him. She was tired and that was causing her to lose her mind.

The Garza case needed her attention, but focus on work seemed as attainable as a hundred-carat diamond necklace.

Thankfully, Aubrey was already fed and back to sleep. At two-months-old her routine consisted of feed, sleep, repeat.

Looking down at her little girl, she couldn't be upset about the amount of work an infant brought. Even facing Wyatt and delivering the life-changing news to him had paled in comparison to the horror of Aubrey being abducted.

Yesterday had been the worst day of Meg's life. She couldn't even begin to process the thought of her baby disappearing forever. Hot tears burned the backs of her eyes.

Coffee.

She needed coffee.

She wiped the moisture from her eyes and stalked toward the kitchen with one mission: caffeine.

Before she took her first sip of fresh brew, Stephanie sauntered into the kitchen and poured herself a cup of coffee. Her hair looked like a lion's mane, thick and golden. The waves highlighted her friend's heart-shaped face and suited her.

"What time did you get the little sprig to sleep last night?" Stephanie asked Meg.

"It's all a blur." Aubrey came into the world weighing almost seven pounds and seemed determined to bulk up. The little angel ate almost every two hours on the nose—still. Meg had learned that she was far less conscious of losing sleep when she had no idea how much she was losing. "Been up on and off since then. How about you? How'd you sleep? I tried my best not to wake you."

"Me? I slept like a log. You must be exhausted after yesterday. I'd offer to take her out this morning so you could get some sleep, but I'm scared after what happened." Stephanie wasn't the type to back down from many things, so her attitude caught Meg off guard.

"That wasn't your fault," Meg reassured. "I know you would never do anything to put her in harm's way."

"Thank you. But she was with me when it happened. Of course, I feel responsible. If anything happened to her, I'd never forgive myself." Stephanie wiped at her eye and Meg figured she was swiping away a tear. She gave her friend some space.

"You're a good friend and the best aunt she'll ever have," Meg said.

"I'm her only aunt," Stephanie said through a half laugh, half sniff. At least she sounded lighter than a moment ago. Meg wouldn't allow her friend to shoulder the burden of some random creep trying to take Aubrey.

The thought gave Meg chills.

"I still can't believe you came home, fed her and worked out." Stephanie faced her and took a sip of coffee.

Meg gripped her mug. "Guess I just wanted to feel like something was normal again. Like I had some control of my routine."

"Did you remember anything about the sketch the sheriff showed us?" Stephanie asked and Meg shot a look. "Never mind. I can see by your reaction that you didn't. I'm in the same boat."

Talking about the sheriff's office brought more tension to Meg's already tight shoulders. Working out had given her a speck of normalcy last night. Maybe discussing work, like they always did over their first cups of coffee, would do the same. "What about the Barber case? Did you get a chance to review the files I sent last week?"

"Not yet. I haven't wrapped up the St. James case," Stephanie admitted.

"What's going on with that one?" Meg asked.

"Looks like he might get off with probation," she said on a sigh. They didn't win justice for every case they took on.

"It's important that our clients know someone cares

about them. We can still get them the help they need to change their lives even if the courts give him a free pass," Meg reminded. She could see the defeat in her friend's eyes. Neither one of them took losing easily and that's probably why they both fought so hard for people.

"He's basically getting a slap on the wrist." Stephanie made eyes at Meg.

"This time. If he messes up with someone else it won't be the same. He has a record now. He won't get off so easily if he pulls anything like this in the future and that's an important win."

Stephanie rocked her head in agreement. "True."

"You made a difference for Adrien and her daughters. Now we can give them the right tools to help break the cycle so they'll have better lives." When Meg took a hit on a case, Stephanie made it her job to pump Meg up and vice versa.

"You're right." Stephanie offered a weak smile, but it was better than nothing. "I'll do a workup on services we can connect Adrien to so that she and the girls can get on their feet."

Meg was grateful to talk about work for a change instead of the haunting image of someone trying to rip her daughter out of her arms. She walked over to the front door. "Did you check the mail yesterday?"

"I forgot after all that happened," Stephanie said.

"I'll do it." Meg opened the door and walked onto the small porch. She glanced across the street and saw something she wasn't ready to deal with this early in the morning, Wyatt's truck. She jumped back inside, closed and locked the door. "What's he doing here?"

"Who? Where?" Stephanie glanced around like she half expected someone to be standing in the kitchen next to her.

"Wyatt's truck is parked across the street." Meg searched for her cell. Where had she put it last night?

Stephanie checked the window for herself.

"At the empty house," Meg provided.

"That one used to be for rent." Stephanie checked out the window and gasped when her suspicion seemed to be confirmed. "Where'd the sign go?"

"What did he say last night?" Meg asked as she continued to unearth pillows, looking for the electronic device that held every important contact she had.

"That he wasn't finished and planned to stick around until you spoke to him," she said.

"You didn't put that on the note." Meg moved to the chair and dug her hands in the seam between the cushion and the armrest. Panic assaulted her.

"Figured I'd tell you when I saw you." Stephanie joined her. "What are we looking for?"

"My phone."

"Oh. I saw that on the counter." Stephanie motioned toward the kitchen.

Meg must've set it down when she was in a hurry to make Aubrey's bottle last night.

Before she could find it, a knock sounded at the front door. Her pulse jackhammered against her ribs.

"I'll get it," she said. For a split second, she wondered what she looked like. The thought was ridiculous under the circumstances. She had on yoga pants and a shirt. She ran her hand through her hair to smooth it down.

Meg stalked to the front door and opened it, thankful she'd had at least one strong cup of coffee before facing Wyatt again.

When she saw him standing there her traitorous heart galloped.

"Meg, this is Dr. Raul. With your permission he'd like to perform a DNA test." Wyatt's expression was stone and his voice gave away nothing. He was steady as steel—just like his eyes—and part of her resented him for being so calm when his presence rattled her to the core.

At least she'd told him about Aubrey. Her secret was out. He deserved to know that he was the little girl's father. And there were so many other issues to deal with rather than obsessing over what his reaction might be today. And yet she was still hurt by his insistence on a DNA test. Was that silly?

What had she expected? Him to take the baby from her arms before getting down on one knee and proposing they become a family?

Right. That was about as smart as dumping acid in the garden and expecting flowers to grow.

"She's sleeping right now, but—"

"There's no need to wake her. I can use a strand of hair from a hairbrush or if you have a recently used bottle available that would work," Dr. Raul said. He was a study in compassion with his rounded shoulders and kind expression. He held a bag in his right hand and she could guess the contents included a DNA sampling kit.

"Fine," she responded. "Follow me."

Chapter Six

Meg opened the door and stepped aside to allow them access, ignoring the chill bumps racing up her arms from the burst of cold air. She walked into the kitchen, making eyes at Stephanie so her friend would know to stick around.

Wyatt and the doctor followed her, and she didn't like the way she could feel Wyatt's masculine presence behind her when he seemed so unaffected by her. He didn't say a word as the doctor went to work, gathering the bottle without touching the tip.

"Who's this?" Stephanie asked.

"A doctor. Wyatt wants a paternity test," Meg said as evenly as she could.

Stephanie rolled her eyes. "Does he know you can get a test at the drugstore and be done in ten minutes?"

"I didn't ask," Meg said with a slight smirk.

"Excuse me if I don't want to leave something as important as this to a dime-store test," Wyatt said on a clipped tone.

Meg didn't offer coffee, mainly because she didn't want them to stick around. As it was she had about an hour before it was time to feed Aubrey again, and she wanted to get in a hot morning shower to ease the tension trapped between her shoulder blades.

"And now a swab from Dad," the doctor said. The word *dad* had an unexpected effect on Meg and she started to tear up. She quickly turned her back to them and reached for the coffeepot. Her reaction most likely stemmed from the fact that she'd never known her own father. He'd ducked out on her and her mother before Meg started school. As much as she didn't want Wyatt to be forced back into her life permanently, she also realized having an attentive father would be best for Aubrey. Based on his reactions so far, when the test came out positive she was going to have to make room for him in her life.

After refilling her mug and getting her overwrought emotions under control—emotions that had been on shaky ground ever since the pregnancy, thanks to all those hormones—she faced them again.

"Seems like you have everything you need," she said, her gaze bouncing from Wyatt to the doctor to the door. If that wasn't subtle enough, she took in a sharp breath and stared boldly at Wyatt.

"Any chance I can get a cup of coffee before I go?" Wyatt asked, holding her gaze. Another dare?

He'd conceded on the last one and she figured she was going to have to learn how to meet him halfway.

She focused on the doctor. "Coffee?"

"None for me, thanks. I have work to do." Dr. Raul held up the specimens. "I'll call with the results as soon as they come in."

"I'll walk you out," Stephanie piped in, and that was not the kind of help Meg was hoping for. She didn't want to be left alone in the kitchen with Wyatt and she couldn't even pinpoint the reason why. Yes, he unnerved her. No, she didn't think they had anything to talk about until he confirmed what she already knew. He was Aubrey's father. Yet, he wanted to stick around.

After the events of yesterday, maybe he just needed to know she was all right.

Meg poured a fresh cup of hot brew and handed it to him, ignoring the frisson of heat when their fingers grazed. She'd give it to him that he looked good, even better than she'd remembered. But—and it was a big *but*—she'd always known he wasn't the stick-around type, and the news she'd delivered yesterday had clearly knocked him off balance.

Heck, she felt the same way. Life was a lot smoother without overcomplicating it with emotions. Okay, sure hers had already engaged, and that confused her even more at the time. It would be just like her to want to start a relationship with another emotionally unavailable person. If there was a Been There Done That T-shirt for picking the wrong type she'd have a closetful. She'd blame her parents for ditching her—and that might partly be true—but she also took blame where it belonged, which was with her. She didn't want to risk her heart by truly falling for someone. Those lines ran deep within her and, if she had to guess, had started when she was ten-years-old.

The worst part was that she wasn't gullible. On some level she realized that she was choosing unavailable men on purpose and the reason was to give her an escape route. Meg didn't get close to people. Period.

Having a daughter was softening Meg. She'd fallen for that little girl the minute she saw those round cheeks and blue eyes, as clichéd as that might sound. Stephanie was the only other person Meg trusted enough to let inside her carefully constructed walls, and the two of them had only become close recently, after Meg had learned she was pregnant.

Meg thought back to the last real friend she'd had before Stephanie. Mary Jane. Her ten-year-old best friend. A tear escaped just thinking about her.

"Hey, everything okay?" Wyatt asked, and she glanced up at him in time to see that he was studying her intensely.

"Yes," she lied, but then decided to come clean. "No. Not really."

"I apologize if—"

"You have every right to expect proof," she said quickly, not wanting him to spell out his distrust of her. Somehow, that would only make things worse in her mind and this was Aubrey's father. For her daughter's sake, Meg needed to find middle ground with him. "It's a lot to chew at once. I'd probably request the same thing if I was in your shoes."

He started to say something but seemed to think better of it, taking a sip of coffee instead.

She needed to redirect the conversation away from the two of them and all that their relationship lacked. "The sketch kept coming back to me last night and I don't know why. I don't think I've never seen him before." She had to consider the possibility that he was someone from her past that she'd blocked out. But who? Why?

"The person who attempted to take Aubrey yesterday did so while she was with Stephanie," Wyatt said, and she could almost see the pins firing inside his brain. He was an intelligent businessman. He'd learned to look at all angles, and he could probably be a big help if she let him in.

Opening herself up even a crack was so hard. Meg had been rejected by everyone she let in.

She studied Wyatt, debating. "Does that mean you think the kidnapping attempt was random?"

"It's a definite possibility. We didn't ask the sheriff if there'd been any similar cases reported in the area or across Texas," he continued, and she liked the way he was thinking. If this wasn't personal, she and Aubrey could be safer. Meg might not have to check the back seat of every car before she got inside or the closets before she went to bed at night. But then, those were habits she'd developed a long time ago and had never been able to shake.

After yesterday, Meg wondered if she'd ever truly feel safe again. "With the holidays around the corner, I read somewhere that infant abductions are more common."

"People start realizing what's missing in their lives and want to fill the gap. Your daughter is beautiful. Those two facts alone could make her a target," he said. Was there reverence in his voice when he talked about Aubrey? "A sad fact of this time of year is that situations like these happen. People who are desperate to have a child are sometimes willing to pay any price without realizing what that might do to someone else. Some have no idea and don't care how they get a baby, just that they get one."

"How do you know all this?" Had he gone back to the sheriff last night?

"Started searching around on the internet last night when I couldn't sleep," he admitted. "Wanted to figure out a profile of someone capable of this. Thought that maybe I could help move the investigation along if I found the right information."

"Did you call the sheriff?" She couldn't hide her shock.

"Before the sun came up," he admitted.

Meg grunted. She would've liked to have been a fly on that wall. "How'd Sawmill take that phone call?"

Wyatt cocked an eyebrow. "What makes you ask?"

"Most of my cases are outside of Cattle Barge and that's one of the main reasons I live here. I like to keep work and home separate. But I've had a few—"

"Like the Garza one you talked about yesterday?" he asked.

She nodded.

"Most law-enforcement officers have a hard time with people they consider outsiders poking around in their business," she said. "Many already feel they have constant eyes on them, be it citizens complaining or those cameras that both help and hurt them when they record everything that's happening. Being an advocate for victims' rights puts me across the table from law enforcement sometimes."

"Which doesn't faze you," he said, but it came off as more question than statement.

"I've gotten used to being the opposition," she admitted, and maybe that was another way to keep people at arm's length. "Because the people I work on behalf of deserve someone strong sitting across from investigators who may have mishandled an investigation. Or don't deserve to be subject to a law that offers more protection to the guilty person than the victim."

"You're passionate about your work." This time, he was examining her like he was looking at her for the first time, and she didn't want to acknowledge the sensual shivers skittering across her skin or the awareness causing her breath to catch.

She couldn't afford to notice the hint of appreciation in his eyes, either.

"I can't imagine wanting to be a mother so badly that you'd be willing to take a child from someone who loves her. The pregnancy caught me off guard and, believe me, I considered all my options more times than I care to admit. In the end, I decided to keep her—obviously—and hoped that I wouldn't mess up being a mother too badly," she admitted, a little unsure why she'd gone there. She hadn't told a soul about her misgivings about parenting before, and she'd already spilled more about her work to him than she anyone in her past.

But, then, things had changed between them. This was Aubrey's father now. Maybe a piece of her wanted him to get to know her so he wouldn't be tempted to fight her for custody. If he saw how hard she worked and how much she cared for their child he'd be more compassionate.

Because when it came down to money, he had buckets more to spend on lawyers than she did. It also seemed like he was in the same boat since the parenting news had been dropped on him. And maybe that was another reason she started talking. She wished she'd had someone to lean on when her entire life had been turned upside down with the news. Part of her wanted him to know that she'd had a similar reaction.

Or maybe it was selfish and she felt he was the only other person in the world who could truly understand her feelings. They were the only two involved even if they were in different places. They were on opposite sides of the same boat, rowing toward some unknown future.

Aubrey deserved the best both had to offer.

There he was, studying her. There was something else in his eyes, too. Something that was familiar. Maybe intimate.

"Whatever else happens," he started, and took a step toward her. Goose bumps sprouted on her arms, and she was very aware of how close they were now. "I know you're an amazing mother. I can see how much you love her and she's lucky because not every kid gets that."

"She's worth it." If she looked into those steel eyes much longer she'd be in even bigger trouble than she already was. Suddenly, the rim of her coffee cup became interesting.

Wyatt took another step toward her and she could see

the tips of his boots as she focused on the tile floor. She felt his finger graze her chin as he urged her to look up.

She resisted at first because the heat pinging between them would give away her reaction to him and she didn't want him to know how much her body missed the feel of him, of kissing him, of his weight on top of her while they made love. She took a step back but was stopped by the counter. He followed and by the time she looked up, she could see him angle his head as he brought his lips down to crash against hers.

The second their mouths touched, warning bells sounded, but they were muted by the heat rising between them as his body pressed against hers. There was so much heat in the kiss that she was rendered breathless. Fighting against her feelings was no use when he was this close. Besides, she had wanted this since seeing him again even though she knew better.

He dropped his hand to her waist and made a sexy little grunting noise against her mouth and Meg got lost.

Stephanie cleared her throat in the next room, an obvious attempt to let them know she was coming back.

Wyatt sidestepped and turned around to face her. Meg brought her coffee cup up to take a sip, thinking she liked the way it had tasted on Wyatt's lips a few seconds ago, mixed with his toothpaste. Knowing those thoughts were dangerous.

Kissing him was a mistake, a distraction they couldn't afford. She could feel his presence in every bit of her body, especially as it still hummed with electricity even after they'd broken physical contact.

"The doctor said he'd get the results to you in a couple of hours," Stephanie said to Wyatt. Her voice was curt as she shot a warning look toward Meg. Her friend was watching out for her and Meg was grateful. The last thing she needed was to fall down that slippery slope of having feelings for Wyatt again. He'd been clear that he didn't do long-term from the start.

Perfect, Meg had thought, because neither did she. Her heart had betrayed her, wishing for more than she knew better to expect.

A dull ache started forming between her eyes and she needed ibuprofen. She checked the pantry.

"Are we out of pain relievers?" she asked Stephanie.

"I took the last one yesterday," Stephanie said. "Put them on the list for this week's shopping, which isn't doing you any good right now."

Wyatt stood there cool as he could be with his legs crossed at the ankles and his hip leaning against the counter.

Meg's heart fluttered like a trapped bird.

WYATT NEEDED TO find the brake pedal when it came to his attraction to Meg. Or at least downshift to Neutral. Kissing her was a big-time mistake and he tried to convince himself that it had more to do with all the other things in his life careening out of control. That it was a way of getting his hands back on the wheel and his backside in the driver's seat. A grab-the-bull-by-the-horns approach to life. Because that had worked in the past. Anytime he'd had a hiccup— and there'd been plenty starting a business from the ground up—he'd faced his issues head-on.

Case in point, at the end of his first real expansion, when he'd moved to five taco stands, his manager, Tim McGowan, had decided to put his hand in the till. Tim had been the closest thing Wyatt had had to a close buddy, which made the betrayal sting all that more.

Turned out, Tim was selling items without ringing them up and blaming his employees for the inventory not matching the register receipts. Meanwhile, he was pocketing the difference. The worst part was that Tim was blaming a sixteen-year-old—a kid he'd hired—for messing up the balance sheet.

When Wyatt had first been alerted to the problem, he'd been back at home in Austin for the first time in six months, staring at an empty calendar and bed. He'd had the kind of exhaustion that made his eyelids feel like sandpaper rubbing against his eyeballs. And nothing seemed more important than pulling the sheet over his shoulders and hibernating for a solid week to catch up on sleep.

Tim had called to let him know he was checking into a problem that "the kid," as he'd called Dwayne, had noticed. The minute something felt off with Tim, Wyatt didn't hesitate to hop in his truck and head to Brunson Falls. He drove for five hours after filling his truck with gas even though he was personally on an empty tank. Caffeine and pit bull determination to be successful had been his fuel.

When he'd arrived at the Brunson Falls location he immediately knew something was off. Tim acted cagey and made a few inappropriate jokes. Wyatt had trusted a handful of people and Tim was one of them. It was clear to Wyatt now that his judgment had been off.

Trying to dim his attraction to Meg—even now after her out-of-the-blue announcement that he was the father of her child—should've dimmed his attraction to her. Facing it head-on was like pouring gasoline onto a raging fire, and his body was still having a reaction to standing so close to her. He'd blame it on autopilot or muscle memory, but he'd wanted to kiss her and he was a little too aware of the fact.

He grinned as he stared into his coffee cup.

Damn.

Time to refocus.

Locking onto Meg's gaze almost caused him to rethink what he was about to say. Call it cowboy code, but he couldn't walk away from Meg and her daughter while they were in danger. "Whether that kid is mine or not, I'm planning on sticking around until I know you're both safe."

A flicker of impatience crossed Meg's eyes. He held up his hand to stop her from speaking. "I know what you're about to say, and I have no doubt that you can take care of yourself and her. Think of me as insurance."

"Is that why you rented the place next door?" Her bottom lip had a slight pout, the same one he'd seen before when she was frustrated.

"Yes. And I have other business in Cattle Barge to address," he added.

Her cheeks were still flushed, her lips still full and pink. He fisted his free hand to stop it from reaching out to touch her again. Call it instinct, habit, muscle memory. Or maybe *stupid* was a better word because he'd learned a long time ago that touching a hot stove burned him, and yet there he'd been ready to do it again with Meg. If Aubrey turned out to be his child, he needed to keep a clear head and oven mitts handy. He had no plans to fan the flame burning between him and Meg.

"The fact that you're a Butler?" Meg asked, and mention of that family went a long way toward that direction.

"I'll never be a Butler," he said low and under his breath. But he might actually be a father. The word caused his blood pressure to rise.

The timing of Aubrey's birth was spot on from when they'd been together. He'd calculated the dates a dozen times last night. They'd been careful, like he always was, but he remembered a pair of times things got so hot and heavy between them neither noticed when the condom broke.

To be fair, either time could've resulted in pregnancy.

"It's a big family," Meg said, cutting into his heavy thoughts. "I've heard good things about them. They do a lot of charitable work in the community and seem like they really want to make a difference in people's lives."

Nothing good could come of his having Maverick Mike Butler as a father. "How well do you really know them?"

"I don't. Just what I've seen in the news and on society pages. They seem to stick together, and I guess I wish Aubrey had that kind of support. All she has is me," she said, and her honesty caught him off guard.

The baby cried from the next room and, before Meg

could disappear, Stephanie was bringing the little girl to her mother. Stephanie went to work making a bottle while Meg soothed the infant.

If Aubrey turned out to be Wyatt's daughter, she was going to have a helluva lot more than just Meg for support.

Finances wouldn't be a problem, either. He'd be ready and willing to take care of expenses, put them in a nicer house and newer SUV. His mind was already clicking through other financial needs the girl might have, like braces, dance classes and college.

Money was the easy part. The rest was barbed-wire complicated. Move too fast and the barbs would dig deeper into the skin. Fight against them, get the same result.

Thinking about Maverick Mike Butler, the man who'd donated his sperm, stirred emotions in Wyatt's chest that he didn't want to explore. Something hard, like a stone being tossed at him, nailed his gut every time Wyatt thought about the man.

What kind of father abandoned his own son? His thoughts went to Madelyn.

A dark thought struck. Would history repeat itself, only this time Wyatt would be the jerk dad pulling the disappearing act? Was he doomed by his DNA to be as big a letdown as the senior Butler had been?

The thing that bothered him the most in the past five years was the words his mother had said to him on her deathbed after he'd told her about his expansion plans. She'd beamed up at him with something that looked a lot like pride and said, "You're going to be so successful. Just like your father. You remind me so much of him."

How was that for shooting a lead arrow through his heart?

Wyatt reminded his own mother of the man who'd abandoned them both. Figuring out what that look of pride had been about had cost Wyatt countless nights of sleep, though he wasn't much on sleep when he could be working instead.

Hold on a second. Why was he already clicking through all this in his mind, anyway? There'd only been a statement, not proof, that the little girl was his.

Was it because deep down he realized that Meg wasn't the type to make a false accusation?

But that was no reason to lose his mind. He needed to think clearly in order to get to the bottom of this.

So, why did that child's eyes haunt him so much?

A little voice said, *Because they belonged to him.*

Chapter Seven

"Before, you said that you were worried about the possibility of Aubrey being targeted due to the Butler name," Meg said, and there was a strained quality to her voice as she watched him. She'd witnessed his entire thought process and it must've played across his face, because she'd stopped feeding the baby and was studying him as she draped the little girl over her shoulder and patted her on the back.

"It crossed my mind. It seems most want a piece of the Butlers these days." Wyatt stood and tried to shake off the heavy thoughts. He needed air and a damn good session at the gym. Since the latter wasn't possible he decided instead to take a few steps away from the situation. All he needed was a fresh perspective, and yet something warned nothing would ever be that easy again. "Can we talk about that later?"

"Okay."

"I can run out. Pick up a bottle of ibuprofen," he offered.

"I'll just get a few dollars," Meg said with a curious glance.

"No need." He threw on his jacket and palmed his keys, impatience edging his tone. Fresh air would do him good. He plugged in the request to his GPS and located the closest store. "Shouldn't take too long. You'll be okay until I get back?"

"We'll be fine." Meg's face muscles were pulled taut, belying her words.

Wyatt walked out the door and climbed into the driver's seat of his truck. The two-bedroom bungalow-style house had many of Meg's personal touches, from the oil-on-canvas painting on the wall she'd told him she was painting last year to the worn-in warm tones in the furniture. The place was just big enough to still be considered cozy, and her kitchen was functional. The place even smelled like her, a mix of lavender and clean and fresh air that was somehow all Meg. He'd never known the difference between lavender and any other herb until he'd asked.

Thinking back to the easy way they had of relating in the past and the white-hot passion in the bedroom brought back other memories, unwanted memories. Like when he'd finally convinced her to sleep over at his place and woke with her in his arms. He'd liked waking up to having a cup of coffee on the balcony of his place overlooking the Austin skyline. And he'd wanted to show her the home that was being built.

But then she'd slowed down and had refused to stay over again. Not long after, he'd wondered if he'd overstepped some invisible boundary with her. It had made him laugh at the time because those thoughts had never crossed his mind before her. He'd reminded himself to get a grip and done his level best to convince himself his feelings weren't hurt when she'd said she was too busy to meet him for dinner the next day.

Hadn't his thoughts derailed?

Wyatt tried to maintain focus on the problems at hand by stuffing his past down deep. He had a media mess brewing with the Butler news threatening to surface at any minute, and he might even enjoy the fireworks his presence seemed to ignite within the famed family if it weren't for the fact that his life was careening out of control.

The announcement of the reading of his father's will on Christmas Eve was another in a long list of things that didn't sit well, and Wyatt had never been a big holiday person.

What he couldn't figure out was…why? Why include him?

In life, the man had never once tried to forge a relationship or help Wyatt's mother in any way. She'd had to live day to day and do without even though she never complained. He'd seen it in the worry lines in her forehead and the way she often paced while figuring out finances. Growing up watching his mother trapped in a powerless situation built a lot of residual anger in a kid, in a man.

He'd used it to fuel his need to be a success on his own even more. He'd developed an amazing ability to shut out the world and zero in on one thing—success.

As his first taco restaurant reached its major success milestone, his mother was barely clinging to life. He'd been in the process of buying a proper house for her as a surprise. She'd been sick for a while but hadn't told him about the terminal diagnosis until the very end, leaving him with tremendous guilt for not spending time with her.

He'd built a successful food franchise on his own and had no plans now or ever to lower himself to the point of getting in line for a piece of the Butler estate. He would never give the man or his family the satisfaction of thinking that he needed them in any way.

A fifteen-minute drive on underdeveloped roads made him appreciate his truck even more. He thought about Meg's older model SUV. It was good enough to get by for now. She'd need something newer with recent safety features. That was an easy fix. She must like the model she owned or she wouldn't have bought it. He'd order the latest and have it delivered.

The convenience store was on the corner of one too many farm roads if anyone asked Wyatt. He also noticed that he'd been down that same road yesterday on his way to the Butler ranch and that was most likely what had him riled up, thinking about them.

Calling this place *convenient* was just about laughable when it would be a thirty-minute ordeal, round trip. The drive would do him good. Thinking about the past had him tense. The air was cold and he didn't like winter. It didn't help that his least favorite holiday came at the start of it. Wyatt clenched his back teeth and moved inside. He located a bottle of pain reliever and paid at the counter.

Walking out to his truck, he cursed when he saw the front flat tire. He must've picked up a nail. No surprise, given the quality of the roads and all the construction going on. Texas was booming. He was used to it living in Austin. There should be something to patch it up in his toolbox. He unlocked the door and pulled out his tool kit. Then he remembered that he'd used the last of his can of aerosol tire inflator after visiting the Brunson Falls job site two weeks ago. He'd been meaning to buy a new one.

He bent down to examine his right front tire and cursed under his breath.

"Can we help?" The voice was familiar. It sounded like the Butlers from the other day and hearing it had the same effect. It grated on his nerves.

He leaned back on his heels and turned his head to look at Dade and Dalton. They'd kept enough distance that he figured they were showing him that they weren't trying to sneak up on him and he appreciated the gesture.

"It's just a flat. I'll take care of this in no time."

"We can help put on the spare," Dalton said.

He'd taken out the spare, but he figured there'd be something he could buy in the store that would have him on his way in a few minutes. "I don't need a hand."

"You sure? We could knock that out in a minute together or give you a ride anywhere you need to go," the other one said.

"I know how to fix a flat." Wyatt was being a jerk. Seeing them reminded him of Maverick Mike Butler and the heavy thoughts he'd been having on the way over.

Everyone needed to be very clear that Wyatt could

handle himself in any situation. There wasn't a case where he believed it necessary to ask someone else for help and especially not a Butler. Maybe his stubbornness came from being an only child and learning to depend on himself early in life. He'd always been the keep-to-himself type, the loner. People were under the misguided impression that a man who liked to be alone was lonely.

In Wyatt's case, the opposite couldn't be truer. He happened to like his own company. He didn't need others to validate him. And he sure as hell didn't want anything from a Butler, and that included their time.

"In case you change your mind," one of them said.

"I'm clear on what I need. I don't need your help." Wyatt had started to say *handout*. That was odd.

One of the twins bent down, set a small card next to Wyatt and placed a rock on top so it wouldn't blow away.

Wyatt glanced down. It was a business card with a cell number on it.

Hell would catch him on fire before he'd call that number.

CHANGING THE TIRE turned out to be more complicated than buying a can of aerosol and plugging up a small hole. First of all, the store was out. Figure that. With all this construction, he should've at least considered the possibility.

Waiting for another customer to show up and be willing to take him to a big-box store near the interstate took almost twenty minutes.

Fixing the tire was the easy part after he'd secured the right materials, except that it had started to drizzle and his hands nearly froze before he'd finished and was on the road again.

By the time he made it back to Meg's, his arms were covered in dirt and he was in one hell of a fine mood.

It took a few minutes for her to answer the door, and when she did she looked like she'd been hit by a truck while he was gone. She had to squint to look at him. Movement looked to cause tremendous pain.

"What happened?" he asked out of concern.

"Headache," she responded, holding the baby. "It got worse." She hadn't seemed to be in that much pain when he'd left more than an hour ago. Now he really felt like a jerk for taking so long to get back. He reminded himself that he'd had no idea she would get this bad, but he wasn't ready to let himself off the hook. Last year, she'd canceled dinner plans more than once complaining of a headache. Even then, he'd believed she was working herself too hard. From the looks of it, she hadn't slowed down since having the baby.

They needed to have a conversation about her taking better care of herself.

Stephanie pushed past him as he followed Meg into the kitchen. Her friend glared at him as he held out the small bag.

"You're a little late, don't you think," she said, not bothering to mask her anger.

"I had a flat tire," he said.

"And, what? No spare?" she shot back.

"It's okay," Meg interrupted, her face crinkled like it hurt to speak.

Wyatt apologized again.

She looked at the bag in his hands like he was handing her a bomb. "It's fine. I don't need them anymore. Stephanie borrowed a couple from the neighbor. They'll kick in any minute. I'm already starting to feel better anyway."

This was better? Wyatt's extended hand stood between them.

She glanced at him and then the bag awkwardly. "Thanks anyway."

"You should've called," he said.

"What good would that have done with a flat tire?" Stephanie said from her spot next to the coffee machine. "Besides, I could say the same thing to you."

Wyatt wasn't used to answering to anyone else and he had to admit to being offended. There was a reason he lived in a house with one coffee mug.

And yet he still felt like the biggest jerk for not checking in.

He set the bag down on the counter beside Meg as she poured a fresh cup.

Looking at her struggling through pain was a knife stab to the chest. It would be better if he was the one suffering. That would be easier for him. Watching her, feeling helpless was the worst.

A memory broke through. He was standing beside his mother's hospital bed as she pushed the morphine-release button repeatedly, complaining of severe pain. He could see it written in the carved lines of her forehead, the pinched muscles of her face. No matter how many times she pushed that button in a row, none came. There was only so much narcotic it could dispense before it became dangerous and her pain seemed to stay above that threshold.

Meg's cell phone buzzed and she quickly answered, balancing the call and the baby. Stephanie cut across the kitchen and took the sleeping infant from Meg's arms with a disgusted look toward Wyatt. Was he supposed to know what her problem was?

He would've offered to hold the baby if it weren't for the fact that he was afraid he'd hurt the little thing. She wasn't much bigger than nothing wrapped in that tiny blanket. He'd never held something so small and so innocent in his arms.

And something with the potential to rock his world so completely.

His cell buzzed in his pocket. He fished it out and checked the screen. Dr. Raul. Based on the side of the conversation he could hear, Meg was on her phone with the sheriff. Two calls that had the potential to change Wyatt's life. The odds of both of them coming in at the same time on a normal day were ridiculously low. But this week, on *this* day any good luck he'd experienced in his life up until now could come crashing down around him.

"What did the test say?" Wyatt asked after perfunctory greetings.

The doctor hesitated before saying, "Congratulations, Mr. Jackson."

"There's no other possibility?" Wyatt wasn't sure

why he asked. Part of him had known since he first put eyes on the little girl that she was his. She was an exact match to his baby picture. He expected to be disappointed by the confirmation. Confused. Hell, angry.

Strangely, he wasn't any of those things. It was as if puzzle pieces clicked together and the picture made perfect sense.

Would he have chosen this particular time in his life to have a child? The answer was simple. No.

But she was here. She was beautiful. And he'd figure out how to move forward with an arrangement between him and Meg to make it all work.

It was most likely his practical nature and not real feelings for his child that snapped him into focus so quickly.

"These tests are never one hundred percent certain, but statistically speaking the probability that you're not the father is insignificant," the doctor answered.

"Thank you." Wyatt ended the call as Meg almost fell against the counter.

Her face was drained of color. He was grateful Stephanie was with the little one. He got to Meg's side in time to catch her, but she lost her grip on the cell she'd been holding and it crashed against the tile.

"What did he say?" Wyatt asked, ready to catch her if her legs gave out. Somewhere in the back of his mind it registered that the two of them would need to have a serious conversation about the future now that he was a father, but he drew a line around the knowledge and marked it as off-limits for now. Separating his emotions was a survival skill he'd developed as a small child out of necessity.

"The hair ribbon." Meg was trembling.

"The what?" He searched her face for something…

"It belonged to Mary Jane," she said so quietly that he almost couldn't make out the words.

"Who's that?" he asked as she started to sink toward the floor. He tightened his grip around her waist as the sound of the baby crying blasted from the room down the hall.

For a split second it dawned on him that *his* child was crying. Again he had to contain his emotions and the strangeness of the thought in order to focus on Meg.

Wyatt took most of her weight as he helped her to the kitchen chair.

"Who's Mary Jane?" he asked again.

It took a few seconds for Meg to speak, and he assumed she was gathering her courage as her gaze darted around the floor. "We were kids when she was taken. Ten years old. She was my best friend."

She looked up at him with a look of complete terror.

"He's back. He can't have my daughter," Meg said in that determined voice of hers. "He can't take Aubrey, too."

"No one's taking my daughter." Wyatt didn't know why those words sprang out, but he wouldn't take them back if he could. This news changed things because he also realized that Meg and his daughter were being targeted. Or someone was taunting her. Could the man who had taken her friend have returned? It was a possibility too real to be discounted. Had the abductor left the ribbon on purpose? Or had the person done that to throw off investigators?

Meg gave him a look that said she knew what the doctor had told him.

"I'm guessing they never caught the guy," he said to Meg. Was this why she worked on behalf of children and women who couldn't fight for themselves? Her best friend had been abducted and the perpetrator was never brought to justice.

"We were together that day." Meg focused out the window, her gaze fixed, and she looked lost.

A shot of anger burst through him. He clenched and released his fists to stop from reaching out to touch her, to be her comfort as tears slid down her cheeks.

"What happened?"

"I don't know," she said quickly, and there was desperation in her tone. Her eyes widened and more tears fell. "I keep trying to remember. All I recall is climbing the tree. I tried to convince her to follow but she was too scared. I should've gone down to play with her but I didn't." Meg stilled. "Next thing I remember I'm in the sheriff's office being grilled about who took her. The deputy thought I knew what happened and was being insolent."

"But you didn't remember so you couldn't help," he reassured. So much made sense about why she'd chosen her line of work and then there was her tenuous relationship with the sheriff's office.

Had a monster returned? Solving a cold case that had occurred almost two decades ago might just lead Wyatt and Meg to the truth about what was going on now. But if she didn't know then what had happened, how would she remember now?

"Aubrey needs a bottle." She pushed up to her feet as the sounds of the little girl's whimpering neared.

Wyatt had no idea how to do that, but he was ready for a crash course. "Sit down until you can stand without losing your balance. Tell me what to do."

"No, it's okay—"

"The DNA test confirmed what you knew all along. Aubrey is my daughter. I owe you an apology, Meg." He softened his tone when he said, "If you'll let me, I'd like to learn how to feed her."

Meg called to her friend, who brought the baby into the room and pulled up a chair next to her. The baby wound up to cry and released a scream that shredded Wyatt's heart. He'd never heard a more gut-wrenching sound than his own daughter crying. *Daughter.* That word would take some getting used to.

"What do I need to do?"

Stephanie started toward him, but he waved her off and then washed his hands. "Give it to me one step at a time."

"The clean bottles are there on the counter. Put a packet of formula into the bottle and fill it with the distilled water from there." Meg pointed to the water purifier next to the bottles.

Wyatt did it, pleased with himself for the progress. At least there was one area in which he could contribute, maybe ease her burden. A burst of light penetrated the wall inside his chest. "Now what?"

"It needs to be warmed. There's a warmer which I set

on a timer after the last feeding. Put the bottle inside and the light will turn green when it's ready." Meg motioned toward the contraption that was smaller than a toaster.

Thirty seconds later, he was handing over the bottle to her. Thankfully, the color returned to Meg's cheeks as she looked at her daughter, *their* daughter.

The hungry baby settled as soon as she got the first drop of warm liquid in her mouth, and something that felt a lot like pride swelled in Wyatt's chest.

He didn't normally do emotion, but there was something primal and satisfying about getting this right, providing food for his child.

Wyatt was caught between a rock and a hard place. Seeing Meg look so vulnerable was chipping away at the walls he'd constructed—walls that he had no intention of bringing down except where his daughter was concerned. But there was a kicker. Could he let Aubrey in without permanently cracking the casing around his heart?

Looking down at the helpless little bug, he knew instantly that he'd do whatever it took to protect his own, including keeping his feelings for her mother balanced. He'd been totally unprepared for the surge of attraction he felt toward Meg earlier. But that would have to stay in check.

He had to keep a clear mind in order to protect her and the daughter who'd stolen his heart from the second he'd put eyes on her. Damn. Parenting. Wyatt had never felt less prepared for any task. And a question loomed…

Could he keep all of them alive long enough to figure out who was targeting Meg and her baby…*his baby*, and why?

Chapter Eight

Holding Aubrey, hearing her baby's cries, jolted Meg away from the dark pit she'd been free-falling into. She marveled at the power the little child had over her.

Trying to remember the past took a physical toll, and she couldn't imagine doing any of this without Wyatt, either.

If she'd done one thing right in her life other than have Aubrey, it was call Wyatt when she did. He might be the added security she needed to keep her daughter safe, and Meg would make any sacrifice to put her daughter's needs first.

Was the kidnapper from her past closing in? Or did someone else know?

"The ribbon changes everything," she said to Wyatt as Aubrey drained the contents of her bottle.

"What else did the sheriff say?" he asked.

"That he would put every available deputy on the case and he'd like us to come in to discuss it," she said.

"That doesn't sound reassuring," he admitted.

"Not to me, either. There's been too much going on in this town," she said. "It used to feel safe, but not anymore. It sounded like he's rethinking his strategy in the investigation, but who knows what's really going on in his mind."

"You and the baby should come to Austin with me," he said after a thoughtful pause.

"To do what?" She couldn't see how that would help. Besides, seeing him with Aubrey made her wish for things she knew were impossible, like a real family. Watching Wyatt's protectiveness also made her realize how much her life was about to change. Their future was going to be about shared custody and spending every other Christmas with Aubrey. The thought brought tears to her eyes, but she kept them in check. Those were good problems to have in comparison to what she faced now.

"It would keep you both out of danger until we figured this out," he said. "Look, news that Butler is technically my father will break any day now if it hasn't already and that's going to bring a lot of unwanted attention to both of us. The media has been struggling to find anything worth printing, but every publication will want to be first to break the story when the sheriff finds the killer."

"Which makes going to your place seem like an even bigger mistake," she said. "Our every move will be chronicled and that could put us in a vulnerable place."

He stood up, paced. "You have a point."

"I have a couple of cases going to trial early in the new year I need to prepare—"

Wyatt was already shaking his head. "Work is going

to have to take a back seat. Staying here isn't an option, either."

As much as she didn't want to admit it, he was probably right about setting her caseload aside. *For now.* Maybe Stephanie could take over for a little while until it was safe for Meg and the baby to surface. They were most likely being overly cautious, but taking unnecessary risks with Aubrey wasn't an option. Meg would have to figure out something for her cases, though. She couldn't walk away from the people depending on her any more than she could turn her back on her own child.

"Then, where do we go? What else do we do? I wish I could remember the past. I could make all this go away for everyone's sake. Most of all, Mary Jane's parents deserved closure. I couldn't give it to them then, and I can't now. There isn't squat I can do about it even though it makes me crazy and now my daughter is in danger." Aubrey shifted position in her arms and blinked. Meg realized she was getting a little too worked up. If babies could sense emotion, she certainly didn't want her daughter to pick up on her anxiety level.

Meg took a deep breath and refocused on her daughter's face. Too many times in the past eight weeks she'd looked to that little angel when Meg doubted she'd be any good at being a mother. Her own had taken off when Meg graduated high school. Apparently, eighteen years with her was more than enough for the woman.

Shaking off that heavy thought, Meg looked up at Wyatt. He stood there, in her kitchen, his hip against her countertop, and there was something that looked so right about him being there. She took it as a good sign that maybe they'd be able to work together when it came to Aubrey. At least she prayed they could set their differences aside and figure out a way to coparent.

His arms were folded across his muscled chest, and the fabric of his shirt stretched over hard angles.

"I'm sorry that happened," he said quietly. Reverently?

"Thank you," she said.

"Someone could know that story and be trying to taunt you," he said.

"It's highly possible," she admitted. "But how would they get her hair ribbon if this person didn't take her?"

"We need to ask the sheriff," Wyatt said. "What if I take Aubrey to Austin for a while until this whole thing settles—"

Luckily, she didn't have to interrupt him. He stopped on his own.

"The determined look on your face as you hold her tells me there's no way you'd ever want to be apart from her," he supplied. "I heard what you said before but I still think my place is a good option. No one will get past security and you'd have privacy. Media aside, it's still safer than here."

"I don't hate the idea. Your town house isn't built for an infant, though," she countered.

"My house in the hills is finished. With a few adjustments, I'm sure we could make do," he said. "Whatever isn't there can be ordered. Most anything can be delivered within twenty-four hours between online shopping and lightning-fast delivery."

"I can't even think of everything she'd need," she admitted. "There's so much."

"Does that mean you're considering the idea?" His brow shot up.

"Yes. Considering, not agreeing," she clarified.

"Let's start with the basics. Where does she sleep?" he asked, and she realized that she hadn't shown him anything in the house other than the open-concept living room and kitchen. He had a lot to learn before he could be left alone with Aubrey. The thought was strangely reassuring because it would give her more time. The thought of shared custody and holidays without Aubrey was almost unbearable.

"During the day Aubrey sleeps in a bassinet in her room. At night, she stays with me. There's a crib but she's usually in bed with me," she said. The idea of getting away from Cattle Barge for a few days was growing on her. What about her caseload, though? The people who depended on her? There was no way she could let them down and his place wasn't necessarily safer, especially once the Butler news broke. "As nice as it sounds to go to your house, I was just thinking that I need to be here for work. I'm not taking on anything new, but I can't abandon the people depending on me."

"What can't be done online?" he asked.

She needed to think. Recent events, his presence and lack of sleep were clouding her judgment. She needed a good workout to clear her mind. "I can study the files and arrange services from anywhere, but I need a lot of help with the baby, and Stephanie usually takes a few feedings so I can work or take a power nap."

"When do you actually sleep?" His brow hiked.

"All the time," she countered, but just thinking about a soft pillow and warm blanket made her want to curl on her side and sleep for two days straight.

"Based on what I've seen so far, I'd have to disagree." He folded his arms across that broad chest.

"What do you think we should do next?" she asked as she placed her—*their*—daughter over her shoulder and gently patted her back.

"I'm still trying to figure out our next move," he admitted. "I see problems with going to my place, but we definitely can't stick around here. Before this update I'd been planning to speak to Garza. See if I could get a good read on him. He seems less likely now."

Stephanie walked into the room wearing workout pants and a hoodie.

"I'm going for a run." She pulled an earbud out of her ear and checked her watch. "I'll be back in half an hour or so."

"Take your phone with you in case I need to reach you," Meg said.

Stephanie patted the front zip pouch of her hoodie. "Got it right here."

"Be careful," Meg warned. "And stay warm. It's gotten colder out there."

Her friend nodded with half a smile. "I'll be right back."

Stephanie pulled the strings to tighten the hood around her face before taking off out the back door. From the window, Meg could see her friend stretching outside. She'd replaced her earbuds and her head was slightly bobbing to the music.

"Do you have family nearby?" Wyatt asked, and she realized how little she'd shared with him even though they'd dated for several months last year while she spent weeks at a time meeting with lawmakers in the capital. She knew surprisingly little about him, as well.

"I never knew my dad," she admitted. "Mom took off after I graduated. Afraid it's just me and Aubrey. That little girl is all the family I have aside from Stephanie, who is more like a sister than a friend. What about you? What's going on with your family?"

"You already know who my biological father was." He raked a hand through his bronzed curls. "Mom passed away five years ago."

"Then we're in the same boat as far as parents go," she said. "The main difference is that you have brothers and sisters."

"No, I don't." An emotion flashed in his eyes that gave her a shock. "I have a daughter and that's the only family I lay claim to."

"Didn't you have a meeting with the Butlers the other day? What happened?" she asked.

"Nothing I wanted to hear."

"It's fine if you don't want me to know," she said a little more briskly than she'd intended. If they were going to coparent it was reasonable to learn about each other's family history. The pediatrician had already asked questions about Aubrey's father's side of the family that Meg couldn't answer.

"Believe me, there's nothing to tell." The bull in Wyatt came out in full force. The man had a stubborn streak.

A shrill scream pierced the air.

"Stephanie." Meg stood and bolted for the door.

"You stay here and lock the door behind me," Wyatt warned, blocking her exit until she nodded agreement.

Meg did as he suggested. The baby stirred. The sudden movement must've startled her awake, but Meg was grateful her daughter was in her arms. Any hope yesterday's attack could've been random shot out the window. She scrambled to the front room and looked outside, wishing she could see something.

Pulse racing, Meg scanned the area looking for someone, something, some kind of threat. But there was nothing and her worst fears came into play. Had Stephanie been abducted?

Meg forced back the tears threatening. A sob escaped anyway. Her body shook with fear.

Nothing could happen to her friend.

For a split second, Meg wondered if the attacks were meant for Stephanie, but that wouldn't make any sense given the ribbon. And then she really thought about it. It was her best friend who had been abducted all those years ago. And now her current best friend had been targeted. Maybe, as odd as it sounded even to her, the person behind these attacks was trying to make Meg pay by hurting those closest to her.

It was a farfetched theory, but that's what she could come up with while this tired, even with adrenaline pumping through her body.

Aubrey belted out a cry and made a face so pitiful that Meg's heart squeezed.

"It's okay, sweet girl," she soothed before feeling her daughter's forehead. Aubrey wasn't warm and that was reassuring. She'd caught a cold at two weeks old and that had nearly scared Meg to death. Everything had turned out to be fine, except for Meg's nerves. She feared they would never recover, and after the events of the past twenty-four hours hope dwindled further.

Meg gently bounced up and down and that seemed to soothe the baby enough for her to close her eyes again. There was no sign of Wyatt or Stephanie, and that fact sent cold chills racing up her spine. *Please be okay. Both of you.*

Minutes ticked by with nothing, causing Meg's pulse to spike with every tick toward the new hour. And then she saw them. Stephanie was being carried by Wyatt, who was almost in a dead run.

As soon as he hopped onto the porch, Meg opened the door. The blast of cold entered before they did, and Meg shivered. Seeing Stephanie sent Meg's heart into a free fall. Her lip was busted and her cheeks were red from blunt force.

"Lock the door and call 911," Wyatt said before setting Stephanie down on the couch.

"Is she—" Meg put Aubrey in the swing, started it so the baby would stay comforted and then palmed her cell. She punched in the three digits reserved for emergencies and listened as the line rang.

"Unconscious," he said, and she noticed for the first time there was a lot of blood covering his hand. He moved swiftly as he went to work, locating supplies like clean towels and wet wipes. "The person who did this to her ran away when he saw me coming. He just dropped her and she went limp like a rag doll. I started to go after him, but he was too far and she was in bad shape. Plus, I didn't want to take the chance he could somehow get to you and the baby before I got back. I don't know this area well enough, so I picked her up and brought her home."

Meg relayed the information to the operator, requesting an ambulance and the sheriff. When the call ended, she ran to Stephanie's side. "What can I do?"

Wyatt scanned the door and then the windows. "Make sure all the doors and windows are locked and that no one enters who isn't wearing a badge or looks like an EMT."

"I couldn't tell if her chest was moving or not. Is she breathing?" Meg asked as she double-checked the locks.

"Yes." He pressed a clean white towel to her skull. A few seconds later, he pulled it back and the white had transformed to red. He replaced the cloth with a fresh one immediately.

Meg moved to his side and took the soaked rag.

"She has a cut above her forehead and foreheads are bleeders." He cleared a little of the area and the cut immediately bled. "It probably looks worse than it is."

Stephanie blinked her eyes open and mumbled something unintelligible. She needed to stay away from Meg if she wanted to be safe from now on. Meg would figure out a way to make that happen. She would do whatever was necessary in order to keep her friend out of danger.

Memories assaulted Meg. Her brain hurt and all she could see was fog.

"He called me Meg," Stephanie said, trying to blink her eyes open. "He thought I was you."

Meg gasped. "I'm so sorry this happened."

Wyatt shot a look meant to be reassuring. Nothing could console Meg. She was toxic to everyone she cared about.

"Did you see who did this to you?" Wyatt asked Stephanie.

The sound of glass breaking in the kitchen caused Meg to jump.

"Stay with her," Wyatt instructed with a narrowed gaze.

Meg was already by Stephanie's side, holding her hand. The noise must've roused Aubrey because she started winding up to cry.

"Go," Stephanie said, and it sounded like it took a lot of effort.

"I'll be right back," Meg said, feeling torn between caring for the immediate medical needs of her friend and attending to her baby who was startled but otherwise fine.

Sirens burst through the chaos. Clearly the emergency or law-enforcement vehicle was still at a distance, but the sound was wailing closer. She could only pray the noise would run off whoever had broken the window. The world felt like it had collapsed around her in the past half hour.

"Help is coming," she said to Stephanie, who was

already trying to sit up. "Stay put until someone can take a look at your head."

Stephanie tried to roll over to her side. "I might be sick."

"She's not well," Meg shouted to Wyatt. She couldn't leave her friend's side, not while she was in this bad a shape and trying to get up.

The sirens were getting closer and she realized an ambulance was almost there.

Wyatt bolted into the room. "If there's someone out there, I didn't see him."

"What was the noise?" Meg asked.

"A rock was tossed through the kitchen window. I'm guessing the sirens scared him away," he supplied, dropping down at Stephanie's side. "Stay right here. You're going to be fine."

With Wyatt there to care for Stephanie, Meg discarded the bloody towel and used baby wipes to clean her hands. She picked up the baby, who was trying to suck on her fingers, and located a pacifier. Aubrey calmed down almost instantly.

"He confused the two of us," Meg said to him as she rocked the baby across her shoulder. Between the sirens, the stress and her child's crying, Meg was one step away from losing it. She took a few calming breaths.

"From the back, I can see where he might," Wyatt said. Frustration and stress creased his forehead.

No one was safe near Meg anymore.

"We have to split up, Wyatt."

Chapter Nine

Wyatt stared at Meg, who looked to be standing guard at the door to Stephanie's room in the ER. Wyatt had played enough football in his youth to know that a blow to the head needed to be taken seriously. Stephanie was resting peacefully for now. A deputy had taken her statement during the brief time she was awake. The doctor had been optimistic for a full recovery as long as Stephanie took it easy for a few weeks.

He contemplated Meg's earlier comment about splitting up. There was no way he could let her or his daughter out of his sight without going insane. But the time for the conversation was not now. Stephanie's well-being was top priority.

Meg paced another lap around the room.

"They're keeping her overnight for observation, but where will she go when she's released? I don't want her going home alone and she moved in with me six months ago when she left her boyfriend." Meg's voice wasn't much more than a whisper, but he picked up on the seriousness. Of course, she would want to take care of her friend. Stephanie was in trouble because of her association with Meg. Given her past, Meg would take that to heart.

Besides, she made a good point. Stephanie had been a good friend to Meg during her pregnancy and these early weeks with the baby. He wanted to do something to help her out.

It was easy to see that Meg bore the burden of guilt, blaming herself for everything that was going on. He didn't want her to feel that way. He wanted to somehow ease her stress, telling himself that it wasn't because he cared about Meg but that it wasn't good for the baby.

"What about your contacts? Part of your job is to place people in care while they sort out their lives," he said.

Meg's eyes lit up. "Of course. I know the perfect person to call." She glanced down at the sleeping baby in her arms and then back to him. "Could you hold her for a minute?"

Wyatt took the baby in his arms, worrying he would crush the little thing. "She can't weigh more than ten pounds."

"She's twelve-point-five pounds according to her doctor last week," Meg clarified.

"That seems small," he said, although he had no idea how much a baby was supposed to weigh.

"She's right on target and pretty average for her age actually." Meg sounded a little put off. Hell, he wasn't trying to offend her. Aubrey was the tiniest thing he'd ever held. Under different circumstances, he might find Meg's defensiveness sweet and a little bit funny. Sexy, too. Right now, all he could focus on was keeping her and the baby safe while making arrangements for Stephanie.

"If you think she's so light, try carrying her around for two hours straight. Your arms burn and they feel like they're going to break off," Meg added.

"You're good with her," he said by way of apology.

"I've had eight weeks of practice," Meg conceded as she dug around in her purse for her cell. She located it and started toward the hallway.

"If you don't mind, I'd like you to stay where I can keep you in full view," he said, not wanting to cause undue stress but at the same time realizing it was difficult to manage holding a baby and still be ready should someone sneak past security and come at Meg. However unlikely the scenario might be, Wyatt wasn't taking any chances.

Meg nodded with a somber expression and he knew she understood fully the reason he'd asked. Even with hospital security on alert, someone could sneak in. It was a big place. If not the attacker, then media could slip past the front desk and the guard at the nurse's station. Bringing attention to anyone connected to Meg or the baby right now wasn't advisable.

He glanced down at the little bundle in his arms. She was secured in a tight blanket, sleeping peacefully. Another burst of pride filled his chest. How could something so tiny break down his carefully constructed walls so easily? He still had no idea what the future held, but he knew this little girl would play a large part in it.

Meg smiled for the first time today, and there was something satisfying about being the one to put it there.

"We've done a lot of work with a women's shelter. Ava Becks is the director. She's good at keeping people out of sight and under the radar while keeping some sense of a normal life for them. She's set up this entire compound where women can do things like shop for food, clothing and get a haircut without ever leaving the safety of the complex. Maybe Stephanie can hide out there until everything blows over. She'd be able to work remotely in order to keep her cases going and keep a schedule. She can go for a jog without being afraid someone will attack her."

The place sounded like the promised land for battered women. While Wyatt hated there was a need for such a facility, he appreciated what was being done. His fists nearly balled thinking about the reason innocent women and children would need such a place. When this was all over, he'd look into setting up an annual donation. His general manager, Marcus Field, had mentioned the employees would like to join together for a volunteer day around the holidays. He'd put Ava's shelter on the list. With twenty-five profitable locations of his restaurant across southwest Texas, he could do a lot of good for the charity and he'd do it in Aubrey's name. Which also gave him another idea. This one he didn't like as much...

"You and the baby could join her," Wyatt offered, taking a hit to the chest at the suggestion even though it was his suggestion. "I'd like to come, too. I know you mentioned splitting up earlier but I'd rather not. Now that I know about her I'd be crazy with worry if I couldn't see that she was safe."

Meg was already shaking her head. "Now that I think about I've changed my mind. It's too risky. I don't want to bring any unnecessary attention to Ava's operation. I could jeopardize her entire staff, not to mention her tenants, who rely on the place being off the radar. Ava's amazing at what she does for people, believe me, and I want my situation to be as far away from her and her people as possible." Meg looked at Stephanie. "And her. She's been lucky twice. If anything happened to…"

Emotion seemed to get the best of her. She turned her back and sniffed.

"Nothing will. She'll be tucked away on one of my properties, out of sight and kept safe." He wanted to tell her how strong she was for making that decision. She was right, too. In a weak moment, he'd considered making a call to the Butlers to see what they could offer. But how would that help? There was a swarm of media on their doorstep and Mike Butler's killer still hadn't been found. For all Wyatt knew he was right under their noses and no one in the family had figured it out. Not exactly his idea of a safe place for Stephanie, Aubrey or Meg.

"As soon as Stephanie wakes, we'll fill her in on the plan," Meg said, her smile still in place. It didn't reach her eyes, but it was a start.

He glanced down at his daughter. The thought of Aubrey being his only living family hit harder than he expected. Maybe knowing he was a father now was softening him. He wished his mother was alive to meet his little girl. The expansion of his restaurant chain had consumed him and, if he was being honest, gave him a good reason to set aside his grief.

He'd seen to it that his mother had had a proper funeral that year and then he'd buried all his emotions with her. He'd become a workhorse, a machine that never needed sleep.

For the first time in his life, he felt tired.

"I CAN MAKE COFFEE," Meg offered after feeding the baby again.

Checking into an all-suite hotel should keep them under the radar for the time being. The one-bedroom was well-appointed and had all the basics, including a nice-sized bathroom and generous living/kitchen area with a full-size fridge and microwave.

"Don't get up," he said, noticing the dark circles cradling her eyes. He needed to keep his distance because he kept thinking about the kiss they'd shared. It hadn't felt like a mistake at the time. Now, he realized it had felt a little too right.

"I need to set her down for a little while before my arms fall off," Meg said. They'd requested a crib and within ten minutes of their arrival one of the maintenance men had arrived to set it up next to the bed, for more convenient nighttime feedings.

Seeing how caring for an infant was a round-the-clock necessity made him tired thinking about it. He could be honest with himself. He had no idea how Meg was doing it. She took care of a baby who fed every two hours. The feedings lasted for almost a half hour and then she was right back at it an hour-and-a-half later. On top of that, she was co-running a successful organization.

He'd only found out he was a father a few hours ago and he was already tired from worry—worry that had been foreign to him until he found out that Aubrey was his child. Then worry had heaped on top of him, covering his arms like cement.

Wyatt's relationship with the little girl's mother was a work in progress, a challenging one at that given his back-and-forth feelings, but they had time to figure things out, right?

Not if a maniac gets his way, Wyatt thought.

Meg crossed her arms and leaned against the counter. He caught her studying him.

"Ready to go to the sheriff's office?" he asked. He'd told Sawmill that they'd stop by to give statements.

"I can't believe my house is a crime scene," Meg admitted with a yawn. "I don't want to disturb the baby yet."

Looking at her while she stood there, Wyatt could see that his feelings weren't the only issue. Her body language said she was closed off. Given her history, he doubted if she'd ever truly let another person in other than their daughter. Meg was on guard at all times and it finally dawned on him that was the emotion he'd picked up on last year. He'd never met a woman with walls constructed higher than his own and chalked both up to crazy childhoods.

"Tell me the truth. How long has it been since you've slept?" he asked.

"Me? I'm fine," she responded, biting back another yawn.

"Close your eyes and try to get some rest." He had no intention of letting Meg or his daughter out of his sight and he could stay awake as long as he needed to.

"Every time I close my eyes I think about her, about my friend. The recent attempt on Aubrey and the sheriff finding the ribbon seemed to be bringing up painful memories from the past." Meg looked at him with an expression that stirred something deep in his chest.

"Will it help to talk about it?" he asked.

"Can't hurt," she said. "I can't help but wonder what kind of monster would take a child. For eighteen years I haven't forgotten he existed. I'd hoped he was dead. I'd see Mary Jane's family in the store not long after it happened. She has a brother two years older than me. I never knew what to say to him. He tried to talk to me a few weeks after Aubrey was born. He seemed upset. He kept looking at Aubrey and then me." She paused. "After all these years I still couldn't face him. I ran out of the store so fast there was no way he could catch up to me. My cart was there by the checkout. I'd spent half an hour in the store before abandoning everything but my daughter."

"What happened when you were young wasn't your fault." He'd read the article she'd pulled up from over the summer. Every tidbit of news had been drudged up from the past it seemed ever since Maverick Mike was killed, including Mary Jane's kidnapping and death.

"And neither is any of this. You didn't do this to her family. This happened to you, too. Both of you were little kids at the time."

"That may be true, but I sure didn't offer much help to find her. I must've seen his face. I was right there." She stared at him. "Why can't I remember? How hard would that be? Maybe law enforcement could've gotten to her in time, rescued her before he killed her and she disappeared forever."

"You were a child. Didn't you say that you were ten-years-old? Again, I don't think you should blame yourself because law enforcement—who were grown men and women, by the way—didn't do the job they were supposed to," he countered. And then a thought struck. What if someone had figured out that Aubrey was his child? What if that person was trying to kidnap her with the intention of getting ransom money? "Do you think there's any possibility the attempt on Aubrey could be related to the fact that she's a Butler? If that's true these cases wouldn't be linked."

"They have to be. Where else would her hair ribbon come from? What are the chances it would be at the attempted kidnapping scene of my daughter?" She had a point. He was trying to offer other explanations.

"It's possible the ribbon was stolen from an evidence room," he said, trying to throw out other options. "Someone could be trying to rattle you or throw you and the sheriff off. Hell, they could be trying to shake up local law enforcement."

"Let's just say that's possible. Who would benefit from doing that?" she asked.

"You work as a family advocate in abuse cases. We need to look harder at the fathers and dig deeper into your cases. It's still possible this could be motivated by revenge and has nothing to do with what happened when you were a child. Someone could be trying to manipulate your feelings. Throw you off balance."

Her eyes widened. "I guess I didn't even think about that."

It looked like her mind was clicking through possibilities.

"Based on what I've heard so far of your work, the list of people not thrilled with your operation is long."

"Are you blaming me for this? Saying I somehow deserve it?" Her lips thinned.

"Hold on. I didn't say anything like that," he defended. "We need to examine all angles, and sometimes the obvious one is the right one."

She looked exacerbated and he couldn't figure out...

Hold on.

Did she think he was trying to dig up dirt so he could fight her for custody? The way she'd bucked up for a fight had him going down that path.

"I've worked on a few cases in the past year. There are always threats in the early stages, and blame and anger. It's usually directed at me in the beginning." She sighed sharply.

"Let's look at the most recent and we can work our way back from there," he said, and he was relieved when his suggestion seemed to calm her rattled nerves a little bit more. If he could do that more often, it would be good for their little girl. Those last three words still sounded foreign.

Wyatt needed to get used to the idea he had a daughter. Granted, Meg had had nearly a year to prepare herself for this day, and all this had been thrust on him in the past twenty-four hours, less if he counted since he'd received confirmation.

He'd risen to meet bigger challenges.

Patience and logic were all he needed to overcome any obstacle.

And that's what he needed to do now. Take a step back. Evaluate the situation. Come up with a plan of attack.

He glanced at the screen of his phone. "If my calculations are correct, the little bug in the next room is going to need to eat again in approximately forty-five minutes."

"That seems to be all she does right now," Meg said. She added quickly, "The doctor said it's perfectly normal. She's perfectly healthy."

Meg wrung her hands together.

"We don't have a lot of time before she needs attention and I'd rather not discuss the case when she's awake," he said.

"Or in the room at all," Meg added.

"Agreed." They'd just made their first decree as parents. It wasn't as difficult as Wyatt thought it might be. Meg was an intelligent and reasonable woman. Her mind was the first thing he'd been attracted to. Okay, fine, it was her eyes. But he'd noticed her intelligence the minute she spoke. They'd talked music—she loved a good old bluegrass melody—and current events.

And she knew how to cook. Not that he was a sexist jerk or bought any of that nonsense about women belonging in the kitchen. But there wasn't anything much sexier than a beautiful woman who was confident in the kitchen and actually enjoyed the process of creating a meal.

He glanced at the counter, remembering the pasta machine she'd brought to his place on their second date. She'd rolled out dough from scratch. She'd flattened it and fed it into the machine, catching the long strands of fettuccini noodles as they came out the other end. The look on her face, the enjoyment at creating something that she knew would taste better than anything he'd ever seen on a plate. And he was no slouch. But his culinary skills were limited to meats on the grill—which were his specialty—and ended with the perfect taco, around which he'd built his entire fortune.

He thought about the expansion. The problems. The lake house that seemed out of reach.

His work headaches were racking up, but they paled in comparison to the thought of anything happening to his child. Strange, he'd only been a parent for a few hours and his priorities were already shifting.

He wanted to get his bearings as a father. It wouldn't do any good to demand rights when he had no experience caring for an infant. He didn't even have friends with kids.

Hell, when he really thought about it he didn't have any close friends, either. He'd had a few beers with a few of his managers from time to time, called it a meeting. Wyatt had thrown everything he had, including all his time and energy, into making his chain a success. Looking back, he'd always been somewhat of a loner.

Somewhat?

He almost chuckled out loud. He'd preferred his own company to most of the young guys in high school. He never could relate considering he'd had a job since he was old enough to string together enough odd jobs to help out his mother with a few of their bills.

And speaking of money. He'd jumped the gun when he'd accused Meg of wanting to get a hold of Butler money the other day. Her reaction had seemed genuine. He'd hurt her feelings without meaning to. It had been a knee-jerk reaction and he regretted it.

Moving forward, he'd keep a better handle on what he said.

He needed to apologize for being a jerk. "I've been way off base and an apology doesn't begin to cover it, but it's a good place to start. I'm sorry, Meg. I've been acting like a real pain when I should've been supportive. I could make excuses, blame my past, but that doesn't cut it."

"We're both working through some intense emotions," she said. "I think we know better than to go down that road again. Kissing was a mistake."

Confusion struck him. She'd changed gears on him so fast he hadn't had time to hit the clutch.

Because that kiss was the first thing that had felt right to Wyatt in a long time. It was a dangerous sentiment considering he and Meg would have to figure out how to care for a child and stay on good terms.

Leading with his emotions would be a bullet through his chest when she pushed him away again. And she would.

For that little girl's sake, he wouldn't allow that to happen. No matter how much he wanted to haul Meg against his chest and kiss her again.

Chapter Ten

Aubrey was fed and burped. Wyatt had just arrived at Meg's house in order to drive the three of them to the sheriff's office.

The little girl made a face—*the* face—and Meg frowned. "She's going to need a diaper change."

"I'll take care of it." Wyatt looked a little uncertain.

"It's no problem. It'll take me two seconds," she said, holding on to Aubrey a little defensively.

"I have to learn to do it sooner or later," he countered, holding his arms out awkwardly.

Meg took a fortifying breath. He was right about one thing. He needed to learn how to take care of Aubrey, and diaper changing was a big part of the deal. At least she could stand over his shoulder and guide him through the process.

Reluctantly, she handed over Aubrey and Meg half expected her little angel to cry. Her doctor had said something about babies being sensitive to their environments and able to pick up on the emotions of others. For as awkward as Wyatt looked holding their daughter, he must be steady as steel on the inside because Aubrey didn't so much as flinch during the exchange. Of course, she was busy doing something else. The product of which wrinkled Meg's nose. *Okay, buddy. Here goes full-force fatherhood.*

"Diapers are in her bag and—"

Wyatt waved her off.

"Don't you think you should let me help you?"

"I can figure it out," he said dismissively before disappearing into the next room.

Meg wanted to chase after him and tell him that he'd been a father all of twenty-four hours and that diaper changing wasn't easy with a squirmy baby. Plus, as soon as that diaper came off Aubrey had a tendency to finish her business. She stopped herself. He wanted to do this on his own. So be it. Far be it from her to stop him.

Impatient, she tapped her toe on the carpeting while standing by the door. What was taking so long?

Meg knew better than to poke the bear and especially while he was handling their daughter. Plus, she really didn't want Aubrey to pick up on the tension between her parents. *Parents?* The word still seemed like Meg was talking about someone else and not her and Wyatt.

The proof was in the other room, most likely giving her father a hard time.

Under different circumstances, it might be funny. But then if she and Wyatt had met again without a baby in the picture she was pretty certain a whole lot of other things would be occurring in the bedroom instead of diaper changing. Things that had started her down a bad path a year ago.

For Aubrey's sake, Meg needed to find middle

ground with Wyatt. The thought of someone else being in her daughter's life was a little jarring. Did he deserve to know his daughter? No question. Did Aubrey have a right to know her father? Absolutely. It was the shared custody, the part about spending every other Christmas away from her little girl that broke Meg's heart. She had never envisioned having a family like this. But, then, Aubrey hadn't been exactly planned. And Meg had never seen herself as the house, minivan and two-point-five-kids type.

She glanced at her watch. If this diaper changing process dragged on much longer it would be time for Aubrey to feed again. "Everything okay in there?"

"Of course," came the slightly too-urgent response. It was the sound of someone who was most likely drowning trying to play it cool.

Okay, Wyatt. Let's see what happens.

Wyatt reemerged, almost immediately handing Aubrey over. He looked like he'd just been through a Cross-Fit class at the gym as he raked his hand through his hair—the sure sign he wasn't as in control as he pretended to be.

A small part of Meg was relieved because those first few weeks with her little angel had been hard. Getting the hang of diapering and every other duty that came with the role wasn't exactly second nature to Meg. She'd grown up alone, without younger siblings or cousins to learn the ropes with. The nurses had had to teach her all the basics before leaving the hospital and she'd watched what felt like a hundred videos on the internet for reference. Then there were the mommy blogs she frequented. Becoming a mother felt like showing up to a job interview in her underwear. But, a few weeks in, Meg had started to get the hang of things. It was amazing what twenty-four-hours-a-day on-the-job training did to bring a person up to speed.

Meg cradled her daughter and stared at the sweet face cooing up at her. Her stress levels calmed enough for her to say to Wyatt, "Ready?"

She didn't want to look at the diaper because it was pretty haphazard and she could only imagine what waited underneath that blanket. Besides, he'd get the hang of it in time, and the look on his face was priceless, no matter how much he tried to cover. He was stressed. Under any other circumstance, they'd be laughing right now. Maybe even enjoying the fact they'd brought this little miracle into the world.

But the circumstances they faced were far from funny.

WYATT PUT HIS considerable size between the members of the media and Meg and the baby as soon as the trio arrived at the sheriff's office. He knew full well the extra attention wasn't going to help matters for them. His high profile could place Meg and the baby in worse jeopardy, but walking away and leaving them to fend for themselves wasn't an option.

Thinking of Aubrey, another pang of regret filled him that his mother wasn't around to meet her granddaughter. When his child had looked up at him and smiled out of the right side of her mouth, it was his mother's smile. Renee Jackson's life had been tough.

She'd done the best she could. If Wyatt's no-account father had been around or had sent even a little support her life would've been so much better. Since Wyatt wasn't the lick-his-wounds type, he was grateful that he'd been shown the bad side of humanity. It had caused him to learn early on that he was the only person who could dig himself out of his own circumstances.

And he'd done pretty well for himself.

The sheriff looked as tired and overworked as the last time Wyatt had seen the man.

"Thank you for coming in," Sawmill said. "Please, make yourself comfortable."

Instead of pointing toward the chairs opposite his desk, he motioned toward the sofa on the other side of the room.

The little girl in Meg's arms started balling her fists and punching some unseen object in the air. She looked like she was about to cry and Meg seemed distressed. She checked her bottom and then pulled her hand from the baby's bottom, soaked.

Meg stood and her blouse was wet, too. To make matters worse, the diaper practically fell off.

Now the baby was crying. Her mother was shaken. And Wyatt only had himself to blame. Diapering his daughter turned out to be trickier than he'd expected, and his damn pride had kept him from asking for help. He'd wanted to show her he could figure it out for himself and instead had made a literal mess of things. Damn.

Wyatt could see that he was going to have to make some changes if he wanted to coparent the right way.

He apologized to Meg. He would've been frustrated if the shoe were on the other foot. It was a good lesson in humility. He was starting to see that he didn't have to take everything on alone when it came to Aubrey.

Ten minutes later, the baby was dry and secured in her mother's arms sucking on her fingers. Meg looked natural holding a baby. Or maybe that primal part of him thought she looked natural holding *his* baby.

Once everyone was settled again, the sheriff continued, "Can I get you a drink? Coffee? Water?"

"No, thanks," Meg said.

Sawmill folded his hands and leaned forward, resting his elbows on his knees. "Forensics was able to pick up a DNA sample from the hair ribbon."

Meg gasped and her face paled. "And?"

"I have a name. Clayton Glass." The sheriff paused before showing a photo.

It looked as though Meg was searching her memory for recognition. Seconds stretched on as she seemed to come up empty. She shrugged with a helpless-sounding sigh.

"I shouldn't be surprised you don't recognize him," Sawmill conceded. "He isn't from around here. He said that he happened to be driving through the city that afternoon eighteen years ago when he saw the two of you. He denied having any previous interaction with either of you prior to that day and it seems as though we can take him on his word."

Tears streamed down Meg's cheeks as looked at the photo of the man who'd taken her friend's life and devastated so many others. Wyatt took the baby from her and when Meg made eye contact, a fireball swirled in his chest. Intense emotion churned behind those blue eyes of hers. An urgent need to protect her, to take away her pain, ripped through his chest. His muscles pulled taut and hot anger licked through his veins.

The baby cooed and he had to force a sense of calm even though what he really wanted to do was show Clayton Glass what it was like to take on someone his own size instead of preying on innocent children. The damage he'd done to Mary Jane's family was irrevocable. As a new father holding an innocent little girl in his arms, Wyatt's heart clenched thinking about what had happened.

"Did he say what he did to her?" Meg asked, and Wyatt picked up on the devastation in her voice.

The sheriff bowed his head as though steeling his resolve. "According to his confession, she's been gone for quite some time."

"I could've stopped him," she said through a sob.

"No, you couldn't have." The sheriff didn't miss a beat. "He confessed to watching and waiting for you to climb the tree. He baited Mary Jane to get her across the street without alerting you. You were reading a book and seemed absorbed by it. In the interview, he bragged about being able to slip her out from underneath everyone's noses."

"If I'd been paying attention," she continued, unwilling or unable to accept that she wasn't at fault, "she would still be here."

"He saw an opportunity and took it," Sawmill said, his voice even. "That wasn't anyone else's fault but

Glass's. He's evil through and through. And he'll never see the light of day again."

"So, you have him in custody?" Meg's apprehension mirrored Wyatt's own. "It's over?"

"We do." Sawmill nodded. "And we have had for some time."

"Meaning?" Meg pressed.

"He's been in lockup at Huntsville prison for a little more than ten years. I'm sorry," Sawmill said with sincerity.

"What about the ribbon? How'd that turn up the other day?" she asked.

"We lost evidence to several cold cases last year. One of my deputies believed the boxes had been marked wrong and were destroyed," Sawmill admitted.

"I need a minute," Meg said, looking as though she was fighting a breakdown.

"Take all the time you need," Wyatt said.

She excused herself and disappeared down the hall toward the restroom.

It took a full fifteen minutes for her to return, and Wyatt's heart squeezed when he saw her red-rimmed eyes. The boogeyman who'd haunted her for most of her life had a name. The truth was out. Wyatt could only imagine what that might feel like.

Meg reclaimed her seat but kept her head down.

"Are you okay to move forward?" the sheriff asked, after offering more sympathy. "We can do this another time."

"Enough time has passed and I need to know who's after my little girl if not him." She'd pulled the baby's burping cloth from her diaper bag and held on to it so tightly her knuckles were white.

"Has anyone from the Fjord family reached out to you in the past six months?" he asked.

"Me? No. Not officially. I bumped into Jonathon at the grocery store over the summer, but we didn't speak. Besides, I'm pretty sure that I'm the last person anyone in that family wants to see, let alone talk to," Meg admitted. She seemed caught off guard by the suggestion. "Why?"

"I spoke to Mrs. Fjord," he supplied. "I'd like to speak to the entire family again more in depth. Time can sometimes offer perspective, and there might've been something missed on the initial round of investigations."

"Like what? You have a name. What more could you want?" she asked.

"He might've been working with a partner. Someone who is still out there," he said.

Wyatt noticed the sheriff didn't mention that would be the person trying to taunt Meg now. But what would be the motive?

"If not for Mary Jane's crime, why is Glass in prison?" Meg's voice shook but she seemed determined to finish the interview.

"He had a laundry list of charges. The biggest was armed robbery, and that's what he's currently serving time for," he supplied.

Wyatt glanced from Meg to the sheriff. "If the guy responsible for murdering Mary Jane is in prison, then who had access to the evidence room?"

"We're checking into the logs from around that time

as we speak, which, unfortunately, takes us back to square one with this investigation." Sawmill looked at Meg. "I'd like a list of acquaintances and anyone you've had a disagreement with recently. It could be a coworker or client. If anyone so much as cut you off in traffic and you have a name I want it."

"As far as coworkers go, you already know Stephanie. We have a receptionist, Amy Sharp. I can write down her contact information for you," she started.

"Does she have any reason to have a grievance with you?" he asked.

"No." Meg rocked back and forth a little faster as the questions continued, and he could tell that she was getting worked up. She was working the cloth in her hands pretty hard.

"Did you check into the name she already gave?" Wyatt asked, referring to the Garza case.

"He was coaching a team in a holiday tournament in Houston at the time of the attempted abduction. There are twenty witnesses," the sheriff supplied. "We broke up the list and each person was contacted by one of my deputies."

Wyatt appreciated the thoroughness.

Under the circumstances, he couldn't blame Meg for being unsettled. He wanted to be there for her and shield the baby, which seemed an impossible task. Since he wasn't capable of caring for the eight-week-old on his own, he resigned himself to the fact she'd have to go everywhere with them.

The sheriff turned to Wyatt. "How are you connected to this case?"

Wyatt glanced at Meg, who seemed to catch on because she nodded slightly, and he took that as permission to keep talking. "I'm Aubrey's father."

Sawmill's eyebrow arched. "How many people knew you were a Butler before you came to town?"

"Only the Butlers and their lawyer as far as I know," Wyatt admitted.

An emotion flickered behind the sheriff's eyes that took a second to discern. He remembered the articles about Cadence Butler trying to run Madelyn Kensington off when she'd first come to Cattle Barge. Cadence had pulled a stunt to try to scare the former reporter so she'd leave town and the Butler family—along with her inheritance—alone.

"You think one of them would get involved with something like this? To what end?" Wyatt asked.

The sheriff's gaze bounced from Wyatt to Meg, but to his credit he didn't comment. Wyatt didn't care if the man was in law enforcement, if he made Meg uncomfortable over their situation the two of them would have words. His and Meg's relationship might be complicated, but judgment was off-limits to outsiders.

"As to your question about who knew Maverick Mike was my sperm donor, you're asking the wrong person." The sheriff needed to talk to the people at the ranch. "My last name is and always will be Jackson."

"I'll have Janis check news outlets and see when they

started reporting, so we can get an idea of the scope," Sawmill said.

Meg made a noise. "News about you, us, is out?"

The sheriff nodded.

"That complicates things, doesn't it?" she asked Sawmill.

"It could," he admitted. "We'll focus on those closest to you first. Without any evidence other than the hair ribbon, we have nothing else to tie the killer in. It could be a sick prank or someone trying to get revenge."

"You asked if I had any contact with her family before," she continued. "Her parents haven't spoken to me since…"

"We're in the process of tracking her brother, Jonathon, down now," Sawmill said. "His mother said he moved out of town for his work as a bricklayer."

Wyatt couldn't imagine the pain Mary Jane's family had gone through losing their little girl so young. Looking at his own daughter, his protective instincts flared at the thought of anything happening to her. Now that he knew what Meg had been through he wondered if that's what had made her pull back from him when things started getting interesting between them. He didn't do long-term, but he'd liked spending time with her, and his current attraction most likely was crackling embers from the flame that had burned brightly a year ago.

Watching her recover after his mess-up with the diaper made him want to work together with her. It also made him feel like a jerk for not accepting help when she'd offered. He'd been so intent on figuring everything out for himself that he'd made everything worse.

Wyatt wasn't used to depending on anyone else. It made him feel…helpless…and reminded him of how awful he'd felt when he couldn't do anything to ease his mother's pain before her death.

Being stubborn had made him the success he was in business…

Speaking of work, his phone hadn't stopped buzzing inside his pocket since they'd walked into the sheriff's office. That didn't signal good news. The longer this day wore on the worse it got.

And just when he thought the crap-day limit had been hit, Dade Butler knocked on the sheriff's door.

"Can I come in?" the Butler twin asked with a nod toward Sawmill.

Sheriff Sawmill stood. "My apologies in advance, but Mr. Butler asked me to let him know when you came in. He said he has an offer for both of you and that you need to hear him out."

Meg shot a confused look at Wyatt.

"There's nothing for us to hear," he said.

"Can I speak to my half-brother alone?" Dade asked the sheriff.

Sawmill excused himself.

Wyatt stood between Meg and Dade, shielding her and the baby from what he wasn't exactly sure.

"I'm here to offer any assistance you need," Dade said with a sincere look.

"You were sent?" Wyatt arched his brow.

"I volunteered, but that's not the point." Dade folded his arms. "The way I see it, you can use a hand."

"I'm afraid you'll have to fill me in," Wyatt said, unmoved. He had no idea what kind of game the Butlers were playing, but he had enough on his plate without adding them as complications. "What help have you decided we need?"

"All the media attention surrounding our father's murder has brought out a lot of crazies. Several of our family members have already been targets and we've been fortunate so far that no one has been hurt," Dade said with that same look of sincerity.

"My daughter isn't a Butler," Wyatt countered. "And neither am I."

"That may well be in your eyes, but not everyone might see it that way," Dade said. "I read someone attempted to kidnap her."

"Her name was never in the news." Wyatt had double-checked this morning to be sure.

"We put two and two together and so will others if they haven't already," Dade said. "It's not exactly a safe time to be connected to this family and whether you like it or not, you are."

"All the more reason to keep my distance," Wyatt said.

"That ship might've already sailed," Dade retorted, and his defenses seemed like they were flaring.

To be fair, Wyatt stood there glaring at the guy like a matador waving a red flag at a bull.

"There was an item found near the site, which links the incident to Meg's past," Wyatt informed him. Either way, he wasn't inclined to accept help from anyone in that family.

"We think we can help with the investigation and

at least offer protection until the case is solved." Dade tapped the toe of his boot on the tile floor. "If you won't take our help, she should still hear the offer and decide for herself."

"Her place is with me," Wyatt interrupted.

"Agreed," Dade said. "Which is why we'd like to offer all three of you full access to one of our guest houses."

"Correct me if I'm wrong, but your father was murdered on the ranch," Wyatt stated. A twinge of regret sluiced through him the instant he saw how deeply that comment cut. Dade's split-second reaction before he recovered was a mix of hurt and wounded pride. The man was there with a peace offering. It wasn't his fault Maverick Mike was a jerk. Wyatt could concede that point.

"That's correct," Dade said.

"The sentiment is appreciated, but we'll do all right on our own." Wyatt glanced at Meg and her surprised reaction caught him off guard. Didn't she trust that he could keep them safe? "We're done here."

"Suit yourself, but if you change your mind my number is on that card I gave you," Dade said.

Dade seemed like a stand-up guy. Wyatt had to give it to him. But he could take care of his family without the help of a Butler.

Wyatt excused the three of them and headed to the truck, realizing that the sheriff had set them up.

Frustration barreled through him, but he needed to keep it in check in front of the baby.

Once inside the truck, Meg said in a reverent tone,

"Mary Jane's family deserves to finally know what happened to her."

"At least they have answers. They have closure," Wyatt said. His personal affairs paled in comparison to the thought of losing a child, but he understood closure. He'd never gotten it from Maverick Mike. "I let her down." The look she shot him said that didn't matter. And that guilt would keep her from moving forward with anyone in her life. She'd never stop blaming herself for what had happened and she would always construct walls to keep people out.

"I said it once and I'll say it again. You were a kid." He caught her gaze and held it. Wyatt told himself the only reason he cared about Meg keeping everyone at a distance was for Aubrey's sake, but there was more to it than that. It was wounded pride that had him wanting her to open up a little more. Being with her brought up feelings he didn't want to acknowledge, didn't want to have for anyone.

His cell buzzed again. It was no doubt work related. He was distracted and letting things slip.

After parking at the hotel, he said, "I'll be right up."

Meg nodded. "I'll feed the baby and put her down for a nap."

As she closed the door, he checked the screen on his cell keeping one eye on her until she was safely inside the building.

There were several texts from his lawyer, Alexander Kegel. Rather than spend time texting, Wyatt called Alexander.

His lawyer picked up on the first ring. After perfunctory greetings, he said, "The shell corporation that owns the lake house is impenetrable. How much time and resource do you want to spend on this?"

"Keep digging," Wyatt instructed, which meant until the lawyer found something.

"Got it," Alexander said. "Also, I'm taking the city of Bay to court over the construction block and refusal to issue permits."

"On that one, retreat." Having a foothold in Bay wasn't as important to him now that he had a daughter. He had other priorities. "One town over, Centreville, has reached out. Let's change course. The Centreville location is still close enough the current employees will be able to commute and keep their jobs. I dug into the data last night and it turns out many of them live closer to Centreville than they do to Bay anyway. It makes more sense to go where we're wanted and appreciated."

"I'll get on the phone with Ladd as soon as we hang up," Alexander said. Hazel Ladd was the head of construction for Tiko Taco Limited.

"Good. I don't want the men standing around waiting for permits that may or may not come," Wyatt said. He'd always been the decisive, cut-his-losses type. "Let's keep them on the clock and working so they can continue to put food on the table for their families."

"We'll make it happen. Is there a specific location you're looking at?" Alexander asked.

"There's land for sale a block off the downtown area. Check into that first and make sure we have the right zoning to ease the transition," he instructed.

"Done. What else?" Alexander was his make-it-happen guy and an important part of his business. Their relationship worked because they kept it professional.

There was no gray area, no confusion.

"That's all for now." Keeping emotions out of their exchanges was the reason they worked so well together.

He'd hold on to that thought when it came to Meg.

Because his emotions had him wanting to run his finger down her generous curves and see if she still mewled with pleasure when he grazed a trail up her neck with his tongue.

With everything on the line between them, that was just dangerous and stupid.

Maintaining a safe distance was the only logical move.

Chapter Eleven

The air outside had been cold and gusty.

The baby had been fussy while Wyatt was in his truck. Did she miss her father? The thought was illogical, Meg knew that, but not entirely impossible. *Right?*

The boogeyman who had been haunting Meg for eighteen years had a name. Clayton Glass. The worst part? An internet search hadn't revealed any photos or information about him. The only thing she knew for certain was that he hadn't been the one to try to abduct Aubrey.

So, who was it?

Wyatt walked inside the suite and tension sat thickly between them.

On top of that, Meg's throat hurt and she sneezed five times in a row. It was probably just allergies with all the wind blowing every possible allergen into the area, but Meg couldn't be certain and she didn't want to risk getting the baby sick if she was going down herself.

"Do you mind holding her for a second?" Meg asked Wyatt, handing over their daughter. He took the baby from her, cradling Aubrey in his arms, looking more at ease than the last time. If Wyatt had been irresistible before, he'd jumped into a whole new stratosphere now while holding the infant against his muscled chest in such a contrast between innocence and strength.

Meg knew from experience just what his skin felt like, silk over steel. And her fingertips had reacted to grazing his skin as she'd handed over the baby.

His fierce, protective look only enhanced her attraction to him—an attraction that had no business distracting her at the moment.

"I've been reviewing my most heated cases from the past six months." She retrieved her laptop and moved onto the couch next to him. Another sneeze and she scooted to the opposite end. She cleared her throat and tried to speak again. "Hold on."

Meg set her laptop in between them before getting up and moving into the kitchenette.

"Can I take a look?" he asked.

"Absolutely not," she said a little too quickly.

"I wouldn't normally ask, believe me. I respect what you do more than you can realize. But our daughter is in danger," he continued, clearly hoping she'd have a change of heart.

After heating water in the microwave and squeezing a lemon wedge into the cup, she returned. "You're right. Technically, only employees can read those files."

"Hire me." It wasn't the worst idea.

She drummed her fingers on the side of the cup.

She sat down beside him.

"Create a board. Put me on it. That would qualify." He was right about that.

"Okay. You're right. I have to do whatever I can to ensure Aubrey's safety. I'll speak to Stephanie about the board. For now, you can fill in for her."

He stared at the screen for a long moment. "Why didn't you go to the police before?"

"About which part exactly? I get threats in this line of work," she said.

"Between those and men hitting on you, I'm not sure…" He didn't finish and it looked like anger was getting the best of him. And there was another emotion present. It looked a lot like jealousy.

Meg dismissed it as her imagination taking over or some maternal desire wishing for more from Wyatt, like a happy family. And the only reason she wished for that was for Aubrey's sake. Plus, her hormones hadn't readjusted.

Moving on.

She cradled the warm cup in her hands.

"How do you deal with this kind of abuse on a daily basis?" There was so much anger and indignation in his voice.

"It's just part of the job," she admitted on a shrug. "I fight against bullies. They push back."

"No one should have to put up with this, let alone you. You're a decent person, despite what this idiot thinks." He motioned toward the screen.

She suppressed a chuckle. "Those people are the reason my job is so important."

"What can you possibly get out of going head-to-head with…*jerks*…who can't even spell your name correctly?"

"I don't do it for them. Most of them are angry and

used to getting their way because of it. To be honest, I'd rather they take their frustration out on me instead of my clients." She perched on one leg. "The kids are why I do my job." She scooted a little closer and minimized the screen to her wallpaper, which was covered in photos of smiling kids cuddling dogs or cats, or sitting on Santa's lap wearing the biggest smiles.

"These are your clients?" he asked, and his tone was much softer now.

"Yes. They deserve to have someone fighting for them, someone who won't be intimidated by an abusive or neglectful parent," she said. "That's what I do."

"It's one of the things I respected about you when we first met," he said in a low rumble of a voice. "When you talked about your work your eyes sparked, and I could tell you were doing something you believed in. I've never met anyone else with that kind of passion."

She didn't remember saying much about it before. Meg always liked to keep her professional life quiet and she could never discuss details for obvious reasons. It was easier not to mention what she did. When she really thought about it, she had opened up to Wyatt about her personal life more than she had to anyone else in her past.

Stephanie knew the most about Meg's caseload, but she'd kept her on a need-to-know basis as far as threats went. There was no reason to rile everyone up over a bully.

Wyatt maximized her email, covering the screen. "I'd like to check the list of names you gave the sheriff."

"Most of what's on there is just venting," she said.

"They don't mean any of it. They're used to having a punching bag and I've taken that away from them. It's just words. They don't mean any of it."

It occurred to her that she'd just repeated the phrase, *they don't mean any of it.* Was she trying to convince herself?

"I'm not so sure and after reading a few of these, I'd like to meet some of these—" he looked to bite back a few angry words "—people personally. Especially this one." He pointed toward a name. Hector Findley.

"He's on the list," she admitted.

"How many names did you give Sawmill?" he asked.

"Seven," she said on a shrug, trying to pull off non-chalant.

"There are at least six more Hectors?" Wyatt's full lips thinned.

Aubrey stirred.

"We shouldn't talk about this in front of her," Meg said. "I read somewhere that babies are constantly reading our moods. If she feels tension every time we talk, she might think we're not getting along."

Wyatt glanced down at the baby and then his gaze bounced back to Meg. "We can do better than that."

"Is she asleep?" Wyatt asked as Meg entered the kitchenette. A half hour had passed since Meg had disappeared into the baby's room to put her down for a nap. He poured a cup of coffee and handed it to her.

"Yes, thankfully." Babies must have a sixth sense about when their parents needed to talk or get something important done, because every time Meg needed her daughter to sleep the little girl fussed instead.

Wyatt moved to the table, sat down and repositioned the screen on her laptop so that both of them could see. "I've narrowed it down to three names I think pose an actual threat."

He pointed toward the first.

"We already mentioned him." Hector. "Tell me more about his case."

"I can't do that without violating confidences," she warned. "It would be unethical. Besides I've already overlooked your digging into the files without my permission."

"Protecting your cases is important. You don't have to tell me specifics. Just why these men are writing threatening emails," he said.

"Because when I testify they'll lose people they view as their possessions," she stated matter-of-factly. "In Hector's case, he repeatedly hit his common-law wife in front of her daughter. My client is nine, Wyatt. He told her that he'd hunt them down and make her watch him kill her mother if they left him. Her mother said that he always feels bad later and that's why she stayed with him. He'd cry and tell her that he was going to get help. And then he'd be really nice to her and my client. The peace usually lasted a month, sometimes two, before something would set him off again. The mother felt like it was partly her fault. She grew up in an abusive household and came to expect it from a relationship. They'd fight. He'd go out drinking, wake the house up when he got home and repeat the cycle of abuse all over again."

His lips thinned and his eyebrows drew together, but he didn't speak.

She glanced at the second name. "Rodney Straum. He works as a youth-group leader. My client is the only one who's come forward. Forensic evidence corroborates his story."

Wyatt white-knuckled his coffee mug and anger seethed behind his normally cool steel-gray eyes. "How do you do it?"

"What?"

"Take up cases like these? I've heard about two so far, and it's taking everything inside me not to look these jerks up and teach them a lesson about being a real man," he said.

"Hearing about the abuses that occur, that's the hard part of my job. If that's all I focused on I'd be in trouble. I mean, these stories make what I've been through seem like nothing," she admitted, realizing she'd slipped. She didn't discuss her background with anyone. Maybe he'd write it off as her experience with Mary Jane and not relate it to the emotional suffering that came after when her own mother had rejected her. "Here, let me show you something."

She moved closer to the computer, ignoring the heat skittering up her arm when her left shoulder touched his right as she repositioned to get closer to the keyboard. Showing him this would hopefully make him feel better because it was the only thing that kept her going when all she wanted to do was cry for the children involved.

"Here's an update from Alicia Rose's mother." The

file opened to a smiling, healthy fourteen-year-old at summer camp. "Her biological father tortured them both. He's locked away in a place he can't hurt another woman or child, thanks to tougher laws that we lobbied for."

"She looks happy," he conceded.

"Alicia's taking hard classes at school and is an honors student. She has a close circle of friends. None of that seemed possible when she was ten years old," Meg said, and she could hear the pride in her own voice. "When these men are faced with losing control, they lash out. Anger is how they deal with life. Usually, that means they come at me."

Wyatt issued a grunt.

"I'd gladly take the brunt of a few angry emails in order to protect people who are weaker than I am," she defended. "None of those words make me lose sleep."

"Until now..." Wyatt glanced up at her. "I wish you'd told me about this sooner. You never said anything or gave me the impression anything like this was going on."

"We dated a few months. What was I supposed to do? Spill my whole life story?" she asked, but she knew it was a cop-out. A glance toward him said he knew it, too. Okay, she'd kept parts of her life from him...*most* of her life from him. Guilt stabbed at her, but she deflected. "It's not like we were serious."

Wyatt shot up out of his seat so fast his movement startled her. He raked his fingers through his bronze hair. There was enough stubble on his chin to reveal he hadn't shaved in at least twenty-four hours. "No. We weren't."

He scooped his cup off the table and refilled it with coffee.

Why did his words sting so much?

They'd had a fling. It was supposed to be a stress reliever. So, why did all her plans come back to bite her in the back side? Her fling had turned into what could've been real feelings and they'd made a baby. Neither was supposed to be on the table.

"We were both busy with our careers. We didn't have time to get to know each other any better," she said, and there was more defensiveness in her tone than she'd intended. Besides, what had been up with the fact that he only had one coffee mug at his place? Who only had *one*?

Wyatt looked at her. No, the right word was *through* her. And it looked like he was about to say something significant. Whatever it was seemed to die on his tongue. Instead, he cracked a smile and shook his head. "No. We didn't. Which makes even less sense why we have a baby together."

Okay, that hurt. "Aubrey's a beautiful little girl and none of this is her fault." Yes, she was being defensive.

"Never said it was. It's ours."

Oh, was that what he thought? That their child was a burden?

"You don't have to be involved," she defended.

The look he shot could've frozen gasoline. "Then you really don't know me."

"I'm just saying that I didn't tell you to force you to

be involved or get money out of you. I have enough to take care of her," she said, hating how shaky her voice sounded.

"My child won't want for anything." His tone was final. "I don't place the blame on you for this happening."

He didn't?

"I take full responsibility," he said. "Wish you'd clued me in sooner, but we're here now. That little girl stirs something in my chest I've never felt before. She deserves to know both of her parents. She deserves to have the benefits of a father who has the means to make sure she has access to a good education and is brought up in a nice house. She deserves to have parents who find a way to get along if for no other reason than for her sake."

He was making sense and saying the words Meg thought she wanted to hear. So, why did they sting?

"We can split her expenses fifty-fifty," she said.

"With all due respect, I can do better than that." His tone was final, and she didn't like the implication that she couldn't pull her weight when it came to their child.

"We can work out those details later," she said with a warning glance.

He stood there for a long moment before he reclaimed his seat. "Tell me about Zach Brandt."

Chapter Twelve

"Brandt is bipolar and drinks to numb his pain," Meg offered. Changing the subject was probably for the best. Opening up and talking about herself, about their non-relationship, felt like poking a bruise with a stick, pointless and painful with nothing to gain.

For Aubrey's sake, they would need to interact and be strong. If she could get to a place where her body didn't hum every time he was close, she'd be a lot happier. And there'd be a lot less stress.

"What's the story?" he asked.

"When he's up, all is well. When he's down, it gets pretty bad. Paranoia. There are no physical bruises, but once he decided that aliens were trying to read his mind so he blocked out all the windows with aluminum foil and made 'hats' from the same material in order to block transmission," she said. "He would go several days without food or water, saying that the aliens were contaminating the food supply in order to control everyone's minds."

"He sounds like a complete nut job," Wyatt said.

"Social services keeps urging him to go to the doctor. As soon as he shows the slightest bit of stability, they return his two children." Frustration nipped at her.

"This is the last person on earth who should be caring for children," Wyatt said.

"Agreed. His kids are two and four," she continued. "They're too young to fight for themselves."

"How'd you get the case?" His brow arched.

"Part of my job is to review social workers' caseloads. In their defense, they like to keep families together and they also have limited resources to work with. They can't be certain that kids who end up in foster care or with adopted families end up doing much better. Especially the ones who end up in foster care," she admitted.

"This seems like a no-brainer. Take the kids, right?" he asked.

"In this case, I agree one hundred percent. Nothing good can come from this guy keeping his children. They're young and adoptable."

"So, basically, if you can't find parents these kids could end up passed around in the system without ever finding a real home," he said on a sharp sigh.

Meg nodded.

"Sounds hopeless if you ask me. Even if you win, they could lose." He stared hard at a point on the wall.

"How would any of them know about the ribbon? I mean, it's the *exact* color and kind of ribbon she wore the day…" A sob escaped before Meg could suppress it. She stood and turned her back to Wyatt with a mumbled apology.

She knew he'd moved behind her even before his

hand touched her shoulder. His scent—a mix of out-doors and clean and masculine—filled her senses, rob-bing her of the ability to think for a split second. Wyatt had that effect on her, which made him dangerous. She could work with him for Aubrey's sake but, dammit, she couldn't go there with her emotions no matter how much her body trembled underneath his touch. And it did tremble.

"Surely the ribbon was in the news. Someone could find a past article and dig up information about it," he said, and his voice was a low rumble against her hair. The only parts touching were his hand to her shoulder and yet she could feel his presence as though it was wrapped around her.

"I guess we won't know until forensics tells us," she said. It was a valid point. One they wouldn't have an answer to for a while or until they nailed the bastard and got a confession.

Her arms had goose bumps, and a trill of aware-ness shot through her when he closed the distance be-tween them.

The hand on her shoulder moved her hair to one side, and he dipped his head and pressed a soft kiss on her bared shoulder. Heat flooded her and her thoughts shifted. Muscle memory had her wanting to turn around and reach for him, to feel him on top of her pressing her into the mattress. To feel safe again. It had been so long since she'd felt she could count on someone else.

It was so easy to get lost with Wyatt standing there, his lips lighting a hot trail up her neck to her ear. She could feel his warm breath sensitizing every place it touched, and her own mouth went cotton-ball dry.

"Meg," he said, and his voice was gravelly.

The baby cried and Meg's heart lurched. She pushed off Wyatt and mumbled another apology as she darted toward the hallway. The thought of anything happening to her girl—no matter how improbable that was given she was being watched over by the two of them 24/7—caused her heart to jump into her throat.

Meg raced to the crib in time for another ear-piercing scream.

"What it is?" Wyatt said, and there was so much concern in his voice.

Meg made it to her daughter before the next burst of tears sprang from the little girl's face. Aubrey was fine. A glance at the clock told her everything she needed to know about what was going on with her daughter. "She's hungry."

"Right. Milk. I'll make a bottle." There was so much relief in his tone. He disappeared, his deep baritone a cover for how shaken he'd been earlier. A relationship between her and Wyatt wouldn't amount to more than hot sex…and the sex would be smoking hot. But real feelings? Sexual chemistry was one thing and they had that in spades. And that's where it skidded to a halt. Wyatt wasn't capable of more, she reasoned.

Except when it came to Aubrey.

His feelings toward his daughter seemed genuine enough, especially with the determined look he got every time he talked about keeping Aubrey safe. She had no doubt that he'd do everything in his power to protect that little girl and give her a bright future.

Meg prayed it would be enough to keep their daughter safe through this nightmare.

She gently bounced up and down, soothing Aubrey as best she could. The little girl cried, but even that was a sweet sound to Meg. Being able to hold her daughter after almost losing her...

The thought of anything happening to Aubrey caused hot tears to spill down Meg's cheeks.

Wyatt returned a few minutes later with a bottle.

"I can feed her," he offered after getting a good look at Meg.

Covering the fact she was crying with a cough, she blamed her watery eyes on allergies. "I've got this."

She would have to learn to share Aubrey in the very near future. Now, though, she couldn't go there. Meg needed to hold her daughter in her arms.

Aubrey latched on to the nipple immediately and settled with the first drop of warm liquid in her mouth. Meg walked to the bed and perched on the edge, gazing down at her little miracle.

A dark feeling settled over her as thoughts of Mary Jane's kidnapping resurfaced.

Had her kidnapper been working with a partner? Or had past news coverage of the crime brought a different kind of boogeyman out from under the bed? One who wanted to see Meg suffer before killing her?

WYATT MIGHT BE brand-new at this parenting thing but he knew Meg well enough to realize that she needed to hold her daughter. He closed the door behind him and moved into the kitchen.

After pouring a cup of coffee—because he could face facts, there'd be no sleeping tonight—he moved back to the laptop. His own work was piling up, but Alexander was handling the bigger tasks and nothing was more important to Wyatt than keeping that little girl in the next room safe.

His emotions had gotten the best of him earlier. Emotions…sexual chemistry? Hell, he couldn't tell them apart anymore when it came to his reaction to Meg. The two had had great sex last year. No question. But he was beginning to realize just how precious little he really knew about her.

In her defense, there was no way to work into conversation the kind of horror she'd been through as a child. And he could see why she'd want to distance herself from all of that and never bring it up again.

Then there was his complicated family dynamic to deal with. His personal business was being splashed all over every front page of most every news outlet. Maverick Mike Butler was big news. Even more reason Wyatt didn't want or need to be included in that family.

Since going down that route was as productive as trying to milk a cat, he refocused on the screen. Families were complicated as hell. The thought of his own daughter going through any of that nonsense sent a wave of rage surging through him.

He didn't know the first thing about parenting, and his role model for being a father was a complete failure at the job. Further, Wyatt didn't know the first place to begin to figure it out. His mother had been a decent person. Poverty hadn't given her a lot of options, and he'd often wondered how on earth she'd met Maverick Mike let alone struck up an affair with the man. But, then, based on his reputation, Maverick Mike had taken up with quite a few women and hadn't seemed to mind walking away.

Anger was a hot poker pressed to Wyatt's chest thinking about a rich man taking advantage of his mother. And yet part of him wondered how that could've been. She'd been one of the strongest people he'd known, making it difficult to imagine anyone could get one over on her.

He wondered how Butler had taken the news that Wyatt's mother was pregnant. How vulnerable his mother had had to be to tell Butler in the first place.

Now that was ironic.

Wyatt flashed to the morning Meg had told him about Aubrey. He'd been about the biggest jerk a man could be under the circumstances. Damn. It was becoming hard to condemn his own father considering how Wyatt had handled the conversation.

Meg was proud, like his mother. Had his mother refused support, too? Had Butler even bothered to offer?

Maybe that's what set Wyatt apart from the Butler family. He took responsibility for his actions. No amount of arguing would stop him from taking care of his child. He expected nothing less of any guy who called himself a real man.

"Find anything interesting?" Meg's voice cut through his heavy thoughts. He glanced up to see the baby being gently held over Meg's shoulder as she bounced and pat-ted the little girl's back.

"I need to say something," he started. Finding the right words was hell. He settled on, "I'm sorry I wasn't here for all of it."

"It's not your fault," she said without hesitation, and he appreciated her letting him off the hook so easily. He couldn't.

"Yes, it is."

Now she turned to him and he half expected her to check his forehead for fever.

"Hold on. Before you assume I've lost it, hear me out. If I'd been a better man, you would've come to me sooner," he said.

Meg looked floored.

"I appreciate you being willing to take the fall for that, but I should've let you know the minute I found out," she argued.

"You would've if I'd made you feel safe enough."

MEG ALMOST DIDN'T know what to say in response. Was that true? Could she so easily shift blame to Wyatt for her actions?

No. Because if she let him take the fall for this, then what else would she blame others for?

"I appreciate the sentiment. I really do. But we're going to have to agree to disagree on this. I should've been stronger. I panicked. Not that I don't love Aubrey with all my heart. I do. But I completely freaked out when I learned I was pregnant and backed off," she said.

"Because I didn't make you feel safe."

Okay, repeating those words weren't going to make them come true. Plus, they riled her up. Call her a feminist, but his actions didn't dictate hers, she thought stiffly. But she could see that he was making an effort to take some responsibility for where they were emotionally and she respected that. Plus, they did need to find common ground for Aubrey's sake. Learn to work together better so their daughter didn't pay the price.

"I appreciate what you're saying. And I want to work together, too. If we get along and make joint decisions, Aubrey's life will be better for it." Aubrey would never feel she'd been responsible for her parents not getting along or being married. So much for feminism. Meg could bring up her daughter on her own. Aubrey would always feel loved by her mother...

And that stopped her in her mental tracks.

How great would it be for Aubrey to feel loved by her father, too?

Meg had to admit the notion brought warmth to her chest and a sense of calm came over her. Having someone else for Aubrey to count on seemed almost too good to be true. Meg had no memories of her own father, so this was new territory. He'd ditched both her and her mother long before Meg was old enough to recall anything about him. Pain pierced her chest.

"What's wrong?" Wyatt was staring at her. One of his brows was arched like he was looking at a puzzle he couldn't quite figure out.

"I'm okay," she said quickly. A little too quickly. "Look, I'm new at this whole 'having two involved parents' thing, so forgive me if I'm no good at it."

"Same goes here."

"Your father was Maverick Mike Butler," she said. "And you never shared that with me when we dated before."

"Would it have made a difference?"

"No. But that's not the point." She wished he'd trusted her enough to tell her.

"Then I'm lost. What is?" he asked, that same puzzled look on his face. He really had no idea what she was talking about.

"Forget it," she said. "Let's just promise to keep working together until we figure this out. I'm sure co-parenting is like anything else you do for the first time. It takes practice in order to get it right."

Being in a room with Wyatt when her nerve endings hummed with need probably wasn't the best idea. It had been a long time since she'd had sex and not because of an outdated belief that single mothers should stay home 24/7 but because the reality of caring for a baby left her too exhausted to leave the house.

And then there was Wyatt. Sex with him had been over-the-top incredible at least in part because of their physical chemistry. Wyatt was sex in a bucket with his easy charm, devastating smile and brilliant mind. His sense of humor and good looks had been so good at seducing her. She'd let her emotions get away from her on something that was supposed to be a stress-relieving, take-time-out-for-herself fling.

The minute she'd realized her mistake in developing real feelings for him, she'd retreated. She could see now that she'd hurt his feelings, which caught her off guard. Or maybe he was just still stinging from her rejection. She highly doubted that Wyatt was the type of guy to lick his wounds for too long when it came to any woman.

Yet, she couldn't deny there was something she couldn't quite put her finger on that seemed genuine about his emotions. It had to be more than her wishing it to be true.

Chapter Thirteen

Meg needed to keep up her guard. Experience had taught her that she had the power to hurt others she was close to, break them, really. Like after Mary Jane's abduction when her own mother started drinking. She'd lost her job and then their home. Nothing had been the same afterward and Meg knew that her mother had secretly blamed her. And that was ironic, too, because Meg already blamed herself.

The new "uncle," who had had so much promise, according to her mother, cut his losses. He'd left town for a new job and said he'd send for them. Not long after, his cell number didn't work and he all but disappeared.

Meg had watched her mother sink into a deeper depression, drink more, stay in bed long past morning. It wasn't long before social services started regular visits. Her mother had been able to get her act together enough to apply for welfare and keep up appearances, but their relationship was never the same.

The day after Meg had graduated from high school, her mother took off. She left two hundred dollars along with a note, telling her she'd be better off on her own.

The two hadn't spoken since.

Meg could place blame on her mother for leaving. Having stuck around for the next eight years after the life-changing incident had seemed to drain the life out of the woman.

Speaking of which, Meg picked up her phone and called Stephanie.

"I just wanted to call and see how you're doing," Meg said. Her friend's voice was a welcome relief from heavier thoughts.

"Better," Stephanie said. "I appreciate everything you've done for me, but I can go back—"

"It's best for you to stay where you are for now at Wyatt's place," Meg said. When Stephanie didn't respond, Meg added, "As a favor to me if nothing else."

The line was quiet.

"Stephanie?" Meg's fear radar jacked up.

"I'm here," she reassured. "I'm sorry about your friend."

Meg hadn't checked online, but she feared her story had been slapped across headlines by now. The sheriff wouldn't release an important detail but there were others at the scene of Aubrey's attempted kidnapping. "Thank you."

She cringed, waiting for the accusations it had been her fault or the judgment that came with knowing she was there and couldn't remember or help.

"It's unfair that happened to both of you. And so young." There was kindness and compassion in Stephanie's voice.

"Did you get any rest?" her friend asked.

"Some," she responded. "But I'm more worried about you right now."

"Me? I'm fine. I slept twelve hours last night and woke feeling the best I have in months. But what I'm hearing from you is that you haven't slept yet." Stephanie knew her a little better than Meg was comfortable with at the moment.

Meg stood with her back against the counter. "Not really. But I did lie down for a while and feel more refreshed."

"How's the baby?" Hearing how Stephanie's voice morphed from overprotective mama to basically a glop of goo almost made Meg chuckle. Under different circumstances, she would do just that but nothing had been funny in her life for a long time.

"She's been great under the circumstances," Meg admitted.

"And the cowboy?" There was a hint of admiration in her voice.

"You mean Wyatt?"

"Yeah, that guy. How's he doing with all this?" Stephanie asked.

"How do you know he's still with me?" Meg didn't mask her surprise.

"I saw the way he looked at Aubrey," she said.

Meg could admit to witnessing the same. There was something warm and reassuring about another human being loving her daughter so much. Meg's world had consisted of her mother and no one else. When she lost her mother to drinking—drinking that was Meg's fault—the world had tumbled down around her. A surprising tear sprang to her eye just thinking about the past.

Meg wanted—no—*needed* so much more for her daughter. She saw her daughter surrounded by people who loved her. She saw birthday parties with kids playing and laughing. She saw Wyatt doting on their daughter. And a little piece of her heart saw a wedding band on his finger.

It was a childish fantasy to think that a child's parents had to be married for life to feel complete. All Aubrey really needed was two parents to love her. It didn't matter whether they lived in the same house or not. Heck, some kids thrived with one involved parent, and Meg had seen all too many cases where one parent was a detriment to the child.

Meg had already made up her mind that her past relationship with Wyatt had nothing to do with Aubrey. How silly was that? He was Aubrey's father. And the two of them were certainly going to have to continue to work at figuring out how to parent together.

It was probably a mix of almost losing her daughter coupled with the emotions of the pending holiday and the past being dredged up that had Meg ready to abandon reason for fantasy. Aubrey had a mother who loved her and that was so much more than Meg had had.

"You know she can stay with me here at the complex," Stephanie offered. "Since you didn't hear me the first time I said it."

"Sorry. I'm distracted." She faked a yawn. "I don't want to draw any more heat to Ava's operation. She's already doing us a huge favor by taking you until this… situation…is cleared up."

"It's quiet there," Stephanie conceded. "You should lie back down and seriously try to sleep. You know she'll have you up every few hours."

"I will." Meg said before ending the call. Why was it that hospital nurses and pretty much every caring-for-a-newborn blog told new mothers to sleep when the baby slept? If Meg did that she wouldn't get any work done, her house would be a complete wreck and she'd—

"What's wrong?" Wyatt stepped into the kitchen, fresh from a shower. His curly hair seemed darker when it was wet and she didn't even want to think about the fact that he'd been naked a few minutes ago.

She cleared her dry throat in order to speak. "Nothing. What makes you think something's wrong?"

He glanced at her hand and then locked on to her gaze. "You're white-knuckling your cell. Did something happen?"

"Oh." Meg tried to force her fingers to relax on the phone. When that didn't work, she set it on the counter. Turning to grab a mug and make a cup of tea, she heard Wyatt walk up behind her. She felt his presence when he got close and her body hummed with electricity.

She took in a sharp breath when she realized how close he was—a breath that ushered in his fresh-from-the-shower masculine scent.

"I'm sorry about earlier," he said, and he was so close she wouldn't have to move much more than an inch to be body-to-body with him.

"It was a mistake." He might be standing so near that

her heart thundered in her chest and her pulse pounded, but she didn't want to give away the effect he had on her. She refused to maintain eye contact as she turned to face him.

He lifted her chin up.

"I've been thinking a lot about that kiss," he said, and her gaze locked on to his.

"It shouldn't have happened," she said, figuring he was about to say the same. This way, she could head him off at the pass.

"I'm glad it did," he said, surprising her.

"Why?" she asked.

"Because it reminded me that I'm alive. I'm human. I make mistakes—"

She held up her hand, effectively cutting him off before he could go all macho on her. "Apologizing for kissing me isn't necessary and it might just hurt my feelings."

"Good."

Meg made the mistake of locking eyes with him again. "So you want to make me feel bad?"

"I didn't say that." He issued a sharp sigh. "I had no plans to apologize. I'm relieved that saying sorry isn't required."

"Why's that?"

"Because I don't want to hurt you," he said. "And I'm no good at feelings."

"You already have hurt me," she countered, but there was no emotion behind the words.

"By doing this?" He dipped his head and captured her bottom lip gently between his teeth.

"Yes." She drew out the word as he released it. His breath smelled like her favorite peppermint toothpaste and a unique mix of all that was Wyatt, because she was certain her brand didn't taste like this straight out of the tube.

Wyatt took a step toward her, closing the small gap between them, and her body stiffened. He looked into her eyes; his were hungry and primal, and she gasped as their bodies pressed against each other. His chest was a wall of muscled steel with a silky exterior, and she should know because her hands gripped him in an almost laughable attempt to push him away. Instead, her fingers dug into his shoulders. Instinct took over and she pulled him toward her.

"What about this?" He dipped his head again, skimming his lips along the line of her collarbone, her neck, across her jawline…

Until he found her mouth and hovered just out of reach. Her lips stung with a need for contact. Every uniquely feminine part warmed, and there was such a strong sense of urgency building inside her, like a tsunami that would obliterate everything in its path when it made landfall. And yet she didn't care about the destruction it would leave. Not when he was this close and her senses overrode rational thought.

Wyatt looked at her one more time with a question in his eyes. His hands came up and cupped her face as they made contact.

She nodded so slightly that she could tell he almost missed it. Almost. Until she realized his pupils dilated right before he kissed her.

Meg parted her lips to allow better access, and he took the invitation immediately, sliding his tongue inside. His tongue slicked across hers. He tasted even better than she remembered and her body cried out for more contact. He seemed ready to take it slow, and that only built up the wave gathering momentum inside her. Her body was strung tight with tension.

Meg dropped her hands and ran her fingers along the strong wall of his chest, letting her fingertips linger on his long, lean muscles. He took a half step back and pulled his shirt over his head in a heartbeat, tossing it to the floor. Speaking of things being better than she remembered, his body was in a whole new stratosphere of muscled strength. She smoothed her palms over his pecs as he unbuttoned her blouse.

She shrugged out of it, and a moment later the thin material joined his on the floor.

A primal grunt issued from Wyatt as he took in her almost fully bared breasts. His thumb ran across the lace of her flesh-colored bra, sending goose bumps racing up her arms. Awareness skittered across her sensitized skin as he outlined the thin material. Her nipples pebbled and her breasts swelled from needing contact.

Urgency was building from a deep place inside her, sending impulses shooting through her sensitized body.

"You're even more beautiful, Meg," he said, trailing his finger around her beaded nipple. He rolled one in between his thumb and forefinger, causing her breasts to swell with need, her body to hum.

The words were appreciated but unnecessary because the look of appreciation in his eyes stirred more emotion and physical attraction.

Without waiting for him to take the lead, she unzipped her jeans, popped the snap and wiggled out of them until she was standing there in her bra and underwear. Under any other circumstance this would be awkward.

With Wyatt, she felt adored and at ease.

Of course, his charm had been all too good at seducing her before, and that same skilled smile overtook his lips now. She pushed up to her toes and kissed him, pressing her body to his before he could say anything.

He leaned against her until her bottom met the hard countertop. Her hands flew to the buttons on his jeans.

It took two seconds flat for him to join her and have his jeans, boxers included, added to the clothing pile on the floor.

His erection pulsed and strained against her midsection as he freed her from her silky bra. She stepped out of her panties next and he grunted another sound of appreciation. Before either could talk themselves out of what was going to happen next, she hopped onto the countertop and wrapped her legs around his toned stomach. He stepped toward her, *into* her, as she guided him inside her slick heat.

He cupped her breasts as she worked her hips to allow him better access. And then his hands dropped to her bottom as he thrust inside her, taking her breath away. He looked into her eyes as he drove deeper.

"I missed *this. You*," he said in a low, gravelly voice.

"Me, too, Wyatt," she said, wishing that it could last longer than today. Knowing that was unrealistic.

In that moment, she didn't care a bit. She tightened her grip around his waist and pressed her body against his. In a swift movement, her bottom left the hard granite and he was carrying her into the master bedroom. The baby slept in the room next door.

They both came down hard on the bed, entangled in each other's arms and legs. Both laughed, but all Meg could really feel was how good he felt on top of her, his solid weight pressing her deeper into the mattress. This was home to her and in that moment she knew he felt the same way. He paused long enough to retrieve a condom and sheathe himself.

He looked into her eyes with so much adoration, her heart stirred, and that was dangerous ground. Sex was one thing, an easy thing when it came to Wyatt. Emotions were a slippery slope they had yet to figure out how to navigate effectively.

Wyatt pressed his lips to hers and drove his tongue inside her mouth in an air-grabbing kiss. All reason, all hesitation flew out the window. All that mattered was the fleeting feeling Meg had right now—love. *Love?*

Meg clasped her legs around Wyatt and bucked him deeper. He responded in kind until they met a fever pitch reaching faster and higher, their bodies so tense she felt like a bomb about to detonate. Meg's body was alive with sensation she hadn't felt in so long…since the last time with Wyatt.

He matched her stride for stride as they climbed to the summit together and stood at the edge not yet ready to trust and completely let go. Need overtook every rational thought…a need to release all the tension in her body.

Instinct and need took over, and Meg relinquished control. She raised to a fever pitch until she could no longer fight the pressure. She dove off the cliff into pure pleasure and sensation, and fireworks being lit at the same time.

Wyatt's body, still taut, drove deeper until, with a primal noise of release, he detonated inside her. She could feel his erection pulsing and releasing until his body seemed drained.

He rolled onto one side and positioned her in the crook of his arm. His breathing was coming out in jagged gasps.

"I'm done for," he said through raspy breaths. "In serious trouble."

She had no idea what he meant by that.

But she hoped it meant more than it probably did.

Curled against him, Meg drifted off into a deep sleep.

Meg couldn't be sure how much time had passed when a sudden noise startled her awake. Meg sat bolt upright. She scanned the dark room and patted the empty bed.

Wyatt was gone.

Chapter Fourteen

The email from Alexander had come in while Meg was still sleeping. The offer he'd made on the land in Centreville had been accepted; permits were being fast-tracked, and construction would be back on track in the new location in a week. Still, no word on the lake house, though.

At least part of his life was coming together…

Meg burst out of the bedroom. The baby in Wyatt's arms jerked awake.

"What is it?" he asked, holding as still as he could considering every instinct had him wanting to jump up and run toward her. She had come out of that room so fast a split-second fear that someone would fly out behind her with a gun struck him.

"I thought you were gone," she said through gasps of air. "A noise woke me. You weren't there. I freaked."

Sweat beaded on her forehead and he could see that she was trembling.

"I'm right here," he said. "I'm not going anywhere without telling you first."

He had to qualify that last part, because there would

come a time when they wouldn't spend so much time around each other. That would be a good thing from the standpoint of the investigation. It would mean Meg and the baby were safe and could get back to their old routine. But what about Wyatt?

The thought of going back to his house in Austin alone sent a strange burning sensation shooting through his chest.

Maybe he could stick around. Put some furniture in that house next door to hers that he'd rented and spend a little time there? It wasn't a horrible thought.

Besides, his daughter was beginning to feel more and more natural in his arms, and he needed to learn to take care of her on his own. He could do bottles and a diaper, but there was a whole lot more involved in caring for a baby than that.

But, hey, getting a diaper on her correctly and securely was something to be proud of. At this point, he'd take all the little wins he could get. He had a feeling this parenting thing wasn't going to be easy. Unlike at work, he could tell people what to do and they would listen. The bundle in his arms had complete control over him, and all he could do—and surprisingly wanted to do—was let her take the lead.

Meg stood there, rooted to her spot, and he could tell she needed more reassurance.

"I'm here. I'm not leaving." That was absolute truth. Not until they had answers.

Watching his daughter sleep, he vowed to give her mother the same peace of mind. They were getting close to finding the truth. Wyatt could feel it. Learning the name from her past and finding out the man was in prison had at first felt like a setback. Not anymore, and he wanted to discuss his theories with her once the baby was down for the night.

"Let's get out of here and grab a bite to eat," he said. There was an out-of-the-way restaurant he'd spotted on the way back from the sheriff's office. Meg needed a good meal and something that felt normal. She needed a fresh perspective and so did he. Taking a break and looking at a problem from a new perspective had always helped him find the answers.

"Okay." She dragged her hand through her hair. "I'll just get dressed."

"This was a good idea," Meg said, after taking the last bite of chicken-fried steak on her plate. "I didn't think I'd be able to stomach anything."

Taking a break from the heaviness of the afternoon was good. They could both use a fresh perspective.

And, besides, Wyatt liked making Meg happy. A decent meal was the least he could give her after all she'd been through.

The baby had slept through the entire meal and tension had slowly eased from Meg's facial features. He picked up the bill the server had dropped off. "I'll take care of this."

"Before we go, I need to use the restroom," Meg said, scanning the room. It was a habit he'd noticed when they'd dated last year. She'd checked the exits of every new restaurant he'd taken her to. At first, he'd wondered if it was just one of her quirks. Then, he'd considered the possibility that she was being overly vigilant with the spate of random crimes on the news in the Austin area. Had he been dead wrong. Her paranoia took on a whole new meaning and he understood so much more of her for knowing about her past.

"I'll take Aubrey," he said, picking up the baby carrier that plugged right into a base forming a secure car seat.

"Okay. I'll meet you out front," she said.

Wyatt handled the bill and walked out to the truck. The air was still chilly, but sun promised to show tomorrow if he could believe the weatherman.

The baby didn't so much as budge as the carrier clicked into place, secured in the back seat.

Until a scream shattered the night air.

Out of his peripheral vision, he saw commotion. He scanned the parking lot of the restaurant. Meg came into focus. A man had her arms jacked up behind her and the glint of metal in the sunlight said there was a gun to her temple.

Wyatt bit back a curse. Make a move and the man could squeeze the trigger faster than Wyatt could literally take a breath. Not to mention the guy could hit Aubrey if he pulled off a shot in Wyatt's direction. Who was this guy anyway? It had to be one of the fathers from her work. Right? Hector? Zach Brandt?

Fighting every instinct inside his body urging him to make a move toward the attacker, he shielded Aubrey with the truck door.

Meg didn't struggle.

"You don't want to do this," Wyatt warned.

"Stay back or she's dead, man." The guy's voice had a hysterical edge to it.

"Listen to Jonathon." Meg winced as the attacker twisted her arms even further behind her back. "Please. Wyatt. Don't follow me. Take care of her."

Jonathon Fjord. Mary Jane's brother. The sheriff had mentioned his deputies were looking for him, and now it made sense as to why he'd gone missing. Had he been plotting revenge? Waiting?

Another thought struck. Meg had said that he'd tried to approach her over the summer at the supermarket. She would've been pretty far along in her pregnancy. Seeing that could've driven him over the edge if he'd been harboring feelings against her all this time. The event, according to Meg, had traumatized him to the point he couldn't function in a normal environment again.

Anger bit through Wyatt.

Tough situation or not, none of this was Meg's fault. She'd been just as much a victim. Her innocence had been stripped that day and Jonathon was too twisted to see it.

How could he let this guy take the woman he loved—loved? Yes, loved.

Without her, nothing in his life made sense. He'd confirmed with one kiss what he'd suspected last year. He was in love with Meg.

But what were his options?

Make a move now and the guy might just pull the trigger. Possibly kill Meg. Aubrey would be without a mother…

Damn.

He couldn't go there. Not even hypothetically.

Plus, there was the other possibility that Jonathon might take aim at the truck and strike Aubrey. If he could trade himself for Meg and know that she'd be safe, no problem.

There was no way he would put their daughter in jeopardy and Meg wouldn't want him to. His mind was spinning with bad options.

In every scenario he came up with, someone he cared about ended up dead. Unless Meg could overpower the guy and somehow knock the gun out of his hand. Wyatt couldn't get to them from this distance unless she made a move and distracted Fjord.

Wyatt had to wait, be ready if an opportunity presented itself. So, instead of taking action, he stood there with an almost overwhelming feeling of helplessness.

One-on-one, Jonathon would go down. No doubt about it. Wyatt didn't doubt his skills for a second. But his attention was splintered between Meg and Aubrey.

Jonathon had the upper hand in this scenario.

Fjord said something to Meg that Wyatt couldn't make out. She winced as his grip seemed to tighten around her neck.

"Don't follow us, Wyatt. He'll kill me," she said with certainty. "Call the sheriff and the second he sees a law enforcement vehicle anywhere near us, he'll kill me. And if you try to follow us, he'll kill me."

Could he trail them without being caught? Not with Aubrey. It was too dangerous.

Standing there, frustration bit sharp lines into his gut.

Wyatt bit back a curse as the two walked around the corner, disappearing from view. He phoned the sheriff but the call went into voicemail. Wyatt texted the details of what had happened and the location before putting his phone on vibrate. His biggest fear was that Jonathon was going to kill her anyway. Why he hadn't done it already caused Wyatt to scratch his head. *Because he wants her to feel his pain.*

Wyatt was reaching for a sliver of hope and the only one he found was in the thought Jonathon wouldn't kill her immediately.

Starting his truck would bring unwanted and dangerous attention, so he unstrapped Aubrey and cradled her against his chest. Could he get a visual on them, some kind of direction, without being seen?

If Aubrey made a single noise, it could be game over for her mother.

His strides were purposeful and silent as he closed in on the restaurant. Could he get around the corner in time? Could he get the make and model of the car? A license plate?

The answer was no. But what if he had? Then what?

That's where he hit a wall. The answer dawned on him as he circled back to the truck. He couldn't do any of this alone. He grabbed his cell and the wrinkled business card from inside his dash where he'd shoved it the other night.

And then he phoned the only person who could assist and said a prayer he remembered from childhood that he hadn't burned the bridge with the few folks he knew in Cattle Barge.

The call went to voice mail.

"I need your help." Those four words rolled off his tongue easily now, and he found, with the right motivation, they weren't difficult at all to say.

Wyatt ended the call and tried to think of someone else. There'd been no response to from the sheriff. There was no one else he confided in or could rely on. He'd constructed walls so high no one could climb over and he couldn't see out anymore.

Damn. Damn. Damn.

He white-knuckle gripped his phone.

His phone vibrated in his hand.

Wyatt recognized the number from the card. Dade Butler.

"Does your offer of help still stand?" Wyatt immediately asked.

"Everyone's here and ready to do whatever it takes to help. What do you need?" Dade responded without hesitation.

MEG'S HEAD POUNDED. It was pitch-black. She struggled to move against the bindings on her wrists. Her hands were numb. Trying to move made everything hurt.

Trying to scream did no good. Her mouth was covered with something…duct tape?

Memories crashed down.

Mary Jane's brother. Jonathon was responsible for attempting to kidnap Aubrey. But why? What did he have to gain?

Revenge?

Did he hate Meg that much?

A light flipped on and she gasped. A quick scan of the room revealed furniture but no person. Where was Jonathon? She was in some kind of container with no windows. A train car turned into a home? She'd seen things like this on TV. Weren't they on those small-house shows where people were looking for inexpensive places to live?

Struggling against her bindings, a voice from behind stopped her. *His voice.*

"You don't deserve to have the kind of life that was taken from my sister," Jonathon said, and he sounded almost hysterical.

Fear shot through her as she tried to work the bindings on her arms.

How many times had she wished she could make it up to the family? That she could've traded places with Mary Jane that day? Survivor's guilt had plagued her since then, stopping her from ever letting herself get close to anyone else.

But Aubrey didn't deserve this. That little girl needed her mother and, somehow, Meg would figure out a way to get home to her.

Wyatt flashed in her thoughts, too. The idea of losing him, of never seeing him again, hit like a physical punch that winded her.

One thing was clear. Arguing her case would do no good. Not even if her mouth wasn't taped shut. Jonathon wouldn't listen. He'd gone to too much trouble to get her, had exposed his identity in the process, and she wondered if either would make it out of this situation alive. He could kill her and then what? Go on the run for the rest of his life? Hide? How did that punish Meg for her best friend's death? And why come after her now after all these years?

She worked her lips trying to make a break in the seal as tears streamed down her cheeks, praying this wouldn't be the place where her life ended.

The thought of not seeing Aubrey again, of her daughter growing up without a mother, stabbed needles of pain through her.

On her side, tears dripped onto the cold concrete flooring.

There was no doubt that she was in some remote location. Most likely somewhere no one would think to look for her.

Had Wyatt done as she asked and stayed put? Part of her wished he hadn't and that he would burst into the room any minute with the sheriff and a few deputies at his side. She'd told him not to follow them and, really, he'd had no choice.

She didn't blame him. He'd done the right thing by Aubrey, and Meg was grateful to see how much he loved that little girl. It was an odd thought but mattered so much to her heart to know Aubrey was going to have a loving parent to care for her if…

Struggling against the bindings, Meg shook with anger and fear and outrage.

"Hold still," Jonathon commanded. She could hear him behind her doing something but couldn't tell what it was.

Like hell she would roll over and let him do whatever he wanted to her without fighting back.

He was going to kill her anyway. What was the difference if she angered him?

Meg fought harder, worked harder.

A piece of tape lifted at the corner of her mouth.

"You don't want to do this, Jonathon," she managed to get out. Her lungs burned from lack of oxygen, and even fresh air hurt as she drew it in.

"Don't you dare say my name," he said, and she could hear his footsteps on the concrete flooring coming toward her.

"She wouldn't want this. We were best friends," Meg said, biding her time until he got closer. Maybe she could wheel around and knock him off his feet. With her hands and feet bound he clearly had the advantage, but if she could knock him off balance, maybe she could do some damage before he killed her and tossed her body away.

"Friends?" The one word came out so shrill it sounded like a trapped animal. And when she really thought about it, he had been trapped in his own mind, his own sorrow.

"Doing this won't bring her back," she said. "And it won't bring peace."

Cold, hard metal pressed against the side of her head behind her ear. All she could think about was Aubrey and Wyatt. At least they had each other. Her daughter wouldn't grow up alone without love. Meg had seen the love in his eyes when he'd been holding their daughter. Part of her wanted to believe he'd had that same look the other day when they'd kissed for the first time since reuniting.

"Mary Jane is dead because of you," he ground out.

"I didn't hurt her. I would never do that," she managed to say on a gasp. Adrenaline spiked and her body trembled from the boost. A knee came down hard on her arm, pinning it to her side. There was no way out and the room felt like it was shrinking. Her lungs clawed for air and she fought to stay conscious. She wanted her last thoughts to be about Wyatt and their daughter, not this creep.

And her sweet friend, Mary Jane.

"She was my best friend," Meg said one more time.

Jonathon's laugh turned to a seething anger.

"Blame me all you want, but I didn't do anything," she said. "Believe me, I wish it had been me that day. That I was the one who'd been taken and not her."

The barrel of the gun traced around her ear and then her forehead, moving her hair away from her face.

"That makes two of us," he said bitterly. There was so much venom in his voice that it seemed no amount of reason could penetrate his hatred for her.

She closed her eyes and prepared for the crack-of-a-bullet sound as the weapon fired. The burst of fire. The explosion when the bullet pierced her skull.

Where she thought there would be panic, anger flooded her, instead. Anger that life had handed her a terrible fate early on that had led her to this place with Mary Jane's brother. Anger that her life might be taken away in an instant and she might not be around for her daughter. Anger for the fact that she'd never know if Wyatt could truly love her since they wouldn't be given a chance. She thought she'd heard him say it when they'd made love. She should've been brave enough to ask, to take the life she wanted and not let go.

And the life she wanted was a family with Wyatt and their daughter.

Meg bucked her body, trying to fight against the certain death hovering.

"Be still," Jonathon commanded. At this point, what did it matter?

"Why? So you can enjoy killing me?" she shot back.

A grunt was issued with a blow to her back. A boot tip?

Meg rolled onto her back. "Look at me when you do it. Mary Jane wouldn't have wanted this. She would be ashamed of you."

Jonathon backhanded her across the cheek and it felt like her eye might pop out.

"Killing me won't change anything," she repeated. "We can't get Mary Jane back no matter how much we wish we could."

"Which is exactly why you're going to suffer," he said.

"She wouldn't want that. Not that you care." Meg was pushing the boundary, but he needed to hear the words again and again until they broke through. "I wish I could've changed things. Been able to remember and give the police a description. But hurting me doesn't punish Clayton Glass. He's already in Huntsville. And when this over, you'll be joining him."

"How do you know who took my sister?" Jonathon's shock twisted his face into angry lines.

There had been no pleading in her tone. She had been stating simple fact.

"Forget it. You're making this up to confuse the issue. You shouldn't have been outside that day," he said. "Mary Jane wasn't allowed and you convinced her to play. Her death is your fault."

"I did nothing of the sort," she defended, for all the good it would do. He'd made up his mind. His sister's death was on her.

Anger flared his nostrils as he straddled her and smacked her again. His legs were like vise grips. "You're a liar."

"Which would still be better than killing someone for the wrong reason," she retorted, and she could tell that his anger was rising. "Mary Jane loved you, Jonathon. You were her big brother. She idolized you."

He stilled as though he was considering her words. And then his gaze bore down on her.

"You're trying to distract me." He belted her again and this time she spit blood.

"Jonathon, think about what you're about to do—"

"Enough," he ground out. And then he replaced the duct tape, securing it over her already raw lips. "You have to pay for what you did."

Meg tensed as the gun barrel pressed between her eyes.

"It was him. The face from the sketch. I couldn't see it before. The sketch made his nose too big and the hair was off but I do now that I know," Wyatt said to the sheriff as he burst into his office.

"Jonathon Fjord," Sawmill said with a bowed head. "Mary Jane's brother."

"He headed west from the restaurant parking lot," Wyatt informed. "At least I think. I checked east and didn't see anyone."

Sawmill made an announcement over the radio, alerting his deputies. Next, he called Janis in and asked her to put out a Be on the Lookout, or BOLO, so that all law-enforcement personnel would be watching.

"What do we do next?" Wyatt asked.

"There's nothing to do but wait." Sawmill shot him a sympathetic look. Wyatt didn't need the man's sympathy. He needed to know where Jonathon was taking Meg.

At least she'd been alive, and he figured Jonathon was keeping her alive for a reason. There was some measure of reassurance there.

That was more than an hour ago. Time was running out.

"How well do you know this person?" Wyatt asked.

"I spoke to the family's neighbors. They described him as a quiet and polite young man. They were in shock he could be involved in anything remotely like this," the sheriff supplied. "Mary Jane's parents moved to the outskirts of town after her disappearance and mostly kept to themselves over the years. We had to do a little tracking to find them. They'd changed their names to avoid being dragged into interviews every time interest in the story picked up again."

"I'm guessing since her brother moved away last year no one suspected him," Wyatt said.

The sheriff nodded.

"What about his parents? Would they have any idea where he'd take her?" Wyatt paced around Sheriff Sawmill's office. He'd made more laps than he cared to count.

"I have a deputy heading over there now, but we didn't get much over the phone interview." Sawmill moved to his desk.

"You said you spoke to them recently. What about that interview?" Wyatt asked, unable and unwilling to sit back and do nothing now that Aubrey was safely tucked away at the Butler ranch and Dade himself watched over her to ensure her safety. It might be overkill using Dade and the Butlers for that job alone but Wyatt wouldn't take chances with his little girl.

"Good point. I'll review the transcript and see if there are any clues as to where he might be taking her," Sawmill admitted as his fingers pounded the keyboard. It was better than the hen-peck method.

Wyatt moved behind the sheriff. "What are the chances he'd cross state lines?"

"It's a possibility we can't ignore, which is why I issued the BOLO."

All Wyatt cared about was bringing Meg home where she belonged. Her life might be here in Cattle Barge, but he was starting to see the possibility that his might be, too.

Whether they were in Austin or here, as long as they were together with their daughter the rest could sort itself out. She could work, not work. Hell, he didn't care one way or another as long as he got to come home to her and the baby every night.

If Wyatt strained, he could see the interview, especially after the sheriff blew up the type and leaned toward the monitor. He must have blown the document up by 140 percent.

He rubbed tired eyes and rolled his neck before straining to read the words.

Wyatt could easily see the interview from his vantage point. Since it was better to ask forgiveness than permission, he scanned the document, searching for a clue to where Jonathon might've taken Meg. All the air squeezed from his lungs thinking about harm coming to her.

The sheriff's personal cell belted out its ringtone.

"Excuse me," Sawmill said. He answered the call and immediately walked toward the hallway.

Wyatt read the entry where Jonathon had taken Mary Jane for her tenth and last birthday. To a property on the lake where the two rode horses, her favorite activity.

The only thing Wyatt was certain of was that the sheriff was on the wrong track. Send in Sawmill or one of his deputies and Jonathon might kill her.

Which left him no choice but to strike out on his own.

Chapter Fifteen

The night was pitch-black and chilly. It was the kind of dark that made it so black outside that the moon wasn't even visible.

Normally Wyatt would see this as a good opportunity to go fishing.

Now he saw it as good cover for hunting—hunting a criminal.

He cut off his truck's engine less than a mile from the site he believed Jonathon had Meg. He'd used his smartphone's GPS to find the place.

The sheriff's deputy was on the other side of the county at an abandoned strip center based on a tip from the Fjords.

On the off chance the deputy hit the nail on the head, that base was covered. Call it gut instinct or intuition, but Wyatt feared the information was wrong. He decided to take another approach in hopes one of them would find her in time.

Any other possibility had to be pushed outside the boundary of possibility.

Besides, if Jonathon and Mary Jane were as close as

Meg had said, it made sense he would take Meg to the last place he remembered spending time with his sister.

According to Mrs. Fjord, the lake was Jonathon's favorite place. The property around the lake—including the stable—had since been split up to sell as lakefront property and this particular spot had been bought by a family for personal use.

When Wyatt had pulled up GPS coordinates of the area, he'd immediately locked onto the perfect building to take a hostage.

Wyatt hoped a family wasn't there or he could potentially be counting a lot of bodies. No, he stopped himself right there. This wouldn't end in tragedy. Anger fired through him, heating his skin against the frigid night air blasting toward him.

Meg had to be all right. There was no other choice.

Getting to the location without using some kind of light was impossible. So Wyatt covered his cell inside his jacket and dimmed the screen as low as it could go without losing all contrast.

Problems were mounting. What if she wasn't there? What if she was? How could he get inside the structure without alerting anyone? He'd seen a demo of shipping container homes once before, and opening the door had made more noise than an oncoming freight train. Not to mention the fact that it brought in unexpected light. He circled the building. This one had a door, at least.

But, there was no way to get any intel without breaching the building. The place was closed up tight, save for the metal door. Wyatt's biggest fear was that he wouldn't be able to see what was going on without alerting Jonathon to the fact that he was there.

Basically, he might be better off if he drove his truck straight into one wall and hoped for the best. Frustration nipped at him. There was too much on the line.

One mistake could cost him the woman he loved.

Taking her to the lake would be a stroke of genius on Jonathon's part. The sheriff had sent a deputy to the strip center and another to the site Mary Jane had last been spotted. No one would think about this place.

Wyatt fired off a text to the sheriff, letting him know that Wyatt was planning to investigate.

Stepping lightly, Wyatt followed the waterline around the lake. At least the ground was cold and hard. Sounds of night, crickets chirping and other insects filled the air. At least on the water's edge there weren't a lot of trees.

A sticky blanket of something pulled at Wyatt's face. A spiderweb?

He didn't want to think about the size of a spider it would take to make one large enough to spread from one tree to the next in this part of the terrain.

At least the cold would ward off snakes. They didn't bother him much. He just didn't need the distraction.

There were other creatures that could get the best of him in these lands. A wild boar caught off guard would be enough to do him in.

Texting the sheriff to ask for backup was the right call but waiting could cost Meg's life. If Wyatt was right and Jonathon somehow got the jump on him, Meg could pay the ultimate price anyway. Trying to do this without alerting anyone to his plans would be stupid.

What about his newfound family? Both Dade and Dalton looked like they could handle themselves in any situation. They were clearly less experienced than the sheriff and deputies but they'd seen and done more than most civilians. Wyatt didn't want to put them in jeopardy without them knowing full well what they would be signing up for.

He'd give full disclosure of the dangers.

They'd offered help before and he'd already trusted them with the care of his daughter.

Without them, he could end up dead, with no parent for Aubrey.

After evaluating his options, he determined that notifying his brothers of his location would be a smart move. Given more time, he could've come up with a better plan of attack.

Time was the enemy and he had no idea if Meg was still breathing.

Again, he wouldn't allow himself to consider the possibility that she wasn't.

He fired off a text, giving his location and brief details about his mission.

Then he put his phone on silent. If he had to sacrifice himself to ensure Aubrey grew up with a mother, he wouldn't hesitate. His own mother had been the rock in his life and most likely the reason he was a successful businessman and hadn't ended up on the wrong side of the law. The line had been blurred a few times during his rebellious teenage years, but he'd come full circle.

He'd made her proud before she died. He'd seen that in her eyes, too. Every child deserved that chance.

Wyatt moved stealthily along the shoreline as though stalking prey, the fight building inside him with every forward step. He'd tucked his Glock inside the band of his jeans and pulled his shirttail out to cover it. He'd learned a long time ago not to show his hand before he had to, and concealing his gun could keep Jonathon off balance should things go south.

He chanced a glance at his phone, checking his location on the map against the target. Having cell coverage here was surprising and fortunate.

The place was dead ahead. Wyatt blacked out the screen and returned his cell to his pocket. Since he'd been walking for more than twenty minutes, his eyes were adjusting to the dark. Another advantage. He'd take what he could get and be grateful at this point.

All the windows were sealed off. Wyatt walked the perimeter trying to get a good feel for the place and what the floor plan might be.

Light spilled underneath the crack of the back door. As he made his way toward the door, it swung open. Wyatt froze.

A male stalked outside and emptied a bucket. Surely, Jonathon wouldn't be so haphazard as to leave the back door unlocked. Had Wyatt made the wrong call in coming here?

Heart hammering, he started to plan his retreat. He'd made a mistake.

The guy went back inside and closed the door. He

didn't lock it, confirming what Wyatt already knew. This couldn't be the right place.

Another thought struck. Was Jonathon too confident no one would find him there?

And then he heard it. The sound, *that* sound. The heartbreaking sound of Meg crying out in pain.

Wyatt doubled back and stood at the door, listening. One noise and he'd be found out. It took all the strength he had not to throw open that door, burst into the room and take Jonathon down with his bare hands. Hell, Wyatt would shoot the man if it meant saving Meg.

Again, tipping his hand could be fatal. So he waited for Meg to scream again, clenching his back teeth so hard he thought they might crack. He fisted his free hand and released, repeating a couple of times to work off some of his tension.

And he waited.

Meg screamed again and Wyatt used the noise to cover any sounds that might come from opening the door. He cracked it enough to see Meg curled in a ball on the floor with Jonathon standing over her. Torturing her?

His gaze flew to Jonathon's hands to check for a weapon. He didn't see one, but that didn't mean one wasn't within reach.

Jonathon sounded agitated as he yelled for her to be still. He was kneeling over her, doing something with that bucket Wyatt couldn't make out.

The room was small. It wouldn't take but a couple of strides for Wyatt to bridge the distance.

Every single muscle in Wyatt's body corded as he

slipped inside the door. And then Meg released a scream that nearly cracked his chest in half.

Wyatt took two giant steps before diving on top of Fjord, knocking him off balance and off Meg. Somewhere in the back of his mind it registered that Meg's hands were bound. Duct tape was over her mouth, and he had to assume that her legs were taped, as well.

Wyatt and Fjord crashed hard onto the concrete. Jonathon was small in comparison to Wyatt, but he was scrappy enough to twist onto his back and launch a knee into Wyatt's groin.

Air whooshed out of Wyatt's lungs as he tried to recover while taking an elbow to the left eye.

Meg was somewhere in the background, trying to wriggle free.

Wyatt climbed on top of Jonathon and captured him in between his powerful thigh muscles.

A fist came up so fast that it barely registered Jonathon was holding something in his hand until the object slammed into his forehead.

Momentarily stunned, Wyatt shook his head.

In the next second, he was being tossed onto his shoulder. The smaller man took full advantage of the blow that Wyatt was recovering from.

"Get out of here," Wyatt said to Meg. Out of the corner of his eye, he saw her scooting toward them. Wrong direction, he thought as something—blood?—oozed over his eye.

Jonathon was pounding Wyatt with fists, kicks. The guy was coming at Wyatt with everything he had.

Wyatt fought back, but a bout of dizziness was making it difficult to keep his bearings.

And then Meg must've done something to get Jonathon's attention because he spun around facing away from Wyatt.

That's all the leverage Wyatt needed. He forced himself to focus and then threw his arms around Jonathon's midsection, clamping his arms at his sides.

Jonathon might've caught Wyatt off guard before, but he wouldn't again.

Wyatt threw his considerable heft into Jonathon, causing him to take a couple of steps forward. This time when he fell Wyatt made sure to secure the squirrely guy beneath him, pinning his torso and arms with his thighs. Jonathon bucked, but he was no match for Wyatt's size.

And then a thought flashed in his mind. From this vantage point, Wyatt could pull out his gun and destroy Jonathon with one flick of his trigger finger.

Being a father must be softening him because he didn't want to explain himself in court or have a news story his daughter could read some day about how her father had killed a man, even this man.

Instead, Wyatt drew back his fist and punched Jonathon so hard his jaw snapped and he lost consciousness.

"Can you scoot closer to me?" he asked Meg, not daring to give an inch in case Jonathon came to and started swinging his fists again. He wouldn't underestimate the man twice.

She mumbled something that sounded like agreement, and he could see her making her way toward him.

When she was close enough, he tugged at the tape covering her mouth until it was free.

"Wyatt," she said on a gasp. "You found me."

"I will always find you."

After untying her and instructing her to call 911, Wyatt looked down at Jonathon. Tragedy had struck his family at such a young age and Wyatt could almost sympathize. Losing his sister at such an early age had broken the man.

"Why did he want to hurt you?" Wyatt asked Meg, wrapping his arm around her.

"He said I didn't deserve a family. He ran into me in the store after Aubrey was born and something snapped. He said he never stopped blaming me for Mary Jane's death but it wasn't until he saw me with my daughter, looking happy for the first time, that he truly broke," she said with a sob.

"What about Stephanie?" he asked.

"He hated everyone connected to me. If you'd been in the picture before he would've tried to hurt you," she explained. "He said he wanted to take away everyone close to me before he ended my life."

That's where Wyatt's empathy for the man stopped. Because everyone was dealt a bad hand at some point in his or her life. Emotions like revenge or resentment made the situation so much worse, poisoning any good left in a person.

The true measure of a man wasn't what he did when he fell down. It was how he got back up and what he made of his life after.

And that made him rethink the resentments he'd formed toward his family. And, besides, the holiday was near. Christmas was a time for miracles…

Chapter Sixteen

Meg could scarcely believe that she was still alive and that Wyatt was standing in front of her. Both of them were completely intact if not a little worse for wear. The EMT had cleared her after treating her injuries and the Butler twins had arrived with reassurances that Aubrey was safe at the ranch. Meg was pleased that her daughter's new family seemed protective of her already.

Meg's left jaw burned from the pain of several blows. Feeling was returning to her hands and Wyatt's coat was the only warmth. She wanted to hold her daughter again so badly her arms ached.

Wyatt was about the most beautiful thing she could ever see aside from Aubrey.

"I don't care where we live or why," he started, taking her hands in his. "All I know is that I want to make everything right for you, our daughter and our family."

And then he looked at her with so much love in his eyes she had to steady herself.

"I have an important question to ask, Meg Anderson." He bent down on one knee, causing what felt like a flock of birds to take flight inside her rib cage.

"I knew I was in trouble the minute we met a year ago. I was an idiot to let you walk out of my life then. But I like to think I'm smarter than that now. That I don't make the same mistakes twice. I love you. It's always been you and it always will be you." He paused like he'd already said too much and there was a moment of uncertainty in his eyes as he searched hers.

"I will never love another man as much as I love you," she said. There was so much relief playing out in his features as she said those words.

"Then there's only one thing left to ask." Another flash of uncertainty danced across his steel eyes, which disappeared the second Meg smiled. "Will you do me the incredible honor of becoming my wife?"

"I want to say yes," she hedged.

"But?"

"How will we know it's real? I mean, my hormones are out of whack and you just found out that you're a father. It's only natural to want—"

Wyatt pressed his lips to hers to stop her from finishing the sentence and she melted against him. He thoroughly kissed her, and when she was out of breath, he pulled back and looked into her eyes.

"Does that feel fake in any way to you?" he asked.

A grin tugged at the corner of her mouth so he kissed her there, too.

"Not in the least," she admitted, allowing the smile to spread. "When did you know?"

"The first time we kissed the other day. Didn't take a half second to realize in my heart that you were the only one I wanted to spend the rest of my life with.

My brain took a little while to get the message, but in here—" he touched her hand to the center of his chest "—there's never been a question. At least not for me."

He released her hand and folded his arms across his chest. "But now it's your move."

The minute she smiled, he had his answer. Hearing the words was even better.

"Yes, Wyatt. I'll be your wife. I love you. It's always been you. I knew last year that I was in trouble, and I couldn't be happier to make the three of us official."

With that, he stood and took her in his arms. He said in almost a whisper against her hair, "I want to spend the rest of my life making every one of your dreams come true."

"Welcome to the family, Meg," Dalton said. It would be strange to have so many uncles, aunts and cousins for Aubrey. Meg's heart danced because she'd be gaining a family, too.

Meg had never seen Wyatt look so happy.

"I was an only child my entire life. I might not be good at being a brother, but I sure as hell promise to do my best," Wyatt said to his brothers.

Dade smiled, embraced Wyatt in a bear hug and offered his well wishes. "Ella said your daughter is the sweetest thing she's ever seen. She's sleeping like an angel and the two of you should take your time coming back." He smiled conspiratorially. "Between you and me I wouldn't be surprised if Ella made her own announcement about a baby any day now."

Dalton seemed shocked. "You think our sister's pregnant?"

"Maybe not now. But she will be. I saw the glittery

look in her eyes when she first held her niece and the way she looked at her husband after."

"Holden's a good guy. He'll make a fine father someday," Dalton said.

Niece. Brothers. Family.

Wyatt completed the picture of everything Meg had ever hoped for. For *her* future and her little girl's. She couldn't wait to start their journey as a real family. There was no better time to start than Christmas.

Ed Staples took his place at the dining table at last. It had been three days since Jonathon's arrest. A wedding date had been set for the morning of New Year's Eve.

"On behalf of Mike Butler, I've been instructed to officially welcome you to the family," Ed said to Wyatt with a glance toward Meg and the baby cooing in her arms.

Wyatt thanked him as Meg smiled before returning her gaze to their daughter.

"As you all know the sheriff hasn't made any progress on your father's case. However, I've been instructed to read this letter to you. So, if everyone's ready." Ed scanned the faces at the table, looking for confirmation.

"Ed's been giving us these letters after Dad's murder, which almost makes me believe that he knew what was coming," Ella said.

"On the outside, your father seemed haphazard with the way he lived life, made his decisions," Ed said after contemplating her words for a minute.

"But I knew him better than that," Ella said.

"Maybe we'll all know at some point but he never

said anything to me. His instructions were clear. If anything happened to him, read the letters he left for me in order," Ed supplied.

"Have you thought about giving them to the sheriff?" Ella asked.

"Your father was clear and he had me build in the controls to keep them out of court. If the sheriff asks, I'm to refuse. It would take a court order, but then I have controls in place to cover that base, too. Your father was always one step ahead," Ed admitted.

"Which leads me to believe that he didn't know who killed him," Ella said. "If he'd known anything was going to happen to him, he had to know there'd be chaos after his death that could put all of us in jeopardy."

"I'll reserve judgment until I open the last letter," Ed stated.

Ella gasped. She had to be thinking what Meg was… Would more Butler children come out of the woodwork?

To her credit, she'd been welcoming to Wyatt and to Meg. It was clear that she was enamored with Aubrey, and Meg suspected that Dalton had been right about what he said before. Ella would be making an announcement of her own before long. She and Holden seemed enraptured with each other, and there was a longing in Ella's eyes when she looked at the baby.

"Two letters are left. And then there's the reading of the will in a couple of days," Ed said.

"I'm guessing you haven't opened that, either," Ella said.

Ed confirmed with a nod. "I'm to open it in the presence of all Mike's children on Christmas Eve."

Conversation stilled.

Dalton finally chimed in. "It'll be strange this year."

Dade was nodding his head in agreement along with their older sister. "Did Cadence say when she was coming home?"

"Christmas Eve. She said she'll be here for the reading," Ella said.

"She's been gone too long." Dade put his hand on the table, palms down.

"We're each dealing with our father's death in our own way," Ella reminded.

Both of the twins nodded. Strange that Meg could already tell them apart. At first glance, they looked so similar it had been impossible. But as soon as she had spent a little time around them she saw the different personalities come through.

"What's in my letter?" Wyatt, who had been quiet until now, asked.

With a half smile and a nod, Ed opened the sealed envelope sitting in front of him.

Wyatt,

I won't make excuses. Your mother did right by you. I didn't. There's no reason in the world I should've allowed that to happen. I've failed as a man, as a father. But—and if you're reading this, something's happened—there is something I did get right in this world. My six children. It is my sincere wish that the children who grew up under my roof haven't adopted my cruelty. I've seen four of them band together because of me. I'm not proud of that, but I am of them. They showed me what it was like to have a family. I'm gone before I had a chance to express that I knew what that truly meant. Seeing them together, the way they supported each other. That's my real legacy. Watching it has been my greatest gift. One I didn't deserve. I hope they can embrace you and Madelyn the same. You deserve that much from me. The lake house you've been wanting is yours if you'll take it. I'd always intended to give it to your mother. She wouldn't accept it or anything else from me. She said the only hope you had of making something of yourself was to grow up like I did, with nothing. I hope you'll consider being part of this family. If not for you, then for your children. Because I can tell you from experience, walking alone in life eventually leaves you lonely.

Yours,

M.M.

Meg looked to Wyatt, whose head was bowed. She could see a tear leak from his eye as his siblings, one by one, came over to shake his hand or embrace him.

"How'd he know that I was trying to buy the lake house?" Wyatt finally asked.

Dade shrugged his shoulders and looked to Madelyn.

"He kept tabs on us over the years," she supplied. "Can't say that I'm surprised."

Meg knew for certain that the family he'd always craved was right there. For him. For Aubrey. For the three of them.

Her heart swelled as they hugged her and took turns marveling at their little girl, touching her cheek or her tiny hand. Aubrey welcomed all the attention.

"Welcome to Hereford ranch officially," Dalton finally said. "This is as much your place as it is ours. Every family member has a home and a job here. And we're looking forward to starting new Christmas traditions with our expanding family."

Dade added, "We can be overwhelming at times but you'll never find more caring than with this crazy bunch. Welcome to the family."

"Glad to finally be home," Wyatt said.

Dalton shook Wyatt's hand before saying, "I'm proud to be your brother. Now let's fire up the barbecue grill and celebrate Texas style so we can plan a proper Christmas together."

Wyatt shot a smile at Meg, a real smile. And she could see that they finally fit in somewhere. Together. As a family. With a real place to call home.

* * * * *

RESCUED BY
THE MARINE

JULIE MILLER

For my father-in-law, Howard Miller,
and his lady, Dotty Robarge.

A Navy veteran and the widow of an Air Force veteran.
Now a fun, lovely couple.

Thank you both for your service to our country.

Prologue

Jason Hunt hung by his fingertips 7,400 feet up in the air. And his phone was ringing.

Another 600 feet and he'd have been out of cell range.

Relying on the strength of his arm, and the sure grip of his hand, he relished the last few milliseconds of silence between each ring. The summer sun was bright overhead, its rays warm on his skin, its heat reflecting off the granite outcropping he'd been scaling for the past hour. Sure, he could have stayed on the marked trail like the tourists, but then he would have missed this view.

Wide-open sky. Miles between this mountain and the next. Snow at the peaks, then silvery-gray granite that gave way to the deep rich greens and browns of the tree line. He even caught a glimpse of Jenny Lake's crystal gray-blue outline from this vantage point. He shifted his grip to swing around the other way, inhaling air that was cooler and cleaner than any part of the world he'd seen. And he'd seen more than he cared to. From here, he could see all the way past the lower peaks into Jackson Hole, the natural valley between the Tetons and Wind River Mountain Range where he'd grown up.

But his phone was ringing.

He eyed the rough granite cliff for the next handhold, doubled his grip of the rock and continued his climb.

His next breath wasn't quite as free and calming, but he grounded himself in the unshakable strength of the rock itself and kept moving. These mountains had endured, and he would, too.

He appreciated the quiet of how alone he was between each urgent ring. Save for the wind whistling through the narrow cave a few feet to his left, he'd found the reprieve he needed today. No mortar fire. No grinding of tank and truck gears, no orders to engage or pleas for help shouting in his ear.

Jason found a toehold and pushed himself up another three feet, nearing the top of the rock face. He lived in these mountains. Worked in these mountains. Escaped the memories that time and therapy could never fully erase. He needed the silence. The solitude. The space. No tight quarters here. No small huts or narrow streets filled with fire and booby traps and too many vehicles and people to know his allies from his enemies.

There was no woman dying in his arms up here.

With every ring, Jason's serenity and forgetfulness was shattered. It was a lonely life here in Wyoming. But it was a life.

Until his phone rang.

Mentally bracing himself for the reality of answering that call, he swung himself up over the top ledge.

He shrugged out of the small pack he carried, pulling out both a bottle of water and his cell. The number was no surprise. Neither was the sudden heavy weight of responsibility bearing down on his broad shoulders. With his long legs dangling over the edge into the Teton Mountains' rocky abyss, he swallowed a drink of water and answered his phone. "Yeah?"

"Captain Hunt?"

He pulled off his reflective sunglasses and squirted

some of the cooling water on his face before squeegee-ing it off his cheeks and beard stubble with the palm of his hand. "We've been stateside for two years, Marty. I told ya you could call me Jase."

"Yes, sir." Marty Flynn was only a few years younger than Jason, and they'd both retired from the Corps once their last stint had ended. But he still spoke to him like the stray puppy he'd first been when he'd been attached to Jason's unit over in the Heat Locker of the Middle East. "Um. Right. Jase."

"What's up, Lieutenant?" Although he already knew. These mountains weren't just his escape now, they were his world.

"Very funny." Yeah. He missed laughter. Not much call to tell jokes when you lived as far off the grid as he did now. "I know it's your day off. Thought you might be locked up in your cabin, shaggin' that pretty girl who was throwin' herself at you at—"

"Talk to me." Like anything resembling a relation-ship was going to happen after losing Elaine over in Kilkut. Like he'd ever be interested in some brainless twit who couldn't talk about anything but the size of his truck and how hard it was to find sexy clothes at the local boutique. He hadn't wanted to hurt the young woman's feelings when his search and rescue team had stopped at Kitty's Bar in Moose, Wyoming, to toast their commander's pending retirement. She seemed to think getting laid by a veteran Marine was some sort of badge of honor. In his book, it wasn't. He'd left the celebration early. Alone.

"So, you and Lynelle didn't hit it off? You wouldn't mind if I—"

"Marty." Jason exhaled an impatient breath. "*You* called *me*. I assume there's an emergency?"

"Right." Marty might be a natural-born flirt, with more charm than discipline in his repertoire, but he was a damn fine helicopter pilot. He'd saved the lives of Jason and most of his men by flying into an ambush to evac them to the safety of the base. That was the only reason Jason put up with his goofy idol worship—the only reason he'd agreed to take the job with the search and rescue team Marty worked for. He owed him a life. "We've got a missing hiker. Family excursion hiking the String Lake Loop. Little boy wandered off this morning west of Leigh Lake. He's been missing four hours now. Parents searched an hour on their own before calling it in."

Jason climbed to his feet, surveying the mountains in every direction. He assessed the quickest path, the weather, the position of the sun in the sky. "It's already midafternoon."

"And it's summer. Kid doesn't have any bear spray on him. No jacket. Nothing but the clothes on his back. Predators will be out after dark. We need to find him before they do."

Jason tucked the water bottle into his pack and pulled out his vest with a large green search and rescue cross on it. "Or he succumbs to exposure or drowns in the lake."

"You got it. The team's been activated, but we need your expertise in the backcountry. We need you to save the day, big guy."

Right. Because he was so good at that. At least, stateside, nobody had died on his watch.

Jason put on his sunglasses, adjusted the brim of his cap and started moving.

"I'm about fifteen minutes away from the clearing up by Solitude Lake. You can land the chopper there.

Come get me. You can drop me at the trailhead, and I'll track the kid from there."

"Will do."

He slipped his search and rescue vest on over his T-shirt and doubled his speed. "Hunt, out."

Chapter One

*Nine months later... The Midas Lodge
outside Jackson, Wyoming*

"Samantha, what are you doing?"

Wishing I was anywhere else.

Hearing her father's tsk-tsking tone above the white noise of conversations, laughter and chamber music drifting in from the reception area of the Midas Lodge's main lobby, Samantha Eddington bit down on the ungrateful thought and stretched up on her toes on the arm of the leather chair she'd pulled from the neighboring window alcove. She closed the back of the mantel clock and screwed the casing shut with her thumbnail before pushing it back into place over the two-story stone fireplace. "Hi, Dad. It stopped at four twenty this afternoon. Fortunately, it was just the batteries." She showed him the oxidized rust stains on the paper napkin wadded up in her hand. "I cleaned them and put them back in, but they won't last for long. We'll need a new set."

Walter Eddington had the build and face of a bulldog, an ironic contrast to the expensive tailored suit and diamond-studded lapel pin he wore. A self-made man who'd served in the Army before Samantha was born, he was as at home in the backcountry with a hunting rifle as he was in the boardroom of the hotel empire he'd purchased on a dare and built into a fortune over the past thirty-five years. Too bad she hadn't inherited either of those skill sets. She didn't share his love for a good party, either, like tonight's shindig that mixed hotel with family business.

But she did love him. Adored him, in fact. After losing her mother when she was seven, they'd become a team—sharing grief and comfort, and helping each other pick up the pieces of their fractured lives. She'd never quite been the tomboy he wanted, nor was she poised enough to serve as the dutiful hostess and helpmate a businessman of his standing needed. And while she understood the numbers and demographics of the lodging and tourism industry, she'd never shared his interest in running a corporation. She loved analyzing the architectural designs and engineering strategies that went into building hotels and resort lodges, but her intellectual acumen and aversion to board meetings, press conferences, and parties like tonight's grand opening celebration with investors and local bigwigs kept her from being the heir he'd hoped for to take over the Midas Group and run the family business one day. Still, Walter Eddington loved her anyway. He was her daddy, the first man she'd loved. And even at twenty-nine, she was his little girl.

"Come down from there." He held out his broad, calloused hand. She took it and smiled as he helped her down from her perch. He dropped a kiss to her cheek, just below the rim of her glasses. "This is supposed to be your party. I realize we're combining business with pleasure by scheduling the grand opening of the new lodge with your engagement announcement to Kyle. But you know how much I want to change the press's perception of you as some kind of eccentric recluse who never recovered from your mother's murder. Hiding out from our guests doesn't help change that image."

"I'm not a recluse. My mind just gets occupied with other things." Too many other things. Like the guilt she felt at putting that worry dimple between his silvering eyebrows.

"I know that," he assured her. "But the last time your picture was on TV and in all the papers, you were only seven. You were so brave. So sad." He captured both hands and backed up to skim his gaze from the loose bun at the nape of her neck to the unpolished wiggle of her bare toes on the woven throw rug in front of the fireplace. He smiled. "You look pretty tonight. All grown up. A woman of the world."

His eyes, the same shade of green as her own, turned wistful. He was losing himself in the past until Samantha squeezed his hands, bringing him back into the present with her. "I miss Mom, too. Tonight of all nights, especially."

Walter nodded, pulling her into his barrel chest and capturing her in one of the bear hugs she'd always loved before he set her back on her feet. He chucked her lightly beneath the chin. "I know you take after my side of the family, but..." He brushed aside a rebellious lock of dark blond hair that had caught in her glasses and tucked it behind her ear. "I see your mother in you tonight. How I wish Michelle could be here to share this with us."

Samantha reached up to straighten the knot of his tie and smooth his lapels, the tender ministrations more of a comfort than a need. "Me, too."

"It's been twenty-two years tonight since that bastard murdered..." Muttering a curse, he blinked away the moisture that glistened in his eyes and pulled something from his pocket. "I want to show you something."

Samantha lit up when she saw the familiar engraved locket on a silver chain that dangled from his fingers. "Mom's necklace. The one you gave her when you got married."

"It'll be yours one day. But tonight, I'm carrying it for luck. That everything goes smoothly, and that Kyle makes you as happy as she and I were. Even if it was for too short a time. I wanted you to know she's with us."

She rubbed her fingertips across the locket's etched surface the way she had as a curious child when it had hung around her mother's neck. Then Walter drew it up to his lips and kissed the heirloom before tucking it back into his pocket. "Don't tell Joyce."

"Don't tell Joyce what?" Samantha's stepmother appeared behind her father in a swish of pale pink satin. "The party's in the other room, you two." She pointed to the lobby behind them. "Where all the guests are."

With a wink that said he'd cover for Samantha, Walter caught his second wife's hand and kissed her fingers before linking her arm through his. "You'll need to speak to the staging crew, dear. Sammie had to repair this clock. It wasn't working. You know I love the beautiful things you selected to decorate the new lodge. But I expect things to do their job, too."

"Of course I will, dear," Joyce assured him. "I want everything to be perfect tonight."

"I opened it up and cleaned the batteries," Samantha explained.

"Cleaned them with what?" She suspected her stepmother was frowning, although her face revealed little evidence of emotion, one way or another. When Samantha showed her the dirty cocktail napkin, Joyce snatched it from her hand and tossed it into the fireplace.

Unlike Samantha, Joyce knew how to work a room and make a business deal as well as Walter did. His successes were hers and vice versa. Samantha had never quite fit into the family equation the same way after her father had remarried and adopted Joyce's daughter, Taylor. "You are the guest of honor, not maintenance personnel. Are you forgetting that I told the press photographers to be in position at eight? After your father gives his welcoming speech, Kyle will go down on one knee and propose. Just like we rehearsed."

Because nothing says romance like a staged proposal. Samantha scratched at the rash itching beneath the stays of her dress. True, she'd been seeing Kyle Grazer longer than any other man she'd dated—not that there were many names on that list. Being the socially awkward, plain-Jane daughter of a wealthy man like Walter Eddington made it pretty near impossible to trust any man who claimed to be interested in her. But Kyle had persisted. They'd become friends after Joyce had introduced them. Then, her father had offered him a job as an executive in the company, and they'd become something more.

So what if she didn't get the topsy-turvy stomach turbulence she'd expected when she fell in love? Logically, they were good for each other. He helped bring Samantha out of her shell, and she offered him a quiet refuge from the heartache of a girlfriend who'd dumped him and the pain of a father who'd raised him with a harsh, unsympathetic hand. Besides, Kyle was immeasurably patient with her inexperience. He praised her efforts to learn more about kissing and seduction, and promised their lovemaking would improve as she developed more confidence in her relationship skills.

Besides, Grazers came from money. Kyle's father owned a chain of hotels on the East Coast, so she knew he wasn't with her just to get a part of her father's fortune. And her father had assured her more than once that the expected merger of companies that would follow the announcement of their engagement would be negated on the spot if he thought for one moment that Kyle wouldn't take care of her and make her happy. Even if there was something she couldn't quite put her finger on that kept her relationship from being everything she'd hoped for, Samantha *was* happy. Wasn't she?

She rubbed her hand over the hives she'd lived with since her father had asked her to make the engagement a public event and schedule it for tonight—the anniversary of her mother's murder. *"I want to create a positive memory for you,"* he'd said. *"Make this a happy day instead of the anniversary of a nightmare."*

For the company, for her father, for her future—Samantha had every intention of saying yes when Kyle proposed in front of the cameras tonight. This would no longer be the day her mother had been kidnapped and murdered. It would be the day Samantha Eddington got engaged and gave her dad a reason to smile. Now if she could just make the hives go away.

"I didn't forget about the time," Samantha answered, explaining why she'd wandered into the anteroom to fix a broken clock. "Tonight's a big night and I'm understandably nervous. I ran out of small talk after I lost track of Kyle. And the lobby was so crowded, I was getting overheated, so I came out here to check the time, look out the windows and cool off."

"Look out the windows at what? It's pouring down

rain out there." Joyce pointed to the bank of floor-to-ceiling windows. "You can't even see the mountains it's so dark."

Samantha crossed to the windows, drawing her finger through the condensation beading there. "You have to admit the rain is cooling things off."

Joyce shook her head, as if the scientific fact made no sense to her. "What do you mean, you lost track of Kyle?" Joyce moved past her husband to straighten the turned-up hem on the embroidered sheer overlay on Samantha's navy blue cocktail dress. "And where are your shoes?" Samantha adjusted her glasses on the bridge of her nose and spied the strappy three-inch heels she'd discarded to climb onto the new resort lodge's furniture. She slipped her feet back into the tan patent leather and fastened the ankle straps, cringing at the sore spots screaming a protest on each of her little toes. "This absentminded professor shtick was cute when you were a teenager, but now it's getting old."

Shtick? Once the wedding was done, Samantha had every intention of becoming a real professor at a reputable university. She'd already earned her PhD. Or, at least she would once she finished her dissertation on the mechanics of waste management design in alpine geographies. If more nights like this one didn't keep her away from her computers and schematic drawings.

"Joyce," Walter chided, joining them. "Ease back on the throttle a bit. This is a big night for Sammie."

"Of course it is. It's a big night for all of us." She batted Samantha's fingers away from her torso when she tried to scratch again. "I've planned everything down to the last minute, from the guest list to the schedule of events to Samantha's dress." A line that could be a dimple or a frown the Botox had missed appeared beside

Joyce's mouth. "Why aren't you wearing the red dress Taylor and I picked out for you? She has better fashion sense than both of us put together. It's more photogenic."

For one thing, Taylor was built like a petite fashion model while Samantha was a feminine version of her father's sturdy build. For another, her adopted stepsister's fashion sense reflected the fact that she could wear anything and look like a million bucks, while Samantha was lucky she'd found heels to match her dress. And finally, "Taylor did help me pick this out."

Joyce waved her hand in front of the embroidered flowers covering the A-line dress. "This one is so busy. It's very sweet, but I'm afraid you look more like a girl going to her first communion rather than a woman who's about to get married."

"I like this dress." Couldn't say the same for the three-inch heels of her shoes that chafed her ankles and squeezed all sensation out of her little toes. "Blues and grays are my favorite colors."

"I think she looks lovely," Walter insisted. "Considering she usually wears pants and a lab coat or she's out at a construction site in muddy coveralls, I think she's very dressed up for the occasion."

"You're right, dear. Of course. It is a pretty dress." Joyce's agreeing smile quickly disappeared. "Could you at least put in your contact lenses? Your glasses will reflect the lights when the photographers take pictures." She made a shooing motion with her lacquered fingernails before latching onto Walter's arm again. "Go upstairs and fix yourself. I'll see if I can find Kyle while your father talks to the lieutenant governor." She tilted her face to her father's. "That's why I came looking for you—to tell you she and her husband are arriving."

"Better not keep them waiting." Her father shrugged

his big shoulders. Maybe he didn't enjoy these big command performances any more than Samantha did. "I'll see you in the spotlight at eight."

Samantha managed to summon a smile. "I'll be there, Dad."

"Excuse me, sir." A big man with dark hair and a perfectly shaped handlebar mustache walked up behind her father. Dante Pellegrino's muscular bulk was accentuated by the holster and gun he wore underneath his suit jacket. The chief of Midas Group security rarely changed his expression from stoic disinterest, so it was hard to tell when there was an emergency and when he was simply relaying information. "Ma'am. Miss Eddington." He acknowledged Samantha and her stepmother. "Walter? A moment?"

"Is this necessary, Dante?" Joyce asked. "We have a schedule to maintain. Walter is greeting guests until seven forty-five, and then he goes to the podium to make a welcome speech."

"I'm afraid so, ma'am. Something unexpected has come up."

"Very well." Not one wisp of Joyce's silvering blond hair moved as she swung her gaze around, scanning the guests through the open suite of rooms. "I'll stall the lieutenant governor for a few minutes." Even though he was twice her size, she pointed a warning finger at the security chief. "Don't keep him long."

"No, ma'am."

As Joyce bustled away in another swish of stiff satin, Dante whispered in her father's ear. Samantha waited expectantly, wondering if something was happening that would compound her father's worries about this evening's success.

Walter's expression hardened to his time-to-do-business face. "Make sure one of your men stays with Sammie. She's going upstairs for a few minutes."

"Yes, sir."

Samantha tugged on her father's sleeve when he would have pulled away. "Is everything okay?"

"Nothing your old dad can't handle. Don't be late. I want tonight to be all about you." He kissed her forehead and strode away to handle whatever situation Dante had whispered to him.

Either her father didn't think she could understand the problem, or he simply didn't want to worry her. Maybe Dante would be more forthcoming.

She tipped her chin to meet his dark gaze. "What is it?"

He chewed once on the gum that seemed to be perennially in his teeth. Maybe the man had given up smoking, or used the subtle action as a stress-reducing ritual. But since her father had hired his firm a couple of years earlier, she'd never once seen him without the sticky wad in the side of his mouth. "Storm's coming up. There'll be more rain tonight. Snow higher up in the mountains."

She arched a confused brow. "You talked to Dad about the weather?"

"It changes plans."

"What plans?"

"Weather like this brings unexpected guests."

Samantha curved her lips into a wry smile. "We *are* a hotel."

"One that's not open for business yet." Dante gave her a look that lacked any emotion—or any real explanation—as he tapped the radio on his wrist and summoned one of the bodyguards who worked for his security team. "Filly Number One is on the move.

Metz? You're up." The bodyguard typically assigned to watch her at public events must have responded in the hearing device wired to the security chief's ear. "Copy that. Pellegrino out."

"Having unexpected guests show up for a party is a security issue?"

"It is tonight." His mustache danced atop his lip as he shifted his gum from one cheek to the other. "It's my job to make sure everything goes as planned. If you're not at that podium at eight o'clock, I'll come get you myself."

Was that a threat? Or just a reminder that she was a commodity in Dante Pellegrino's eyes? Protecting her was no different from guarding the diamond jewelry Joyce and her father were wearing tonight. Grumbling a curse under her breath, Samantha turned and left as quickly as her toe-pinching shoes would let her.

Filly. Although it was a word she was familiar with—she was Number One and Taylor was Number Two when it came to coded security team communications—the nickname only added to her anxiety. She felt like prize livestock tonight, being paraded around for a group of wealthy investors, high-powered executives and gossipy reporters looking for a sensational headline. Joyce was probably hoping that marrying Samantha off would allow her to shift the spotlight over to her own daughter and maybe snag the interest of one of the wealthy guests here tonight to send a son or nephew to come court Taylor. Samantha might have had her fill of socializing, but Taylor would relish all the attention. And she was welcome to it.

Samantha wasn't good enough for her stepmother. She was invisible to the guests. Her father worried too much about her. And she might as well be a horse in the family's stable as far as the security chief was concerned.

"I am so taking a private honeymoon with Kyle," she muttered, hurrying her steps to the trio of elevators. She didn't think her numb toes could handle the staircase up to the mezzanine floor. Even if Kyle wasn't in their room primping for his big moment in front of the cameras, Samantha needed the time away from the people and noise to give herself a pep talk and get her extrovert on. If she was lucky, Kyle would be in the room. A few private words and a kiss would go a long way toward reassuring her that she was making the right choice in saying yes to his proposal.

The bodyguard Pellegrino had summoned appeared in the hallway behind her. Brandon Metz might be the closest thing she had to a friend here tonight. Even though he was part of the elite security team her father had hired to safeguard the family and top executives at the company two years ago, Brandon was usually assigned to her at public events. Although sworn to be discreet, he knew her embarrassing idiosyncrasies. He knew she'd rather be almost anywhere else than dressing up and giving a speech in front of a microphone and flashing cameras.

Samantha pushed the elevator call button as Brandon's long strides quickly ate up the hallway behind her. "Samantha?" he called to her as the elevator dinged and the doors slid open. "What's the hurry?"

If she could get in and close the door before he caught up to her, he'd be forced to take the stairs up to the next floor to keep an eye on her. She darted inside and pushed the button, eagerly anticipating a whole fifteen seconds or so of peace and quiet.

But Brandon caught the door and stepped into the elevator with her. "Didn't you hear me?"

She sagged against the back railing. "Sorry. I just needed a break."

His golden-brown eyes narrowed in a reprimand that she probably deserved. "I know you're crawling out of your skin dancing through hoops for your family tonight. But it's my job to keep you in my line of sight at all times." Ironically, he turned his back on her, facing the front of the elevator while he spoke into his radio. "Filly One is secure. Heading to mezzanine." He glanced over his shoulder to question her. "The anniversary of your mom's death getting to you?"

"A little," Samantha confessed. Although the grief wasn't as intense as it had been growing up, she still felt the hole in her life that the woman who loved her unconditionally was supposed to fill. But if she started down the trail of all the landmark events in her life her mother had missed, and would miss, then she'd become the weepy little girl pushing her way through a crowd of reporters, asking them where her mother had gone. She was years past allowing herself to be that vulnerable again. A tart tone of sarcasm was one of the defensive tools she'd developed as she'd grown up. "I have to go *fix* myself so I'm up to my stepmother's standards and don't embarrass my father when the paparazzi start flashing pictures."

Brandon chuckled and finished his report as the elevator stopped. "Will keep you posted when she moves again. Yes, I know the timeline," he groused. "Metz out." He held the door and checked the hallway before ushering her out ahead of him and following her to the room she shared with Kyle. "And here I thought you were skipping out on the party to go have a rendezvous with Loverboy."

"I wish." She slipped her hand beneath the hem of her skirt to pull her key card from the leg of her shapewear. "I don't suppose you've seen Kyle the last half hour or so, have you?"

"He's not my assignment."

She slid the card into the lock and opened the door to the faint garble of muffled voices. Maybe Kyle had come up here to catch the market report on the news or listen to one of his motivational podcasts. If he'd abandoned her to watch television or psych himself up for tonight's show, she'd be angry, but at least she'd have an explanation for his disappearance. Samantha nodded to the settee and chairs where the private hallway opened onto a dramatic picture window above the lodge's front entrance. "Relax if you want. I'll only be a few minutes."

He nodded toward the closest chair and side table with its fake potted fern. "I'll give you five minutes. After that, I'll come knockin'." With a lopsided grin, he pulled his cell phone from his suit jacket pocket and retreated into the hallway. She heard him calling someone with another *Filly One* update while she locked the door.

Samantha's deep exhale buzzed her lips as she sagged wearily against the door for a moment. The voices she'd heard had gone silent, so no television. No Kyle, either. She eyed his polished shoes that had been kicked off onto the carpet, and his suit jacket tossed in a lump on the rumpled bedspread beside her purse. Samantha peeked around the corner to knock on the bathroom door. Rumpled was not a typical state for her fiancé. Had he spilled something on him and come up to change? Was he not feeling well? "Kyle? Are you okay?"

The bathroom was empty, and the light was off. The inkling of concern that he might be ill faded. Samantha flipped on the light switch and studied her reflection in the vanity mirror, adjusting her glasses on her pale face before digging through her cosmetics bag to dust on another layer of blush. She was going to have to reach down deep inside her to find the strength and grace to make this evening the success her father wanted it to be.

Once she was sufficiently convinced there was nothing she could do to transform herself into the beauty of the family, Samantha set out her contact lenses and saline solution. But she quickly put her glasses back on when a more proactive way to improve her evening hit her. She returned to the bedroom and sat on the edge of the bed, giving her squished toes a break, and pulled her cell phone from her purse. It would be more efficient to text Kyle and ask his whereabouts than to wander around the ski lodge in hopes of running into him, or trust that he was simply going to show up in the right place at the right time to propose.

After she hit Send, a buzz answered from Kyle's jacket.

Samantha frowned. Even more unusual than Kyle tossing his clothes about was his not having his cell with him. She tugged his jacket into her lap. A black velvet ring box fell from the folds of wool. An unexpected twinge of feminine anticipation made her catch her lip between her teeth as she opened the box. The large marquise diamond surrounded by a double halo of emeralds and tiny seed diamonds was much too gaudy for her tastes. She'd never be able to wear this in the lab or out in the field when she was working. She snapped the box shut, trying not to feel too disappointed by his impractical choice. Why hadn't Kyle bought the simple solitaire she'd shown him?

Since her curiosity had gotten her this far, she didn't hesitate to pull out the folded slip of paper she found in his jacket pocket when she tucked the ring box back inside. This was probably some sappy poem or crib notes he planned to use when he proposed, instead of honest, heartfelt words.

Samantha's jaw dropped open and her breath rushed out as her whole future closed in on her in one humiliating, suffocating moment. She read the names and numbers on the paper. This wasn't even a stupid poem. It was a receipt for the ring. More expensive than she'd imagined. Charged to her stepmother Joyce's account.

"Why would she buy my engagement ring?" If Kyle didn't have the money for that shiny eyesore, then he should have purchased something smaller, more tasteful—a gift from the heart she would have treasured. Had he asked her stepmother to visit the jeweler for him because he'd been away on business so much lately and didn't have time to shop?

She crumpled the receipt in her fist. Maybe this wasn't about the money or time. Were her father and Joyce that worried about her? She was going through most of this for them. Did they think they were doing all this for *her*? How much of this whole engagement was for the benefit of public relations and the family name? Was any of this marriage bargain real?

Samantha pulled out the velvet box again and squeezed it in her fist. She was sorely tempted to track Kyle down and shove this ring and whatever bargain he thought he'd made with Joyce and her father down his throat.

The whole bed rattled when something thumped against the wall, startling Samantha from her vengeful thoughts. The interruption gave her a moment to temper her emotions, a moment to think more rationally about her discovery. Maybe her own doubts about this engagement were feeding her suspicion of Kyle.

But then she heard the giggle.

Chapter Two

A moment of cold dread was quickly erased by the angry understanding that followed. She should have trusted her instincts. It wasn't the pomp and circumstance of the evening that made her break out in stress hives. It was the idea of marrying Kyle.

When another thump against the wall made her jump, Samantha went to investigate. The door on her side that could be opened to turn the neighboring rooms into one large suite was unlocked and slightly ajar—as was the connecting door into the next room.

She'd like to go back to that whole television-or-podcast-watching theory. But Samantha knew better as she pushed the second door open and entered the room that mirrored her own. Though still hushed, she could distinguish the voices and giggles and breathy moans now. She turned past the desk to the closet door, wishing her hearing was as lousy as her myopic vision.

A woman laughed from inside the closet. "Stop shushing me. You said no one could hear us in here."

Oh, how she wished she didn't recognize that voice.

"Just do it, baby. Do it now." Betrayal drove a stake through her heart at Kyle's gasping reply. "Stop talking and…"

Samantha whipped the door open to see Kyle leaning against the closet wall and her stepsister, Taylor, kneeling in front of his unzipped pants.

Oh, hell. Oh, double hell.

Kyle swore.

Samantha watched her stepsister tumble onto her bottom as Kyle pushed off the wall. She backed away, shaking her head.

Taylor's cheeks burned with embarrassment. "Samantha? Oh, my God. I'm so sorry. I never meant to—"

"Screw my boyfriend?" Seriously? Were those tears? "Or just get caught doing it?"

Kyle made a token effort to button his shirt as he stepped out of the closet. "I can explain."

"So can I." Fortunately, he was in a condition that made it difficult for him to hurry after her as Samantha headed to the connecting doors. "Apparently, you lost track of the time. And which sister you're proposing to."

Kyle grabbed her wrist and tugged her around to face him. "Baby, you know I'm committed to you." He captured her by the shoulders, his handsome blue eyes searching hers. Hadn't he just called Taylor *baby*? *Real special endearment, jackass.* "To us. I will see this thing through to the end. I just needed to get this out of my system before we settle down."

"*This?* You mean having sex with my sister?" Samantha twisted in his grasp, and his hold on her tightened painfully.

Taylor scrambled to her feet to follow them, tugging her dress down to her knees. "Out of your system? What does that mean? You said—"

"Shut. Up."

When Kyle turned to dismiss her stepsister, Samantha finally put those three-inch heels to good use and stomped on his stockinged foot, freeing herself.

He cursed her and the pain, and stumbled into Taylor. While he teetered off balance, Samantha shoved him back inside the closet, knocking Taylor in with him. The two traitors were falling to the floor, pulling coats and hangers down with them, as she hurled the ring box at them and slammed the door. Tuning out both demands and apologies, she wedged the desk chair beneath the doorknob. Blind with rage and hurt and even a little self-loathing that she hadn't seen this coming, Samantha marched back to her own room and locked the connecting door behind her. She just wanted to escape. If she'd needed a reprieve from the social event downstairs, then dealing with this kind of humiliation demanded nothing less than utter and lengthy solitude.

But she wasn't going to find that here. She spared a moment to pull the luggage rack with her suitcase in front of the door to block the exit, further trapping the two on the other side before grabbing her purse and pulling her checkered trench coat from her own closet.

The argument from the next room continued, mixed with knocks against the walls and periodic swearing. "You said you were with the wrong sister. That you wanted me. Was that just a line to get me to—?"

"Shut up, Taylor." The doorknob rattled. He pounded on the wall between them. "Samantha, open this door. We need to talk. You're being a child."

And you're being a bastard.

"I love you," he insisted, in the most rote, carefully practiced and insincere tone she could imagine. "I've told you that countless times."

"If only you meant it any one of those times," she muttered before slipping into her black-and-white coat and exiting into the hallway.

She barely noticed Brandon springing to his feet.

She hated that her eyes were gritty with tears, hated that she cared enough to hurt like this. But her brain seemed to function, even when her emotions couldn't get their act together. Although Kyle couldn't get to her through the room they'd shared, he'd be able to reach her through Taylor's door. No sense risking that he'd be able to break out of the closet and chase after her. She knocked over the side table, spilling it and the silk fern in front of Taylor's door.

"Um, trouble in Happy Couple Land?" Brandon dodged to one side as she dragged the leather chair in front of the door, building a bigger barricade. "Your mother asked me to remind you—"

"Stepmother, Brandon. Joyce is my stepmother. My real mother died." And apparently, so had any chance at a relationship. After swiping at the tears that clouded her glasses, Samantha booked it down the hallway toward the elevators, leaving the banging and swearing and shouting behind. "Tell Joyce and Dad something came up. I'm leaving."

Brandon stayed right with her. "What did that lowlife do? Is he cheating on you again?"

Samantha stopped in her tracks. "Again? You knew he…? This isn't the first…?" So much for protecting her. She tore her gaze away from the bodyguard's pitying brown eyes and punched the elevator button. *Be angry, not hurt.* "I knew something wasn't right between us. I was trying so hard to make it work. I'm such an idiot."

"Where are you going? I can't let you leave on your own. Especially when you're like this."

"Like what? Awake to reality? Standing up for myself? Saving what little dignity I have left?" The strain of the evening intensified the rash on her torso. Ignoring the habitual urge to scratch, she dug into her purse.

"Fine. Then you're coming with me. Here are my keys." She stepped into the elevator, handing them to the confused bodyguard. "Bring my car around back by the kitchen entrance. I'll meet you there. I'm not walking through that lobby and facing all those people again."

"Pellegrino will want to know your destination. He doesn't like changing plans when security is already in place. The rain is pouring—"

"I don't know where I'm going. I don't care if I get wet. I just have to get out of here." She jerked at the crash of splintering wood from down the hallway and punched the first-floor button. "Now."

Brandon grabbed the door to stop the elevator from closing. "What do I tell Pellegrino and your father?"

"Tell them I'm not feeling well. Tell them I'm flying to the moon. I don't care."

"Samantha!" Kyle's shout reached her through the makeshift barriers she'd put up. The closet door was down.

Brandon pulled back his jacket, resting his hand on the gun holstered there. "You want me to stop him?"

At last someone was on her side. But she needed him to do what she needed him to do. "Either get the car right now, or I'm leaving on my own."

He nodded and ran toward the stairs, allowing the doors to close. "I'll meet you under the parking canopy at the kitchen's delivery entrance in back." She could hear him reporting in as the elevator dropped toward the first floor. "This is Metz. Be advised that Filly One is…"

Without even a glance toward the lobby, Samantha hurried toward the kitchen area by one of the lodge's service corridors. With the catering staff out working the party, there was only the chef and her assistant in the kitchen when Samantha pushed her way through the swinging metal door. Ignoring their curious looks and offers to help, she quickened her steps toward the walk-in refrigerator and storage pantry near the back entrance. When the door crashed open behind her and the assistant squeaked in startled surprise, Samantha ran as fast as her aching feet and starched dress allowed.

"Samantha! You have to talk to me."

Kyle hadn't stopped to put on his shoes, and his stockinged feet made no noise as he raced up behind her. She yelped when he grabbed her and spun her around, backing her into a stainless-steel worktable, pinning her there with his hips and hands. His chiseled cheekbones were flushed with exertion, his perfect white teeth clenched as he panted in her face. "I thought you were an adult. Running away is what a child does. You owe it to me to listen."

"I owe *you*?" His fingers clamped down tightly enough to bruise her skin when she shoved at his chest. "Let go of me."

"Clear the room," he ordered the catering staff. When they were too stunned by the argument to budge, he shoved a tray of hors d'oeuvres onto the floor. "Get out!"

Samantha wished she could leave with them as the door swung shut on their backsides. Dishes and pans rattled on the steel table as she squirmed in Kyle's grasp. "You need to let me go."

He released her arms to grab either side of her face, pulling at the pins that held her long hair in place and pinching her scalp, forcing her to look up at him. "You and I are getting married. We have an agreement. Your family likes me."

"Some more than others, apparently."

"Don't get snarky with me. Yes, I screwed up. You have to forgive me."

"Says who?"

"You think there aren't things I would change about you?" he challenged.

How was this her fault? She blinked back the tears that stung her eyes and fought through her emotions to find the words she needed to say. "I'm not the one who's cheating."

"I have a weakness. Okay?"

"No. It's not okay. You didn't even pick out the ring yourself. You couldn't spend that much time on me?"

"I've been busy."

"I can see that."

"With work! I was a little strapped for cash and couldn't afford the ring I wanted to get you, so Joyce helped me out." He was the son of a millionaire and had a good job with the Midas Group. How could he possibly be short of money? Before she could voice the accusation, Kyle touched his sweaty forehead to hers in a supposedly tender gesture, and Samantha wondered how she'd ever found him handsome or charming. "I am committed to us. You know I'm good for you. I help others see beyond the professor and the glasses. We make a good team."

What about needing her? Or wanting her? Or any other stupid compliment that could make her believe he was ever in love with her? The urge to cry disappeared. She let his lips brush against hers, but the moment he thought he was winning her back and his hold on her eased, Samantha twisted from his grasp.

He paused long enough to curse before pursuing her again. "This is a misunderstanding. You need to clue in to how the real world works. I have needs."

She whirled around. "You *need* to keep your pants zipped around other women. If you wanted to get laid, you should have asked me. It's not like I haven't wanted you to…teach me more."

The creep actually smiled. He cupped his fingers against her cheek. "Is that what this is about? Baby, you're too good for a quickie."

She slapped his hand away. "But my sister's not?" She didn't know whether to be flattered or insulted.

"Taylor's young and fun. But she means nothing to me. You mean everything."

"Liar. How many others have there been?"

At least he had the good grace to look guilty. For a split second. Then he was reaching for her again. "Look. Truth. You're learning. Eventually the sex will be great between us, but until you get some confidence—"

She slapped his hand away. "A relationship isn't just about sex. It's about trust and caring and respect. You have no clue—"

When she felt his hand on her arm again, Samantha reached for the first weapon she could find, a heavy skillet resting on the edge of the metal table. She swung around, whacking him in the shoulder. He cursed, grabbing his bruised arm. She knew a moment of guilt, sensing she'd gone too far.

"You are not dumping me." When his eyes narrowed in rage instead of pain, her brain took over.

She had a feeling that escape wasn't just an emotional need at that moment. Shoving the pan into his gut, she forced Kyle back a step. She ordered him to open the refrigerator door. "Get in there. Get in or I swear I'll run straight to my father and tell him you were banging Taylor tonight instead of earning your spot as Midas's newest vice president."

Kyle raised his hands and moved toward her. "You don't want to upset your father tonight…"

"Get in!"

If she'd had any doubts that she was nothing more than a means to an end for Kyle, his willingness to step inside the cooler in exchange for her silence confirmed the truth. As disgusted with herself for being taken in by his promises as she was with the man himself, Samantha closed the refrigerator door and slipped the pin into the lock.

Instead of cursing her or shouting her name, Kyle pulled his cell phone from a pocket and held it up to the window beside his gloating face for her to see.

"How did you…?" Had he broken out through their room? Taken the time to retrieve his phone? Did he have a second cell? Whom was he calling?

Samantha dropped the skillet and opened the back door.

"This is Grazer. I need your help." With the rain beating down on the loading area's metal canopy, she lost the rest of the conversation until he started shouting. "I mean right now! She's taking off. Running out the back door. This *is* plan B!"

Whoever Kyle's ally was, she wasn't waiting for his help to arrive. Slightly breathless with the exertion of fending off Kyle, she scanned the row of employee cars on the other side of the driveway for her silver BMW. The rain fell in sheets on either side of the canopy, blackening the night sky and shrinking her world to the lights beneath the canopy and parked vehicles ahead of her. Her steps stuttered to a halt beside the caterer's van. Where was Brandon? Surely, he'd had time to fetch her car from the lot in front of the lodge to drive back here. "Where are you?"

Although she was out of the elements, the moisture in the air dotted her skin. She shivered with a chill that was part Wyoming springtime and part apprehension. Samantha took out her own phone and pulled up Brandon's number. Should she call him? Give him a few more seconds?

A powerful engine revved nearby. Too big to be her car. Tires screeched against the wet pavement somewhere out in the darkness. Two headlamps came on, their bright lights crystallizing every raindrop, blinding her. Shielding her eyes, Samantha drew back to her side of the driveway so she wouldn't be run over.

Just as she punched in her bodyguard's number to get her out of this madhouse, a black van erupted from the wall of rain and skidded to a stop only feet away, sending a wave of dirty water splashing over her feet. "Hey!"

The side door opened and two men in dark camouflage gear and ski masks jumped out. One was carrying what looked like a machine gun.

Samantha screamed.

"Shut her up!" a growly voice ordered.

She spun around and slammed into a third man. Where had he come from? Strong arms snugged around her like a vise, knocking the phone from her hand. "Let go of me!"

"Get that phone!" someone shouted.

Someone tore her purse off her shoulder. She kicked. Clawed. Twisted. "Brandon! Help! Help me! Ky—!"

A gloved hand slapped an oily cloth over her mouth and nose, forcing her to breathe in some nasty fumes, making her dizzy. Rough hands lifted her off her feet. Her knee cracked against the running board of the van before she was shoved inside. "Help me," she wheezed. The hands let go and she rolled across the floor of the van, slamming into the opposite side. "What's happening? Who are you?"

"Samantha!" Help. Brandon was coming for her. She heard two sharp pops, and jumped inside her skin at the metallic clank of two bullets striking the back of the van.

A man in the front seat thrust his hand out the window and fired a gun that made a whup, whup sound. A silencer. Her would-be rescuer wouldn't hear the man returning fire.

She pushed herself up, tried to warn him. "Brandon!"

The side door slammed shut. The van lurched forward and she fell.

"Glasses."

Cruel hands pulled them off her face, blurring the world around her. "Please… I can't see—"

"I said shut her up." She felt the prick of a needle in the side of her neck. "Get the tracking device." The man giving orders cursed. "Drive!"

Those same cruel hands tugged at her coat. A sharp blade pierced the back of her shoulder. Her world blurred into a woozy haze of faceless men and squealing tires.

Kidnapped. Just like her mother. Michelle Eddington had been taken on a raw night just like this one.

Samantha's brain went dark on one final thought.

Kyle's betrayal, seeing his daughter used and being played for a fool himself, might anger her father.

But this would break him.

Chapter Three

A beer bottle sailed through the air. Jason dodged the flying projectile and watched it shatter against the wood door frame behind him at Kitty's Bar.

He halted a moment to brush off some of the beer that had sprayed his jacket and quickly assessed the combatants of the fight he'd just walked in on. Looked like locals versus outsiders. Located on the outskirts of Moose, Wyoming, Kitty's was usually a quiet hole-in-the-wall where a man could get a drink and meet a friend without running into too many people. But at o-dark-thirty on a Friday night, this place had more people in it than he'd ever seen—and half of them were throwing punches.

"Stop it!" Kitty Flynn yelled from behind the bar as a table tipped over, spilling playing cards and poker chips over the warped floorboards.

He spotted a familiar search and rescue ball cap sliding across the floor before zeroing in on a head of curly red hair. Sure enough, Marty Flynn, Kitty's nephew and Jason's coworker, was right in the middle of it, landing a punch on a blond guy in a three-piece suit before pulling a dark-haired waitress out of Blondie's arms and pushing her toward the bar and his aunt. "You get out of there, Cathy, before you get hurt."

Marty shoved at a dark-haired twenty-something wearing jeans and a flannel shirt. That was one of the Murphy boys, twins who ran a gun shop with their dad. He never could tell Cy and Orin apart. The kid shoved right back, trying to get at a tall, lanky man who already sported a black eye. Jason pulled off his knit cap and shook the rain from the dark hair that dripped onto his collar. He never should have answered his phone.

"Hey, Captain. I've got a woman we need to track down in the Tetons."

"Missing hiker?" Jason had asked, thinking the woman was a fool to risk going up into the high country in the spring before the upper elevations had thawed. But he was already grabbing his go bag to load into his four-wheel-drive truck. Night was the worst time to be lost in the mountains. And all this rain and snow, depending on where she was on the mountain, made this a particularly miserable night.

"Not exactly." Either the woman needed their help, or she didn't. Jason waited for the younger man to explain. "Meet me at Aunt Kitty's place. I'm not calling in anybody else on the S&R team because the guy who wants to hire us says this rescue needs to stay off the books. Hell, I'm not even filing a report with the boss, just getting clearance for a flight plan from the airport. I don't think we need anybody else. And we could make some good money. A lot of it."

Jason didn't care about the money. What he cared about was living with his conscience. Letting another woman die when he could do something to help was his Achilles' heel. Letting anyone die in those mountains when he knew them better than just about anybody in a hundred-mile radius wasn't something he could hide away from, although he tried damn hard to hide from

the world as much as it would let him. He'd found that
five-year-old kid who'd wandered off from his parents
last summer. He'd tracked down a mountain biker who'd
had a run-in with a cougar, carried the guy on his back
to clear ground so he could be life-flighted to the hospital. There'd been skiers and snowboarders who'd needed
his help, and he'd been there, too, for them.

But it was never enough. The debt was still there.
He'd lost too many lives over in Kilkut. No matter how
far off the grid he got, that need to balance the scales—
a life for a life—demanded that he answer Marty Flynn's call. Maybe one day the score would be even, and
the losses he'd suffered in the Corps, the anger and the
guilt, wouldn't be able to find him anymore.

And so, he was here. At Kitty's Bar on the outskirts
of Moose after midnight, walking into the middle of
a bar fight.

Looked like Marty was actually trying to stop the
fight, and was getting cursed and dinged up for his
trouble. Four more locals, judging by their boots and
jeans like Jason wore, were going after four guys in
suits who seemed to be toying with them. One of the
suits, an older man with a square face and silvering hair,
hung back behind the tall guy and a bruiser with a handlebar mustache. Although he seemed mature enough
to avoid duking it out with men half his age, he wasn't
above shouting orders, or answering taunts about getting the hell out of where he didn't belong. Mustache
Man had training. He blocked every punch, braced his
feet when another drunk local charged him and used
his attacker's momentum to shove him off to the side.

Blondie wiped a trickle of blood from his mouth and
grabbed the older man's arm, pulling him away from
two men who knocked over a bar stool and toppled to

the floor. "Stay out of it, Walter. Let the professionals handle these yokels. That's what you pay them for."

"I'm not afraid of a fight." While the older man didn't dive into the thick of swinging arms and wrestling men, he did shrug off the young man's grip, stepping forward while Blondie waved him off with a dismissive curse and pulled out his cell phone.

Marty looked a little outnumbered, since neither side seemed interested in backing down. But Jason's priority was the missing hiker, not bailing Marty out of a tough situation because someone had made a joke with the wrong person, or the city dude had made a move on one of the small-town country girls.

Sure, Jason could handle himself in a fight. The Marines had trained him to do that better than most. And the fact that he was built like a tank and stood almost a head taller than anyone else in the room generally dissuaded all but the drunkest or most stupid from picking a fight with him in the first place.

But he didn't wage war anymore. Only the one inside his head. Not even for a friend from the Corps. Jason backed toward the broken bottle and swinging door. Marty could call in a different favor on another day.

Jason was big, but he wasn't fast. Not fast enough to make his escape, at any rate.

"Captain! Jason. Thank God. This is the—" Another local boy with a dark crew cut and tats lunged past Marty, trying to get at the old man. He recognized Richard Cordes Jr., the son of a militia leader who'd led a remote compound in the area back when Jason had been a boy. "Damn it, Junior, I said back off!"

"Mind your own business, Marty." More glass smashed. "Eddington!"

"Jase!"

Putting every emotional survival instinct on hold, Jason squeezed his eyes shut, inhaled a deep breath and answered Marty's plea for help.

He grabbed the young man who was picking himself up off the floor and shoved him down in a chair with a warning to stay put. Kane Windisch—he was Junior Cordes's cousin. Jason captured the next punk in a neck hold and twisted him out of his path to reach Marty and Junior, who was wielding a broken bottle, ready to cut anyone who got too close.

And that's when he saw the guns. The bulges inside their suit jackets indicated Mustache Man and the lanky suit guy already sporting a black eye were both carrying.

"You shouldn't have come here at all, old man," Junior whined. The young hotshot poked the jagged edge of the bottle at the old man who must be Eddington. Mustache Man pulled back his jacket and reached for his gun. "Accusing me of stuff you know nothin' about."

As Junior lunged forward, Jason grabbed him from behind, lifting him off his feet and trapping his arms at his side, shaking him until his grip popped open and he dropped the bottle. Jason kicked it aside and set Junior down. The kid reeked of beer and smoke, like he'd just come in from camping. Jason shoved him back and pointed a warning finger at him. "You need to sober up and calm down."

Junior smacked his hand away. "Get out of my face, Jase."

"Who are you supposed to be?" Mustache Man sneered from behind him. "The cavalry? We got this covered."

Jason turned on him next, unused to looking men straight in the eye, but not fazed by the man's size, either. He nodded to the gun in his hand. "You need to put that away."

"And he needs to back off," Mustache Man warned.

"These boys aren't armed." No telling how many rifles and shotguns Junior and his buddies had stowed in their trucks outside. But Jason figured Mustache Man already knew that. This guy was a pro, former military if not a trained bodyguard for the old man and Blondie. Like Jason, he probably even knew about the revolver Kitty kept behind the bar for protection and to break up fights like this melee. But that didn't mean Jason would allow him an unfair advantage over a group of young men who were too plastered to think straight. "I said put it away."

"You ain't fightin' any fights for me, Jase." Jason heard Junior squirming against the restraining grip Marty and one of the twins had on him. "I ain't afraid of you, Eddington, or your peacekeepers you brought with ya."

"Dante." The silver-haired man in the pricey suit put a hand on Mustache Man's shoulder. "Put the gun away." But his eyes were fixed at a point beyond Jason's shoulder. "I've been watching you for two years now, Mr. Cordes, and I've been content to keep my distance. As far as I'm concerned, justice was served the day of your father's execution. But if you've done anything to my daughter, I will make it my business."

Junior's lips buzzed with a beer-fueled curse. "Justice, my ass." He elbowed Marty in the gut, freeing himself. "You here to take my land, too? The way you took my daddy's?" He charged the older man. "You'll see how we do justice around these parts."

Dante was definitely Eddington's protector. The big man moved forward to block Junior. With barely a twitch of his mustache, he twisted Junior's arm behind his back, pushing him into the dark-stained pinewood bar and smashing his face down onto the polished bar top.

One of the twins lunged forward to help his buddy. But he pulled up short, raising his hands in surrender as Mustache Man pulled his gun and aimed it squarely at the young man's face.

"Back off," Mustache Man warned.

Enough. Jason pulled the young man out of harm's reach and stepped forward to take his place. The gun was now pointed at his chest, but it didn't waver as Mustache Man's dark eyes narrowed.

"Take a deep breath, mister," Jason stated in a calm voice. The other suit had pulled his gun, too. An MK-23. He hadn't seen a laser-sighted pistol since his last deployment. Didn't know why any man would need hardware like that stateside. These two meant business.

Mustache Man pushed a little harder on Junior's skull to keep him pinned to the bar. The damn gun didn't move. "You are outmatched, my friend. There are two of us, and you're not armed. I am Dante Pellegrino, owner of Pellegrino Security."

"Good for you." Jason wasn't impressed by the posturing.

"Yo, Jase." Marty Flynn materialized at Jason's side, dusting off his cap and plunking it backward on his head. "This is Jason Hunt, Mr. Eddington. The guy I told you about. Served with him in the Corps."

"Dante." Like a superior officer, the bulldog who answered to *Mr. Eddington* spoke to his man in a tone that said he expected him to listen. "Let Cordes go. I need to talk to this man. Put your gun away. Brandon, you, too."

With a deliberate chomp on the gum or chew he held in his cheek, Pellegrino released Junior and holstered his weapon. His sidekick did the same. When Junior sprang toward Pellegrino, Jason tripped him and shoved him out of harm's way, warning him to walk away from the fight before Jason chose a different side.

"You, too, Kitty." Jason's tone was a little more indulgent with the barkeep, since she reminded him of the mother he hadn't spoken to in two years.

"Jason Hunt, if you didn't look so much like your daddy…" With some noisy grousing about people telling her what to do in her own place, she circled back behind the bar and put the revolver away in its drawer. "Cathy, get the broom and dustpan out of the back room." The young waitress eagerly hurried off to do her boss's bidding. "Wash your face while you're back there, too."

"Yes, ma'am."

Only after the weapons were all accounted for did Jason take his eyes off Pellegrino. He glanced over to where Junior was downing a surviving shot of some dark liquor and grinning like an idiot. "Go on home." He nodded to his cohorts who were already gathering their jackets and hats. "One of you sober enough to drive?"

One of the twins—Orin, he thought—nodded. He'd been the one with the gun shoved in his face. He shrugged into a lined denim jacket. "Yes, sir."

But Junior had been the son of a fiercely independent militia leader. In addition to inheriting his father's rebellious attitude toward all things authoritarian, he was a little too drunk to choose keeping his mouth shut and leaving as the wiser course of action. He adjusted his stained and twisted cowboy hat over the crown of his head. "You owe me, Eddington. You owe my family. You don't know who you're messin' with."

Kitty circled around the bar with a tray and wet rag to clean the messy table. "Please, Junior, just go. Drinks are on the house. Whatever beef you've got with these people—"

"You don't need to do me any favors. I ain't so broke that I can't pay my debts." He tossed a couple of bills onto the table before turning to volley one last shot. "You took my daddy from me, Eddington. You watch out or I'll take something from you."

"Damn you, Cordes." The older man surged forward. "If you've harmed my daughter in any way… I'll give you the money right now if it means getting her—"

"You can't give him the cash." Pellegrino moved to intercede, but Jason hooked his arm around Pellegrino's shoulder to stop him from turning this argument into another fight, especially when Kitty would be caught in the middle of it. Pellegrino sloughed off Jason's hold and bounced a warning glare from his dark eyes.

Kitty stepped in front of the older man. "I told you, Junior has been here all night, playing cards. He couldn't have taken your daughter."

Taken? That word left a very bad taste in Jason's mouth. What had Marty gotten him into?

"I'm goin', Kitty. I'm goin'." With his posse urging him toward the door, Junior put on his jacket. He paused when he brushed past Jason's shoulder, looking up as though seeing him for the first time. "I could have taken him, you know." No, he couldn't. Not with the buzz on that clouded his judgment and coordination. Not against firepower like Pellegrino and his man were carrying. "You talk to your daddy recently? You're lucky you still can. I heard Nolan's been to see the doctor a couple of times this last month. You ought to call home sometime, instead of spending all your days building that cabin up in the woods. Or interferin' with my business."

A flash of concern that Jason's father, Nolan Hunt, was facing some kind of health scare he didn't know about blindsided Jason for a split second. He was equally steamed that Junior had chosen to make his screwed-up life *his* business, just because his pride was wounded. But Jason quickly shoved both emotions back where they belonged, relaxing the fist at his side. There was a reason Jason was out of the loop on family matters, a reason why he chose the wide-open space of the mountains over life in Jackson, Wyoming, where his parents lived. And no taunt from a drunken kid was going to make him forget that reason.

"Good night, Junior. Stay out of trouble."

After the door swung shut on Junior and Orin, the older gentleman in the three-piece suit stepped up to shake his hand. "Mr. Hunt. I'm Walter Eddington. Thank you for coming on such short notice. What'll you drink?"

Kitty scooped up her tray and headed back to the bar. "I'll get a fresh pot of coffee brewed for you, Jase, and bring you a cup."

He nodded his thanks and followed Marty and Eddington to join the blond man who'd left the fight to make a call at a large, stained table at the far side of the bar. He hung back when Dante Pellegrino and his sidekick flanked him, refusing to come any closer until they gave him the space he needed. Pellegrino smoothed his thumb and forefinger over the curves of his mustache, sending Jason a very clear message that he was used to calling the shots around his employer. But with Jason not budging, Walter Eddington muttered a choice word and ordered Pellegrino to take a seat. Before obliging his employer, he shifted his gaze to his hireling and nodded toward the bar's front door. "Metz. Check outside to make sure Cordes and his boys drive away and don't come back. I don't want any surprises."

"Yes, sir." As the younger man buttoned his suit jacket and jogged toward the door, the ladies' room door opened in the back and the drama of the evening took a turn into Circus Land.

Two women who looked as out of place in this beer-scented joint as daisies in a patch of weeds came out of the ladies' room. A twenty-something blonde in a shiny silver dress wheeled out a duffel-shaped overnight bag, while an older, equally dolled-up version of sophisticated beauty murmured something dismissive into the cell phone at her ear. The older woman met Jason's assessing gaze before ending her call. While Marty pulled out a chair for the young woman, the mature blonde sat next to Eddington at the head of the table. "I'm assuming it's safe to bring the money back out now that Mr. Cordes and his unpleasant friends are gone?" She squeezed his hand. The proprietary gesture and white gold band of diamonds on her hand told Jason they were husband and wife. "Are you certain they have nothing to do with Samantha?"

"I'm not certain of anything anymore." Eddington pulled her hand to his lips to kiss it. She reached over to brush a strand of silver hair off his forehead with a lacquered fingernail. The tender gesture drew attention to the older man's weary expression. His skin had been ruddy with emotion during that standoff with Cordes, but now his face had a gray quality to it, as if the toughness he'd summoned for that confrontation at the bar had faded away. "Mr. Hunt, this is my wife, Joyce. My younger daughter, Taylor. And I don't believe you met Kyle Grazer. He works for me at the Midas Hotel Group. He was supposed to become my future son-in-law tonight."

"Supposed to?" Grazer paused in the middle of pulling out a chair beside the younger woman. "Nothing has changed in my plans for Samantha. They've only been delayed." He picked up the heavily packed duffel bag and dropped it into the middle of the table, rattling every glass and earning a glare from the older man. "This isn't even what they asked for. Screw your principles. If we do what they tell you, we'll get her back. Otherwise—"

"Kyle." Joyce Eddington shot him a look that forced the young man into his seat. Clearly, the woman was very protective of her husband. But the outburst triggered a gasp and a sniffle from the young woman. Joyce tutted a reprimand behind her teeth, but put an arm around her daughter's shoulders. Jason suspected that one reason for the trip to the bathroom had been for Taylor Eddington to apply a fresh coat of makeup to mask the puffiness around her red-rimmed eyes. "Taylor, dear, I need you to be stronger than this. Kyle, we need your handkerchief."

When he hesitated, Marty pulled a blue bandanna from the pocket of his jeans and held it out to the petite blonde, sliding into the empty chair across from her. The young woman slid a quick glance up to Grazer's glaring expression before softly thanking Marty and dabbing at the moisture on her face. "I'm all right, Mother. I'm just worried about how Samantha is doing. She must be so frightened. And we're still sitting here, talking about what we should do when she might already be—"

Joyce squeezed her hand, shaking her head to keep her daughter from finishing that sentence.

Before anyone else snapped or glared or cried, Jason reached over the table to unzip the bag. He didn't have to open it very far to see the bundles of cash packed inside. Ransom. A far cry from a cache of high-tech weaponry and intelligence info, but the bargaining chip was the same—a woman's life.

His blood scalded like acid in his veins at the vivid memories he couldn't escape. He wasn't sure he could do this again. Marty thought they were going to make some easy money. He had no idea what he'd signed them up for. How much it could cost them if they failed.

But once a Marine, always a Marine. Jason was hardwired to be mission-oriented, and a shot at redemption was as tempting as it was unsettling. He closed the bag and pulled out a chair, swinging it around to straddle it beside Walter Eddington. "Who's been taken?"

"Straight to the point. I like that. I'm a military man myself. Served a stint in the Army back in Vietnam." For a brief moment, Walter Eddington looked truly old. But with a deep breath that expanded his barrel chest, he pulled out his phone and slid it across the table in front of Jason. "This was texted to me at midnight. My older daughter, Samantha."

Eddington turned away, unable to watch the screen. He pulled a silver chain from his jacket pocket, running his thumb over every link as if he was counting rosary beads. That wasn't a good sign. Jason's jaw tightened as he took the phone and played the video message.

Hands that belonged to unseen men plucked a black hood off a woman's head. She put her bound wrists up to her face and squinted against the sudden brightness of the lights shining on her, lights that also obscured her captors and their surroundings. Long ash-blond waves tumbled down one side of her neck while straighter strands still caught beneath hairpins floated upward with static electricity. When the gloved hands pulled her arms away from her face, she winced, but didn't cry out.

An off-camera voice muttered something unintelligible and she blinked open big green eyes. She ran her tongue across her full bottom lip and cleared her throat, as if she was thirsty and struggling to speak. "I can't even see the camera without my glasses, much less read that scrawl of yours."

"Give 'em to her," the muffled voice ordered.

She glanced blindly about until the gloved hands reappeared and thrust a pair of tortoiseshell-framed glasses onto her face. As Samantha Eddington blinked the world into focus, she whispered a soft "Thank you."

Jason fought the urge to bolt. This was Kilkut all over again. The hair and eye color might be different, but with those glasses, she looked too much like... The memory of a bullet hole through the shattered lens of a woman's glasses superimposed itself over Samantha Eddington's face. He curled his fingers into a fist, fighting off the past and focusing squarely on the present reality of those big green eyes.

"Say it." The harsh voice wasn't muffled now.

Samantha nudged her glasses into place and looked into the camera. "Dad? Um, I got myself into some trouble here. Never should have left that stupid party. I'm so sorry. Is Brandon okay? He tried to help. I know you're thinking about Mom right now. I felt like I needed to get away before I exploded, but I never thought any of this—"

"Cut the sentimental crap and read it."

"Will you take me to use the outhouse if I do? My bladder's about to bust."

Her answer was the distinctive sound of a bullet sliding into the firing chamber of an automatic handgun. "Read it."

Her green eyes widened and locked on to someone off camera beside her, no doubt holding a gun on her. Samantha Eddington was pale, scared, dressed in some nonsense fancy dress that curved over her generous breasts and left her visibly shivering. Or maybe that was fear. But other than the edge of a bandage peeking out beneath the flowery strap over her left shoulder, at least she didn't appear to be injured.

She turned her focus to something at the right of the camera and started reading. "We—these men, of course, not me—want five million dollars. Wow. That's a million dollars apiece. You must think—"

"Stop ad-libbing." The barrel of the Sig Sauer pointed at Samantha entered the camera shot, inching closer to her caramel-blond hair. "Word for word."

Although this was hard to watch, Jason was learning more about the situation in the few seconds he watched the nearsighted socialite on camera than he'd learned in the previous few minutes with the rest of her family and employees. At least five men, armed with pricey hardware, were holding her someplace that had an outhouse. So not in town, and not anyplace where a military-grade weapon like that would be noticed. There were snowflakes dotting the black camouflage material on the arm holding that weapon. Snow meant they were at a higher elevation. Samantha Eddington was smart—maybe a little too clever for her own good if her kidnappers caught on to all the clues she was dropping and punished her for it.

With a jerky nod, she lowered her gaze to the script. "If you don't pay us the money, you'll lose your daughter…" She hesitated, twisting her lips into a frown, blinking back tears before reading on. "…just like you lost your wife. I'm sorry, Dad. I know how hard this is for you. If anything happens to me, promise me you won't blame—"

"Read it!" The gun ground against her temple and she froze.

Tilting her head away from the gun, she continued. "We'll call tomorrow morning at eight with an account number where you will deposit the money. Once the deposit has cleared and we're out of the country, we'll call again and give you Samantha's location. If the money isn't there by noon, all you will find is her body." A delicate muscle rippled down her throat as she swallowed again. "Unless…the scavengers find her first." She shook off the terror that threat must engender and read on. "No cops. No FBI. Don't send your fancy security force after us. It's time to pay up. Five million for your daughter's life." Her green eyes darted toward the camera. "I tried to fight them, Dad. But my toes are freezing up here. Remember when you tried to teach me how to hunt? I wish I had that gun now—"

"Shut her up."

The gloved hands whisked the glasses off her face. "Please, don't. I read what you wrote. You don't understand what my father's been through. He won't pay—"

"He damn well better."

She was struggling with her captors now. And losing. The men pushed her down to the floor and the camera followed.

"Stop! Please… No!"

"We'll kill her if you don't cooperate, Eddington," an off-screen voice promised.

Another pair of hands pushed her loose hair off her face, exposing her long, creamy neck to the syringe they held. She grimaced when the needle pricked her skin. Her words were already slurring as she looked toward the camera. "I love you, Dad."

The screen went black before a cue icon beckoned Jason to replay the disturbing images. But he'd already memorized any useful intel he could get off the video. His blood simmered as experiences from the past were already painting a dark outcome for Samantha Eddington's future. He'd put his fist through the table if he watched it again. If he couldn't block these emotions, he'd be no use to anybody. And clearly, Samantha desperately needed somebody's help. His kind of help.

But Jason wasn't sure he was mentally fit to handle this kind of dark ops rescue mission anymore. He handed the phone back to Samantha's father. "You got five million dollars?"

"I do."

"Pay the ransom." He rose from his chair, giving the best advice he could, even as he tried to save his sanity and make an exit.

"I won't give in to their threats." Eddington was sentencing his daughter to death on some kind of principle? The older man stood to block Jason's path to the door. "You may not know who I am, Captain Hunt, but this isn't the first time I've gone through this. I paid a million dollars to Richard Cordes and his militia for my wife Michelle twenty-two years ago. The kidnappers killed her, anyway."

Twenty-two years ago, Jason had been a middle-schooler, discovering girls weren't icky, counting the days until his father returned from his latest deployment and not paying attention to the news. But even now, he had a glimmer of a memory about the dead woman who'd been found in a gully outside Cordes's militia compound. He glanced over to the table where Richard Jr. had been playing cards. "You came here to accuse Junior of taking your daughter?"

"Yes. He and I were both there the day his father was executed for Michelle's murder. He said things... I know he blames me for his father's death. He thinks I cheated his family when I bought the militia's land to build a ski resort. Of course, they didn't own it. They were squatters who'd taken over government land. I had a legal deed and I paid a fair price for every acre. But I'm sure that's what his father preached to him his entire life. I didn't want to argue with him. I just wanted—"

"Samantha back." Joyce rose beside her husband as his shoulders sagged. She took over the conversation when Walter couldn't immediately continue. She dragged the duffel bag across the table. "I told Walter we should come prepared to make a deal. He scraped together over a hundred grand in cash. But Mr. Cordes was insulted by the offer. Of course, he was also drunk and hitting on my daughter."

"Mother." Taylor Eddington seemed embarrassed to be any part of this conversation.

Kyle Grazer, however, didn't seem to have any problem making himself heard. He pounded the table with his fist. "Pay the damn ransom, Walter! All of it. Your stubbornness is going to get her killed."

The accusation galvanized the older man. His cheeks flushed with anger as he pushed his wife aside and met the younger man nose to nose. "You have no say in this. If you had stayed by Samantha's side tonight—"

"I'm the one who tried to stop her from leaving."

Taylor burst into tears and dashed off to the bathroom while Joyce Eddington urged the two men to behave like gentlemen and Pellegrino inserted his shoulder between them and forced Grazer back a step. The younger man tipped his chin up to the mustachioed bodyguard and swore. But, as Jason suspected he would, Grazer backed off.

Pellegrino's dark eyes never left Grazer's as he put the microphone on his wrist up to his lips and called his man back inside. "Metz? If the coast is clear, I need you in here to walk Mr. Grazer out to the limo."

"Save your damn escort," Grazer whined. "You can afford to lose five million, Walter. Can you afford to lose anyone else you love? If anything happens to Samantha, it's on your head." He pulled out his cell phone and stalked toward the bar's swinging door, exchanging a sour glance with Brandon Metz on the way out as the younger bodyguard came in.

Metz shrugged in confusion, but joined them at the table when Pellegrino waved him over. "Grazer can walk it off." He reached for the duffel bag of cash. "I need you to secure this."

"Yes, sir."

But Eddington was taking charge again. He pulled the duffel bag from Pellegrino's hands and shoved it into Jason's chest. "Mr. Flynn says you're the best. Consider this a down payment. I'll give *you* the five million if you bring Samantha home alive."

Pellegrino immediately intervened, taking the bag back into his custody. "Whoa, Walter. I said my men and I would go after Samantha. This guy will be our guide. You can't pay some stranger to rescue her."

"The message said specifically not to send you. No cops, no FBI."

Mrs. Eddington wasn't about to be left out of the argument. "I think Kyle is right. We should pay the ransom. Make sure Samantha is safe. Then worry about bringing these men to justice."

Walter raised his voice. "I want her home before the next phone call. Before it's too late."

Jason shot a look across the table, catching the wry apology on Marty Flynn's face. Damn Marty for getting him involved with this. But he couldn't walk away. He couldn't live with another Elaine Burkhart on his conscience.

"I'll do it."

His nostrils flared with a deep breath as he summoned the years of training in both the military and search and rescue that lived inside him. Those skills triggered the muscle memory and do-or-die mind-set that turned him into a man he didn't want to be anymore. But he had to become that man to do this job, to salvage his conscience, to save an heiress with pretty green eyes so he'd be able to sleep at night. "I need to know everything about your daughter's abduction, and an explanation for those clues she was feeding us on that video." Jason felt a clock ticking now. Whatever needed to be done would have to happen within the next few hours, before the 8:00 a.m. deadline. "Did you take Samantha hunting? Stay at a cabin with an outhouse?"

"She didn't have the right shoes on that trip." With Jason's urging, Eddington processed the information from the video. "When she was twelve, I took her up past Marion Lake and showed her how to use a gun. She didn't want to aim at any of the birds we were after, but she'd shoot at a paper target. She liked the mechanics

of the weapon. My girl always did like to tinker with
gadgets and fix things. Sammie spent more time taking her rifle apart and cleaning it than she did with any
actual hunting. I'd rented a cabin for the weekend. She
was tucked in and asleep by the fire before I realized
she'd worn her tennis shoes instead of the boots I'd got
her. Her feet were soaked and her toes like ice before I
got her warmed up."

"Where was that cabin?"

"On the trail going up to Teton Canyon." Walter
shook his head. "That place was torn down six years
ago. They can't be holding her there."

"But if she's familiar with that area, that could be the
connection she was making." The national park alone
covered 485 square miles. It was imperative that they
narrow down the search area if there was any chance of
rescuing Samantha before the kidnappers called again.
"There are supply cabins and a handful of rental properties all along that trail. The kidnappers could be holed
up in any one of those."

"At the time that video was made," Pellegrino
pointed out. "They could have moved on."

And she could already be dead. A plan was forming in his head, but Jason needed to get up to speed as
quickly as possible. He wasn't going to wait until it was
too late to go after Samantha Eddington. Even if this
mission had been forced upon him, he wasn't going to
have another hostage rescue gone to hell because somebody else kept him from doing his job. "How did they
get their hands on her?"

"That's on me." Brandon Metz glanced at the door
before answering. "I was waiting for Grazer to come
clean. But since he weaseled out… The two of them had
a blowup, and she decided to leave instead of going back

to the party." He exhaled a rueful sigh. "I'm pretty sure there's not going to be an engagement."

"That son of a bitch had the nerve to sit here at this table—"

"Walter." Joyce Eddington interrupted her husband before he sprang from his chair. "We don't know what happened yet. We'll straighten things out with Kyle. We might need his help with Samantha."

The long-limbed bodyguard gave a reluctant nod. "Grazer was the last person to see her. He said she lost her temper, was behaving irrationally. He called the security team for help."

Pellegrino confirmed as much. "I'm the one who let him out of the walk-in freezer where she'd locked him up."

The woman had fire. She'd have to in order to survive this bunch. She was resourceful, too, if she could end an argument with the other guy locked up. And even with a gun to her head, there'd been nothing random about the intel she'd fed them on that video.

But any awareness of those haunting eyes or admiration for his target's intelligence would be distractions that could derail this mission. "Get back to the abduction."

Metz continued. "Men were waiting for us in the parking lot."

"They ambushed you?" With something as spontaneous as an argument to drive her out of the lodge, away from witnesses, the abduction indicated inside knowledge of Samantha and the people around her, or someone monitoring her movements. Like a fiancé. Or a family member. Or a bodyguard.

"The rain masked their approach. Two men pulled me out of the car. I put up a fight, but they knocked me out, removed my weapon. I grabbed my spare sidearm out of the glove compartment as soon as I could get to my feet, but they fired on me. The shots came from a black van. I managed to get off a couple of shots before they turned west onto Highway 22. I called it in to Pellegrino and went after them."

"Heading into the Bridger-Teton National Forest." Jason knew the area well. But that was still a lot of miles to cover in a search for the missing woman. "You get a plate number?"

"A partial." Metz gingerly tapped the swelling at his temple. "My vision was a little out of focus."

Pellegrino dismissed his employee. "Go outside and keep an eye on Grazer. He's a loose cannon. I don't trust the guy."

"Sir, I want to be part of the team that goes after her," Metz argued. "She was taken on my watch."

"Outside. Now."

Metz's mouth opened as if he wanted to respond to that directive. But he wisely snapped it shut and headed for the exit. "Yes, sir."

Pellegrino watched his man leave before taking over the briefing. "You can't blame him. These guys are pros. Samantha's cell signal went dead around the time she was taken. The kidnappers used a burner phone we can't trace."

"You thinking of hiking up to the high country tonight, Jase?" Marty finally added his voice to the conversation. "I can't fly the chopper and do a visual search until sunrise. That's still a lot of ground to cover before that eight o'clock call."

Pellegrino paced to Jason's end of the table. "Maybe this will help. As a security measure, Walter had himself and his family chipped with tracking devices." He pulled up an image on his phone and showed it to Jason. "We tracked Samantha's to a location at a gas station near the Snake River. Discovered the abandoned black van with the tracking chip still inside it." Jason gritted his teeth against the picture of a plastic bag holding a tiny microchip that still had bits of blood and tissue clinging to it. That must account for the bandage he'd seen on Samantha's shoulder in the video. "A local there said a small group of men with a load of cargo switched vehicles to an all-terrain SUV and four Arctic Cats on a trailer. He didn't get a license plate."

Snowmobiles. Useless in the mud or on paved roads. That many men and equipment like that left tracks. Tracks and high country just tipped the search into Jason's favor. If the tip was legit. "Did this local actually see Samantha? Could be a misdirect to throw off any rescue effort."

Pellegrino pocketed his phone. "He saw crates, rifles, gas cans...and a lumpy, rolled-up rug. Everything else was state of the art. I'm guessing that rug was Samantha."

Jason nodded. Chances were, he was going to come away from this unsanctioned mission with blood on his hands. But saving Samantha Eddington might go a long way toward atoning for the lives he hadn't saved in Kilkut. For Elaine Burkhart's life.

"I'm not a cop," Jason reminded them. He wouldn't be bringing these men in for justice. "If I have to break a few rules to extract your daughter—"

"I have friends in the county sheriff's department," Eddington assured him. "And the lieutenant governor is an old friend from school. If there's any trouble, I'll make sure it goes away."

Jason wasn't sure how much faith he'd put in any

of these people. But his decision had been made. He pulled his knit cap over his head. Then he opened the duffel bag and tossed a stack of bills across the table to Marty. "Gas up the chopper. I'll call in once I've secured a rendezvous point. You're flying at first light."

Marty turned his cap around, tugging the bill into place, a sign he meant business. "I'll be ready."

As Marty jogged to the exit, Eddington stood to hand the duffel bag to Jason. "Take it."

"Money isn't what I need. Donate it to a veterans' charity and survivors' scholarship fund."

"Done." Walter extended a hand. After a moment, Jason reached out to take it. He was surprised to feel the older man transfer the chain and locket he'd been holding into the palm of his hand. "So she'll trust you. Bring my daughter home."

With a sharp nod, Jason pocketed the necklace and strode out the door, heading to his gray 4x4 pickup. The rain limited his scan for activity up and down the street. He wasn't surprised to see that Junior and his crew had driven off in their trucks and SUVs. He *was* surprised that there was no sign of Metz or Grazer. Had they ducked behind the tinted windows of the Eddington limo to avoid the elements? For two men so interested in Samantha Eddington's well-being—or maybe just their standing with the family—they hadn't waited around to find out if he'd agreed to Eddington's rescue request. Unless one or both men had gone off on some fool's errand to track down Samantha himself. Jason paused with a hand on the scratched-up paint of the truck's door handle. A wildcard like a guilt-ridden fiancé or eager-to-please bodyguard could be problematic to the speed and focus of his mission tonight.

And his focus was already compromised. He might

be dealing with snow instead of sand, freezing nights versus mind-cooking heat—but the resolve to complete this mission was the same. He'd failed Elaine.

He squeezed his eyes shut as if that could blank the memory of the embedded reporter his unit had been sent to rescue. He and Elaine had spent a lot of late nights together, talking about work at first, then home and hopes and how crazy it was that they should find each other and fall in love over in the Heat Locker. Yeah, she'd talked about her affair with her bureau chief back in Stuttgart, and how she ought to feel guilty for getting close to one of the jarheads in the unit she was covering. But for those few weeks they'd been together, those precious nights they'd shared, the world and the war hadn't mattered. If she hadn't been so dedicated to putting her job first, she wouldn't have been taken. If he hadn't waited for orders to come through before going after her…

"Mr. Hunt? Hold up." Jason shook off the painful memories, turning to see Dante Pellegrino jog across the street. "Metz isn't the only one who wants to help make this rescue happen. It's my job to protect this family. I started this security firm on my own dime. The reputation of my company is at stake here. It'll put me out of business if we lose Eddington's daughter, and I can't afford that." If Pellegrino was as good as he claimed, Samantha Eddington wouldn't have been kidnapped in the first place. "What do you need from me and my crew?"

"Nothing." Jason wasn't about to trust anyone's chain of command but his own. He didn't care about Pellegrino's reputation or the financial solvency of his business. All he cared about was a frightened woman with glasses, and putting old nightmares to rest. "The fewer people I'm responsible for, the faster I can move."

"You don't want any backup? Weapons? Night-vision goggles? A newer truck to tackle those roads?"

Jason reached into the bed of his truck and picked up one of the logs he stored there to add weight and give the back axle more traction. "This baby's gotten me through plenty of bad weather and rough terrain."

Pellegrino thumbed over his shoulder toward the bar, indicating the patrons inside. "You can talk miracle rescues all you want in front of those civilians. But I know the risk you're taking. You're going up against dangerous men who don't care who gets hurt." Jason watched the drops of rain beading on that ridiculous mustache. "There were at least five men involved in Brandon's attack and the kidnapping. Probably more. The second they hear your approach, you'll be a dead man."

Jason tossed the log into the back of the truck and opened the truck door. "They won't hear me."

"No one expects you to go up against those kinds of odds alone. Let us be part of your team. My men are trained to deal with mercenaries like this."

Jason climbed up behind the wheel. "They're not trained to deal with that mountain. It'll be the only ally I need."

Chapter Four

"Mama?"

Samantha's shivering and her empty belly filled her sleep with familiar dreams. The sedative working its way through her system morphed those dreams into nightmares.

"Mama, where are you?" She was a little girl again, searching through every room of the house for her mother, smelling her sweet perfume, wondering why she wasn't coming upstairs to read her a story and tuck her in. All the rooms were dark, every door locked. She heard thumps and footfalls and angry growls from shadowy corners, but she couldn't see the monsters lurking there. She only knew the monsters were real, lying in wait for a little girl who was all alone.

The house was so cold. Her long hair hardened into shards of ice that poked her neck and shoulders. Her glasses fogged over, and she could barely see. She rattled every doorknob, pounded on wood that wouldn't budge. She fled from one closed room to another, scratching her way through locks and doors until her hands bled. She threw herself against every barrier, breaking through only to find more darkness. She felt the cold, fetid breath of the monsters as they stirred from the shadows and pursued her.

"Stay away," she murmured.

She always slept deeply, securely, when her mother sat on the bed beside her, reading until Samantha's eyes grew heavy and her head tumbled onto her pillow. But tonight, she was running, searching, panicked, bleeding. "Mama?"

She couldn't sleep. She wanted a story. She wanted to melt into the warmth and softness of her mother's body next to hers. She wanted to hear that gently articulate voice in her ears, filling up her head with magic and science, imaginary worlds and characters whose ideas and adventures Samantha wanted to be part of one day.

But she couldn't find her mother. Her tears had frozen on her cheeks. Her pajamas itched against her skin, and every desperate step she took hurt. She was trapped in the darkness. Trapped with monsters, alone and afraid. A cold hand closed around her arm, but she shook it off. Ran. "I can't find you, Mama. Help me."

And then she found a door with light blazing outward from every crack around it. Someone was awake. Someone was alive. She wasn't alone.

"Mama!" Samantha ran, raw nerves stabbing her frozen feet with every step. But hands reached for her from the shadows. Fingers, gnarled like tree limbs, crawled against her skin and tangled in her broken hair. Large hands, strong and unforgiving, closed around her arms and dragged her back into the darkness. "No!"

She fought against the hands. Shoved. Twisted.

The darkness exploded with a loud crash and Samantha screamed. Only the sound stopped up her ears and rang against her skull. She fought to get to the light. Fought to get to her mother. To warmth. To safety.

The shadows closed in all around her, suffocated her.

The terrible hands pulled her down, down, snatching at her, grasping her, burying her in the darkness.

"Mama!" she cried out, the timbre of her voice sounding wrong. Older. Deeper. Hoarser.

"Quiet." Not a sound of comfort. Something deeper. More dangerous. A warning.

Too many hands, reaching, grabbing, wanting a piece of a little girl who'd already lost the most precious thing in her life.

False hands, pretending to love her, but offering pain and betrayal, using her.

Rough hands, lifting her off her feet, pushing her inside a van, stealing her ability to see. Hands that didn't care if she was hurt or cold or tired or afraid. Too many hands.

Samantha squirmed and twisted and kicked against the nightmare.

The monster cursed.

"Damn it, woman. I'm not hurting you."

She fought through the dark fog of her brain. She fought for her mama, fought for her freedom. Fought against her kidnappers.

She was trapped, pinned beneath the heavy weight of all that she had lost, of everything she feared, everything that controlled her. Samantha battled the hands in her dream, wrestling with monsters as she came awake, screaming.

Her eyes opened to the reality of two granite-colored eyes inches above her face, eyes that seemed to capture the haze of moonlight reflecting off the snow outside and glow in the dusty air of the cabin. Such mysterious, masculine eyes.

A man was on top of her. A very large man, with shoulders that filled up the limits of her vision, and hips that pinned her to the floor in the most intimate of positions. A long, muscular thigh was wedged between hers, and something cold and hard poked against her hip. Her arms were splayed over her head on the twisted rag rug where she must have struggled with him. He needed only one hand to pin her cinched-up wrists in place. The other hand had a hard grip on her mouth, cheeks and jaw, absorbing every sound she made. He used the rest of his body to keep her still. It was an effective tool. His chest was as solid and unforgiving as the thick wood planks of the cabin floor.

Her nostrils flared with shock, but her lungs refused to expand. What was happening? Was she still dreaming? Was this a side effect of the drug-induced sleep she'd slipped in and out of for the past several hours?

One of the monsters from her nightmare had caught her.

Samantha squeezed her eyes shut, then blinked them open again. He was still there. This monster was real, pinning her to the floor, his warm breath brushing across her cheek. Clarity rushed in along with fear and the awareness of just how completely vulnerable she was, crushed beneath the weight of the big man's body. His muscular thigh pressed with humiliating familiarity against the most feminine part of her, igniting sensations she didn't want to feel.

Don't hurt me. Please don't hurt me. She tried to speak, but her mouth and jaw were anchored shut by his hard, leather-gloved hand.

Was this some new torture her kidnappers were playing on her? Was rape now on the list of assaults that included threats, guns and drugs?

Only, her kidnappers didn't have faces. They all wore masks. And this man very definitely had a face. Not a handsome one. But taut, compelling, dangerous. Even the dusting of a dark brown beard across his jaw and neck didn't soften the rugged contours of the facade that could have been carved from the same granite that colored his eyes.

A grizzly bear of a man.

"You're awake. No more kicking. And do not scream again," he warned. Her kidnappers didn't have hushed, deep-pitched voices that vibrated from their chests into hers, either.

Samantha nodded her compliance, inhaling a shallow breath as he removed his hand and propped it on the braided rug beside her head. When he released her arms, she pulled her hands beneath her chin, trying to wedge some space between her body and his. The fact that his hips and chest still pressed into hers indicated that he didn't entirely trust her. *The feeling is mutual, buddy.*

"Samantha Eddington?"

She nodded again.

"You hurt? Concussion? Broken bones? Internal injuries?"

She tapped her fingers against the sandpapery stubble of beard that darkened his chin, the only part of him she could reach in this position. "Can't breathe."

He did a push-up, shifting his weight off her, and she sucked in a much-needed breath of air, filling her nose with the scents of pine and cold coming off his clothes and skin. "Scrapes and bruises as far as I can tell." Her voice came out in a crackly rasp. "A little dizzy from the sedatives. Sore throat."

In a surprisingly graceful movement for such a large man, he grasped the hand she'd touched him with and helped her sit up as he shoved aside a limp body that lay on the rug beside her.

A body?

The moment he released her, Samantha scooted away on her bottom, retreating until her back hit the log-and-plaster wall. Whether she was fleeing him or the lump of man at her feet, though, she wasn't sure. She dragged her knees up to her chest, making sure her bare toes didn't touch the lifeless man.

"Who are you? Is he dead? Did you kill him? Did you kill the other guard? There were two of them." But she couldn't hear either one of them now. A chill of absolute panic shivered across her skin, despite the lightweight coat that covered her arms. Had she just switched one kind of terror for something new? Where had this mountain man come from, and what did he want with her? "Are you going to kill *me*?"

"No," he answered, tucking a gag into the limp man's mouth and dragging him into the shadows beyond her line of sight.

The kidnappers must not be dead. There'd be no reason to muzzle a dead man. A knocker-outer was better than waking up to a murderer lying on top of her. Good.

Samantha shook her head, clearing her wandering thoughts. There was nothing good about her situation. She'd been bound and drugged and held hostage in the rickety old cabin in the wilderness somewhere up above Teton Canyon. She was freezing, hungry. And now a new threat had entered the cabin and crushed her beneath every inch of his hard, muscular body.

Why was it so dark in here? The men who'd stayed with her this time had been playing poker on the chipped enamel kitchen table, with a battery-powered lantern illuminating their cards. There was no lantern now, only the glow of the small heating stove that barely reached her corner, and the moonlight streaming in through the window. Samantha hugged her bound arms around her legs, unable to decide which was more frightening— having the big scary man in her face where she could see him, or knowing he was lurking somewhere in the darkness around her. "What do you want from me?" Her throat was raw from too much screaming and try- ing to reason with unreasonable men. She coughed, swallowed against the irritated rasp of her throat and spoke again. "Who are you?"

His deep voice was an ominous growl from the blur of shadows. "I'm not one of them."

"And I'm just supposed to believe that?" Fear and confusion still rattled around her brain. "They leave two men with me all the time, but they've changed shifts three times, so there are at least six of them. These two aren't the ones who took me from the lodge, so that makes a minimum of seven. I can tell because their body shapes and voices are different. There's the bully with the gun and the slimy one with all the lewd comments who thinks he's funny and the little guy who compensates by being extra physical." Samantha gently prodded the bruises on her knees. When her numb feet hadn't been able to keep up with the brisk walk from the SUV to the cabin's front door, he'd dragged her up the porch steps. "They go on patrols outside. They talk about sleeping in the truck because it's warmer. And there's some guy named Buck they keep saying has called, or they need to call, or he's coming here, or..." Lord, she was rattling on like a crazy woman. She pressed her parched lips together to stop the flow of words long enough to make her point. "Are you Buck? Are you the man they answer to?"

She heard a groan from the darkness and soft ratcheting noises she could now identify as the sound of zip ties binding someone into place. She looked at the raw skin beneath the plastic tying her wrists together, but quickly glanced up when the man reemerged from the shadows. A flitting image from her nightmare dissipated with the click of a flashlight. The small beam of light brought hope to her world as he knelt beside her. He unzipped a pocket in his dark gray cargo pants and pulled out a silver chain. "I don't know who Buck is. I don't know who either of these two men are, or the guy in the SUV out front. I'm Captain Jason Hunt. United States Marines. I'm one of the good guys."

Leave it to her father to hire the Marines to come after her. She squinted the coffee-colored hair hanging over his collar into focus. "You don't look like a Marine."

His grim expression turned grimmer. "*Former* Marine. I work search and rescue now."

"Oh." Recognizing the engraved locket he dangled from the end of the chain, Samantha snatched the necklace from his hand. "This was my mother's. Where did you get it?"

"A token from your father. He sent me to find you and bring you home. Said you'd understand why he wasn't paying to get you back."

She ran her thumb over the initials *ME* and *WE* etched into the sterling silver, then opened the latch to study the faded images of her parents, taking comfort in the item that had been so precious to her mother, and therefore to Samantha and her father. Remembrance and relief surged through her system with such force that tears stung her eyes. "I do."

"I need you to do exactly as I say. And no crying.

You'll dehydrate." What the man lacked in reassuring comfort, he made up for in concise practicality. He handed her a water bottle from the backpack looped over his shoulders. "Drink."

After swiping at the tears trailing down her cheeks, she opened the bottle and took several long swallows. Feeling slightly better after having addressed that basic need, Samantha dredged up a smile of gratitude for her rescuer. But he was no longer there to see it. Captain Jason Hunt knew her father. Jason Hunt was here to get her out of this nightmare. Jason Hunt had found her in a remote cabin on the western edge of the Tetons and single-handedly subdued two of her kidnappers. Possibly three, if the man who'd talked about sleeping in the truck was still out there. And now she was alone with him.

Was the man with ghostly gray eyes supposed to make her feel safe? She listened to him prowl about the cabin, cracking open the front door to check outside, rifling through the kidnappers' supplies, disabling what she assumed were weapons and opening the back window to a rush of frigid air to toss small boxes—ammunition perhaps?—into the snow. Her smile faded, and she rubbed at the familiar itch on her torso. Since she was clearly no great judge of whom she should trust, Samantha would be smart to adopt the same wary urgency radiating off her self-proclaimed savior. "Do you work for Mr. Pellegrino? He's former military, too."

"I met him."

Was that a yes or a no? Did that make him a bodyguard? Samantha took another drink. He certainly wasn't much of a conversationalist. Kyle had always been able to fill up the awkward silence of a room and put her at ease when her mouth couldn't keep up with all the thoughts pinging through her brain and she just shut down. Only now she realized Kyle had been nothing but talk—greedy, self-serving, tell-Samantha-whatever-she-needs-to-hear talk. Her heart pinched with the ache of losing the man she'd thought she loved. Or maybe that was her ego, as bruised and tender as the rest of her body from the discovery that she'd been a naive fool.

This man was nothing like Kyle. He was bigger. Rawer. Less about charm and more about efficiency. Was he a cop? FBI? A mercenary her father had hired? Some backwoods mountain man Dante Pellegrino had unearthed to find her? Bearing so little resemblance to her would-be fiancé should be a good thing, right? Maybe Jason Hunt had brought someone else with him who could make her feel a little surer about trusting him. "What's next? Are the rest of your men waiting outside?"

Instead of answering, he knelt in front of her again, holding out a real gift. "I took these off the guy by the door. Didn't look like his style."

"Thank you!" Samantha set down the water bottle to take her glasses from his hand. She hugged them to her chest for a brief, grateful moment before putting them on. "I've been so blind. At such a disadvantage. What…?"

Just as his face and the black knit cap he wore came into focus, he pulled a knife as big as her forearm from his belt. When she shied away from the vicious blade, he grabbed her wrists, pulling her toward him as he sliced through the plastic bindings. Her startled breath returned as slowly as the feeling seeping back into her extremities. "Flex your fingers and toes. Get the circulation going again. Put your shoes on and let's get out of here before the others get back."

"Um…" She picked up what remained of one of her patent-leather shoes. The short, overcompensation guy with a temper had broken off the heel and thrown it at her after she'd gouged a chunk of skin out of his leg during a failed attempt to run away when he'd taken her to use the outhouse behind the cabin. "I didn't exactly have time to pack a change of clothes."

Jason cursed at the shoe that had proved useless in the snow outside, even if it hadn't been snapped in two. "How much do you weigh? I'll carry you." He doused the flashlight and started adjusting his gear around his waist and back. He unhooked his pack and tossed her a pair of thick wool socks. "Put those on. If we can keep your feet dry, there's a chance you won't get frostbite before sunrise."

"There's no one else but you?" She suspected his lack of an answer was her answer. Just the two of them. She nodded her understanding, although she couldn't stop her mind from calculating the odds that were not in their favor. With her glasses giving her twenty/twenty vision again, her eyes quickly adjusted to the dusky cabin to get a clearer look at her surroundings. Yes, Jason Hunt certainly looked fit and capable. He seemed to be nothing but muscle and hard angles and a dangerous, coiled energy. And there was no mistaking the threat of the gun holstered around his thigh or the way he'd handled that hunting knife. But the threat from her kidnappers was very real. And they were outnumbered. "How far away is your vehicle?" No answer. "Skis? Dog sled?"

"Socks." He nodded to her icy toes. Again, no answer. Just a new command. "We need to walk about five miles to get to a buddy of mine with a helicopter. He'll fly us out of here. On your feet."

Five miles? No one was carrying her that far. Hadn't

she been manhandled enough over the past several hours? Besides, she was tired of feeling helpless. Done with feeling like she was a burden that had to be dealt with. Samantha pulled on the socks that came up to her knees and tried to get up, fighting off a wave of nausea as the remnants of the sedative in her system spun the room around her. When the vertigo passed, she gritted her teeth against the subsequent headache that throbbed against her skull and braced her hand against the rough log wall. "Can't we steal their truck?"

"It can't handle the terrain we've got to cover."

Clinging to the wall, Samantha pushed to her feet. No dizziness. Good. But she was far from ready to hike five miles across a mountain. "One of their snowmobiles? I saw four."

"Gone." Snap. Click. He'd lightened his pack by tucking several items into the pockets of his cargo pants and insulated jacket.

"They'll be back. All of them. They said they had another tape they needed me to record before sending it at eight in the morning. They complained about not having any cell service up here, so they must go somewhere else to send it to Dad. What time is it?" She moved away from the wall, testing her ability to walk. The warmth of the socks pierced the numbness of cold and inactivity, shooting tiny sparks through her feet. But the pain shocked the last of the fatigue out of her system. "They're not out patrolling the area?"

"Now that the storm has passed, it's a clear night. We'd hear the noise of the engines if they were close by." Something buzzed on Jason's wrist, and he pulled back his sleeve to turn off the alarm on his watch. "Time to go. Ready?"

One of the men lying near the door groaned. Although they'd been gagged and hog-tied, and Jason had taken their weapons, the kidnapper was stirring. *Stirring* couldn't be good for a successful getaway. Samantha's brain suddenly kicked into a higher gear. Why hadn't she thought of this sooner? She looped the chain around her neck and kissed the locket before stuffing it inside the neckline of her dress. Hurrying as quickly as the stiffness of her body allowed, she crossed to the metal storage cabinet across the room and pulled it open, blindly feeling around on the top shelf for the items she was far too familiar with. Her fingers closed around a small glass vial. "Are they waking up?"

"We won't be here to find out. What are you doing?"

"Buying us more time to get away." She pulled down a syringe packet and tore off the paper, measuring out a dose of the sedative the kidnappers had used on her. She injected Moaning Man, checking his pulse after he quieted. Breathing, but asleep. Then she opened a new packet and injected the second man. "Buying me enough time to do this."

She measured the size of her foot against both men, then sat down beside the one with the smaller boots and started untying them.

Jason's sigh was as impatient as the brisk wind outside the cabin. Still, he surprised her by kneeling beside her and picking up the other boot to loosen the laces. "If these are too big, they'll rub blisters. Then I'll definitely be carrying you."

"I think I'll be okay with these thick socks. A few minutes now will save us time later. You can move faster if you're not hauling me on your back, right?"

She held his gaze until he gave her a sharp nod.

"I so wish I had a pair of pants or long johns." She

pulled off the first boot and lifted the black camo canvas of the guy's pant leg. "You don't suppose—"

Jason grabbed her wrist and shoved the second boot into her hand, ending her search. "It's not that far, and the sun will be up in another hour. Move it, Princess."

Princess? Samantha bristled at the tossed-off nickname. Sure. The party dress and ridiculous heels? A $5 million bargaining chip? He probably had her pegged as one of the society princesses her father and stepmother so desperately wanted her to be. If only he knew.

But he didn't give her time to take offense or correct his impression of her. He pulled the black knit stocking masks off the unconscious men. "You recognize either of them?" he asked.

She spared a quick glance for the two men, a bald one with bruising around the tattoos on his throat and the other with blood matted in the hair at his temple. Strangers. Two men she'd never laid eyes on before who'd hurt her and promised more than once to kill her if she didn't cooperate. Samantha went back to securing the second boot. "No. Should I?"

"They've got fighting skills, sophisticated weaponry…" He picked up one of the syringes she'd discarded and tossed it into the darkness. "…access to drugs. Enough players involved to rotate shifts and carry out different assignments."

"Meaning?"

"Meaning these guys aren't amateurs. Your father said he doesn't care who's responsible as long as my mission is a success. But it would have been nice to know exactly what I was up against."

"Mission?" Samantha tied a second knot to keep the boot secure around her ankle. She looked at her abductors with fresh eyes. Matching black camo outfits. The arsenal of rifles and guns she'd seen. "Are they military?"

The whiny buzz of a distant engine pierced the night. Make that two engines. More than two. She recognized the sound. Snowmobiles. Her captors were returning.

She'd barely acknowledged the terror that suddenly immobilized her when Jason lifted her right off the floor, setting her on her feet beside him just inside the door as he opened it a little wider to peer into the milky darkness outside the cabin. "You *can* hear them," she whispered. Like mutant hornets swarming through the trees. Samantha pushed Jason toward the door. Well, *pushed* was a relative term. She pushed, and he didn't budge. But she was about to be trapped in this cabin. Again. "How far do you think—?"

Jason clamped his hand over her mouth again, tilting her face up to his. Right. That glare meant *shut up, Princess.*

Those mysterious eyes, framed by lines of sun and outdoor living, held hers a moment longer until she nodded. He released her and dropped down to check the fit of her boots, his big hands easily spanning, squeezing, adjusting. On the way back up, he tied the belt of her black-and-white coat, cinching it snugly around her waist. He towered above her for a moment, assessing either side of her face. Before she could question his perusal and what he found off-putting enough to make him grimace like that, he pulled a knit cap off the bald man and plopped it on top of her head, stretching it over pins and tangles until her ears were covered.

Then he turned to the opening and held up his fist. "This means stop. Talking, moving, whatever. I don't care how scared you are, listen to what I say and do what I tell you. Your life may depend on it." He unholstered his gun and gripped it in his right hand, reaching back with his left to pull her onto the porch behind him. The noise of the gunning engines seemed to bounce off every hard surface around her—the cabin door she pulled shut, the forest of trees surrounding the perimeter of the clearing, the cliff wall on the far side of the gravel road and the rocky outcropping just a few yards beyond the edge of the porch—making it impossible for her to tell how far away her abductors were, or even from which direction they were coming. "Walk where I walk. I've already made a couple of false trails in the snow to keep them busy and force them to split up. Move as quickly as you can. Don't say a word."

He stepped off the porch, expecting her to follow. Sinking up to her ankles in the trampled slush and fresh layer of snow, she was glad she'd thought to steal the pair of boots to protect her feet and at least give her a chance at staying warm. "Did my father really send you? Or am I walking off into the wilderness with a stranger, never to be seen again?"

Her head was down, watching each slippery step, when she bumped into his backpack.

Jason had stopped abruptly. He inhaled a deep breath before he pushed her into the shadows at the side of the cabin and hunched down to level his gaze with hers. "I have three rules. Do what I tell you. Don't get wet. And do what I tell you."

"That's only two. Is the fist thing the third rule—?"

He plastered his hand over her mouth again. "Noise carries in this cold air. Those men have friends who will kill us if they find us. They will find us if they hear you. Understand?"

That seemed clear enough. A cloud of his warm breath fogged her glasses, forcing her to tilt her eyes above the rims to see the warning stamped on his hard expression.

"I know you're not used to situations like this. But I am. Let me do my job. I will keep you safe. I won't let these men hurt you again." Was he trying to tell her she didn't need to be afraid with him around? That she needed to trust him? Maybe she'd be safe from the bad guys, but Jason Hunt's size and strength, his terse commands and grabby hands, not to mention the knife and the gun, still made her very nervous. "Keep up. Remember the rules. And I'll make sure you get home to Daddy."

That reassurance would have to do for now. Samantha nodded one more time before he released her. He peeked around the cabin, checking the man sleeping in the truck, evaluating the distance and arrival time of the approaching snowmobiles. This time, when he stepped out, he moved at a quicker pace, forcing Samantha into a jog to stay close behind him.

As the echoing drone of the snowmobiles closed in around them, Jason entered the tree line, moving with unerring speed through the obstacles of pines and terrain. Samantha plunged into the woods behind him—following Jason's broad back into the cold, moonlit night, leaving shelter, her kidnappers and the luxury of doubting this man behind.

Chapter Five

He was a mile and a half from redemption.

Jason climbed on top of the thick lodgepole pine that had been toppled by a forest fire years earlier. Now, the charred trunk gave moss and lichens a place to grow and provided shelter for the squirrel that scurried from beneath it and raced up a neighboring snag, or dead tree that was still standing upright. He watched the little critter leave its tiny tracks in the snow, and instinctively glanced over his shoulder to make sure Sam was still following in his footsteps about twenty yards behind him. He'd led her on a path close to the trunks where the snow wasn't as deep and was already disturbed by animals, drifts, and snow melting and dropping from higher up in the trees, making their boot prints harder to follow.

But he'd pushed the pace to reach the rendezvous point at Mule Deer Pass by 8:00 a.m., and she was getting tired, based on the puffs of breath clouding around her face in the cold air. A short break would do her good. Allowing himself a moment to rest as well, he tilted his face to the pink and gold rays of morning sun that pierced the canopy of dark green branches above him. The stars had long been swallowed up with the grayish haze of dawn. And though the sun had barely crested the tree line of the lower elevations off to the east, Jason could feel the promise of a new day coursing through him—knowing that he was close to completing this mission without a single casualty. He hadn't failed. He'd made a quick hike with a light pack up the crest trail toward Teton Canyon between the south and middle peaks, taking a shortcut to the line of supply shacks that fit the clues from Sam's video and the intel Dante Pellegrino and his man had given him.

The burn in his thigh and calf muscles and the dampness of the brisk morning breeze cooling the skin around his cheeks created a yin and yang of sensations inside him that made him feel alive. Useful. Living squarely in the present. He inhaled a cool, fresh breath that filled his lungs and eased the tightness of guilt and regret he normally carried with him. They weren't out of the woods yet, literally or figuratively, but redemption felt pretty damn good.

His long strides feeling lighter now, Jason stepped down and made a quick visual sweep through the trees in every direction. Not that he'd heard, seen or sensed anyone closing in on their trail.

So far, this op had gone pretty much according to plan. He'd spotted the man sleeping in the truck with the trailer hitch outside the second cabin. It had been easy to surprise him and subdue him with a choke hold before the guy even had a chance to cry out or alert his buddies. The two men inside had been arguing loudly enough over why they'd drawn the short straw and hadn't been able to go down into town with the others that Jason had scouted out the cabin and kicked in the front door before either of them had a chance to draw their weapons. Stooge One had gone down with a blow to the head while his buddy had required a few seconds of hand-to-hand combat before he'd succumbed to Jason's forearm cutting off the flow of oxygen to his brain.

Sam herself had been a little trickier to subdue. He'd needed her to wake up, so she wouldn't startle and alert anyone within hearing range of his presence. A gun butt to the temple or a choke hold around the neck had been out of the question, but she'd come out of her drugged-up sleep disoriented and violent. He had the bruise on his inner thigh, a little too close to the family jewels for his liking, from the kick that had connected before he realized that a friendly nudge awake wasn't going to work. He'd pinned her flailing limbs the best way he knew how without hurting her, and had wound up frightening her even more when she'd come to and found him lying on top of her. The frankly sexual position had achieved his goal of securing each limb so that she couldn't strike him again. But those few seconds of having a soft, curvy woman stretched out beneath him had done something to him, too.

His toe caught a rock and he nearly stumbled at the distracting memory of generous breasts and earth-mother hips plastered against his harder frame. Jason shook off the answering surge of base male awareness that heated his blood and made sure he was centered over his feet again. No matter how long he'd been without female companionship, no matter how long it had been since he'd even hit on a lady, Sam Eddington was a mission objective, not a uniquely attractive woman.

And until he delivered her safely into the arms of her father, he'd do well to remember that.

With a resolute breath, he checked his watch and the attached compass for both time and direction, confirming what the angle of the sun and the years he'd spent hiking these mountains had already told him.

Marty should already be en route to their destination, and within the hour, they'd be landing at the airstrip outside Jackson. The bad guys had taken the bait and split up to follow the false trails he'd left along the service road and down the mountain in the opposite direction. Both were easier paths than the steeper route he was taking south to the high-altitude clearing of Mule Deer Pass. Even if they did find the right trail, the snowmobiles would be the only vehicle that could handle the rough terrain. With all these trees, they wouldn't be able to go full throttle. Plus, there would be no way to mask their approach, giving Jason plenty of time to hide Sam and backtrack along the rocky incline to deal with them if he had to.

But if his luck held, he wouldn't have to deal with anyone but the woman behind him. He pulled his bottle of water and drank a couple of long swallows before attaching it back to his pack. "About three clicks away now, Princess."

The grunt behind him sounded a little different this time, more of a groan of irritation than the slightly winded sound of determination he'd been listening to for the past three miles. "I resent that, you know."

Jason turned to see Sam sit on the far side of the fallen tree trunk, pausing a moment to inhale a deep breath before swinging her leg over the top. Her checkered coat and frilly dress rode up past the edge of the skin-colored underwear that clung to her thighs, and he caught a glimpse of long, strong legs as she plopped into the snow on the other side. At least she was getting one rule right—she followed in his steps, plunging into the snow where it was deeper, and shuffling along a little faster where wind or the dense canopy of overhanging pine boughs had cleared the exposed rocks and hard-packed dirt. As for staying quiet…?

"My feet are doing okay, but I can hardly feel the skin on my legs anymore. Pink skin means they're getting chapped, right?" She tugged her clothes back into place and leaned back against the tree trunk. "I wore this dress for press photographers, not trekking through the mountains. What I wouldn't give for long pants. Or an electric blanket."

"The hike will be over soon," he assured her. "A click is only—"

"A thousand meters. A kilometer. I know. It's about the distance between each line or click on a rifle scope when you're sighting a target." That was an odd chunk of information to have stored away in that blond head of hers. But her father had said she knew her way around guns. "What I resent is the nickname. Princess. I find that offensive. I don't call you Mountain Man or Big Scary Dude, do I?" Was that how she saw him? He supposed the descriptors fit. And he hadn't exactly given her reason to see him any other way. "You don't even know me. It sounds derisive, like you don't respect me, or you don't respect people *like* me. Oh." Sam quieted, pulling out the water bottle he'd given her and taking a sip. Although he suspected the pause had more to do with catching her breath, Jason gave her a once-over to make sure he wasn't pushing her too hard and she could finish the hike. "I fit the stereotype, don't I?"

"Stereotype?" He caught her hands between his as she rubbed them together.

"Poor little rich girl? All dolled up and dumb enough to get herself kidnapped?" Jason tugged his gloves off with his teeth to feel the temperature of her skin. Her fingers had been pink the last time he'd checked how she was handling exposure to the elements. Now, even with massaging them between his palms, they were stiff and pale. "I have two college degrees. But I guess being book smart doesn't make me smart about people. You know who I was running away from last night? The man my father and stepmother handpicked for me to marry. Ooh. I hear it now. Having a *handpicked* boyfriend does make me sound a little like a princess." She winced as he pressed her fingers between his. Or maybe that was the face she made when she realized she was revealing more than she wanted. "I knew something wasn't right between us, but I didn't trust my gut. I found Kyle in the closet with my sister. And they weren't picking out clothes." She tugged her hands from his, and he glanced up to see her eyes widen behind her glasses. "Sorry. That's too much information, isn't it?"

That revelation explained a lot about Kyle Grazer's and Taylor Eddington's behavior last night at Kitty's Bar. If he knew nothing else about Sam Eddington, Jason knew the woman had courage. She'd done what she could to help herself get rescued, even with a gun pointed at her head. She'd kept up with him on this fast trek to freedom. And she'd had the sense to walk away from the selfish hothead he'd met last night. Curvy body. Pretty eyes. A brave heart. There was a lot to admire about…

Mission. Objective. Jason lectured himself silently, halting any thoughts of attraction. Saving Elaine from the insurgents who'd kidnapped her in Kilkut had been all too personal—and she'd died. He needed to keep this relationship distant and professional, or the mistakes that haunted him could become all too real again.

Besides, this mission would be over in about sixty minutes. Hardly enough time to even think the word *relationship*, much less contemplate getting involved with a woman with whom he had so little in common.

He tugged one of the gloves from his teeth and slipped it onto her right hand. "Your legs will survive because there's meat on them. I'm more worried about your extremities." He slipped the second glove into place, carefully avoiding the abrasions around her wrists. "We should have grabbed a pair off one of the men in the cabin. Better?"

"Better. What about your hands?"

"I'm tougher than you are. Bigger. More body heat. Feet?" Jason knelt in front of her to check her boots. He slipped his finger inside and ran it around her ankle, ensuring her socks were dry.

"Aching." She wiggled her toes against the squeeze of his hands, reassuring him that she wasn't suffering from frostbite.

"Blisters?"

"Not that I can tell."

"That was a good call to take these."

"Thank you."

He patted her knee before pushing to his feet. "Let's keep moving. Your dad is waiting for me to bring you home. I don't want to give those guys a chance to catch up with us."

Jason was already continuing his zigzagging path down the mountain's incline when he heard her fall into step behind him again. "I'll call you Jason or Mr. Hunt. And you can call me Samantha or Miss Eddington, but not Princess. And certainly not baby or Filly One."

"Why would I—?"

"Actually, my full name is Samantha Beryl Geraldine Eddington. I know, it's a mouthful. I'm named after both sets of grandparents. Good thing my last name's

Eddington, or there'd probably be an Edwina thrown in there. Sam and Geraldine, Ed and Beryl."

"That's too much to remember." Jason stopped, faced her. He took her hand to help her climb over the next log with a little less effort than the last one before sliding over it himself. He dropped to the ground beside her and kept walking. "How about I call you Sam."

"Beats Princess," she muttered under her breath.

Jason's chest vibrated with a low-pitched chuckle. The woman sure had a lot of words in her. They didn't all make sense when she rattled on like this. But every now and then, her sarcasm made him want to laugh.

Smaller trees that indicated newer forest growth, and the mounds of detritus that had rolled down from a rockslide higher up the mountain, told Jason they were nearing the edge of the cliff that would curve around a deep washout to take them to their destination. He nodded to a small boulder where Sam could rest while he pulled the two-way radio from his pack to call Marty Flynn and confirm his ETA at the extraction point.

"Sierra Romeo Seven One Five, this is Ground Team One. Come in. Sierra Romeo Seven One Five, this is Ground Team One. What's your twenty? Over." The crackle of static was his only response to his request for Marty's location. Jason paused to look up, giving his friend time to answer. Wispy clouds made the sky a pale blue. But even after last night's heavy rain and soft new blanket of snow, the weather was clear enough to fly. "This is Ground Team One. We're approaching the extraction point. Do you copy?" A faint sense of unease narrowed his gaze before he put the radio back to his mouth. "Sierra Romeo Seven One Five, please respond. You'd better not be late, Lieutenant Flynn. Over."

Unwanted voices played in his head.

"We have to wait for air support, Captain!"

"There's no time. Radwan already posted his last broadcast—he's got no reason to keep the hostages alive." Jason unhooked his rifle from his flak vest and readied to make the incursion into Radwan's stronghold. *"I'll go in alone. I can at least scout out which of those blips on the infrared are our hostages, and which are Radwan's men."*

The major shoved Jason back inside the abandoned hut on the edge of Kilkut. *"I have my orders, Hunt. Your girlfriend and her cameraman are going to have to wait until I have clearance to send in any men."*

"It'll be too late."

"We wait."

"They'll kill her!"

"Is there a problem?"

Jason jerked at the husky voice at his elbow, and pulled himself back into the present. He glanced down at the concerned tilt of Sam's green eyes above the rim of her glasses. He wasn't about to explain where his mind had gone. No sense letting her know that he hadn't saved the last woman he'd gone to rescue from kidnappers. And the idea of opening up and talking about all he had lost and how he should have been able to change the outcome of that fateful day grated like a straight-edge razor across his skin.

Without explanation or reassurance, he looked away from those worried eyes and toggled the call button on his radio. "Marty? Forget the code talk. This is Hunt. We're coming up on Mule Deer Pass. Are you reading me? Over."

The crackle of static was the only response he got on either of the frequencies he tried. Since he couldn't hear the telltale whup-whup of helicopter blades in the air, either his red-haired buddy was running behind schedule, or Marty had already landed the chopper. If that was the case, though, he would be in range of Jason's radio signal and he should answer. Clipping the radio back onto his pack, Jason climbed out to the rim of the drop-off and searched the sky and the surrounding gorge. If Marty wasn't in range, that meant there'd been a problem of some kind. Weather at a lower altitude. Mechanical issue. Trouble getting his flight plan cleared.

Jason studied the familiar terrain, evaluating his options. Any delay meant he and Sam would be alone on the mountain longer than planned. Delays meant more time for her kidnappers to come to, gather their full numbers—however many that was—and catch up with them.

He had a really bad feeling about this.

"Your friend's in the Marines, too?" she asked. "You called him Lieutenant."

"We served together." He closed his eyes and tilted his head, training his ear to the echo of any snowmobiles or hikers in the woods, on the ridge or down in the canyon. Nothing. Save for the wildlife and the wind, the mountains were a naturally quiet place—one of the draws that made this part of the world a sanctuary for him. But this was unnaturally quiet. He opened his eyes, studying the slope above and the drop-off below. "Why aren't we hearing the kidnappers in pursuit?"

"That's a good thing, right? That they haven't found us?"

"You're worth five million dollars to them. Why aren't they coming after you?"

She hugged her arms around her waist. It could be

the temperature, but he suspected his words had chilled her. "Because you're really good at what you do?"

If he was really that good, he'd have noticed something was off about this rescue mission earlier. Now he'd noticed. There was no crunch of gravel from vehicles using the service roads, no growl of snowmobiles, no clomp of boots or jangle of gear. He just couldn't put his thumb on what it was he needed to be worried about.

At the very least, Marty's silence was the equivalent of a big red flag. "The pilot's not answering his radio. I'm running ahead to see if I can make visual contact with our ride out of here. Keep a steady pace so you don't get winded. You'll be fine as long as you stay on the trail I make." He grasped her by the shoulders, kneading his fingers into the weatherproofed polyester of her coat and the slim muscles underneath before he backed her several feet away from the rocky overhang and released her. "That drop-off into the gorge is steep. Unless you're half mountain goat, I don't want you tumbling over the edge. Can you remember that while I'm gone?"

She raised her fingers to the edge of her knit cap in a sharp salute. "Yes, sir. Fist means stop. Do what you say. Don't get wet. Don't fall off the mountain."

"And don't call you Princess."

Yeah. Interesting turned pretty when she smiled. "How come my rules outnumber yours? Once I get my hands on a computer or piece of paper, I am so making a list to keep track of them."

But this wasn't the time or place for smiling. He was in trouble already if he was flashing back to Kilkut or thinking she was pretty. This whole op was about getting the job done and easing his conscience. Saving a life in exchange for the one he hadn't. "I'll get you whatever you need once we're off this mountain. Laptop. Pen and paper. Warm clothes."

"A hot shower?"

"Done." He hardened his expression so she'd stop that smiling thing that was getting under his skin and derailing his focus on the mission, then dismissed her with a curt nod. "Stay on my path."

He turned up the mountain and doubled his pace, climbing over rocky crags and around thinning trees until he reached the edge of the relatively flat alpine clearing that had been carved out of the granite eons ago. Relief was far from what he felt when he spotted Marty's red-and-white search and rescue chopper sitting in the middle of the treeless expanse.

"Why didn't you answer me?" he speculated out loud.

Jason paused at the edge of the trees, hanging back in the last bit of cover to assess the situation before he headed out over open ground. Although the rotor was now still, a lot of snow had been stirred up by the chopper blades when Marty had landed, exposing bits of high-mountain grass and glacier lilies peeking up through the ground to reach the sunshine. It was impossible to tell if there were footprints showing he'd left the bird, or that anyone else had approached it. With the tail of the chopper facing him, he couldn't see the cockpit to know if Marty was even on board. Maybe his pal had done something as innocent as walking into the woods to take a leak.

Jason closed his eyes, listening for any sound the young man might make. But the only noises he heard were the crunch of snow beneath boots that were about half the size of his and Sam's openmouthed exhales as she climbed up to the edge of the clearing. "A helicopter. Thank God. I will be so glad to get off this mountain. Is that your friend?"

Jason squeezed his hand into a fist beside his head. Sam stopped behind him, thankfully quiet except for the soft rasps of air as she evened out her breathing.

That is, she was quiet until he unhooked the holster on his thigh and pulled out his Glock. "What's wrong?" Her damaged voice was little more than a husky whisper.

"Something's off. Stay out of sight behind the tree line."

Ten fingers curled around the sleeve of his jacket and nipped into the skin and muscle underneath. "You're coming back, right?"

"That's the idea."

"Good." She tugged against him when he would have gone, and her touch drew his focus down to green eyes that held as much doubt as they did courage. "The last time I put my faith in a man, and he left me… I got kidnapped."

Before he could dismiss the pull he felt toward that brave vulnerability, Jason captured a tendril of toffee-blond hair that had fallen over her cheek and tucked it back beneath the edge of her knit cap, securing it behind her ear. Her eyes widened behind her glasses at the unexpected touch—or maybe that was his own body responding to the sensations of soft, cool skin and silky hair beneath his fingertips. How could a practical gesture feel so much like a caress? Jason curled his fingers into his palm, needing to distance himself from the tender feelings stirring inside him. Emotions had nothing to do with this mission. It was all about saving the girl and reclaiming some measure of solace for his tormented soul—not developing any kind of hormonal attraction or visceral appreciation for said girl. "I'm coming back. As long as you're my responsibility, I'll be close by."

He nudged her toward a trio of scrawny pines and waited for her to hunch down behind them before he moved out. Jason squeezed his gun between both hands, keeping his body low to the ground as if he was clearing a suspected enemy stronghold. His long legs took him quickly to the helicopter, but not only was the mountain unusually quiet, but now his nose could detect a smell in the air that wasn't natural.

He circled around to the front of the chopper, every nerve ending prickling with suspicion when he saw the front door propped open. "Marty? If this is some kind of joke…" He swung his gun around into the opening but lowered it just as quickly. He'd found Marty, all right. "Son of a…"

His lungs burned with a painful breath. The small-bore hole in the side of Marty's red hair, and the spatter of blood on the far seat and window, tried to take him back to Kilkut. But he shoved the memory of all the dead bodies out of his head and lowered his weapon, leaning in to press two fingers to the side of Marty's neck.

Jason swore again. Not only was there no pulse, the pilot's skin was cold to the touch. This hadn't just happened. "Damn it, Marty." He pulled the rim of his friend's blood-soaked ball cap down over his lifeless face. "This was supposed to be easy money for you. Not a death sentence."

So much for doing a friend a favor. So much for redemption.

"Jason? What is it? What's wrong?" He heard Sam's

worried tone a split second before he realized she was out in the open, running toward him.

"What the hell?" Jason met her in two long strides, dragging her in front of him, using the helicopter and his body to shield her from view. "I told you to stay put. You think I want another casualty on my hands?"

"Casualty? Nobody cusses up a blue streak like that unless something really bad… Oh. This *is* really bad." Her back flattened against his chest. Her fingers dug into his forearm still cinched around her waist. "I'm so sorry. This is your friend?"

But Jason was lost in the memories of a war-torn village street where two soldiers and two journalists lay dead among the insurgents who had fallen in the firefight that came too late to save the woman he'd loved. He squeezed his eyes shut against the memory of Elaine's shattered glasses and matted dark hair as he rocked her in his arms. He pulled her tightly to his chest, his hands fisting at the stench of sulfur and smoke filling his head, his whole body clenching with help-lessness and guilt and grief. So much blood. So much death. So much loss. It was more than one man could—

"Jason?" The body in his arms pushed against him, wiggling its way into the flashback. That wasn't right. Elaine was dead. No, Marty was the one who'd died. "Jason." A hoarse voice pierced the veil between the present and the past. He inhaled deeply, his lungs fill-ing with cool air. The air in Kilkut burned. "Hey. You're squeezing the stuffing out of me. Are you okay? He must have been a good friend."

The damn inappropriate reaction to Sam's bottom rubbing against his zipper shocked Jason back to real-ity. He unlocked the death grip he had around her waist and stepped back, giving her room to turn around. "I'm sorry. I…"

How did he explain how damaged he was? How could he share his guilt with a stranger?

But those green eyes were bright with tears now, as if she understood his pain. And the hands rubbing soothing circles up and down his arms felt familiar. "Tell me about your friend. I know he must have been very brave. He was trying to help me."

Yeah. He was a brave kid, all right. "His name's Marty Flynn. I work with him. *Worked* with him in search and rescue. He's the one who called me last night to help your dad find you. Always such a smooth talker. He was hittin' on your sister. And the waitress. He survived two tours of duty, but not a routine flight into… He was barely old enough to…" He turned his nose to the sky and sucked in another cooling breath before looking down into Sam's caring eyes. "This reminds me of…" No. He didn't want to talk about the past right now. Not with her. He took another breath and centered himself back in the present. "Sorry if I hurt you."

"Your hold wasn't any tighter than this corset thing I'm wearing. I'll live." But for how long if he couldn't keep himself together? She meant to tease a smile out of him, but it wouldn't come. "Do you know how to fly a helicopter?"

A relatively easy search and rescue—for him—just got complicated. Marty Flynn was never going to flirt with a pretty girl or bug him like some sort of adoring puppy dog again. And they weren't flying out of here.

Remember the mission. Think like a Marine. With a sharp nod, Jason slammed the door on his emotions and focused on the job at hand. Step one was recon.

Gather intel. Make a plan. "No. I don't suppose you've got a pilot's license?"

She shook her head.

"How'd the kidnappers get here ahead of us?" Jason leaned in beside her to check the helicopter's radio. Marty wasn't the only thing they'd shot up. "We're not calling for backup."

"I slowed you down, didn't I?"

"Not that much. How did they know where the chopper would meet us?"

He pulled back to check the windows and side panel for bullet holes. There were none. The shooter had gotten the drop on Marty the moment he'd opened the door. Or else, Marty had known the shooter and opened the door for him.

He flashed on the memory of a laser-sighted pistol pointed to his chest. A handgun like that could cover almost as much range as a rifle. Whoever shot Marty wouldn't have needed to be that close. But the shooter could certainly be close enough to have them in their sights, too. If he was still nearby.

"They knew we were coming." Instead of following them from the cabin, the kidnappers had gotten out in front of them. But there weren't exactly any road signs indicating the trail Jason had taken to get Sam here. "They knew about Mule Deer Pass."

Beating them to the rendezvous point wasn't the only lucky break the kidnappers had gotten. How had they known when and where she'd be alone so that they could abduct her in the first place?

"You mean Marty told them we were coming here? He's one of *them*?"

Jason drew his weapon again, scanning the landscape beyond the chopper. "He wouldn't do that."

Who all had been in Kitty's Bar last night? Who had Marty talked to between then and now? Who else knew the details of Jason's rescue mission? Who didn't want Samantha Eddington coming home?

Understanding made her skin go pale, and she hugged her arms around her middle. "Are they sending my father a message? Pay up or this is what will happen to me?" Sam straightened under his unblinking scrutiny, then started backing away. "What are you thinking? Damn it, Jase, you're scaring me."

He grabbed her by the shoulders before she retreated beyond arm's reach and pulled her toward the back door of the helicopter. "You afraid of a long walk?"

"No."

"How about a dead body?"

"I don't think so. But I've never seen a guy who's been shot—"

"Close enough." He set her on the running board. "Get inside and stay down. It'll give you a few minutes to warm up while I scope things out."

"You're coming back, right?" she asked, climbing over the seat.

"Get in." He growled at her insecurity, then changed his answer to a succinct "Yes."

Apparently, his word was all the assurance she needed because she spotted something on the floor that caught her interest and she ducked down beneath the dashboard. Good. He had a feeling that out of sight was the best place for Sam to be right now. She was pulling a Mylar blanket from the chopper's medical supplies and covering up Marty when Jason felt it was safe enough to close the door and move away.

Staying close to the helicopter, Jason quickly scanned the top of the ridge. Thanks to glacial ice and rockslides, there was no place for a man to hide up there. Same with the washout downrange of the chopper. But the trees and craggy terrain to either side offered plenty of cover to anyone with a rifle and a steady aim. So where were the kidnappers now? Why hadn't they taken a shot at him yet? If they wanted to recapture Sam for the ransom, they'd have to take him down first.

Why take out the pilot and trap them on the mountain?

His nostrils flared at the pungent odor he'd noticed earlier, and an idea began to take shape. He knelt to swipe his fingers through the snow and soggy grass underneath. Fuel. He visually followed the trail of discolored snow back to the chopper and tracked the oily residue up to the tank near the engine. Marty. The radio. And now the fuel tank—all with nice big bullet holes in them.

A man wouldn't need to shoot them if he could make all their deaths look like an accident. Jason glanced down the incline to see where the fuel had pooled in a snowy depression. This was bad. "Sam?" He pushed to his feet, backing toward the chopper. "Sam?" When he heard rustling in the trees, and spotted at least three upright shadows moving, he ran. This was very bad. He slapped the passenger window. "Sam!"

She popped up, holding a Swiss Army knife in one hand and a backpack in the other as Jason waved her toward the exit. She was stuffing the tool she'd scrounged into the emergency gear bag and hooking it over her shoulder as he slid the door open. "Your friend had a backpack. Warm clothes. A couple of protein bars. Water. Do you think he'd mind if I—"

"We need to go. Now."

She flinched at the crack of a gunshot, tilted her

head to the sky as a flare arced like a comet above the clearing. "Is that…?"

Very, very bad. "Run!"

Jason grabbed her around the waist, set her on the ground, snatched her gloved hand and ran back the way they came. The flare hit the fuel, igniting a fire that ran up the slope like a charging bear. He forced Sam into the race of her life as he lengthened his stride and sprinted toward the trees. They'd barely reached the three scrawny pines at the edge of the forest when the helicopter exploded.

Chapter Six

A shock wave of heat knocked them off their feet. Jason hit the ground hard, catching Sam in his arms as they tumbled over and over down the mountain. He felt the bite of every rock, the punch of every root, the rasp of every frightened breath against his neck until he slammed into the trunk of a fallen tree. But there was no time to do anything more than roll Sam beneath him as fire and debris from the chopper rained down from the sky. The bulk of his pack shielded them from most of the shrapnel, but he felt the sharp nick of something hot burning into his left thigh.

Ignoring the pain, he rolled off her, helping her sit up. Her glasses sat cockeyed on her nose, and he pushed them back into place, willing her eyes to focus and tell him she wasn't hurt. She rubbed at the hinge of her jaw, gently shaking her head. "You okay?"

"My ears…" Yeah. His were ringing, too. She eyed her scraped knees and the tear in her coat before catching sight of the blood on his pant leg. "You're hurt."

He batted her hand away when she reached for the singed slice of material. "I'm fine."

For now.

The first thud hit the tree beside them and Jason swore. He lifted her to her feet in front of him as staccato gunshots joined the roar of the burning flames. "Keep moving."

"Are they shooting at us? I'm worth five million dollars to them."

"Into the trees!"

Jason spared a few precious seconds to swing around and return fire.

"He's armed!" someone shouted.

"Son of a…" It looked like half a platoon, all dressed in black camouflage, darting out of the trees on the far side of the clearing. They carried assault rifles and handguns, wore utility vests and stocking masks like the men he'd subdued at the cabin. Their shots were wild right now, with the burning helicopter and the chimeras of rising heat obscuring their sights. But their intention was clear. Eight? Ten men on the hunt? And he and Sam were the prey.

"Move it!" He caught Sam's hand and ran past her, leading her into the shelter of the trees, wondering how long she could keep up this pace at this altitude, evaluating how long it would take the men to get close enough to get an accurate bead on them, worrying about the number of bullets he had left in his sidearm to protect her.

Sam's breathing was labored now, her steps less sure. Jason's brain was in combat mode, but they were outgunned, outmanned. Standing his ground wasn't an option. But maybe he could even up the odds a little bit.

He pulled Sam down behind the tree where they'd stopped earlier. She was breathing way too hard and her skin was far too ashen. "Did I ever tell you… I don't really…work out?" She sucked in another deep breath. "Never been much of a—"

"Don't talk." Jason placed a hand on her shoulder,

encouraging her to match the rhythm of his breathing. "Deep breaths. Don't panic."

"I'm going to asphyxiate long before I have the energy to panic."

She covered her ears and sank down as he braced his arms on top of the trunk and aimed the Glock at their pursuers. Now he could hear every damn noise in the book. Snowmobiles. Shouts. Running feet. Who were these guys?

"Circle around!"

"Don't lose them!"

Their point man crested the rise above them. Jason fired. Took him out.

"Jimmy's down!" another man shouted. "Jim—? He's dead! That son of a… They're headed north!"

A second mercenary burst through the tree line, whooping with adrenaline as he unloaded a barrage of automatic gunfire. Jason dived for the ground as the wood splintered and flew around them. More shots shattered branches and kicked up tiny explosions of pine needles, dirt and snow. The wild spray of bullets cut a small tree beside them in half before the gun jammed and the man cursed.

"Jason?" That terrified sound in Sam's crackly voice twisted in his gut. "I'm not afraid to admit that I'm pretty damn scared."

He rose and fired off two more shots, forcing the man to the ground, before he yanked Sam to her feet and pushed her into a run ahead of him. "Deeper into the trees."

The noise of the snowmobiles ebbed to an idling growl as they reached the barrier of the tree line. The woods would be swarming with the rest of those men any second now, and Sam was about to drop from a lack of oxygen and fatigue. The shouts were less distinct now, the enemy's movements harder to track.

But Whooping Trigger-Happy Man cleared his gun and stormed down the trail Jason had made no effort to hide. "You won't get the drop on me twice, soldier boy. Where's my money, honey? Come out, come out, wherever you are," he taunted, firing random bursts into the forest around them.

Pine needles and bark and tiny branches paid the price for every gunshot, sailing through the air and dropping like fallout from anti-aircraft fire. Bullets thunked into trees, exploded drifts of snow.

"I got 'em, boss! This way!"

"Watch your target! I want her alive. She's mine!"

"The hell with that! That bitch isn't gonna take a chunk out of me again."

Jason needed a rifle. Air support. A miracle.

This mountain is the only ally I need.

They weren't going to outrun well-armed mercenaries. Trees didn't stop bullets. But granite did.

Jason abruptly changed course and pulled Sam toward the lip of the rocky overhang.

"What are you—?"

"Hold on!" She tightened her grip and Jason squeezed his fingers around her wrist, dragging her to the very edge of the gorge. "Hug the rocks as soon as your feet hit."

"Hit what?" She screamed as he swung her over the cliff face and let go.

Jason spared a quick look at the men in black changing course in pursuit before he scrambled over the edge, catching a grip with his left hand and right toe, righting his equilibrium before dropping the last couple of feet to the narrow granite ledge.

Sam shivered against the rock face. "I can see all the way down to that creek from here. Oh, hell. That's a river, isn't it." Her voice was little more than a rasp of air. "My calculations say that gorge is about a thousand feet—"

"We gotta move." He pried her hand off an exposed tree root and pulled her along behind him as the rapid-fire staccato of automatic weapons tore through the air above the cliff edge they'd just vacated. It had been more than a year since he'd scaled the north face of the canyon, but he was praying that winter weather and rock slides wouldn't work against him. The opening where he'd rested before that last pull over the ledge should be about twenty feet ahead.

More bullets pinged off the granite at their feet. The men followed their path around the rim of the canyon, firing over their heads. The angle wasn't right to hit them yet, but they were getting close. If one of them figured out to run in the opposite direction, getting clear of the rocky overhang, he'd have a clean shot from the side.

Jason wasn't waiting for any of them to grow some brain cells. "Look at the rock face and step where I step. Don't look down."

"Don't look down," she repeated. "There is a way off this ledge, right?"

"Trust me."

"You can't just tell me yes or no?"

Six feet. Three. Two. Jason ducked into a recess beneath the rocky overhang as a final fusillade of whoops and gunshots filled the air with the stink of sulfur and anger. He hugged Sam to his chest, palming the back of her head and smoothing his hand down over her hip to pull the flare of her skirt between them, keeping any part of her body out of the line of sight. She huddled beneath the point of his chin, averting her face from the snow and tiny pebbles cascading past them into the canyon as their pursuers gathered above them. Her fingertips dug into skin and muscle, clutching him tightly as he moved farther into the darkness that neither the morning sun nor enemy eyes could reach.

"Get them!" That had to be the voice in charge. His order echoed off the canyon walls.

"I've got no shot from here."

"I don't want excuses. I want a dead body." Was it just his imagination, or did the boss's voice sound familiar? "Ten grand to the man who brings down that thief!"

"Ten? You promised us ten times that."

"For the Marine, you idiot. You won't get *any* money if we don't get her back."

"I'm not climbing down there. You think I have wings, Buck?"

"He killed Jimmy. All the more reason to end him."

Sam's fingers curled into the front of Jason's jacket. "Buck? That's the guy behind all this. The boss they kept talking about."

Jason nodded. The seed of understanding tried to take root. But solving mysteries wasn't high on his priority list right now. "Do you recognize that voice? How does he know I was a Marine?"

Sam was in survival mode, too, clinging to him as he moved them farther into the cave. "I'm just trying to not get shot right now. Is it important?"

The shooting stopped, and the voices grew indistinct as they put more distance between them and the makeshift army above them. But Buck's orders were clear. "Grab the rappelling gear. We'll trap them inside. Smoke 'em out. You—get me anything that will burn. You—if that guy pops his head out? Shoot it."

"What about the girl?"

"Wing her if you have to. But I'm the one who gets to cut out her heart and serve it to Daddy."

Sam's weight sagged against him at the venomous directive, as if her knees were suddenly too weak to stand. "That sounds a little hateful."

"I didn't sign on for cold-blooded murder, Buck," one of the men groused.

Buck didn't seem to hear the protest. "You get me Walter Eddington on the phone. I don't appreciate him playing games like this. He needs to know the price for getting his daughter back just went up."

"That means hiking back to the truck and driving down the mountain."

"Then get to it!" Buck shouted. "He needs to know I'm carving up another piece of his daughter now for thinking he could get away without paying me. And I want to tell him in explicit detail how much I'm going to enjoy doing it."

"I don't want to kill anybody. Jimmy's already dead. Plus, that guy in the chopper." There was a buzz of conversation overhead, the shuffling of men and equipment. But the man who wanted out was louder than the rest. "Cut me out of the money if you want to. She can't ID us, and you know I won't talk—my pledge is still good. But I'm headin' home."

Jason heard a brief, unexpected moment of silence. Then even he jumped at the crack of a bullet. A corresponding thump gave way to another shower of gravel at the mouth of the cave.

Ah, hell.

"Anybody else want to argue with me?" Buck challenged.

A man's limp body splatted onto the ledge at the lip

of the cave. Samantha screamed at the bloody, blank-eyed face that stared at them for a few seconds before his momentum carried him over the edge into the abyss.

She turned her face into Jason's chest, muffling her next screaming sob. Yeah, these guys were a whole different kind of crazy than poor Marty had suspected when he'd signed them up for this rescue mission. *Buck* had no regard for human life, even a friend's. He was mission-oriented, with his own agenda. And Jason seriously doubted that this was about the money for him. At least, it wasn't *just* about the money. Kidnapping Sam was about pain and punishment. Although if Sam or her father or some other cause was the source of his rage, he couldn't tell. But he understood one thing—the only way Buck wanted this sortie to end was with Sam and Jason dead. And he had the numbers and fire-power to do just that.

Judging by the way she clung to his jacket and sagged against him, Sam understood that, too. Tightening his hold around her waist to keep her on her feet, Jason pulled her deeper into the cave. "This way."

"I'm comin' for you, Samantha," Buck's fading voice taunted. Buck's men were scrambling to obey his commands now. "Get those torches lit. I want a rope here, now!"

Jason still had Sam tucked beneath his arm, their deep, ragged breaths falling into sync as a snowmobile fired up, kicking up another fall of snow and debris beyond the mouth of the cave. The voices faded. Jason paused to unzip a cargo pocket on his thigh.

"I can't see anything," Sam whispered. Thankfully, she hadn't collapsed into tears, and the screams had been more about shock than debilitating fear. "It doesn't sound like they're all going away. Are you sure you know what you're doing? We can't hide in here forever."

"They only think we're trapped." Jason pulled out his flashlight and clicked it on, shining the light into the space between them, quickly assessing the pallor of her skin and how well she was breathing, before covering one of her hands where it rested against his jacket. "I won't let anything happen to you," he promised. "I *can't* let anything happen."

A frown puckered the skin above the bridge of her glasses. "Can't?"

"I'm not losing anybody else on my watch. Come on." Lacing his fingers through hers, Jason turned the light farther into the cave and led her over a formation of broken rock that blocked them from view of the cave opening. They shimmied through a narrow crevasse before reaching an opening where the cave branched off in three different directions. One led back to the cliff face, and the other was a dead end. He paused a moment to orient himself to the correct option.

"My dad must be paying you an awful lot of money to risk your life like this for me," Sam suggested, adjusting her glasses to peer into the darkness with him.

"I'm not doing it for the money." That way.

She planted her feet, tugging him to a halt. "Then why?"

Jason swung the beam of the flashlight back to her face. "Let's just say I'm repaying a debt I owe."

"To Dad? To Marty? Is this a Band of Brothers kind of thing?"

"Partly."

The frown reappeared. "I don't understand."

And this wasn't the time or place to explain. Buck wasn't all that different from the terrorists who'd taken hostages over in Kilkut. And though he blanked the worst of the memories from his mind, the essence of the danger they were facing remained. He had to think like a Marine. He wouldn't resort to Buck's extreme methods of persuasion, but he needed Sam to obey every order.

With a faint pink coloring her skin again, and the distant din of men and gear overhead reminding him they had only a few minutes to rest, he slipped his fingers beneath the necklace hanging at the front of her coat, catching the carved silver locket in his palm. "This means you're supposed to trust me. Remember?"

She wrapped her fingers around his hand, capturing him and the locket he held inside. Even in this dim light, he could see her eyes were far from certain. "I take it there's another way out of this cave? And you're not just leading me down into the dark, scary place so we can die later?"

Jason nodded. "I need you to go on being tougher than you ever thought you could be, and do as I say for a little while longer."

She glanced toward the narrow slant of blackness leading into the deepest part of the cave. "No hibernating bears or other surprises?"

"Can't promise that. That passageway is too narrow for bears. It's coming out the other side where we'll have to be careful."

"Do you have bear spray?"

"I do. And you have me."

She nodded, looking not at all convinced that either his word or his plan were good. He leaned in, obeying instinct, even though an inner voice of experience warned him this was a dangerous miscalculation, and pressed his lips against the cool skin of her forehead.

He lingered there until he felt the pucker of her frown relax. And before that voice of reason could scream any louder, he dipped his head and brushed his lips across the soft curve of her mouth. He breathed in her startled gasp and tugged at the fluttering pulse of her full lower lip.

Her lips closed around his bottom lip, capturing it for a moment in her gentle grasp, waking something dormant and faintly animalistic in response to her tender acceptance. He traced the lean line of her top lip with his tongue. And while he took little nibbles along the same path, she stroked that decadent bottom lip against the scruff of his beard and captured his lip again and again. A sound, like the whimper of a baby animal, hummed in her throat, and she smiled against his skin, as if she was enjoying learning the texture of his face as much as he was enjoying this brief respite from danger, guilt and grief.

But the distant rumble of a snowmobile speeding away across the mountain above them was far louder than any voice inside his head, and he pulled away. "We'd better go."

"You kissed me." Her voice was a breathy sigh that revealed curiosity rather than surprise.

"Yeah? You kissed me back."

"Wasn't I supposed to? I mean, I wanted to." Sam shook her head. "I don't understand you," she admitted, testing the feel of him on her lips with the tip of her tongue. It was an unconsciously sexy gesture that warmed his blood all the way down to his toes with the urge to stamp a more thorough claim on her mouth and discover what she'd be like if he tapped into the passion he suspected was locked up inside her.

An imaginary hand slapped him up the side of his

head as he remembered something important. "Sorry. I know you have a fiancé or boyfriend or something."

"Not anymore."

Jason frowned. "What was his name? Grazer? He was at the meeting where your father hired me."

"Scumbag," she muttered. "I suppose he was acting all brokenhearted at my disappearance."

His gaze narrowed at the roll of her eyes. "I'd say pissed off was more his reaction. He was adamant that your father pay the ransom to get you back."

"My father should pay *him* the money to get him out of my life. Lousy excuse for a man. He undermined my confidence… When I broke up with him, do you know what he said to me?" Her gaze dropped to the middle of his chest. "I don't want to talk about it."

There was something out there she wouldn't discuss? While her condemnation of her ex triggered both relief and concern—neither of which he should be feeling— and reinforced his low opinion of the hotheaded Grazer, Jason was getting used to her rambling tangents filling up the dead space when he had nothing to say. But who was he to urge anyone to talk about things they didn't want to. "Fair enough."

"I'm grateful that you came for me. If I question too many of your dictates, or it seems like I'm arguing, it's just because it's my nature." She twirled her finger beside her head in a universal sign for crazy. "Logical, science-y, engineer brain. I like facts. Not real good at trusting my instincts and reading people, though. But I trust you."

That was what he wanted, right? Her complete faith in him so she wouldn't question any command required to keep her safe? Elaine had trusted him to come to her rescue and save her. Every man in his unit had trusted him to have their back and lead them safely home.

Jason tilted his head to the cave's damp, black ceiling, taking a moment to get his head back in the survival game before he blew this mission, too. "All right, then. Let's move out before Buck and his men rappel down the cliff and figure out which of these passages cuts through to the other side of the gorge."

"*You* know, though, right?" She waved off that moment of doubt. "I said I trust you, and I do. How many rules are we up to now? Six or seven? Keep moving? Step where you step? I've got them memorized now."

"Don't let go of my hand." He couldn't risk her getting turned around and wandering away down the wrong passage.

"No problem with that," she assured him, latching on with both hands. "Lead on."

As Sam willingly followed him into the darkness, he wondered if her ready trust in him would be an even more dangerous mistake than that kiss.

Chapter Seven

Samantha's feet felt like stones at the end of her frozen, boneless legs, dragging through the snow and tufts of brown grass peeking through along the ridge above the South Fork of Cascade Canyon.

Her nose was an ice cube in the middle of her face. Her body was bruised; her skin was chapped. Her shoulder where she'd been cut open to remove her tracking chip ached, and she was certain she was never getting the body-hugging undergarment she wore tugged back into the right places after that last stop to relieve herself, and so things were chafing in uncomfortable places. Her stomach growled with hungry protest. And Jason wasn't talking.

Not that he'd proved himself to be a brilliant conversationalist in the twelve hours she'd known him thus far. But she preferred him barking orders or laying down rules or tossing her over the edge of a cliff without a proper warning to this stoic silence.

No. She preferred him kissing her. Swallowing up both her hands in one of his. Hugging her so tightly to his chest that she knew every bump and hollow of equipment, weapons, clothing and muscle the man carried with such sexy, unapologetically male ease.

She wondered if Jason Hunt even owned a tie. She

couldn't imagine the rugged outdoorsman and former Marine wearing anything close to the tuxedos and tailored suits Kyle favored. Not that he needed any fancy adornment to draw her eyes to those broad shoulders and the tight lift of his butt in those cargo hiking pants she'd followed the last countless miles since leaving the claustrophobic chill of the cave.

It had taken just one of those twelve hours for her to admit she was attracted to him. Even a nerd like her could appreciate tall, dark and not-quite-handsome. Another hour and she'd learned to appreciate his unique skill set as a survivalist, sharpshooter and bodyguard. After only a few hours of knowing him, she felt compassion for the shadows that went beyond the loss of a former comrade that haunted his granite-colored eyes, along with a curious need to know what had put those shadows there and how she could make them go away. His praise was sparing, but genuine, instilling her with more confidence than any of the pretty poetry Kyle had used on her. Patience might not be his strong suit, but he made an effort to explain most of his actions and teach her a few survival skills of her own, rather than telling her to *grow up and get a clue about how the real world worked* or to *fix* herself. At least he had up until he teased her skin with his ticklish beard stubble and claimed her lips in a kiss.

She still didn't know why Jason had kissed her. Maybe he had a thing for four-eyed geeks with wild hair and horrid luck with men. Maybe kissing a socially awkward heiress or kidnap victim completed some notch on his bedpost. Or maybe he'd simply wanted to distract her from her panic for a moment so that she'd calm down and listen to what he was saying to her.

It wasn't lost on her that she was completely dependent on this man for her life. Or that his mood could swing from hero to heartthrob to hermit in the span of these twelve long hours.

Rule one. *Do what I say.* How was she supposed to ensure her survival on this fast trek to only-Jason-knew-where if he didn't give her any directions?

Other than the occasional warning about some bear scat or loose rock hidden beneath the snow, Jason's last words had been about the need to put as much distance as possible between them and the mysterious Buck and his surviving band of mercenaries. Yes, the route through the black, freezing, thankfully bear-free cave would make them difficult to find now, especially since they seemed to be avoiding anything that resembled a road or path. But discovery wasn't impossible. And until she was home in a hot shower and a warm bed, and she was certain her father wasn't blaming himself for her kidnapping or stressing to the point of a heart attack, she intended to do her best to follow Jason's rules.

She had rules five and six down pat. *Step where I step. Keep putting one foot in front of the other.*

But she was getting so tired. Tired of walking and climbing and overthinking everything that had happened to her in the past twenty-four hours. She wanted to know who'd kidnapped her, and if there was any significance to being taken on the night she was supposed to get engaged in front of a crowd of dignitaries and reporters. She imagined she was front-page news. Except for the drugs and bullets and two dead men on the mountain, this might have been a whale of a publicity stunt. Mostly, she wanted to know whether being taken on the anniversary of her mother's abduction and murder was a stab at her father or just a cruel coincidence.

She was tired of worrying about what the next twenty-four hours held in store for her. For her father. For Jason.

Despite the spectacular scenery of the Tetons on the cusp of spring, her vision had narrowed to the wall of Jason's back and the twenty yards or so of tracks and terrain between them. Although she was tempted to ask how much farther she had to walk, she tucked away the whiny voice and summoned the most sensible tone her weariness and sore throat could manage.

"Do you think it's safe to take a break now?" she asked, cursing his machine-like endurance, even as she wondered about the secrets and emotional pain he seemed to crush beneath every step. "I haven't heard a snowmobile or voices or anything but us for ages now. The sun was overhead the last time we stopped, and now it's in front of us. That means a couple of hours have passed, doesn't it?"

Silence. Was this how he grieved? March on and ignore the rest of the world?

"Look, I don't know about you, but I'm starving. I haven't had anything to eat since that energy bar you gave me before dawn this morning. All I need is ten minutes to get off my feet and eat something. I can make do with five," she bargained, when he showed no sign of stopping.

Twenty yards stretched to twenty-five as she stumbled over some uneven ground and her pace slowed. She was getting a little light-headed. Probably not breathing right. Too much oxygen or not enough. Her lungs and brain struggled to find the right rhythm. "I don't know if you noticed this yet, but your legs are longer than mine. It wouldn't hurt you to slow down every now and then, would it? Jason? Can you hear me?" Either her voice was too raw to carry the distance between them or he was so focused on finding the safest route between men who wanted to kill them and civilization that he couldn't hear her.

Although they were gradually working their way down the mountain, the course he'd charted for them was more like a roller coaster—up one rise and down the next, circumventing one rock formation while climbing over another, avoiding one stream of icy water and hiking straight across the next one. As her stride shortened and every breath strained her lungs, she watched him climb a winding path through the trees up to the next ridge.

A flat rock sunning itself in a clearing a few feet up the slope beckoned. Without the surrounding pines to shade it, even last night's snow had melted away to expose dry gray rock with hundreds of sparkly specks that beckoned like a neon sign. The ancient chunk of granite had been pushed ahead of a glacier eons ago and worn smooth by erosion. Samantha pulled off her borrowed glove and spread her palm against the surface. The sun made it warm to the touch, certainly warmer than the air around it. It wasn't her bed, or even one of the stiff new leather chairs back at the lodge. But it was warm and she wasn't, and the chance to sit for a moment was too inviting to pass up.

"I'm taking a break," she announced to Jason's back. He had a way to go to reach the top of that rise yet. She could make do with a two-minute respite.

Obeying the needs of her body, Samantha climbed onto the rock and stretched her legs out in front of her, relishing the warmth seeping into the back of her thighs and bottom. She heard the whoops and chirps of small songbirds, and the screech of a raptor—an eagle, maybe?—soaring overhead. She let her vision blur out of focus and listened more carefully. Underneath the sounds of animals and wind, she heard the splashing of water. No, it was more like splashing times a hundred. There was gushing water running someplace nearby. Someplace where the water was thawing better than she was. A waterfall?

This was a beautiful part of the country, she admitted. Rugged, hard, but worth the effort to see and hear and understand it. Not unlike her stony mountain guide. Even if he did refuse to talk to her. Or acknowledge her fatigue. Or slow down.

Her eyes drifted shut and her chin dipped forward until her head grew too heavy, and she jerked it back. She'd be asleep in those two minutes if she didn't keep her thoughts and at least some part of her body moving. Forcing her eyes open, she spared a few glorious moments to look straight out over the tops of the trees into the greening valley and frothy lines being drawn across a pond far below before her gaze traveled up the next slope beyond the dark tree line to the mountain's snowy peak. That pond was probably a lake. The creek feeding into it was most likely a river, maybe attached to the waterfall she heard. Those lines were probably boats motoring across the surface. If there were any people down there, they were too tiny to make out. Everything looked small from this altitude. She felt small, too, surrounded by towering trees and endless miles of mountains, snow and sky. "Get out of your head, Sam," she chided herself. A pity party had no place in her life if she wanted to survive this endless hike and the cruel, greedy men and dead bodies in their wake.

She was probably down to one minute now. Working as quickly as her gloved hands would allow, she pulled the pack she'd taken from the helicopter into her lap and unzipped an outside pocket. "Thank you, Marty."

Smiling at the pair of water bottles there, she opened one and toasted Jason's friend before taking a long drink. The next pocket revealed a stash of protein bars. She ripped into the first one and gnawed off a chunk of the bone-dry granola, oats and nut butter mix. She swallowed it down with some more water and felt it sink all the way down her gullet. It wasn't tasty or easy to eat, but there was something heartening about the feel of a food-like substance in her stomach again.

Rest, water and two bites of sawdust improved her spirits enough to risk conversing with Jason again. He was a tall gray figure in a black knit cap, pumping his long, strong legs from snow to grass to rocky precipice through the trees. "This tastes like cardboard, but I was getting to the point where I was worried the growling in my stomach would give our position away." No laugh. No response. She drank some more water, soothing her throat before reaching out to him again. "I am so eating a steak and mashed potatoes when I get home. What are you looking forward to when we get back to civilization? Are you a cake or pie man? Crème brûlée? A beer?" She lowered her voice to a grumble and forced down another bite. "Right. Super Scary Mountain Man doesn't need food or water or rest like us mortals do. Probably doesn't even know what civilization is."

Samantha cringed when she heard the words coming out of her mouth. "Sorry. I didn't mean it," she apologized, even though he hadn't heard her weary complaint. "Are you hungry? Do you want part of this? I can share…"

Jason was a good forty to fifty yards ahead of her now. Invisible threads of panic tightened Samantha's chest even as her breathing evened out and more oxygen reached her brain. She took stock of her surroundings the way a practical engineer would.

The depth of snowfall was thinner here. As their altitude dropped, the late afternoon sun was melting more snow, leaving gaps of bare ground and exposed rock instead of the oversize boot prints she'd been following for miles now. She glanced behind her, surveying the path they'd made through the trees. Even though she saw no armed men in black camo gear, she was too far away from Jason to feel safe. And if she lost his trail, she might accidentally wander off the edge of another cliff or come face-to-face with the bear who'd been marking this part of the mountain. Panic became thick cords that nearly choked her. In another ten yards, the people down below wouldn't be the only ones she couldn't see.

"Jason, wait up!" Samantha zipped the water bottle back into its pocket. Slinging the straps of the pack over her aching shoulders, she scrambled off the rock to catch up with him. "Are you upset about Lieutenant Flynn? Is that why you're not talking? I can't tell you how sorry I am he got killed trying to help me. You didn't even get any time to mourn. When we get home, I'll set up a memorial for him. Or help his family. Whatever you think is right." Her feet, back and leg muscles were really protesting now as she pushed herself to close the distance between them. Why had he set such a relentless pace? Had she said something to offend him? Did he know something about the men following them he wasn't sharing? Could it be…? Ah, hell. "Are you mad about that kiss? Did you break some gentleman's or mountain man's code? I didn't mind it, I swear. I liked it. A lot. It took my thoughts off everything else for a few seconds and I wasn't quite so scared.

I know that doesn't mean we're dating or anything if you're worried about me crushing on you. No pressure, okay? I can pretty well guess that I'm not your type. It was just a peck on the lips."

A peck on the lips combined with that full-body hug and that rumbling deep voice that had tickled her skin and warmed her from the inside out. Kyle had had his tongue down her throat and her blouse unbuttoned, and she hadn't felt anything like the ignition point in the pit of her stomach that had jolted through her blood like a combustion engine turning over the way she had when Jason had teased her lips. It must be the thinner air at this altitude that made her think that kiss could have turned into something much more significant if he hadn't been so quick to pull away.

"If it wasn't a good kiss, it's my fault. I mean, I don't think my ex was that great of a teacher. I thought he was, but you know, there's a reason he's an ex, and I just never seemed to catch on the way he wanted, so he was kissing other women and boinking them and... Jason?" She froze for a split second when he crested the rise and disappeared down the other side. She was alone. He'd left her alone.

She wadded up the wrapper of the protein bar and stuffed it into her coat pocket so she could use her hands to balance and help pull herself up the slippery rocks. When she reached the top, she exhaled a noisy sigh of relief. Not a sheer drop-off this time, but a gentle, shadowed slope that angled down to a frozen creek bed. Indirect sunlight left the snow knee-deep as she half climbed, half slid down to the bottom of the ravine. The icy crystals got into the tops of her socks and beneath her dress, chilling her skin. But cold was good. Cold meant she was feeling and awake—awake enough to be concerned.

Jason stood on the opposite side, his pack and radio sunk into the snow at his feet. He stared into the blackness between the trees while she searched for a narrower point to cross than where he'd obviously leaped from one bank to the other. "Did you hear anything I just said?" she asked, carefully testing a protruding rock for ice before using it as a stepping-stone over to his side of the creek. "Please don't ignore me. I know I'm rambling, and I'm sure it's annoying. But all these thoughts are going through my head, anyway, and saying them out loud is what I do when I get worried or need to think things through…"

He wasn't fixated on the space between the trees; he was focused on the gnarled trunk of the lodgepole pine right in front of him. Her hand instinctively went to her torso for one nervous scratch.

"Is everything okay?" Samantha lowered her voice to a whisper as she crept up behind him. "Is your fist supposed to be up?" She stepped to one side after a moment with no answer, to see if there was some sort of message carved into the tree. Or blood or a chunk of fur or some other clue that told them they were in imminent danger. "I haven't heard anyone behind us since we climbed out of that cave, so I think we lost them. Did you find that bear?" She took another step, peeking around his shoulder to see his jaw clenched so tightly, it shook. Was he having a seizure of some kind? Was he angry? "I'm sorry I ignored rule number six and stopped back there. I didn't think I could take another step, and the front of my stomach was trying to eat the back half—"

All at once, he punched the tree.

"Jason!"

"There's a damn bullet hole in my pack and the radio doesn't work. I can't call for an extraction or radio our position, even though we're close to being within range. It'll be nightfall in another hour, and no way can we reach a search and rescue station, or get within cell phone range by then."

While he rubbed his bruised knuckles, Samantha picked up and eyed the broken device, wondering if the pocketknife she'd stolen from the helicopter had the right tool to open the casing and pry out the bullet wedged inside. Maybe the radio could be repaired. Finally, something she was good at, something that might be useful up here. "Let's not give up hope yet. Fixing things is a hobby of mine."

She ran her finger around the hole. That hole could have been in her. She glanced up at the broad target of Jason's back. Her snack sat like a rock in her stomach, and she suddenly felt light-headed again. The bullet could have lodged in his spine or pierced his heart.

Although she'd known it, she hadn't really *felt* it until this moment—those men wanted to kill them.

"Hope? You're stuck with me, Princess." Ouch. Okay, she deserved that one for calling him a Scary Mountain Man back on the rock, even though she doubted he'd heard her. "And that sure as hell isn't the best news I can give you."

She knelt to flip over his backpack in the snow and poked her finger into the clean round hole the bullet had made. "Thank God the radio was there, or you'd have been shot." Losing Jason up here in the wilderness would surely sign her death warrant, as well. Losing him, period, messed with her equilibrium again. She shook off the dizzying emotions of fear and relief and shrugged the bag she carried off her shoulders. If it was simply the power cell that had been damaged, she could cannibalize parts from his flashlight and get the radio working again. "We'll figure out something else. Like you did with the cave and getting away from Buck. We'll walk all the way down the mountain if we have to. It'll be all right."

"All right? *Nothing* about this mission is all right." Foul words spewed through his gritted teeth. "It's *not* supposed to go down like this." With every negative word, he punched the tree. Samantha jerked at the violence of each blow, gasping at the pain he must be feeling. She shot to her feet. Did she grab his arm? Was she strong enough to hold on to all that muscle and stop him? "First I lose Elaine. And now Marty."

"Who's Elaine—?"

"Too many damn people have died on my watch. I *can't…*"

"Captain!" When he pulled back his fist again, she leaped into the space between him and the tree, bracing her hand at the middle of his chest. "Stop."

His fist froze in midair, his face contorting with grief and rage, his nostrils flaring as he sucked in deep breaths of brisk, cooling air. He dropped his hand to his side. Of course, he wouldn't hit her. But the tree and his hand deserved kinder treatment, too. His eyes, dark with the emotions that must have been building inside him as they walked, darted in every direction before his gaze settled on her. He pulled her hand away from the rough texture of his jacket and released her. "You can do better than me, Sam. You should have better than me to keep you alive."

Better than him? How could that be? What happened

to that confidence he never once had to brag about the way Kyle had?

"I'm sorry about your friend." Tears made her eyes gritty, and she had to swipe them away to keep her glasses from fogging up. "I'm so sorry you hurt like this." She tenderly grasped his fist. He'd split two knuckles open and two more were swelling. "But please stop hurting yourself."

She reached into her coat pocket to pull out a tissue to dab at the oozing wounds. A single drop of blood trickled down the side of his hand and dripped into the snow. The moment it hit, he pulled away. But before he fully retreated, Samantha reached up to touch his face. She cupped the side of his neck and jaw, feeling the friction of his beard rasping against the palm of her glove as she tilted his face down to hers.

"Jason, I need you." His wild gaze snapped to hers. She felt the tight muscles vibrating beneath her touch as he held himself still. She gently brushed her fingertips across the sharp angle of his cheekbone, soothing the tension there. "I have no idea where I am. I don't know how to survive in the wilderness. I don't know how to beat the bad guys. I need you to save me."

He huffed a wry sound. "What if I can't?"

"I need you to try."

His splayed his big hand over hers, holding her against his skin. "My last mission…" He squeezed his eyes shut against a memory he couldn't shake. "Before I was discharged…" His eyes opened again, pleading with her. "I don't think I can handle losing anyone else. I can't fail again."

Samantha considered the best way to respond to the pain in that taut whisper. "Then don't."

"Sam—"

"Are we alive?" He nodded. "Are we lost?" He shook his head. "Then I'd say you're doing your job, Marine. And I have every reason to believe that you will continue doing that job."

Her reasoning seemed to take him aback for a moment. But then he nodded. He squeezed her fingers before pulling them from his face. "Nice speech. You're officer material. How tired are you?"

"What's the next stage beyond exhausted?"

The lines in his face softened with half a smile. "You've got a wicked sense of humor, woman. It takes a lot of spirit to make jokes when we're in such dire straits. Sorry I've been such lousy company." He stooped down to pick up the radio where she'd dropped it, then tucked it into his pack and pulled out a first aid kit. He opened a roll of gauze to tie around his bleeding knuckles. "I've…got some issues from my time in the service. Sometimes, I… I've got a lot on my mind."

Samantha pulled off her gloves and knelt beside him. "Losing your friend reminded you of that? The explosion? The guns? They triggered something inside your head, got you to thinking about memories that upset you?"

He nodded. "Post-traumatic stress syndrome. Marty's not the first man I've lost. He was air support for my unit in Afghanistan. He saved my life on my last mission. Even though I lost…" His eyes darkened and he turned away. "Marty flew in to evac my team when no one else would. Too bad I couldn't return the favor here."

"Those action movie bad guy wannabes are responsible for Marty's death. Not you."

"I do better when I'm not around people. Nobody gets hurt."

"You didn't hurt me just now when you easily could have." She smiled, taking over bandaging his hand. "I do better when I'm not around people, too. I don't mean to make light of what you've gone through. I'm just saying I understand the need to retreat sometimes."

"From your cheating ex?"

"Kyle? You were listening to all that stuff I was saying?" Feeling her cheeks flooding with heat, she kept her face down, concentrating on tying off the gauze dressing.

Her blush intensified when Jason smoothed aside a lock of hair that had fallen across her face and tucked it behind her ear. "Kind of hard to miss the conversation when we're the only two people here."

For a split second, she didn't know what to say. But then, as the thoughts tumbled in, her mouth started working again. "I knew something was off with that relationship. But on paper, he was perfect for me. I wanted to make it work." She shrugged. "I think my dad worries I'm going to be a lonely old maid. It made him happy to see me with a man in my life."

"Did Grazer make *you* happy?"

She thought about that. "Maybe at first. The attention was nice." But even then, she'd had trouble believing his interest in her was sincere. Only her stepmother's unfailing support of Kyle and his family pedigree had convinced Samantha otherwise. "I thought he found my quirks endearing. That we complemented each other. It never occurred to me that he was trying to change me into someone else. Maybe that's why Joyce, my stepmother, likes him so well. She'd been trying to mold me into a pretty princess for years. That's what she knows. That's what she thinks I should be. Looking back, I think the only thing Kyle loved about me was the vice-presidency that comes with marrying me."

Jason let out a low whistle. "That explains a lot."

"What does?"

"His behavior last night. He was desperate to get you back. Maybe he was just desperate to get his meal ticket back in hand. Unless…"

"What?"

"Grazer disappeared before the meeting with your dad and security chief was over. I thought maybe he knew something about your kidnapping"

Samantha frowned. "What would be his motive? Kyle comes from money. Why would he need it?"

"To get you out of the way so he could be with your sister?" When her hands stilled at the dark possibility, he took out a small pair of scissors to cut the end of the gauze.

Her dad had promised Kyle an important position in the company when he married *her*. But he could marry Taylor instead and get the same deal if she was out of the picture. How had this pep talk for Jason turned out to be about her? Shaking off the malaise that threatened to overwhelm her at the idea she'd been set up by someone so close to home, so close to her heart, she plucked the scissors from Jason's fingers and finished the bandaging job herself. "I can't picture Kyle going by the nickname of Buck. Besides, I would have recognized his voice if he was one of the men on the mountain."

"Things got pretty crazy there for a while. No telling what we heard. But you're probably right. Could be Grazer was just worried about your dad finding out about them fooling around. I wouldn't say concern for you was his priority."

"It wouldn't be. I was never going to make him

happy. I just wish I'd wised up sooner." She exhaled her humiliation on a deep sigh before reaching over his bent knee to pick up his backpack and pull it into her lap to put away the first aid kit. "I have almost three college degrees, but I'm dumb about people. I have a hard time figuring them out. Who's being real? Who's sucking up to me? Who thinks I'm an asset, and who thinks I'm a burden?"

Jason watched her every movement, hanging on to every word intently enough to make her squirm. "You're not a burden to me."

"What would you be doing today if you weren't stranded on this mountain with me?"

"Working on my cabin. My dad and I started building it before my last deployment. I'm finishing it on my own now."

"What happened to your dad?"

"We had a falling-out."

She suspected there was more to that revelation than he let on. But he'd just revealed his struggle with post-traumatic stress—he probably wasn't ready to share whatever family drama had made him choose such a solitary life.

"My mom was murdered when I was a little girl. I still have nightmares about that sometimes. I was in the middle of one when you found me in the cabin. I don't know your experience, and you don't have to tell me unless you want to. All I'm saying is, I understand how traumatic events can get in our heads and mess us up." She clutched her fingers against her stomach for a moment, confessing every shortcoming. "I break out in hives when I get stressed. I ramble on to fill up the dead air because there's a very insecure part of me that thinks I'm not acting the way I'm supposed to be. And when

I don't know what to do, I tinker or talk or make jokes or…get myself into trouble. The only thing I'm good at is being smart, so I get frustrated when I don't have the answers. People don't understand me. They feel sorry for me or I intimidate them, or the money does. I keep thinking my mom…she would have taught me how to be normal. My dad tries, and I know he loves me, but he doesn't know how to fix me. My stepmother's tired of trying." She zipped the pack shut and held it out to Jason, finally raising her gaze to his. "Don't blame yourself for anything you've done with me. I come this way—a little odd and eccentric, but tough enough. And I can learn anything if you give me a chance. We'll just keep putting one foot in front of the other and deal with the bad memories. Maybe we should make that another rule. No matter what happens—from the past or the present—we won't judge each other, or ourselves. We'll deal with it and support each other. We'll get through this. Together." She thumbed over her shoulder. "And we won't hurt any more trees."

His eyes held hers for an endless moment.

He thought she was an idiot.

He was probably still replaying everything she'd said inside his head, trying to make sense of it all. He was probably deciding right then and there whether she was worth the time and trouble and grief she'd caused him. Maybe he was even trying to think of a nice way to tell her to shut up.

But Jason did none of those things.

He dropped the first aid kit into his pack and reached for her. By the time she felt his hands on her shoulders, he'd covered her startled lips in a kiss. It was no tentative exploration this time, either. If he was trying to calm her down, the moist heat of his mouth moving against hers was having the opposite effect. His arms snaked around her waist, pulling her to him as he stood, lifting her right out of the snow.

Samantha fell against him when she lost her footing. Her fingers latched onto the collar of his jacket, hanging on as he speared his tongue between her lips. Her mouth opened and his tongue slipped in, swirling around the soft skin inside, testing the hard edge of her teeth before sliding against hers in a needy claim. He touched that unknown ignition point inside her again, melting away the shock of the unexpected kiss, triggering a tingle of heat in her blood and breasts and the notch of her thighs.

The tingling scattered her thoughts. Suddenly, Samantha wasn't thinking. She was feeling. She was learning. Jason was teaching, and she was an apt student, following instinct instead of logic. There were no notes to take, no rules to remember. There was just Jason and need and a kiss.

As the taste of him filled up her mouth, the scent of him filled up her head and the heat of him filled her entire body. She wasn't just hanging on. She was grasping, pulling. Twining her tongue with his and suckling on the firm lip that moved between hers. She skimmed her sensitive palms along the rough textures of his neck and jaw and tangled her fingers into the thick strands of his hair. Jason moaned into her mouth at the needy tug of her hands, and she answered back as the deep-pitched sound vibrated against her lips. His hands slipped lower, palming her butt and anchoring her against the trunks of his thighs, creating a friction that kindled even more heat in sharp contrast to the cool air at her back, and the crispness of their clothes rubbing the skin of her legs between them.

This full-body contact was a new experience for her. It was a graphic reminder of all the differences between male and female, and she relished the discovery of all his hard places with her own soft curves. Her nipples beaded to tight, almost painful, nubs, and she felt weepy and heavy inside. The sandpapery stubble of his beard was a seductive abrasion against the delicate skin of her lips, the stroke of his tongue a soothing balm. His nose caught beneath the rim of her glasses, nudging them up so he could press a warm kiss to the apple of her cheek, the corner of her eye. She kneaded her fingers against the back of his neck before sliding them beneath the grip of his cap to cradle the warm, masculine shape of his head and pull his lips back to hers.

She went after his mouth this time, replaying every nibble, tug and stroke that he'd used on her moments earlier. He answered every touch with one of his own. The give-and-take made time stand still. Samantha lost track of where she was. There was no past, no future, only now. Only Jason and this kiss.

And her rumbling stomach.

Her eyes blinked open at the intrusive noise and she pulled her hands back to his shoulders, mentally cursing the noisy growl of reality. She squiggled out of Jason's grasp, the cool air rushing between them as much of a shock as the initial kiss had been. But even as she sank ankle-deep in the snow, he steadied her with his hands at her waist.

"I'm sorry," she apologized, feeling a different, far less pleasurable heat coloring her cheeks. "That's embarrassing."

Seductive just wasn't a talent of hers. She glanced down at her smudged coat, torn dress, men's boots and knee-high socks. She knew her makeup was gone; her hair was a mess and she hadn't brushed her teeth since dinner last night. Plus, there was that whole never-ending question-asking thing that was probably bugging the hell out of him. Wow. She was all kinds of *not*-seductive.

He dipped his head to press a quick, dismissive kiss against her tender lips, pausing to study her expression for a moment before releasing her. "You okay?"

"Of course. Yes." She pressed a hand against another growl of her *not*-seductive tummy. "Hungry, I guess."

"You're right to let me know when I'm pushing you too hard." He unzipped one of the pockets in his jacket and pulled out a plastic bag filled with dried fruit. Opening the bag, he invited her to sample a pineapple, apricot or banana. "It's not the steak and potatoes you want, but the fructose will give you some energy."

Steak and potatoes? He *had* heard that whole whiny, stream-of-consciousness ramble earlier.

"Thank you." He tossed back a few bites, too, while she chewed and savored the sweet, tangy fruit. The apricot was more flavorful than the cardboard-flavored granola bar, but not as delicious as the taste of Jason. She stuffed the whole thing into her mouth, averting her gaze from the rugged lines of his face. When did she become such a devotee of kissing? And when had she ever thrown herself into an embrace without thinking about whether she was getting it right or not, or even if she was welcome to try?

Her brain seemed to be misfiring. Maybe it was the drug the kidnappers had shot her up with.

"You don't have to fill up the dead air for my sake. But if it feels better to talk, it doesn't bother me. At least I know what you're thinking. I don't have to be a telepath." Jason offered her another handful of dried fruit before tucking the bag back into his pocket. "I like the husky sound of your voice. I know it's not a hundred percent because you've damaged your throat. But it's kind of sexy."

"Sexy?" Had the man just applied that word to her? She choked the last bite of pineapple down her throat. "Me?"

"Nothing's wrong with your hearing, is there?"

"No, but—"

"Just watch if you get light-headed or dizzy. Talking expends more energy and lets more cold air into your lungs, dropping your body temperature faster." In the span of a few seconds, he'd kissed her senseless, tended to her needs, complimented her matter-of-factly and explained a valuable survival skill. What more could a woman want? Samantha followed his gaze as he glanced up at the sky. The sun was moving closer to the horizon. "And it will get cold again. The temperature is going to drop thirty degrees once night falls. We need to find shelter. Buck and his men shouldn't be able to track us after dark. I know a place where we can stay the night. It should be far enough off the grid to be safe." He dropped his gaze to hers, catching her staring at him. But her fascination with his rugged profile, ability to truly listen and his different sort of intelligence didn't seem to faze him. Or maybe he wasn't aware of just how badly she *was* crushing on her rescuer. "Let's amend that last rule. You believe in me, and I'll believe in you."

"I do believe you'll keep me safe."

He nodded. He made a scan of their surroundings, quietly slipping back into mountain man mode, into the serious, taciturn former Marine who had promised to get her home. He stooped down and handed her the gloves to put on again. "You think you've got another mile in you?"

Samantha exhaled a heavy sigh. "I guess I have to." She pulled on the gloves while he adjusted his pack on his back and checked the gun holstered to his thigh. "Could you talk to me a little more while we're walking?" He arched an eyebrow in apology. "You won't talk…?" Wait, what was he apologizing for? He turned toward the steeper terrain that followed the rise of the creek bed. "We're hiking?" He pointed to the rock face, about fifty yards north, where the water cascaded over a ledge, its plume frozen in midair. "We're climbing? That?"

Jason laughed, a deep, rich sound. She decided then and there that he was just as good-looking from the front as he was from the back. And she wondered why eliciting a smile from Kyle had never given her such pleasure.

"We'll deal with it. Together."

"That kiss was to bolster my courage to tackle rock climbing?"

"No. That kiss was about thanking you. For getting me out of my head where I'm my own worst enemy, and giving a damn about me even when I'm being a total jerk."

"You weren't."

"I was." He helped her into her pack, hanging on to her shoulders for a moment before spinning her around to face him. "And for the record? You don't need me to bolster your courage. You've been through more in the past twenty-four hours than most people endure in a lifetime. But you don't quit. You make jokes when most women—hell, most men—would be crying. You're grounded, Sam Eddington. You were the anchor I needed today. You care—even when a washed-up nut job like me goes off the deep end. A lot of people run from the kind of scary I can be. You ran *to* me."

"It seemed like a matter of survival. For me." She brushed her fingers against the back of his uninjured hand in a tentative touch. "But, for the record—when you lost it, that really did scare me."

"Scares me when it happens, too. We'd better get moving." He tightened his grip around her hand, leading her to the craggy rocks he wanted her to scale. "And one more thing for the record? Sometimes a man just wants to kiss a woman. He wants to feel her in his arms. Feel her softness, her strength. There isn't always a reason. Your ex is an idiot if he never taught you that." He tugged her to a stop. "I don't know what lessons Grazer was teaching you. But there isn't a damn thing wrong with the way you kiss."

Chapter Eight

A fist of guilt punched Jason square in the gut.

"I thought you said you weren't hurt." The emergency lantern from his pack cast enough light through the murky shadows of the hunting shack off Pinewood Trail that Jason could see the bruises up and down Sam's arms, along with the shiner on her shinbone, scraped-up knees and the soiled bandage on her shoulder where her tracking chip had been removed.

"Jason!" It wasn't like there were any walls in this place. He'd already changed into a clean T-shirt and shorts before sliding back into his cargo pants and thin-knit sweater and tying on his boots. He hadn't expected to catch her half-naked. The arm over her sweet, full breasts and a hand in front of the boxer shorts she'd scrounged from Marty's go bag did little to hide her beautiful, battered body from his worried perusal. "A little privacy, please?"

He obediently turned away, although the image of every curve, every strand of toffee-blond hair hanging loose and finger-combed into unruly waves, and every injury he should have prevented was indelibly imprinted on his brain. It didn't help that he could hear her moving behind him, finishing a sponge bath with a moist towelette.

"I am so setting up a memorial fund of some kind to honor your friend Marty," she said, followed by a quick gasp. He peeked over his shoulder to see her hooking her bra back on and tugging it into place. "The water, snack bars and extra clothes he packed in his bag are lifesavers, as far as I'm concerned. And an unopened toothbrush? That's the best treasure I ever could have found. Jason!"

He held her gaze for a charged moment, feeling the temperature in the tiny cabin rise, even though he'd nixed the idea of building a fire in the structure's crumbling fireplace. He liked her better in that bra she'd rigged with straps from cutting up the girdle thingy that had cinched her body from shoulder to thigh, covering up all the best parts of her rounded, earth-mother figure. He'd like it even better if those boxer shorts she was wearing were his.

The rush of interest stirring in his groin finally made him politely turn away to face the door. Whoa. Where had that possessive thought come from? He hadn't been with a woman since Elaine. Hadn't really been interested in finding anyone—partly because he'd been raw with guilt and grief for a long time after Elaine's death, and partly because he didn't want to saddle anyone with all the mental garbage that came with getting involved with him.

But a day with Sam Eddington had him thinking about the connections that were missing from his life. She had him wanting to be physical with a woman again. She had him opening up and sharing things he'd talked about only with his therapist. She had him wishing he had the right to do more than protect her, wishing he could explore where this surprising attraction between them might lead. She had his priorities all twisted up in a way he hadn't felt in two long years.

But twisted-up priorities weren't exactly something he could indulge in right now. Not with Marty Flynn and his radio dead, and his cell phone useless until they dropped down another thousand feet or so. His extraction plan had been shot to hell. And eight to ten well-armed men eager to recapture Sam and kill them both lay in wait somewhere on this mountain, hunting them.

That sobering assessment of the situation was enough for Jason to set aside his interest in this oddly fascinating woman and remember those priorities. He faced her again. Job one was survival, not sating his awakening libido or respecting her Puritan need for privacy. She was using the Swiss Army knife she'd taken out of the chopper to cut a length of cord she'd slipped through the belt loops of the man-sized jeans to cinch them around her waist. She chided him with a silent glare before turning her back on him to roll up the pant legs to her ankles.

"Don't get many women up here in this neck of the woods, huh?" she tried to joke. "Is that why you keep staring at my girlie parts?"

"Stop." He wasn't in a joking mood. The gauze bandage that had been taped over her shoulder was caked with blood and had come loose. He closed the distance between them in three short strides. "I want to check your injuries before you get completely dressed. Especially that cut on your shoulder. Looks like it's been bleeding. You should have told me the pack was rubbing against it."

She batted his hand away and picked up the gray T-shirt that had also been rolled up in Marty's pack, clutching it in front of her like a shield. "So you could carry both packs? It's bad enough I got you into this mess. I want to do my part to help."

"You didn't get me into anything I didn't volunteer for."

"Yes, but you thought you'd be home in your cozy little bed tonight. You weren't expecting so many well-armed men to be waiting for us. And I know you didn't expect them to kill your friend." No. This supposedly easy op had gone south almost from the get-go. When he didn't respond, she reached out, probably to share more of the compassion she needed to keep for her own strength. Needing to take care of her more than he needed taking care of, Jason moved away to pull the first aid kit out of his own pack. Rebuffing her concern only made Sam transfer her worries in another direction. "Do you think Dad has called in reinforcements by now? Other members of your search and rescue team? Pellegrino and his men? The sheriff's department? FBI?"

Jason pulled out the supplies and set them on the pine bench that passed for a seating area in the old shack. "I hope not. They have no idea of the kind of firepower they'd be running into up here, and we have no way to warn them. At this point, it's easier, and probably safer, for us to hide and wait out Buck than it is to try to co-ordinate a new rescue plan. We'll send the authorities in to round them up once I know you're safe."

"Dad must be worried sick that he hasn't heard from us. He has a heart condition, you know. I hope Joyce is making him take all his meds because the stress could kill him." Her eyes were focused on some far-off place as she pulled on the T-shirt. "The similarities between last night and my mom's kidnapping are creepy. They feel almost intentional. She and Dad were at a party like

I was. She left early by herself because she wasn't feeling well. Never made it home. It was a business reception celebrating his first new builds in Wyoming—just outside Yellowstone and Teton."

"The land Cordes accused him of stealing?" Sam looked surprised that he knew that, so he explained. "Richard Jr. was at the bar where I met your father last night. The two of them were arguing when I walked in."

Sam's cheeks went a scary shade of pale. "Did he hurt Dad? Threaten him? Do you think he's behind my kidnapping? In retaliation for his father's execution?"

"Pellegrino and his boy Metz kept Cordes away from your father." Jason made no mention of the role he'd played in breaking up the fight. It hadn't been any big deal to step in where he'd been needed. But it wasn't modesty that left him analyzing the antagonistic behavior he'd seen at Kitty's. "I've never known Junior to go by *Buck*. And he didn't seem interested in your father's money. Plus, he's got an airtight alibi for the time you were abducted. But I don't like coincidences like that."

"Maybe he hired those men to kidnap me. Maybe Buck's a friend of his."

"Or a cousin. Lord knows there are enough of Cordes's old militia group, their kids and grandkids, still scattered around the area."

"It sounded like this was personal for Buck. You think this is about revenge instead of money?" She sank onto the far end of the bench. "Dad already blames himself for Mom's death. I know he's blaming himself for me. Hasn't he been hurt enough?" Her gaze kicked up to Jason's. "I have to get a hold of him and let him know I'm okay. I have to get home."

Did she ever think of herself first?

"One step at a time, Sam," he cautioned, straddling

the opposite end of the bench. "I want to keep you in one piece first."

"Do you think the kidnappers contacted him at noon like they originally planned? Even though I wasn't there to make the video for them? I can imagine they'd say some vile things to upset him. Maybe even lie and say they'd already killed me because he wouldn't pay the ransom. They could have videotaped me when I was passed out from the drugs—I probably looked dead."

Jason remembered his own advice to himself. "Priorities, Sam. We'll figure out the who and how later. And I promise we'll contact your dad as soon as we're in cell range. But right now, we need rest. And I want to err on the side of caution and check your injuries. It's not like there's an emergency room I can take you to up here if an infection sets in. We're still a full day's hike down to civilization—and that's only if we don't run into Buck and his friends again."

Nodding, she let him steer the conversation away from her concern for her father. "All right. I'll let you tend my wounds if you let me change the dressing on your hand and check that spot where the flying helicopter part burned through your pant leg."

"The metal was hot enough, I'm sure it cauterized the wound."

"Fine." She got up to retrieve the silver locket from the pile of her discarded clothing and looped the chain over her head. Then she reached for the moth-eaten sweater they'd discovered, along with a few other abandoned, second-rate supplies, when they'd searched the shelves in the cabin. "I don't take care of you, you don't take care of me."

"Sam." He caught her wrist, tugging her back to the

bench. "We're doing this. You know I can outmuscle you if you don't do what I say."

"Yes. But I don't think you will. Despite every effort to be a big, badass Marine on a mission, I think you're a nice guy. The only time you've used your size and strength against me was when you were trying to save me, and you didn't have time to explain what was going on. Clearly, the fact that we're having this conversation right now means you don't have to rush me. Even when you lost it back at that tree, you didn't hurt me. And that means you won't bully me into something I don't agree with."

Sucker. Couldn't argue with logic like that. He released her and gestured to the bench, inviting her to join him again. "Well, then, I guess we're going to be playing doctor with each other."

Her eyes opened wide and she blushed, all the way down to her cleavage. Yep, watching that woman react to a suggestive remark or a simple touch wasn't going to get old anytime soon. He wasn't sure what she'd seen in Grazer, but he knew her ex was the one who'd lost something special when she'd rightfully dumped his selfish, cheating ass.

She sat with her back to him and Jason peeled off the gauze and tape and tossed them at his feet. He opened a bottle of water and poured it over the small, ragged gash to irrigate the wound. "This is going to hurt a little." She winced when he dabbed at the cut with an alcohol wipe but didn't complain. Without the means to put any stitches in the wound, he settled for gluing the jagged little hole shut, hoping it'd stay sealed once they got moving again. He covered it with a fresh bandage and cleaned and put ointment and bandages on the worst of her scrapes before he realized that she'd been quiet for an uncharacteristically long time. He helped her shrug back into the T-shirt and holey but clean sweater before he tugged down his pant leg to let her put ointment on the burn that had indeed sealed the cut the shrapnel had made in his skin. "Just so you know, I haven't always lived off the grid. I've seen plenty of *girlie parts*."

"It sounds silly when you say it."

"It sounds silly when anyone says it." When she pulled his beat-up hand into her lap to unwind the field dressing, Jason captured the waterfall of blond curls that masked her downturned face and draped them behind her shoulder, so he could read the expression in her eyes. "If you're being funny, fine. But if you're denigrating that fabulously generous figure of yours, stop it."

"Fabulously generous? You mean I need to lose fifteen pounds."

"I mean, you've got the kind of body fantasies are made of."

She finally looked up to meet his assessing gaze. "Fantasies…? No, I don't."

"Is that something Grazer told you?" Yet another reason to smack that guy straight into Sunday for saying or doing anything to make her doubt herself or think she was anything less than a sexy, attractive woman. "He probably told you that old saw about women who wear glasses, too."

Ah, hell. He had. "He asked me to buy contacts. They're better for photo ops. And, you know, boys don't make passes at girls who wear—"

He pressed his fingers against her lips to stop her from finishing that untruth. "Men do."

Her eyes widened with the same anticipation that suddenly raced through his blood like a fast-running river breaking through an ice jam.

And then he replaced his fingers with his lips, claiming her soft, responsive mouth. Her welcome was instant and unhesitating. Her fingers cupped the side of his jaw, stroking against the beard stubble there, pressing into the skin and muscle underneath. He tunneled his fingers through the weight of her hair and clasped the nape of her neck, drawing her into the vee between his legs, knocking trash and the first aid box to the floor as he lifted her onto his lap. He'd never had an addiction before, but kissing Sam was quickly becoming something Jason couldn't say no to.

She tasted like minty toothpaste and heat and hope. Her responses to his touch were as natural and powerful as the mountain beneath their feet. She mimicked each thrust of his tongue, answered every press of his lips. Innocent as he suspected she was, Sam didn't just meekly give back the caresses he offered. She ventured out into new territory, too, exploring his growling response to her teeth nipping at the jut of his chin, testing just how many times she could pull on his bottom lip and tug on his hair before he crushed her squarely against his chest and deepened the kiss.

Her breasts pillowed against him, her nipples pebbling into decadent little morsels of hard candy he wanted to touch and taste. Her breath quickened with every heartbeat, and that telltale hum in her throat told him she was enjoying this full-body contact as much as he was. Her exploring hands skimmed along his neck and shoulders before tangling with his hair again. Her needy tugs pulsed through him, heating his blood and stirring things up behind his zipper.

His lips scudded along her jaw as he tugged at her sweater and T-shirt to get his hands on bare skin. He found the nip of her waist, the smooth skin of her back.

And while she was cool to the touch, his skin heated like fire when she tugged at the hem of his sweater and slipped her hands beneath to latch onto his waist. He skimmed his palms up to the edge of her bra and slipped his thumbs beneath the heavy weight of her breasts. He lifted her to spread her legs over his lap, nestling her feminine heat against the part of him that wanted to be inside her. He closed his teeth over the lobe of her ear and she giggled, a sound that was part delight and part overwhelming sensation.

He felt more like a man than he had in years when she responded to him like this. He felt more human.

He smiled inside at the pleasure she took in the simplest things. Quiet conversations. The tactile differences between his body and hers. The discovery of a particularly sensitive spot at the base of her throat. There was no calculated seduction in the way she kissed, no subterfuge he could misinterpret that might come back to bite him in the butt. Sam wanted to kiss and be kissed. She wanted to touch and be touched. When she tipped her head back, offering the creamy arch of her neck to feast on, Jason did a little exploration of his own, chasing that needy hum of arousal.

Jason slipped his hands into the tight space between them, rubbing her nipples with the pads of his thumbs and cradling the sweet, sexy weight of her breasts in his palms. "Oh, Jase. This is so...so good."

She squirmed in his lap, her hums becoming breathless gasps of pleasure that fueled his own desire. He reclaimed her mouth as he rocked helplessly against her. There wasn't a part of her body he didn't want to taste—no part of his own where he didn't want to feel her touch.

But this was crazy. This was piss-poor timing. It was

selfish to see this lightning bolt of electricity arcing between them through to its inevitable conclusion. Warning bells from his past sounded an alarm. He moved his hands away from bare skin but clutched the flare of her hips instead, pinning her thighs around him. He tore his lips from the delicious grasp of hers but ended up peppering her face with a dozen little pecks instead because he wasn't ready for this to end. Her heat called to his, and with a few flicks of his thumb at just the right pressure point, he could turn that humming passion into the release she craved. Would she come with a breathless moan? Would she cry out his name in that husky voice of hers?

Focus on the mission, Marine.

"Sam, we can't do this." It did him no good to indulge this need if there was a chance his feelings could get involved and distract him from the job at hand. It did her no good to promise something with his body that his broken heart and fractured brain might not be able to give. She found the button of his pants and unhooked it, dipping her fingers into the front of his shorts, her knuckles sliding against bare skin. Jason had to grab her wrists and pull her free before he couldn't think with his brain anymore and this turned into a mutual hand job. "Samantha," he growled with a mix of want and regret. "We need to stop."

"No."

"We have to." He lifted her from his lap, pushing her back across the bench. He made a token effort to pull her sweater and T-shirt back into place, but when she scooted back toward him, he held up his hands to ward off the temptation of her primed-and-willing passion. "I'm sorry." His nostrils flared with deep breaths, but he needed a slap of cold outside air to cool his jets and make this crazy craving for her go away. He gingerly swung his leg over the bench and stood, rebuttoning his pants. "I can't afford to forget what's at stake here. Your life."

Sam hugged her arms around herself, as if she was feeling the chill he so desperately needed. "Not the sweet nothings I was hoping for."

"I don't do sweet nothings." Jason raked his hands through his hair, pulling at the tangles she'd made there. The sharp pricks on his scalp were a welcome deterrent to the heat coursing through him. But the pain was an equally clear reminder of what a turn-on her grasping fingers had been. He forced himself to walk away to the storage shelves where he'd dropped his pack and jacket.

"I kind of figured that. I'm the one who's sorry. For pushing you into something you don't…that we're not ready…" Sam pulled her glasses off and rubbed at her eyes a moment before her face stretched with a wide yawn. "I don't have the energy to do this right, do I?"

Exactly. She was exhausted and probably not thinking straight about where this make-out session had been leading. He needed her strong to face the trek that lay ahead of them tomorrow, not drowsy and replete with the orgasm he'd wanted to give her. Plus, giving in to passion now would only make things more awkward between them when he needed her to listen to every word he said and take action when he gave the order. He turned his back to her, carefully adjusting his pants while he recovered, before picking up his jacket and shrugging into it.

"Did you want me to do something else?" she asked in a voice that sounded decidedly different from the *"Jase, this is so good"* that had nearly sent him over the edge a few moments earlier. "Kyle said I should be more—"

Uh-uh. Jason pulled Sam to her feet. He captured her face between his hands, maybe a little more roughly than necessary, and tilted her face up to his. He needed her to understand this. "You don't need to be *more* anything. I stopped because my first priority should be keeping you safe, not getting inside your pants. I stopped because I don't want you to feel I'm taking advantage of your situation. You don't have to give me your body to make sure I protect you. Even if you hate my guts, I'm still going to get you home." He inhaled a sobering breath before resting his forehead against hers. "I stopped because I'm not sure I'm the best man for you to get involved with. I'm not sure I'm ready to get involved, but I'm feeling like I want to, and that makes me wonder if my motives for lusting after you are as pure as they should be."

Her eyes darkened like a rich alpine meadow at twilight. "Lusting…?"

Damn straight. What did she think that was that had nudged against her thigh? Jason dipped his head and captured her mouth in a hard, quick kiss, reminding her that he didn't play games the way her ex apparently had. "That man's name is never to come up again when I'm in the middle of kissing you. When you're with me, I want all of you with me."

She might have swayed when he released her, but damn, it made him angry to think that she'd sat there evaluating every moment of that embrace, wondering if she wasn't measuring up to his expectations. Considering he hadn't expected anything to happen between them, he wasn't quite sure if he could explain the way being with her had awakened something inside him and turned him inside out.

Jason pulled his cap on over his head and strapped his gun and military-issue holster back into place around his thigh. She put her glasses back on and knelt to pick up all the medical supplies they'd scattered. Then she moved on to layering together a makeshift bed out of a moth-eaten blanket and a dusty sleeping bag with a broken zipper the former inhabitants of the cabin had left behind. He was geared up at the door when he realized she hadn't said a word for several minutes. Was she focused on her work? Asleep on her feet? Had he said something that hurt her? Ah, hell. Maybe his own ego had gotten the better of him here and he was assuming things about Sam that he really didn't know. Kissing him could just be some affirmation-of-life thing. Or maybe that logical, science-y engineer brain of hers saw kissing another man besides Grazer as an experiment, comparing what she knew with other possibilities. "Do you miss him? Were you thinking of him when I kissed you?"

Sam shot to her feet. "No!"

Thank God for that. "Then don't make me think of him, either. He hurt you. He used you. It makes me want to punch something. Preferably him." He curled his fingers into a fist, then flexed them straight, testing the bandage she'd wrapped around his knuckles. "You're better than he deserved, Sam. You're better than I deserve."

"Don't say that." She waved aside his protest and crossed the cabin to lay a hand on his arm. "Rule number ten. No more mentioning what's-his-face. Thank you for thinking of what's best for me. For both of us.

It wasn't that hard to get carried away by the opportunity since I've been lusting after you, too."

He didn't need any games or tricks or coy seduction. Straightforward worked for him. "Yeah?"

"Yes." The rosy blush on her cheeks belied the directness of her upturned gaze. "In some ways, I can't imagine anyone more different from me. On paper, we just wouldn't work."

"True." She *was* a smart woman.

But before he could leave, she tightened her grip on his sleeve. "But in other ways... I can't imagine going through this with anyone but you. Maybe you're just tolerating me because you don't have any choice, but I feel like I can talk to you. I feel safe with you. And kissing you is—"

"A little rough around the edges?"

"I was going to say really hot. I can't always think straight when you're holding me—and I'm used to being able to think things through. I've never had chemistry like that with anyone. Certainly not with what's-his-face."

Jason laid his hand over hers and squeezed it. "It's the situation. Could just be gratitude or the thrill of something—someone—different, someone who's not part of the world you were running away from. Danger intensifies anything you're feeling."

"Or maybe it strips away all pretense and leaves you with honest emotions. I care about you, Jase. I think I care about you more than I probably should."

Leaving that bombshell hanging in the air between them, she went back to making the pallet. She rolled her sadly abused party dress into a bundle and tucked it against the wall. Then she rolled up her checkered coat and set the bundles side by side, making pillows

for them both. Without a fire to warm them, he'd rec-
ommended they share a bed and their body heat tonight.
She'd agreed, saying that sleeping together was a sensible solution. Despite the limited, no-frills resources
available to them, the domestic picture she made left
Jason wondering which of them was right. Were they attracted to each other *because* of the circumstances surrounding them? Or *despite* them? In the outside world,
where she was a society princess and he was a recluse,
where she worked with her brain and he worked with
his hands, where she was close to her family and he
was estranged from his, would they have anything in
common? Would they even have noticed each other?
Would he be feeling this inexplicable pull toward hope
and salvation that Sam seemed to offer? Would he have
spent enough time getting to know her that he'd look
beyond the geeky exterior to discover her intriguing
mix of brave compassion and almost shy vulnerability?

"Who's Elaine…?"

The question jerked Jason from his thoughts. Wow.
That woman sure knew how to throw an emotional
punch. Maybe he needed to rethink that straightforward quality he admired.

She hugged the Mylar blanket from his pack to her
chest. "You mentioned her when you were giving the
tree a beat-down. She was important to you, wasn't she?
You said you'd lost her. She died?" He nodded. "Is that
what happened? You were in a dangerous situation like
this one, and your feelings for her intensified?"

That's how their affair had started, but after a while,
Jason's feelings for Elaine had become all too real.
Maybe Sam had a right to know why he'd wigged out
on her at the tree. She was counting on him for her survival. She had a right to know why he'd ended that kiss,

why keeping her safe was more important than any lust or emotions she made him feel. "I knew Elaine when I was in the Marines."

Sam spread the Mylar on top of the pallet before sitting in the middle of it. She hugged her knees to her chest, patiently waiting for him to answer her questions. "Tell me about her."

Jason scrubbed his palm across his jaw, fighting the urge to bolt out the door. "Is this part of that doctoring agreement?"

"Does it need to be?"

Closing his eyes, Jason inhaled a deep breath. Her expectant gaze was on him when he opened them again. He moved to the bench and took a seat facing her. Curiosity and concern created that pucker of a frown between her eyebrows. "Elaine Burkhart was a reporter imbedded with my unit when I was stationed in Afghanistan. I loved her. Huge no-no when it comes to military protocol, but I loved her anyway." He leaned forward to brace his elbows atop his knees, twisting his hands together as he unlocked the memories. "We had an affair. I vowed to keep her safe—we were in a dangerous part of the world, and she wanted to be on the front line. To get the real story. She'd been negotiating an interview with one of the imams in a village near where we were camped. Radwan. She was determined to present all sides of the story. Turned out Radwan was a double agent, connected to a group of insurgents who didn't want a military presence in their part of the world. Radwan and his men kidnapped Elaine, her cameraman and their two Marine escorts."

Jason remembered when their Afghani guide had run into his tent to report the abduction. He was already suited up and ready to roll out on a half-formed extraction plan by the time the Major overseeing his unit had made the announcement and put the unit on standby until an official incursion plan came down from command. "My superiors wanted to negotiate their release. They didn't want to risk alienating their source to enemy movements." Jason shook his head at the precious time he'd lost. He should have risked a court-martial and disobeyed those orders not to go after the hostages. "You don't negotiate with terrorists. They value life differently than we do. It's about the mission for them. It's not about the people. They said they wanted weapons and intel in exchange for Elaine's life. The Corps wasn't about to pay it. By the time we got clearance to enter the village and raid Radwan's home…"

"Oh, my God." Sam was on her hands and knees, crawling toward him. "Jason…"

When her hands closed around his, he pulled her into his lap, needing something to hold on to. She wound her arms around his neck, weeping softly against his ear.

"They were already dead. It was a setup. We were all sitting ducks by the time we got into close-quarter fighting. There were villagers and insurgents, and we couldn't always tell them apart. I got Elaine's body out. We brought them all home, but…" His hands clenched in the folds of her scratchy wool sweater. "So many people died. Marty's was the only chopper that showed up to evac us out. I'm pretty sure he violated orders, too. I should have gone in as soon as I knew. Maybe it was already too late. I promised to protect her. And I let her die."

"No. I'm so sorry." Her hands rubbed at the tension in his neck and shoulders before she hugged him tight. "And now I'm putting you through this again. You don't love me, of course, but… A kidnapping? A rescue? Those men dressed and armed like soldiers? Marty?"

"I found you alive. And I will get you home that way."

She nodded as if she understood how much he needed to succeed with this rescue. After a moment, she sat back, pulling off her glasses and swiping away her tears. "You didn't kill Elaine. Those terrorists did. I don't suppose that's much comfort, though. You didn't just lose someone you felt responsible for—you lost someone you loved. And today, you lost the friend who helped you. I don't know what to say."

"It's war. It's a horrible hell of a thing a lot of men and women have to deal with. It stays with you when you come home."

She looked him square in the eye, close enough that she didn't need her glasses to focus on him. "You're getting help with this, right?"

He caught a lingering tear with the pad of his thumb and summoned what he hoped was a reassuring smile. "I saw some Navy doctors. I've got a therapist in Jackson I go to every now and then. I've got the wide-open space and clean air of these mountains so the heat and small spaces and too many people I don't know can't get to me again." He studied her verdant eyes, absorbed the intimacy of her warmth and caring, surrounded by the silence of the cabin and night around them. This was pretty good therapy, too, and an unexpected calm centered him in the present again. "I knew this mission would push some buttons for me. I'd hoped I could handle it better. You need me to."

"I need you to be okay. I don't want to make your recovery any harder than it already is." She put her glasses back on and tucked her long hair behind her ears as if she was gearing up in a flak vest and helmet, prepping for battle. "I promise I won't die on your watch. I just have to follow the rules, right?"

Jason nodded. Hopefully, it would be that simple. Although, in reality, he couldn't even remember all the rules she was talking about beyond *Do what I say* and not mentioning what's-his-face by name.

"What about your dad?" she asked. "You said you had a falling-out with him? I would think family could be a big help with what you're going through."

The woman could fill up the air with more words than he'd use in a week. Maybe even a month. But she *was* a good listener. She hadn't forgotten anything he'd said, not even in passing.

But he was still raw from sharing his memories of Elaine and Kilkut. Right now, he couldn't handle the shame he felt at being a third-generation Marine who'd failed his duty and come home without his head screwed on straight. "One touchy-feely conversation at a time. Okay? Besides, it's getting late. We both need sleep. I want to get moving at first light."

"Okay." She scooted off his lap and Jason stood, missing all the different kinds of closeness she'd shown him today. She shooed him toward the door. "I know you need some space right now. You go out in the cold and get your mountain man back on while you're checking the perimeter. But be careful out there. I've got an idea about how I can rig the door since there's no lock on it. At least we'll have a few seconds' warning if anyone tries to break in. I won't set it until you get back."

Jason planted his feet and pulled his gun from his holster. A jerry-rigged alarm wasn't protection enough against the danger that lurked outside, waiting until sunup to track them down again. He placed the Glock in her hand. "Your dad said you knew how to use a gun."

"He taught me. But I haven't held one for years."

"You afraid of it?"

"A little."

"Good. That means you'll respect it. It's a deadly weapon. I want you to keep it with you while I'm scoping out the area and laying a few traps of my own—extending your early warning system into the trees." He pointed out the important elements. "I refilled the magazine. I just put a bullet in the firing chamber. Don't touch the trigger unless you're ready to use it. Shoot anyone who comes through that door who isn't me. I'll be back in half an hour."

"But you'll be unarmed out there."

Jason pulled out his hunting knife. "No, I won't." Risking the temptation he hadn't quite been able to shake despite common sense and that nightmarish trip down memory lane, he dipped his head to kiss her again. The kiss was basic, brief, but he liked how she always latched on as if she was never quite ready to let him go. But she had to. No, *he* had to. Jason opened the door. "Stay inside. Stay away from the window. Stay safe."

Chapter Nine

The last time Jason had spent the night with a woman sleeping in his arms had been that last night before Elaine's kidnapping in Kilkut.

Despite resurrecting those memories so he could explain to Sam the kind of messed-up he was, it had also been the best night's sleep he'd had since Kilkut. He'd awakened a couple of times to make sure the cabin was secure, but when he'd crawled back onto the pallet beneath the Mylar blanket, Sam had turned her cheek onto his shoulder and snuggled in as if he was her own personal fireplace. He'd barely noticed the hard floor at his back, or her soft snore of exhaustion. Sure, he'd been aware of the heavy weight of her breast pillowed against his side and the light grip of her fingers resting against his chest. But what stayed with him as the sun rose was that the nightmares hadn't come—not one flicker of a firefight, not one raging shout, not one image burned into his brain. Instead, he'd dreamed about big green eyes and fishing with his dad and a fun night he'd shared with Marty and some of his flyboy buddies at a pub outside the base in Germany.

The bad memories had eased their grip on him for a few hours, allowing the good memories to surface and be discovered again. They eased their grip, it seemed, because determined, surprising, sexy Sam had never loosened her grip on him.

Peace was the best way he could describe what he'd felt last night. And he'd known far too little of that these past three years. He didn't know whether it was all the talking, being emotionally spent or having a trusting woman fastened to his side that had left him feeling this way. Sam's absolute faith in him coaxed at the trust he'd once had in himself to be the right man to get the job done. The woman was all kinds of unusual—maybe Jase-whispering was another one of her unique talents. Jason wasn't about to thumb his nose at the rare gift. He'd wound his arms around Sam's sleeping form and held on as if she was an anchor in the storm of his life.

And he'd slept. The way he suspected most men slept. Free from guilt and grief for a few hours. Content in the moment. Looking forward to the possibilities of the next new day.

He hadn't forgotten the danger on the mountain with them, the threats Buck had issued, the guns and casualties, and the fact he was the only thing standing between Sam and the men who bartered with her life without caring what a funny, smart, special woman she was. Until he could get within cell phone range to call for backup, or get her to a search and rescue station, it was up to Jason to protect her. As badly as he wanted to unmask Buck and find out who in her inner circle had set Sam up to be kidnapped, he knew his first priority was keeping her safe and getting her home to her father.

Although his motives for saving Samantha Eddington were a little muddled today, his mission was as clear as it had been the night before last. Checking the time on his watch, Jason hoped Sam had been right about the twenty minutes she needed to get ready to move out this morning.

He tightened the cap on the second bottle he'd filled after breaking through the top layer of ice to reach the clear, cold water of the creek and tucked it into his pack before tipping his face to the sky. Although the air still held the chill of the night here in the shadows among the trees, the rosy dawn had burned off the lingering clouds from the last few days of snowfall. Today would be bright and sunny and a few degrees warmer than yesterday's hike.

A warm, clear day meant three things. As long as they stayed dry, the risk of frostbite and exposure dropped exponentially. As they continued their winding descent and dropped in altitude, the snow would be melting or gone, meaning they could move faster. And without footprints and disturbed snow trailing in their wake, they'd be that much harder for Buck and his men to track.

Tucking the water into his pack, Jason looped the straps over his shoulders and studied the red fox that had come to the water to drink about twenty yards upstream from him. The little guy was probably on his way home from what he suspected was a good night's hunt, judging by the tiny bits of dark fur that dotted his muzzle. Jason held himself still, so as not to startle the animal before it drank its fill and returned to its burrow before the larger predators, like bears or cougars, came out for their morning meal. That little black nose and those wide, triangular ears were a far better tracking system than GPS or infrared technology. And when one of the furry ears flipped back, alerting to a noise in the trees behind him, Jason paid attention.

The fox scurried into the underbrush, and Jason

ducked behind the cover of the nearest tree, quickly covering his tracks with the sweep of a broken pine branch. Tossing the branch aside, he tuned his ears to the sound of footsteps crunching over hard-packed earth and snow. That wasn't a larger predator creeping up on four legs. That was the sound of two feet. A man.

The fox wasn't the only hunter on the mountain.

Jason automatically reached for the gun on his thigh. But his hand slapped an empty holster. Damn. He'd left it with Sam. He crouched down, quickly assessing the man's location and in which direction he was headed. Buck's men had gotten here faster than he'd anticipated. Of course, *men* was a relative term. So far, he'd heard only the one set of footsteps.

This guy wasn't making much of an effort to mask his approach, so he hadn't spotted Jason. But Jason had no problem pinpointing the man emerging from the trees on the far side of the creek. Dressed in black camo like the kidnappers holding Sam at the cabin and the men pursuing them yesterday, he carried a rifle over his shoulder and wore a pistol at his hip. This guy's black stocking mask had been rolled up above his ears, but that didn't mean Jason recognized him, or could even give an accurate description at this distance.

But the guy had a walkie-talkie pressed to his ear, and his drawled response was loud enough for Jason to eavesdrop on the conversation, even with twenty yards and the rocky creek bed between them. First there was a crackle of static, followed by something about *blood in the snow* and *they must have stopped here*.

Jason eyed his bandaged knuckles, silently cursing his explosive reaction to Marty's murder. He hadn't policed the scene. Hell, he shouldn't have lost it like that in the first place. He'd let his needy reaction to Sam's insistent words and touch distract him from the basic mission—keep Buck and his men from finding her before he got her home to Daddy.

The clear morning air also carried the distinct growl of at least two snowmobiles in the distance. Search parties. That's what he'd do if he was hunting the enemy and had this much territory to search—split his men up and send them out in different directions to scout for their location. Only, he was the enemy this time. And he had no intention of letting any one of those scouts get a bead on Sam's location and radio back to Buck and his compatriots so the whole group could converge on them again.

One man he could take out. But facing off against seven or eight men by himself? That meant picking them off one by one.

Leaning back against the trunk of the tree, Jason unsnapped the sheath of his hunting knife. He hoped it wouldn't come to using lethal force, but if he couldn't get behind that guy and subdue him with a choke hold the way he had the men at the cabin, then he intended to do whatever was necessary to keep him from radioing in his position and calling for backup.

"Copy that," the man reported, moving upstream to the narrowest part of the creek to cross over to the bank on Jason's side. "I'm about a mile from the forestry service road. No visual yet. But the signal's getting stronger."

Signal? Jason paused in the shadows as the man moved up the bank into the trees. What signal? Had they found some other way to track them besides that computer chip they'd cut out of Sam? The man shifted course, moving along the edge of the tree line. Fortunately, the few boot prints Jason had left were farther in. But the man's course correction was far too accurate for his peace of mind. He was on an intercept course with the shack where Sam was right now. Brushing her teeth. Tying her beautiful hair into a ponytail and erasing all trace of their stay there last night. And Jason had no way to call her and warn her. Nobody was that lucky. Or that good at tracking up here. Except him.

He slipped farther into the trees, mirroring the man's path along the creek bed. He had to stop him before he found his trail and went to investigate.

"I'm going silent on my end," the man reported. "Switching channels to listen in. I'll call in when I get her twenty." The man twisted the knob to pick up a different frequency on his walkie-talkie. "This is ranger station twelve. Please repeat that request. Hello?"

Her twenty? There was no ranger station twelve. And no officer in the park wore anything that resembled a black camo assault uniform. Hell. This was no lucky guess. That guy had Sam and the shack on his radar, and he was heading straight for her location.

The time for stealth had passed. Jason needed to make his move. Now.

With all the lumbering grace of a bear waking from hibernation, the man hiked into the trees, his gear clacking together against his back, his boots breaking twigs and pinecones in the shallow snow beneath his feet, making it easy for Jason to slide around him without being detected. He followed him several yards until the man spotted the first print of Jason's path through the snow and knelt to check it out.

Taking his cue from the silent little fox, Jason crept up from behind and looped his forearm beneath the man's chin. In the same move, he yanked the rifle off his shoulder and slung it beyond his reach. Jason cinched his arm tighter, lifting the startled man off his feet, using the guy's full weight to hang himself. He sputtered and cursed, clawing at the sleeve of Jason's jacket. But the guy wouldn't pass out. He'd misjudged the smaller man's bulk, forcing him to use two hands to secure the choke hold.

But what the man lacked in brute strength, he made up for in agility. When he gave up the fight to free himself, he went limp, slipping through Jason's grasp to make a grab for his pistol. Jason clamped his hand over the guy's wrist, twisting until he cried for mercy. But the guy wouldn't let go. In the two seconds Jason had shifted his focus to the gun, though, the guy jerked his head back against Jason's jaw, the back of his skull splitting his lip.

"Son of a…"

The gun fell to the ground. One of them kicked the weapon into a bank of snow that clung to the shady side of a rocky outcropping. The guy changed tactics, jabbing the point of his elbow into Jason's ribs, spinning around to land a swing-kick against Jason's injured thigh. But facing him gave Jason's fist an easy target, and he plowed his fist into the middle of the guy's face. He felt the pop of his nose breaking, stunning his opponent. Jason backed off, swiping the back of his hand across his bloodied lip, giving the dazed man some space as he stumbled to his knees and landed face-first in the snow. Either this guy was trained in hand-to-hand combat or Jason was off his game.

But Camo Man was down, not out. Shaking off the effects of his bloodied, broken nose, he rolled away from Jason, diving toward the rocks where the gun had landed. Jason didn't waste another second evaluating his opponent or his own rusty skills. When the man rose with the weapon in hand, Jason charged again, hitting him square in the chest and tackling him to the ground.

They traded punches and fought for control of the gun. They rolled over tree roots and pinecones. Snow abraded his skin and got inside his jacket. But the cold revived him. Sharpened his senses. He took a fist to the cheekbone and a knee to his aching thigh before he got both hands on the gun and smashed the guy's grip against the frozen ground. Once. Twice. On the third smack, his grip popped open and the weapon skidded into a snowbank.

Now Jason had the advantage. He braced his forearm against the man's throat, using his full weight to choke him into unconsciousness. The guy's stocking cap and walkie-talkie were long gone. His skin was flushed. His lips were pale. His bruised blue eyes laughed with arrogance as he stared up at Jason.

"It's you or me, bounty," he rasped, no doubt refer-ring to the $10,000 promise Buck had made to get him out of the way. "It ain't gonna be me."

When he saw the man's fingers crawling across his belly toward Jason's knife, he pulled the weapon himself and put that to the man's throat. "Who are you guys? Who is Buck? Who wants Sam Eddington dead?"

Blue Eyes laughed, even as the edge of the blade pricked his skin. "You better kill me, or I'll find your woman. Too much money at stake. Me or somebody else is gonna—"

"I'll kill any man who hurts her." It wasn't an idle threat.

The walkie-talkie, lying somewhere off to the side, crackled to life. A voice, husky and sweet and far too familiar, came across the line. "I'm calling the nearest ranger station or sheriff's department or search and rescue. Please. I can transmit, but my receiver is damaged. Is anyone getting this message? There are two of us stranded on this mountain. We've been hiking south from Mule Deer Pass. Men with guns are pursuing us. They blew up our rescue helicopter. We need help. Over?"

Blue Eyes laughed out loud. "Guess who she's been talking to."

Jason's blood ran as cold as the snow soaking through to his skin. Sam had fixed the damn radio. Just like she'd promised. No telling how far her signal had been broadcasting. Was this yahoo the only one who'd heard her or…?

Jason raised his head to the growl of snowmobiles. Not so distant now. "Ah, hell."

Blue Eyes was playing him for the lovesick fool he was. "Buck's gonna enjoy cuttin' her up. Maybe he'll make you watch before he puts a bullet in your head. Unless I tell him you're already dead."

He twisted under Jason's blade, slamming his knee into Jason's thigh, ignoring the shallow cut the movement sliced across his jaw. He kicked again, knocking Jason onto his backside before another vicious kick clipped his wrist and knocked the knife into the snow.

Blue Eyes lunged for his gun. He swung the barrel around, squeezing the trigger.

But Jason was faster. The shot burned through his arm as he scooped up the knife and thrust it into the man's belly. With a feral roar, he shoved to his feet, lifting him with the blade before dumping his opponent at his feet.

The gun dropped to the ground and Jason picked it up, tucking it into the back of his belt. Those blue eyes were wide, dazed, dying. "He won't…stop… He's sick with wantin'…to kill…"

"Who is?" he demanded.

Jason was bruised, breathless as Blue Eyes bled out. But he sucked in deep gulps of air, clearing his head of the violence, blood and death. He stooped down to clean his blade in the snow before briefly checking the burning gouge where the bullet had grazed the meat of his shoulder. Like the reopened gash in his leg, the thing throbbed like a son of a bitch. But he'd been hurt worse. He needed to move.

"I just heard a gun go off." Sam's voice held a tinge of panic as Jason dug through the snow to find the discarded walkie-talkie. "This is an SOS. My friend could be hurt. Help me, please! I need a ranger station or sheriff—"

Jason picked up the walkie-talkie and switched on the call button. "Damn it, Sam. Get off the radio."

Static was his only reply.

There wasn't any time to waste. Jason grabbed his pack, stretching his legs into a flat-out run as the growl of engines became a roar.

Chapter Ten

Samantha opened the screwdriver attachment on the Swiss Army knife and tightened the wire connecting the anode with the battery pack she'd cannibalized from the flashlight Jason had left with her. This should be an easy-peasy fix for her, but her hand shook. The reverberation from that gunshot she'd heard had rattled the false sense of security she'd felt since waking up with Jason's arms wrapped around her.

This wasn't some rustic Garden of Eden she was sharing with the rugged veteran. Yes, she'd had a good night's sleep. She felt closer to Jason Hunt than she'd felt to any other human being for a long time, and she was probably already more in love with him than common sense said she should be. Funny how she trusted him more than she trusted her own feelings. But feelings weren't the priority here. She wasn't safe. Neither of them was. She scratched anxiously at the torso of her sweater. There was only one reason why anyone would be shooting up here. And she wasn't so hopeful to think that a hunter had suddenly shown up on this part of the mountain this morning.

"Damn it." The shattered transceiver was beyond repair. There was no way to change the frequency, no way to have a back-and-forth conversation. She had no idea if she was talking to anyone but herself, but she stuffed the knife into her pocket and tried again. "This is an emergency. My friend may have been shot. We need help."

Samantha didn't hear the charging footsteps until they hit the wood planks of the shack's front stoop. She rose from the bench and picked up Jason's gun, bracing her feet and aiming at the door when it swung open. In one breath, she'd been numb with fear. In the next, she was light-headed with relief as Captain Jason Hunt of the United States Marine Corps barged in.

"Sam?" Her early warning contraption tangled Jason in a bunch of cords and noisy cans. Swearing, he pulled them off his body, ripping the nail they'd been connected to out of the wall.

She quickly lowered her weapon and ran toward him to help. "I heard the gunshot. Are you hurt?" She saw the blood wetting the tear in his jacket, more oozing through the stain on his pant leg. "You are. What happened? How can I—?"

"Flesh wound. We'll fix it later. How long have you been broadcasting our position?"

"You heard me? Who shot you?" There was dried blood in the scruff of his beard and a scrape across his bruised cheek. She peeked around him to look out the door. "Is he following you?" Finally free of her web, Jason caught her by the shoulders and pushed her to the center of the room. "Please tell me the other guy looks worse than you. What are you—?"

He knocked the radio off the bench and stomped it beneath his boot. His gray eyes drilled her for a second before he plucked the gun from her hand and moved away to pick up her coat and backpack. "How long were you transmitting that SOS?"

"A few minutes, I guess." She raked her fingers through her hair until she met the knot of cord securing her ponytail. Clearly, she'd done the wrong thing here. "I thought I was helping." She caught the coat he'd tossed at her, eyeing the shattered bits of plastic and wire on the floor. "You could have just switched it off. I don't think I can repair that."

He shoved her pack into her chest. "You're brilliant. I get it." He ejected the bullet from the firing chamber of the gun he'd taken from her and stuffed it into her pack, zipping it shut. She saw now that he had a second handgun secured in the holster at his thigh. Even before he explained himself, she was getting a pretty good idea of what had happened to him out there. "I don't know if anybody down in Moose or at the ranger station heard it, but Buck and his men sure did. At least one of his reconnaissance men was tracking you on his radio."

Samantha batted his hands away and took over gathering the loose supplies into her pack while he moved to the door to scan outside. She recognized the droning echo of snowmobiles in the distance. The hornets were swarming again, closing in on their position. Her entire body itched with regret that she'd unintentionally put them in this position. "I didn't mean… I'm so sorry."

"Your timing sucks, that's all. I shouldn't have snapped. I…" He wanted to say something more, but the urgency of the situation changed his mind. "They're on their way here. We have to go. Now."

He didn't need apologies. He needed her to move. She pulled her coat on over the moth-eaten sweater and hooked her pack over her shoulders. "I'm ready."

He eyed the top of her head. "Hat? Gloves?"

She pulled the knit cap from her pocket and met him

at the door. "I can put them on while we're running. Hiding? Leaping off another cliff?"

"How did I luck out to rescue an heiress who doesn't know how to quit?" Heaving a breath laced with exasperation, he slipped his hand beneath her ponytail, palming the nape of her neck. She'd barely braced her hands against his chest when he pulled her onto her toes and covered her mouth in a hard, quick kiss. He squinted his eyes and grunted against her lips as if the pressure there hurt him. But he kissed her again before releasing her and letting her heels slide back to the floor. Then he pried her fingers from the front of his jacket and turned his grip to pull her along behind him. "Stay close."

She didn't intend to do anything else. "You're the safest place I know."

He scanned the clearing outside before jogging into the trees, retracing their steps down toward the creek from the day before. "Come on. I want to get to the river." Once he was certain she could keep up, he released her, allowing her the use of both hands to balance herself as they half climbed, half slipped down the steep, uneven terrain. "There'll be less snow there, and the ground is still frozen enough we won't leave footprints."

"The river? As in the bottom of the gorge?" She'd have to sprout wings and fly if he wanted her to cover that distance in a hurry.

"Creek flows into it about a mile from here. Before it hits the waterfall." She'd heard the running water yesterday when she'd stopped to rest, although she hadn't been able to place its location. But she trusted that Jason knew exactly where they were going. "Then it drops down."

"About a thousand feet!"

"A series of waterfalls, not one big one. There's plenty of river in between. We'll be more exposed, but we can cover the distance faster. Flatter terrain. Fewer obstacles. They won't be able to cross it with their vehicles unless they backtrack several miles. Keep moving. These rocks are loose." He pointed out the hazard even as he ordered her to follow him across. They created a mini-rockslide and Samantha glanced up the slope behind them, wondering if the noise and movement was loud enough for the men to track. She grabbed onto an exposed root to slow her skid toward the next tree trunk. Then she hurried after him toward the rock face they'd scaled the evening before.

"Thank you for explaining the plan to me." The consideration was a far cry from the bossy, taciturn man who'd pushed her to her limits without so much as a *please* or *You hangin' in there?* the day before. He wasn't a hard man, cruel and uncaring and all about the job as she'd initially thought. He was a wounded man, guarded with his thoughts and words and feelings because he'd been hurt so badly and had lost so much.

Yet he'd held her and kissed her and shared a part of himself last night. He listened when she talked, conceded when he could, and now explained when he couldn't. Samantha's heart pounded a little harder in her chest, and it wasn't just from the exertion of their quick descent. This was more than a crush she was feeling for Jason.

If she was completely honest, this was more than she'd ever felt for Kyle. Her feelings for her ex had been about excitement and discovery and the satisfaction of pleasing her father and alleviating his concern. She'd felt useful. She'd thought Kyle needed her. But that had all proved superficial, a ploy to gain her trust and make her feel something for him. On the surface, Jason didn't need anybody, certainly not a self-conscious citified brainiac who thought and talked too much. But now she had an idea of how isolated he was from the world—another survival tactic. She understood now that what he needed was compassion, acceptance, maybe even forgiveness for the tragedies in his past he blamed himself for. In all the months she'd known Kyle, he had never touched her heart the way these few hours with Jason had. Kyle needed her money and her connections to her father. Jason needed *her*. To listen. To hold. To trust. The idea that she could mean something to a man like Jason was as frightening as it was empowering. Although her experience with men was next to nil, what she felt for Jason Hunt seemed a little scary, yet it was more precious, more profound than anything she'd felt for the man she once thought she'd marry.

"Eyes on me, Sam," her beat-up mountain man reminded her, interrupting her thoughts. *Her* mountain man? Talk about errant thinking. He pointed to a knob of exposed granite. "That's your next handhold. Step where I step."

Focusing on the demands of the moment, she obeyed his every order, facing the rocks as he did when the trees thinned out. Although she imagined real rock climbing required a level of upper-body strength she lacked, he made it easy for her by pointing out toeholds and tiny gaps and protrusions where she could grip the rock.

Suddenly, the woods were eerily quiet. Samantha stopped, standing on her tiptoes on a small lump of granite, her gloved fingers flexing around the outcrop where she clung. She held her breath and tipped her face up toward the trees, unsure whether she should risk feeling relief. Had Buck's men gone the wrong direction? Had Jason's knowledge of the mountain saved them yet again? "Do you think we lost them?" she whispered on her next exhale.

"I think they found the shack. They'll be on our trail soon enough. I didn't take the time to hide anything when we left." His hands closed around her waist and he lifted her down to the flatter ground beside him. The brief sensation of heat at his touch, and the surprising flare of confidence she felt at discovering just how close she'd been to reaching the bottom on her own, vanished as soon as he tugged on her hand to get her moving again. "They won't be able to drive down this steep slope. They'll have to split up to cut us off one direction or the other or pursue us on foot. And we're not slowing down."

Only, they were. At first, she thought he'd slowed his pace to accommodate her shorter stride. But now she saw he was limping. So much for cauterizing that shrapnel wound. The bloodstain on his pant leg was spreading, and the rip at his shoulder was oozing blood, too. Jason had clearly fought with one of Buck's men. Had he been ambushed? Just how badly had he been hurt? "Did you have to kill someone to get away?"

"Him or me," he answered matter-of-factly. "I chose me." She remembered yesterday's arduous trek across the mountain. Yesterday, his strength had seemed indomitable, his skills unparalleled. Today, he seemed a little more human. A little more vulnerable. His breathing seemed more labored than it had yesterday. Jason was hurting. What was this rescue assignment costing him? And not just physically.

"He's the one who shot you?"

"It's just a graze."

He squeezed his hand around the wound on his left shoulder, wiggling his left fingers as if they might be going numb. That wasn't a good sign, was it? His right palm came away bloody before he dipped it in the icy water to wash it off. That definitely wasn't a good sign. Samantha's heart lurched in her chest to think of all he had suffered on his mission to help get her home. But he didn't complain about the pain or what he'd been forced to do. He was a machine again, hurrying along the bank, testing which rocks weren't coated with a treacherous sheet of ice before climbing across and jogging up to the next line of trees through the snow.

Samantha followed along, grateful for the long, baggy jeans instead of the soiled dress she'd worn on yesterday's hike. The cool temps shouldn't sap her energy quite as quickly today. But it was still a challenge to keep up with Jason's relentless, if uneven, pace. "That arm's still bleeding," she admonished, unable to hide her concern. "You need stitches. Antibiotics, too, I'm guessing. At least let me pack it off for you. When was your last tetanus shot?"

The air around them was suddenly alive with the growl of gunning engines, moving closer. Snowmobiles. When they heard a series of rapid-fire gunshots and angry shouting in the distance, Jason cursed. Buck's men had found their trail again. Samantha turned toward the sound. With the noise echoing off the rocks and trees, it was hard to tell which direction they were coming from. She was only certain that there was more than one vehicle moving through the forest now. Had they split up like Jason had suspected? Could they be surrounding them? Getting close enough to shoot at them again?

She startled at the brush of Jason's fingers sliding against hers. "Less talking. More running."

Keeping hold of her hand, he hauled her up the creek bank and led her into the trees again. Despite his injuries, he lengthened his stride, forcing her to push herself into a faster speed.

"Is one ahead of us?"

"Above us. On the forest service road that runs parallel to the river. If he gets ahead of us, he can cut us off before we reach the walking bridge across the river. The others are searching the trees. They'll figure out where we are any second." He pointed to the right. "Remember downhill. That's where the river is. If anything happens to me—"

"Nothing's going to happen to you!"

"—go that way. Stay out of the snow and follow it. You'll be in cell range before you hit the next drop-off."

"I don't have a phone!" she gasped. A staccato of bullets thwapped through the tops of the trees over their heads. Instinctively, she ducked as bits of twigs and pine needles rained down on their heads. "Jason!"

"They're firing blind. Hoping for a lucky shot."

The shots were too damn close to be any kind of luck for them. "If they're shooting this way, they must know we're going to the river."

"There isn't any other way out of here unless you packed some rappelling gear I don't know about."

Another spray of bullets chopped up the snow a few yards behind them. "Jase?"

They were running now. Endlessly running. Samantha's vision narrowed to the broad strength of Jason's back. There was only Jason and running and deafening sound. Gunfire. Engines. Shouting. Their boots slapped against the frozen, hard-packed dirt as the layers of snow thinned, and every breath was a noisy gasp. Snow and danger was up the slope to their left. She caught glimpses of the river, of their escape route, off to their right through the trees now. But as the noises grew louder and the enemy closed in, it seemed farther and farther away.

But that distance was an illusion. As was the promise of safety. She could hear some of the words Buck and his men were shouting now. Or were those radio communications?

"River."

"Can you see them?"

"This way!"

"Nobody touches her but me. I'm the one who's going to make her daddy pay."

The creek and ribbon after ribbon of melting snow running off from the higher elevations poured into the river, and the river widened. They were close enough to see water splashing against the rocks and loose chunks of ice bobbing along the surface. But it was already too wide for them to simply walk across on stepping-stones as they had the creek. The current picked up speed as the water deepened, transforming the tinkling sweetness of a slow-moving stream into a thunderous crash of water against rock that vibrated through the mountain itself.

The loudest sound of all was her pulse pounding in her ears as her heart raced and her legs pumped to keep pace with Jason's. But he was faltering. She was lagging behind. Blindly guessing their location or not, the bullets and voices and snowmobiles were closing in on them. They'd never reach the river and the walkway bridge across it in time. They weren't far enough ahead of Buck and his men to get to the open ground where

she and Jason could move faster. She'd never quite understood her father's love of hunting, and now that she'd
spent the last forty-eight hours of her life as somebody's
prey, she knew she'd never be a fan of the sport.

Yet as fear crept into her mind and fatigue claimed
her body, the instinctive adrenaline of survival pushed
it aside and cleared her thoughts. Her brain was her best
weapon. *That's* what she needed to listen to.

They couldn't outrun bullets or snowmobiles.

She slowed to a jog. "Jase? I've got an idea."

A crazy one. Full of risk. Until they got off this
mountain, though, every decision was a risk.

He snatched her hand again, urging her into a run.
"We need to get out of this snow, so they have to move
on foot."

"No. We need to go toward them."

"Honey, we—"

"Listen to me." She tightened her grip and jerked him
to a stop. The fact that he winced at the sudden stop and
rubbed at his injured thigh told her this was the right
plan of action. She curled her fingers into the front of
his jacket, asking him to hear her out. "You can't keep
up this pace when you're hurt and losing blood like this.
I can't keep up this pace."

His heavy breaths stirred a tendril of hair that had
fallen out of her ponytail. "Then we're looking at a
shoot-out, and the odds aren't in our favor."

"We have to outsmart them. Not out-shoot them.
Can you take out one of the men on a snowmobile?"
She picked up a dead branch, holding it up like a base-
ball bat.

"If we get close enough, yeah." Then his expression
changed. Maybe not so crazy, after all. "Yes." Nodding,
he plucked the branch from her fingers and took her

hand again, pulling her up the incline toward the service road. "We need transportation. That's half a great idea."

"What's the other half?"

"Can you swim?"

"The second rule you said to me was that I shouldn't get wet."

The growl of the snowmobiles got louder as they neared the service road. "Right. You'll freeze. We'll both freeze. Can you swim?"

"Yes."

"Then I know how to buy us some time and get us off this mountain faster."

He released her when they reached the flat surface of the snow-covered gravel road that had been carved around the curves of the mountain to give emergency vehicles access to the wooded slopes, as well as create a natural fire break. Her attention was drawn to the ominous buzz of the approaching engine while Jason scanned the trees on either side of the road.

Deciding on his best vantage point for the attack, he led Samantha across the road, obscuring their tracks by dragging the branch through the snow behind them. "Get behind that tree." He pushed her back against the trunk, hugging his body around hers, shielding her from view from any angle. She clung to the front of his jacket, holding him close so that he'd be hidden from view, as well. "Be ready to go on my mark."

It was only a matter of seconds before the Arctic Cat and a now-familiar armed figure in black camo came around the bend in the road. Jason's gray eyes locked onto hers for a moment. He inhaled a couple of deep breaths. Steeling his nerves? Schooling his energy for the blitz attack? Reassuring her?

When she released her grip on him and nodded, he smiled. And then he was gone.

Even if she'd had a clear view of the road, the next several seconds would have passed by in a blur. The snowmobile was almost upon them when Jason charged, swinging the thick branch as if he was aiming for the bleacher seats. The wood caught the rider squarely in the chest, and between his speed and Jason's strength, the man went flying.

As the unmanned vehicle careened off the road and plowed into a snowdrift, Jason tossed the branch and raced toward the stunned man. The man in black staggered to his feet, clutching at his rib cage. He muttered something just as Jason tackled him and they rolled into the ditch beside the road.

Although Samantha's heart was telling her to go to Jason to make sure he was safe, her brain told her he was expecting her to stay away from whatever fight was taking place. Since securing the snowmobile had been her idea in the first place, she ran in the opposite direction. A quick examination of the vehicle revealed a dent in the front fender, but the gas tank hadn't been damaged, and the engine was still idling with power. She straightened the runners, climbed on board and shifted it into Reverse, backing out of the drift and centering it on the road for their escape.

"Ah, hell."

She shifted into Neutral and jumped off, hurrying to Jason's side. "Are you hurt?"

"I'm okay."

"Then what…?" She ran up behind him, resting her hand against his back and assessing the degree of pain on his face as he knelt over the unmoving man. When he didn't answer, she followed his gaze to the stocking mask he clenched in his fist and on down to the man's scraggly dark beard. There wasn't a single line marring his face. Samantha frowned. "He's younger than I am. This guy wants to kill me? Why? I don't even know him."

"I do."

When he didn't elaborate or change the somber disappointment in his expression, Samantha squeezed his shoulder. "Jase?"

The walkie-talkie hooked to the young man's pack blared to life. "Murphy, you got them? Damn it, cuz, answer me! Everybody, head east!"

She felt the energy galvanizing the muscles beneath her hand. Jason stood, towered over her, pushed her up to the road. "Get back on the snowmobile." As she straddled the seat, he climbed on behind her. "You know how to drive this thing?" Samantha nodded. This model was fancier than the one she'd ridden in college on a spring break ski trip with her father, Joyce and Taylor, but she understood how an engine worked. She kicked it into gear and turned in the direction of Jason's hand. "That way."

They zoomed down the road, zigzagging a few times to dodge the spots where the gravel was starting to peek through. Even with her glasses secured to her face by the knit cap she wore, she squinted as the wind whipped past them. Under different circumstances, she might have enjoyed the feel of Jason's hands at her waist, the warmth of his body at her back as they raced along in the cool, crisp air. But these circumstances were starting to feel far too familiar. Men shouting threats. That swarm of hornets, albeit smaller now, still pursuing them.

She turned her chin to her shoulder, shouting to be heard. "How many of them are there?"

"I counted eight to ten men, including Buck, up at Mule Deer Pass. They're down to five or six now."

"Won't they give up if you keep killing them?"

"Orin's not dead. He's unconscious."

"Orin? Who's Orin?"

She automatically ducked as a pop of gunfire shattered the air behind them. Jason hunched his shoulders over hers. "Drive!"

There was someone on the road behind them now, and he was picking up speed, firing random shots as he steered the snowmobile and tried to take aim. "I got 'em now, Buck!" he shouted. "That five million is ours!"

Samantha spotted a small supply shack marked with the forestry service logo ahead on the right. Jason tightened his grip at one side of her waist and pulled his gun from the holster on his thigh. She felt him twisting in the seat, reaching back to fire off a couple of dissuading shots of his own.

But trading bullets at this speed wasn't the only thing she was worried about. She could hear the thunder of running water skipping over rocks and breaking off chunks of melting ice as it tumbled over the edge of a precipice beyond the trees. They were heading straight toward the river and the walking bridge that arched across it. "Jase? That bridge won't support us." Stopping didn't seem like an option right now. "Do I turn upstream? You don't want me to turn around and play chicken with him, do you?" As the trees thinned near the water, she saw nothing but a drop-off and the water tumbling over the edge of the cliff into blue sky. They were running out of road. "Jase?"

"Hang a right." He fired off two more shots.

"Are you kidding me?" Cliff? Waterfall? Blue sky?

"The river runs pretty deep this time of year." He lurched behind her, squeezing the sentence through gritted teeth at her ear. "It runs a good distance before dropping off into the canyon."

"But—"

"Rule one!" A second man had joined the chase. Jason traded shots with him, too.

"Do whatever you say."

"We're going to be okay, Sam." He slapped his hand over hers, opening the throttle up as high as it would go. "Gun it!"

"Oh, I am so moving to sea level." Samantha tightened her grip and veered off the road, screaming every inch of the way as the edge of the cliff raced up to them. At the very last second Jason's arms cinched around her and he jerked her off the back of the vehicle. They hit the ground hard and rolled as the snowmobile sailed off over the waterfall ahead of them. A split second later, she tumbled over the edge of the embankment, locked in Jason's arms.

What had she thought earlier about sprouting wings and flying? She got a glimpse of the snowmobile crashing into the rocks on the opposite bank of the river. Flames erupted, and black smoke billowed up, filling the air with the pungent stench of burning fuel.

But a glimpse was all she got. She had one moment to notice the stink and heat of the fire in the air, and bruises and scrapes dotting her skin.

And then she was plunging into the frigid water. Shock knocked the breath right out of her and she swallowed a mouthful of water. The current tossed her forward even as she sank until her feet hit the gritty bottom. She grabbed for her glasses and clutched them to her face, even though there was little to see.

Before she could orient herself, she felt a jerk on her shoulders. A long, strong arm reached down through the water for her. Once she understood that Jason had grabbed the strap of her backpack, she kicked toward the surface, helping them both swim upward until their heads cleared the surface. She coughed her aching lungs clear and tread water to keep her head above water while the current quickly swept them downstream. Jason left his arm threaded through the straps of her pack, linking them together. He coughed a few times, too. Water dribbled from his beard stubble, and his skin was pale, probably like her own.

"Keep moving so we have some chance of staying warm." The din of hornets in pursuit faded. They left the burning heap and angry, greedy men behind them as they bobbed along down the river. "Stay afloat. Let the current take us. Stealing the snowmobile was a good idea. No way can they catch up to us now. We'll be in civilization before they do."

Samantha circled her arms in front of her and kicked from time to time, despite the cold seeping into every pore of her body. "What about the next waterfall?"

"We'll be on dry land before we get there. Trust me."

"Always."

She didn't know how many yards, maybe even a mile or more, they'd floated, slowly descending the mountain as the river raced toward the valley before Jason paddled toward the shore and her feet touched solid land again. True to his word, they'd left the river before faced with the next obstacle of a taller, more powerful waterfall and its potentially deadly drop. But her teeth were chattering, and he was shivering as they crawled up the bank to more even ground and rolled over onto their backs, blinking up at the clear, sunny sky.

She went willingly when he turned her into his arms after a little bit and hugged her tightly against his chest. He pressed a kiss to the crown of her head and she nestled close, trading comfort as well as the last vestiges of body heat. "Bet you never thought in a million years you'd do something like that."

"It wasn't exactly on my bucket list."

She smiled at the soft rumble of laughter vibrating through his chest. If she wasn't so exhausted, she'd join him. When he went still beneath her cheek, she had the vague notion of dozing off with him for a few moments.

No, wait. Dozing was bad. Falling asleep might mean hypothermia. They needed to get up and get moving. Pushing against the ground and his chest, Samantha sat up. When she saw Jason's eyes were closed, a frisson of concern sparked a different sort of heat inside her. "Jase? Wake up." She gently tapped at his cheek, urging him back to consciousness. "What do we do now, mountain man?"

His dark lashes fluttered against his cheek and one granite-colored eye popped open. "Mountain man? I thought we weren't doing nicknames, Princess."

Silly with relief to hear him joking, she leaned down and kissed him, carefully avoiding the swollen cut on his bottom lip. He, however, seemed less concerned about any pain she might be causing him because he palmed the back of her head and held her lips against his as he deepened the kiss, sliding his tongue alongside hers until the cooler temperature of his skin registered and she pulled away. "All right. I deserve that one. I've followed the rest of your rules. Tell me what to do or I'll think you don't care about me anymore."

"I care." He answered the teasing challenge by sitting up, the lines beside his eyes deepening with the seriousness of his tone. "About getting you home. About doing right by you."

"You haven't failed me yet," she assured him, wondering if he'd been this hard on himself before losing his girlfriend when he'd been in the Corps. "You won't. Tell me what to do."

"Empty the water out of our boots. Wring our socks dry as best we can." After spending a few minutes doing just that, he pulled her to her feet. "And then we walk. As far and as fast as we can. If we're lucky, Buck will think we're dead. His men will search the crash and the river. Look." He pointed to the green grass and tiny shoots of wildflowers and succulents pushing up through the dirt. "No more snow. Unless they get a visual on us, they won't find any tracks. If we're really lucky, we'll run into a forest ranger or somebody out hiking or camping. Keep your head covered. If you lose sensation in your toes or fingers, let me know. But moving should help us warm up."

Jason forged ahead along the top of the riverbank, his fingers staying near his gun. His gaze swiveled from side to side, continuously looking for any sign of Buck or his men, even though she saw nothing but the scenery and heard nothing but the wind through the trees and the river powering its way down the mountain beside them.

That scenery included keeping her eye on the man ahead of her. Despite the afternoon sun rising high overhead, slowly drying the outer layers of their clothes to the extent that she shed her coat and he tied his jacket around his waist to let the warming air dry the sweaters and T-shirts they wore underneath, Jason's pace was slowing. And where the ground was uneven, he stumbled, catching himself with a muttered curse. His injuries and constantly being on alert were taking a toll on him. When he tripped again, Samantha looked down at the ground and uttered a choice word herself.

"Jason?" She pointed to the drops of blood on the ground. "You're leaving a trail."

When he turned, she saw a crimson blot about the size of her fist staining the front of his sweater, just above his waist. "So that second guy may have clipped me with one of those shots. The cold water slowed the bleeding for a while. But now that we're warming up—"

"Damn you and your stubborn Marine-headedness." She marched up to him and pushed to the nearest rock to sit him down.

"Marine-headedness? Is that a thing?" He looked down at her, watching her slide his pack off his shoulders and pull out the first aid kit. The fact that he was making light of his newest injury probably meant he was hurt worse than he was letting on.

"Be honest with me," she ordered, dumping the wet contents of the kit and a little stream of water in her lap. She needed something dry to stanch the bleeding. She untied her coat from her waist, pulled out her Swiss Army knife and started ripping it apart at the seams. "How badly are you hurt?"

"It may have nicked a rib and torn some muscle, but this one went through."

He lifted his sweater and T-shirt when she moved around him, inspecting the neat, finger-sized hole in the lower-left part of his back. She cleaned the wounds and folded the shreds of her coat lining into two small packets. She had him hold one over the wider exit wound in the front of his flank while she tied them both into place with the belt from her coat. "Stop getting hurt."

"Not my intention, honey. But better me than you."

"No. Not better. I need you alive. I need *you*." Before she could analyze all the ways she meant that last confession, she dug into his pack for anything else she could secure the bandages with. "Your phone!" Her fingers closed around his cell phone and she pulled it out. "Do you think we have cell service yet? I'm calling 9-1-1. Or my father. He'll mobilize the National Guard if we need it." She was frustrated to see the black screen that refused to light up. Water dripped from the battery casing when she opened it up, as well. "It's as wet as we are. Unless we can dry out the components, it won't work."

"I've still got one of their radios."

She used nearly every inch of tape in the kit to secure the bandages around his waist before she pulled his T-shirt and sweater back down to cover the makeshift bandage. "The river might have ruined it, too. The battery pack won't make a good connection."

"Don't worry. You'll fix it." After repacking what was left of their things into one pack, she looped it over her shoulders and helped him up. He draped his arm around her shoulders, partly for warmth, partly for support. Samantha wound her arm around his waist, sharing whatever strength she had. He pressed a kiss to her temple and started walking, leaning on her a little as he limped along beside her. "If you can fix me, Sam, you can fix anything."

Why didn't she think he was talking about bullet holes?

Chapter Eleven

Never in a million years would Jason have guessed that a nearsighted heiress, with clothes that didn't fit, no filter on her thoughts and a seriously sweet set of lips, would be helping him hike the gravel road from the foot of the Grand Teton past one of the elk preserves outside Moose, Wyoming. He was the search and rescue expert. He was the tough-as-nails Marine, trained to do or die to complete his mission.

Sam Eddington had more backbone than any man or woman he'd served with. She was braver than any officer he'd served under. And she was more resourceful than anyone he knew, period. He'd sorely underestimated the challenge of this mission. Even more, he'd underestimated the woman he'd been sent to rescue.

Sam was funny, compassionate, frustrating, surprising, strong and sexy in ways he wasn't sure she fully comprehended. But Jason did. He wasn't sure exactly how he was going to walk out of her life and return to his solitary ways once he'd safely handed her over to her father. He was damn sure he wasn't going to forget their time together. Whether facing down danger or facing his past, she hadn't once retreated. But it wasn't like they had anything in common beyond having a band of mercenaries hunting them across the mountain. He was hardly the stuff relationships were made of, and he wasn't likely to fit in at the latest Eddington soiree or Midas Group board meeting. And he still wasn't certain he could handle being with someone if there was the possibility he could lose her again.

Not for the first time during these past days, he wondered if he'd finally achieved the redemption he'd sought for losing so much in Kilkut. While he tried not to lean too heavily on her shoulders as his wounds left his balance and stamina a little iffy, he wondered if redemption was enough. Or if there was an outside chance that his life could be about something more.

He smiled down at the top of Sam's head as she broke that silence that had lasted for oh, say, the last fifty yards. "You're certain you recognized the man on the snowmobile?"

"I'm certain. Orin Murphy. He's a friend of Richard Cordes Jr.'s. His cousin, I believe."

Sam nodded. "I heard Buck call him 'cuz' over the radio when he was chasing us. Do you think Buck is the same guy you called Junior? Buck wasn't in the van or on the mountain when I was first taken to that cabin. He could have been at the bar with you and Dad, and then he could have joined the group later once we went on the run."

"Orin's and Junior's dads were both part of that homegrown militia that kidnapped your mother." Jason squeezed her shoulder, apologizing for the sad and frightening memories this discussion she kept coming back to must trigger for her. But she wasn't the only one who needed to understand why this had happened. "This isn't about the money at all. It's about revenge."

"It's probably about the money for some of them.

I'm guessing Junior hired whatever help family loyalty couldn't buy. Five million dollars can be pretty persuasive."

"Your father would never hire anyone he knew was related to Cordes. So how did he get a man inside your circle of friends and family?"

"What if Dad didn't know? Dante Pellegrino could organize something like a kidnapping and mercenaries. And Kyle would probably do it for the money. Or to get rid of me so he could have Taylor and still be a part of the Midas Group. Could Taylor have dated one of Cordes's friends or met him in college?"

"It's all speculation until the FBI launches an investigation and we can get answers." Jason dutifully put his thumb up when he heard the vehicle approaching from behind them. But the minivan filled with tourists was smart enough not to pick up hitchhikers in this remote stretch of wilderness in the southeastern edge of the national park. It skirted into the far lane and drove on past.

Sam's weary sigh echoed his own. "How much farther do we have to go before we reach a farmhouse or some kind of road-stop business?"

"Don't think about it. Just keep walking."

"That's rule number six, I think. A raised fist means stop. Do what I say. Don't get wet. Don't fall off the mountain—"

"Enough. Am I really that much of a bossy jerk?"

"Yes. Well, the bossy part."

When he laughed, he winced and grabbed his side, forcing them to stop as pain radiated through him. Sam tried to get him to rest on the shoulder of the road, but Jason shook his head, breathing through the pain. At the rate his reserves of energy were failing him, he might not get up again if he sat down. Besides, this terrain was far too flat and open for him to feel he could protect her here. "We need to keep moving. Find shelter if we can't get help."

"We'll get help," she insisted, wrapping her arm around his waist and taking more of his weight as they continued at a slower pace.

And, as usual, she talked. "I've only met Richard Cordes Jr. one time. At his father's execution. Dad wouldn't let me go to the trial. How does a virtual stranger plan a kidnapping? How did he know where I'd be that night? How did his men know when I'd be alone? When they could abduct me? They were waiting for me at the lodge. It wasn't any spur-of-the-moment thing."

"An inside job."

"You think somebody I know…somebody I trusted… is working with Buck? Do you think my father knows we have a traitor in our lives? Is he safe?"

"I don't know. All the more reason to get you back to Jackson. I want to know who set you up."

"Get in line behind me." She startled when a car honked at them, warning them to move onto the shoulder of the road before racing around them and kicking up a cloud of dust and stinging gravel they had to shield their eyes against. He was guessing the word she uttered wasn't welcome at Eddington parties, either. "Even if they don't want to pick up strangers who look as raggedy as we do, you'd think someone would at least stop and call the authorities for us."

"Might be the gun I'm wearing."

"Or the blood." He hated that he should be any part of the worry that puckered that little frown above her glasses. "Shoulder, stomach, back, thigh. You're pretty scary looking right now."

No doubt. "Want to split up? You're more likely to flag down someone to help on your own."

"You never left me. I'm not leaving you."

"I doubt these guys will try anything this close to civilization. They don't know we don't have a working cell phone and haven't called for help. If they're smart, they've already packed their gear and are heading north across the border as fast as they can get there before we sic the authorities on them and round up all the dead bodies."

"What if they're not smart? Buck or Richard Jr., or whatever he wants to call himself, seemed adamant about slicing and dicing me and serving me up on a platter to my dad. I'd feel better if we weren't out in the open like this." Good. Some of his survival skills were rubbing off on her.

"Want to try the radio again?"

"There's nothing else in this pack to cannibalize that will make it work."

As the dust from the last car settled, Jason noticed a second plume of dust kicking up behind a speeding vehicle. "Pickup truck at twelve o'clock. We'll try again."

"Hey! We need help!" Sam waved at the approaching black truck. It was an older model, but well taken care of by the sound of the engine. "Is he slowing down? He is." The truck flashed its lights at them and Sam waved. "He is!"

The pickup pulled off onto the opposite shoulder of the road. He averted his face as momentum carried the moving cloud of dust around the truck, obscuring his view of the driver. But as soon as it skidded to a stop, Sam was moving. Jason tightened his hold on her when she would have run forward to meet the man opening the grubby black door. "Let's see who we're dealing with before… Sam?"

"I know him." She broke free and ran across the road. "Brandon? Brandon!"

Jason recognized the lanky bodyguard who'd been ambushed the night Sam had been taken. Looked like he was wearing the same suit he had that night at the bar, only now his shirt collar was open, his tie was gone and the dark-haired man needed a shave.

"Samantha?" Metz climbed down from the running board and checked both ways for traffic before hurrying across the road to meet her. "I haven't been able to sleep for three days. I've felt so guilty. I've been looking everywhere for you."

"Thank God it's you." When the tall man bent slightly, Sam launched herself into his arms.

Even in his weakened state, Jason's instincts buzzed on high alert. This was wrong. Metz being here was wrong. Or maybe he was just having an irrationally possessive reaction to another man scooping Sam up and hugging her like that.

Pressing his fingers to the leaking bandage at his waist, Jason limped across the road to face Metz over the top of Sam's head. "Pellegrino and Mr. Eddington have run out of ideas to retrieve Sam beyond randomly driving around Wyoming?"

"Not random." Metz ended the hug but kept his arm around Sam's shoulders. "I knew which direction those men had taken her. Walter called in the FBI, despite the threats on that video, as soon as we got word that your man had crashed his helicopter and you two were stranded in the mountains."

"That man was Marty Flynn. His death was no accident. He gave his life trying to help us."

"I didn't mean to imply that he'd screwed up." The younger man raised his hands in apologetic surrender, releasing Sam long enough for Jason to pull her back to his side. "I'm sorry about your friend."

"You got a cell phone?" Jason prompted.

"Jason's hurt," Sam said. "He's been shot. Twice. Call an ambulance."

"Of course." Metz smiled down at Sam before reaching inside his jacket to pull out his cell.

Jason shook his head. "Call Walter first."

"Sure. You look like you're hurt pretty bad. Let's get you inside and off your feet." Avoiding Metz's offer to help, Jason leaned on Sam and walked around to the passenger side of the pickup. By the time he'd climbed onto the cracked white vinyl of the bench seat, Metz was standing there with a bottle of water. "Drink. If you've lost as much blood as I think you have, you need to replenish your fluids."

Jason took the water and thanked him for that, at least. "Make the call."

"May I talk to Dad?" Sam asked.

"Let me explain the good news to him, see how he wants me to handle this." He punched in a number and put the phone to his ear. "In the meantime, there's a blanket in the back of the truck. We don't want your friend here going into shock."

"Right."

As Metz's call went through, Jason turned his gaze to the rearview mirror and watched Sam lower the tailgate and climb into the back of the truck. He'd promised to get her back to her father, not to one of the family's bodyguards. His need to protect her hadn't diminished. Not by a long shot. But she didn't need to be married off to ensure her future. She didn't need to settle for a loser like Kyle Grazer. She could damn well take care of herself. The confidence that had been missing from their first meeting now radiated through every determined step and sharp-eyed glance.

It was those big green eyes meeting his gaze in the mirror through the back window that warned him a split second too late that his instincts had been right.

Sam scrambled over the side of the truck, carrying a black stocking mask in her hand. "There's a black camo uniform in a bag—"

"I know." She followed his gaze across the bench seat to see Metz at the driver's side door, pointing a gun right at him. "I found your inside man."

SAMANTHA GLARED THROUGH the windshield of the truck at the dark-haired psychopath who'd made it his life's work to punish her father for the death of his father.

Richard Cordes Jr. seemed to have an innate instinct as to what caused people the most pain. Watching him strike another blow to Jason's broken rib and open wound when the man she loved was already kneeling in the dirt with his hands bound in front of him cut through her as deeply as the length of Jason's knife plunging through her heart. Brandon had thrown that knife into the ditch along with the two guns they'd carried, leaving Jason completely unarmed before he forced him to drink the water from the bottle he'd given them—water which must have been laced with the same sedative she'd been injected with. At least she hoped that's why her savior had passed out on the long, bumpy ride into the Wind River Mountains on the other side of Jackson Hole. She couldn't bear to think that Jason might be dying because of the wounds Junior and his men had inflicted on him each time they'd gotten close to recapturing her.

Since her dad had bought the land once illegally claimed by Junior's father, Richard Cordes II—he preferred the tougher-sounding nickname Buck to the diminutive *Junior* he apparently had grown up with—had secured a ramshackle house on what she assumed was an abandoned farm, based on the weedy fields and empty pastures they'd passed before the sun had set. She'd heard enough of his posturing through the open truck window to know he thought of this place as his new compound. He'd build an empire bigger and stronger than his father and aunts had owned, and no one, not even a *rich old bastard like Walter Eddington* or the US government, would be able to take it from him.

She recognized Orin Murphy from the mountain, too. Although his black eye and the tender way he carried himself indicated he was still feeling the effects of his run-in with Jason and a tree branch, he, like three other men in black camo gear, stood in a circle around Jason. Apparently, there was no electricity running at this remote location, either, because the men had all parked their trucks in a semicircle around Jason and the side of the house, spotlighting Junior—she refused to do him the honor of calling him Buck—while he rattled off some wild manifesto about the Second Amendment, injustices, and his vow to honor his father's legacy and avenge his death by the man who'd stolen that legacy— her father.

Brandon had parked his truck in the semicircle, too. He was one of these nut jobs with a skewed idea of right and wrong. His traitorous butt was so getting fired once she got back to her father. *If* she ever got back to him. Beyond that, she'd make sure there was jail time for each one of Junior's accomplices. They'd left three of Junior's men dead on the mountain, but they might be the lucky ones once she was done testifying about all she'd seen and heard and been subjected to, and the money and connections her father wielded made sure the very best lawyers in the country prosecuted them.

Of course, that kind of real justice depended on whether she survived this night. And even if she lived through it, she didn't think she'd survive if Jason didn't live through it, too.

Junior smacked his fist across Jason's face, knocking him onto his side on the ground.

"Stop it!" Sam yelled, distracting Junior from the torture.

But the young man with the pistol at his waist and the rifle hanging across his back merely looked at her through the windshield of the truck and laughed. "Aw. Does this upset you, rich girl? Seeing your big man bleedin' in the dirt? Just imagine how much fun I'm going to have doing the same thing to you."

"Damn it, Buck," Brandon complained, taking a step toward his cousin. "Quit playing games. You promised me a million dollars to bring Samantha to you. You already screwed up any chance at getting paid the ransom. Let's cut our losses. Finish them both off and at least let me turn her body back in to Eddington for a reward."

"A reward?" Junior turned his full attention on his cousin. "You think I want Eddington to have any kind of closure? Any kind of comfort?"

Oh, no. Brandon pulled back his jacket, bracing his hands on his hips, making sure Junior saw that he, too, carried a gun and knew how to use it. This was about to turn into a violent confrontation—some sort of Wild West shoot-out—and Jason would be caught in the crossfire. How could she get him out of there? How could she protect him?

Samantha's hands chafed against the rope that bound them. Brandon had left her in the truck trussed up like prized prey at the wrists and ankles when he'd pulled a semiconscious Jason out and thrown him to the ground at Junior's feet. *"You promised ten thousand dollars to the man who brought you Hunt. Pay up."*

Ten thousand dollars. She nearly cried remembering that taunt. Jason's life was worth so much more than that. His heart, his spirit, his soul were priceless. He'd served his country. He'd sacrificed his friends, the woman he loved and even a little part of his sanity. He'd saved her.

She had to save him.

As she struggled to slide across the seat to reach the locked door, Samantha's fingers brushed against the bulge in her front pocket and she froze.

Jason might be unarmed. But she wasn't.

"Bless you, Marty Flynn." She contorted her body to get her hands close enough to her pocket to slide her fingers inside. "You're going to save us, after all."

While Brandon stood his ground and Junior spewed more vitriol about her father and how her mother deserved to be taken from him all those years ago, Samantha opened Marty's Swiss Army knife and sawed at her bindings.

"You never even would have thought you could get money like that until I put the idea in your head," Junior bragged. "I'm the one who said you needed to become her friend, so she'd turn to you when the opportunity came. I'm the one who told you to capitalize on her boyfriend's infidelities."

"Eddington trusted me," Brandon argued. "I had a

good thing going there. Hell, given enough time, I could have ingratiated myself with the family and married Samantha myself. I didn't need you to do anything for me. I let you take a swing at me to make that kidnapping look real. Fired a couple of shots at the van while your men sped away. I did what I did for the money, so you could have your revenge. You owe me."

"I owe no man," Junior spouted, possibly quoting something his father had once said. "I am what I am because of who I am. And no greedy bastard will ever take my pride, my land, my manhood from me."

Brandon reached for his gun. "Shut up, already."

But Junior was faster. Samantha jerked, dropping the knife, catching it between her thighs when the gun went off and Brandon crumpled to the ground beside Jason.

She watched Jason's big form roll away from the dead man. Not only was he still alive, but he roused the strength to push himself up to a sitting position. In the light from the headlamps, she could see one of his handsome eyes had swollen shut, and the circle of blood on the front of his sweater had spread to cover nearly half his torso. He was bleeding badly. He needed her help.

Moving the knife back to her fingers again, she sawed away at the rope.

"All I wanted was Samantha Eddington at my mercy." Thank goodness Junior was more interested in hearing himself talk than in paying attention to her now. "I wanted to send pictures to her father and watch Walter's grief when he discovered what was left of her body. I had to stage it as a kidnapping, so I could convince these idiots to help me. Promised them each a ton of money. I'd have taken it, too. Enjoyed every penny. It's the least Eddington owes my family."

Jason's voice was low, yet surprisingly strong. "How'd

you ensure their loyalty once they knew the ransom wasn't coming?"

"I lied. Just like I lied at Kitty's Bar in Moose that night you got mixed up in this. Set up my own alibi while my cousins and friends took Samantha. Right from under Eddington's nose. I've got no quarrel with you, Jase. But you keep getting in the way of what I want."

The ropes scraped across her skin as she broke free.

"I will protect Sam until my dying breath."

"That's what I figured." Junior raised his gun. Samantha jammed the pocketknife's blade into the ignition and turned it.

Junior looked her way, startled to hear the engine roaring to life.

But that wasn't half as startled as he looked when she stomped on the accelerator with both feet and plowed into him.

The wall of the house caved in as she pinned him against the rotted siding.

Bits of roofing and a rusted gutter rained down on the hood of the truck. Tears burned down her cheeks and she swiped them away, unsure why she was crying now when she'd already been through so much.

But as she cleared her vision and shifted the truck into Park, she realized she'd made a tactical error. Junior was trapped, but he wasn't dead. And despite the way his body sagged between the truck and the house, she hadn't caught his arm in the crash. The arm that still held the gun.

With the slow deliberation of a madman, he dragged the gun up onto the hood of the truck and aimed it through the windshield. "You just have to die," he slurred as blood appeared in his mouth.

Samantha dived for the seat as the windshield shattered. There was a second explosion. Two gunshots.

She tried to shift into Reverse from the awkward position, not wanting to raise her head above the dashboard while he kept firing.

But after two shots, she heard no more.

She heard only Jason's deep voice, ragged with pain. "It's okay, Sam. You can come out. You're safe."

She slowly sat up, averting her gaze from the gruesome sight of Richard Cordes's dead body slumped over the hood of the truck. She looked out the side window to see Jason on his knees, the barrel of the gun he held still steaming in his hands.

A closer look revealed that Brandon's holster was empty. Jason had taken the gun off the slain bodyguard and saved her, even as she'd saved him.

She looked beyond him as he swung the gun around to see Orin Murphy toss his weapons on the ground. He collapsed on the running board of his truck, cradling his middle as if the bones inside were cracked or broken. The other three men in black camo followed suit, dropping their weapons and kneeling with their fingers laced above their heads as Jason instructed.

Samantha wasted no more time. She retrieved Marty's knife from the floorboard and cut her ankles free. Then she was out of the truck and hurrying to Jason's side.

"Jase? Are you all right? Please tell me you're going to be all right." She inspected his face, lifted his shirt to check his wound. She took the knife to the ropes at his wrists, freeing him the way he had once freed her. "Why aren't you saying anything?" she demanded, tossing the bindings aside.

"Because you're doing all the talking, woman." He

caught a loose tendril of hair and rubbed it between his fingers and thumb. "If you're okay, I'll be okay."

"I'm okay. You're okay, too, right?" She nodded, knowing that was a lie. Her hair fell from his fingers and he collapsed to the ground. "Jase?"

She picked up the gun and pointed it at the men who'd surrendered their weapons. "You all know who I am?" They nodded, chiming in with a few hesitant *yeah*s and saying her name. "I'll pay a hundred grand to the first man who gives me a working cell phone and the keys to his truck."

All four men held out their phones.

Chapter Twelve

"I love him, Dad."

Samantha hugged her father in the hospital's second-floor waiting room outside the surgical ICU. There wasn't anything this fine hospital could do to make her feel better after the kidnapping and survival ordeal than a shower, clean clothes and a hug from her father could. The bright, sunny afternoon and news that Jason had come through his surgery without any unexpected complications didn't hurt, either.

Walter Eddington pulled back, capturing her face between his beefy hands and offering her a wry smile. "You know, you never once said that about Kyle."

Samantha was even feeling generous enough to share a smile with her stepmother and Taylor, who'd brought the change of clothes to the Jackson hospital and had waited with her until the surgeon had come out to give her a report on Jason's condition. "I don't mention what's-his-face anymore. It's one of the rules Jase and I agreed on."

He caressed the silver locket and chain she'd returned to him, a little worse for wear after a long dip in a cold river, and slipped it into his pocket. "Captain Hunt makes you happy?"

"I think he will, Dad." If she could convince Jason of that.

"That's all I need to know. And we'll never mention what's-his-face again. It'll be like he never existed."

"I can live with that rule," Taylor agreed, turning a hopeful smile to her older sister. "I'm sorry for what I did. He said that he loved me. I don't know how I can ever make it up to you—or get over how stupid I feel for believing him."

Understanding exactly how her sister felt, Samantha reached out to hug her, too. "What's-his-face always seemed to know what to say. He just never learned how to listen. You and I will work on our relationship. We'll be okay."

Walter shook his head. "Looking back to the night you were taken, the way he was on his phone so much—I thought he might be involved in the kidnapping." Samantha grinned at the choice word he uttered. "With everything going on, he was more worried about himself. All those calls to his mother, playing the sympathy card of losing you to get back into his family's good graces."

Joyce slipped her arm through Walter's. Even her chemically peeled expression looked apologetic. "I for one am glad he moved back to New England. He wasn't hardy enough to thrive out West. To think his father didn't share that he'd cut Kyle, er, that man we can't mention, off from his trust fund and any future with the family business until he straightened up his act and stopped sleeping with his investors' wives and daughters. No wonder he was so desperate to marry into the family. You'd think that man had some kind of sexual illness."

Walter squeezed her hand where it rested on his

arm. "I think that illness is called being a self-centered jackass."

Tipping her face to her father, her stepmother actually blushed. "I think you're right, dear." She raised her right hand and turned to Samantha and Taylor. "From now on, I leave my daughters' matchmaking…to my daughters. I'm just glad we're all together again, and we're all safe."

"I second that." Walter dipped his head to kiss her cheek. Samantha approved.

"Sam!"

She smiled. Finally. There was that voice. Bossy and deep, expecting answers and demanding action.

Jason shouted her name again from his room. Samantha stood there, her eyes tearing up with the emotional relief of all her fears and concern.

"Sam!"

Her sister giggled as her stepmother slipped her a tissue and her father nudged her toward his room. "You'd better go."

"Now stay put," a voice warned. A nurse brushed past her, mumbling something about hardheaded men as Samantha entered the recovery room. "Thank goodness you're here. Talk some sense into him."

She found Jason swinging one leg off the bed, trying to untangle himself from the monitor cords and IV attached to his hand. "What are you doing?" She rushed to his side, helping him settle back against the pillows. She adjusted his blue-and-white gown and pulled the covers up around his lap. "You're supposed to be resting."

When she checked his IV and the monitor clipped to his finger, he turned his hand to grab hold of hers. "I didn't have eyes on you. And that stupid nurse wouldn't answer any questions about you because I'm not family. Are you all right? Were you admitted to the hospital? What happened to Orin Murphy and the others at the compound?"

She perched on the side of the bed, appreciating the rugged lines of his cheeks and jaw that had been shaved so the doctors could address some of his injuries. Although she did miss the wiry scruff of dark stubble that had tickled her lips and palms.

"I'm okay," she assured him, cradling his hand between both of hers. "A doctor checked me out for exposure, hypothermia. They drew blood to see if there's any residue from the drug they used on me in my system—there's not. And they doctored a few scrapes and contusions. You're the one who was in surgery for three hours. Two broken ribs, a nick in your kidney, debriding wounds, stitches and staples—it's a wonder you're still alive and causing so much trouble."

"Don't joke about this. I know I was in and out of consciousness. Cordes didn't hurt you? You're really okay?"

"I'm really okay." Maybe if she changed the subject, he'd relax, and ease the convulsing squeeze of his hand around her fingers. "Dad's here. He's having a long conversation with Mr. Pellegrino about his hiring practices."

"My conversation with Pellegrino would be short and sweet. I don't know if he's ignorant or incompetent, but he can't be in charge of your security anymore."

She could feel him calming down enough to risk teasing him. "Maybe we'd better let Dad oversee diplomacy. You can be in charge of keeping me safe."

"You're offering me a job as a bodyguard?"

"I'm not offering you a job. I… What I want is… What I mean to say…" Since when did she get tongue-tied? Even when her words made no sense, she'd never had a problem getting them out.

"Hey." Jason pulled her hand onto his thigh, capturing her against the warmth of the blanket and the man underneath. "Come on. Seventy-two hours on that mountain with you, and I never once had to wonder what you were thinking. Talk to me."

Samantha nodded, heartened by his indulgent smile. Strengthened by the knowledge that he always had, and always would, listen to the truth behind what she had to say. She scooted closer. "Thank you for accepting me for who I am, and how I am. Quirks and baggage and all."

"Not a problem. You accepted me, and I will put my baggage up against yours any day."

"Agreed." Her fingers danced against the cotton blanket. She hadn't expected this to be so hard. Maybe it was hard because she suddenly realized his response was the most important thing in the world to her, right after learning he was still alive and would fully recover.

"What else, Sam?" He stilled her nervous fingers. His beautiful granite eyes locked on to hers, touching her with the same gentle strength of his hand. "I dumped everything on you. You can tell me anything."

"You really do listen to me." She reached up to touch his face. He smiled. Suddenly, this was easy. "Do you believe a person can fall in love in seventy-two hours? That you can know a person, inside and out, trust and respect that person, and lose your heart in that short a time?"

"Yes." He didn't hesitate to answer. He pulled her onto his lap and tucked her head beneath his chin, holding her close. Although he didn't protest any strain against his injuries, she held herself as still as possible and snuggled into his warmth and strength. "It happened to me. I love you, Sam. I didn't know I *could* love anymore. Sure as hell didn't think I was worthy of it. But you make me feel and want and I'm…better… when I'm with you. A better man. Better at saying what I think and admitting what I feel. I've been avoiding life and people and caring for a long time. But I don't want to anymore. I want to live and laugh and love and be with you. I'm probably still going to be a mess some days, but…" When he realized she was crying against his neck, he wiped away her tears. "I want to be a better man for you."

"You save people, Jason. You saved me. There isn't anything better than that."

"You saved *me*. In more ways than you'll ever know. You have more money than I'll make in my lifetime, but I don't want a penny of it. I want to live in the mountains—I don't think I could handle the city. I'm damaged, you're crazy smart or maybe just crazy, but I love that about you. I want to be your man. I want you to be my woman. If there's any way in hell you think this would work."

Samantha smiled then.

"I think…if we lay down a few ground rules…maybe different ones than mountain rules…" She stroked her fingers across his lips, finding an unbruised place where she could press her mouth against his. "With your experience, my brains—and our love—I think we have a very good chance at making this work."

Epilogue

Seven months later

October in the Teton Mountains was a beautiful time of year. At the lower elevations, the trees were a riot of red, gold and orange leaves, while the evergreens higher up stood out in sharp contrast against the first layers of new snow.

Samantha cradled the steaming cup of coffee between her hands to warm them as she stood on the front porch of Jason's cabin—their cabin now—and surveyed the beautiful, rugged wilderness that reminded her so much of the man she loved. These mountains had once nearly killed her, but now she was beginning to think of them as her home.

As for any lingering fear or worries that she could be kidnapped again, Samantha tempered her new alertness to the people and places around her with a bone-deep trust that Jason Hunt would always have her back. He was more than enough security for her when they were alone like this. Even when she was at a Midas Group function surrounded by her father's new security team, she knew there was no one more focused on keeping her safe than Jason. And though their fears might stem from different causes, she took pride in knowing that she provided the emotional security Jason seemed to need, too.

She heard a whisper of sound as the door opened behind her. "I'm ready to head out." Jason had a deep, growly, sexy voice in the morning, and simply hearing it made her shiver with awareness.

Samantha set her mug on the railing and faced him, crossing the porch to check the zipper of his jacket and make sure he was wearing several layers of clothing. "Good morning to you, too. And goodbye, I guess. Got your gloves? Hat? The temperatures are starting to drop higher up the mountains."

"Who's the mountain guide and rescue expert here?" he teased, capturing her hands against his chest and smiling down at her. "What will you be doing while I'm rock climbing? Working on that eco-friendly waste disposal system you designed?"

"Uh-huh. Thanks for letting me experiment on your home."

"Hey, if I didn't know how good you are at tinkering with things and making them work, I wouldn't let you near the place."

"Liar. Rule one is to always be honest with each other."

"Okay. Truth is you can do whatever you want to my plumbing." The double entendre wasn't lost on Samantha. And when he dipped his head to steal a kiss, she wound her arms around his neck and let him take whatever he desired.

He'd loosened her hair from its ponytail and backed her against the post, before he finally pulled away, leaving the taste of him on her lips. "I'd better be going if I want to make it back in time to clean up for dinner with our parents."

Ignoring the frissons of passion still lingering from that kiss, Samantha turned the conversation to a more serious subject. "I know you need a little alone time before you tackle whatever's been on your mind these last few days. You do know you can talk to me about anything, right?"

"I know. The counselor says I'm continually improving. I'm doing better with groups of people. I'm able to talk more about some of my experiences when I first came home from overseas—like the day I went after the mailman because he gave my mom a package and I thought it was a bomb." Samantha reached for his hand. He might be making light of the frightening story he'd shared with her a month ago—how he'd scared his mother so badly that day that he'd moved out and hadn't looked back until reconnecting after Samantha's kidnapping. But she knew he was still dealing with some of the effects of his post-traumatic stress. He squeezed her fingers, silently thanking her for her support before releasing her. "I like the doctor's suggestion of adopting a pet, too. Maybe a big dog. One who'll go hiking with me."

"I'm just glad you're working on the relationship with your parents. How was Nolan's visit to the dermatologist?"

Fortunately, the illness Jason had been worried about was treatable. "They think they got all the melanoma cells off his face now. He'll have a scar that looks like a question mark. But that just makes him look cool."

She pulled a tube of sunscreen from the pocket of her jeans and stuck it in his backpack while he tugged his knit cap over his short, dark hair. "You should be watching your exposure to the sun at this altitude, too. Are you tackling the north face again? Or will you be working on clearing more of that trail up to Mule Deer Pass?"

"Neither. I'm just going for a day hike. Clearing my head."

"Why do you have to clear your head?" Samantha walked into his chest, wrapping her arms around his waist and snuggling beneath his chin. "Are you sure nothing's bothering you? Have I overstayed my welcome? Made the cabin too crowded for you?"

"No." He leaned back enough to capture her chin and tilt her lips up to his descending mouth. "Never."

Several minutes later they were back inside the cabin. The door was locked. Clothes were dropping as they made their way to the bedroom.

Jason skimmed his hands over her hips and rump and dragged her naked body up against the hard ridge that tented his shorts. Her breasts pillowed against the wall of his chest and her nipples caught in the wiry curls of his chest hair. They pearled into sweetly painful peaks that demanded the squeeze of his hand and the warm, moist stroke of his tongue. While he roused every cell, every nerve ending with the sweep of his big hands and greedy mouth, she caught his bottom lip between hers and nipped at the firm, masculine curve.

He moaned against her mouth. "You make me crazy when you do that."

"Crazy good?"

"Very good." He scooped her up and she hooked her legs around his waist, opening her heavy, weeping center to the fiery heat of his body.

They fell onto the bed together and they battled to find each other's most sensitive spots. The best angle for a kiss here. The lightest touch for a caress there. She was a tingling, quivering bundle of nerves, just waiting for the release she knew he could give her when he abandoned her for a moment, just long enough to shuck his shorts and roll a condom over his straining arousal.

"Are you sure you want to go hiking today?" she teased, her voice a husky, erotic plea.

"You're what I want today." When he returned to the bed, he flipped her onto her stomach, crawling behind her and entering her in one long, deep thrust. Samantha clutched a pillow in her fists, waiting helplessly for him to send her over the edge.

When he slipped his fingers beneath her, pressing against the nub of her arousal, she did just that, burying her face in the pillow and screaming his name as all sensibility shattered and she rode wave after wave of pleasure between his body and hand. Moments later, he groaned against the nape of her neck and poured himself out inside her.

It could have been seconds or minutes or even half a day that she lay there, sandwiched between Jason's body and hands, secure and replete in the weight and warmth of him spooned against her.

"I knew I'd like sex," she admitted on a satisfied whisper, rolling onto her back as he settled in beside her. "I just never knew it could be this good."

"That mouth." He kissed it soundly before climbing off the bed and crossing into the bathroom to wash up. "The sex is good because it's you and me. Everything is good because it's you and me."

Samantha put on her glasses and tucked the top sheet around her, sitting up to watch him pull on his shorts. The scars were still pink on his stomach, thigh and shoulder. But as far as Samantha was concerned, they were badges of honor, testaments to his bravery and commitment and just how lucky she was that he was a part of her life.

"If you're going to look at me like that, then I'm never going to get up that mountain."

"Like what?"

"Like you love me."

"I do."

"Here." He picked up his cargo pants from the floor and pulled a ring box from one of the pockets before sitting beside her on the edge of the bed. "This is why I've been a little distracted lately. I was going to do this tonight in front of Walter and Joyce and my parents. But I can't wait." He opened the box to show her a small, square-cut diamond in a white gold setting. "I love you, Sam. Will you marry me?"

The ring was as simple and beautiful and perfect as his proposal. "Yes."

* * * * *

COMING SOON!

We really hope you enjoyed reading this book. If you're looking for more romance, be sure to head to the shops when new books are available on

Thursday
18th October

To see which titles are coming soon, please visit
millsandboon.co.uk

MILLS & BOON

LET'S TALK
Romance

For exclusive extracts, competitions
and special offers, find us online:

f facebook.com/millsandboon

⦿ @millsandboonuk

🐦 @millsandboon

Or get in touch on 0844 844 1351*

For all the latest titles coming soon, visit
millsandboon.co.uk/nextmonth

*Calls cost 7p per minute plus your phone company's price per minute access charge